SEALED WITH A KISS

BOYS OF THE BAYOU GONE WILD

ERIN NICHOLAS

The Series

Crazy Rich Cajuns
Must Love Alligators
Four Weddings and a Swamp Boat Tour

Boys of the Big Easy
Hot single dads in the sexy city of New Orleans

Easy Going (prequel)
Going Down Easy
Taking It Easy
Eggnog Makes Her Easy
Nice and Easy
Getting Off Easy

MAIN AND RECURRING CHARACTERS

Andre LeClaire: Naomi's nephew, Michael's son.

Armand LeClaire: Naomi and Michael's grandfather. One of Leo's best friends.

Bennett Baxter: partner in Boys of the Bayou, married to Kennedy, millionaire/philanthropist/politician. (Crazy Rich Cajuns)

Charlotte (Charlie) Landry: granddaughter of Ellie and Leo, cousin to Josh, Sawyer, Owen, Kennedy, Fletcher, Zeke and Zander. In love with Griffin Foster. (Otterly Irresistible)

Cora Allain: Ellie's best friend and business partner, Maddie's grandmother.

Dax Marshall: friend from Iowa, engaged to Jane, part-owner in Fluke, Inc/ Warriors of Easton. (Forking Around, the Hot Cakes series)

Didi Lancaster: grandmother to their friends from Iowa. (the Hot Cakes series)

Donovan Foster: Hero. Griffin's brother. Wildlife rehabilitation expert. Former reality TV star and current internet sensation.

Ella Landry: Josh and Tori's baby daughter, Ellie and Leo's great-granddaughter.

Ellie Landry: owner of Ellie's Bar, matriarch of Landry family, married to Leo.

Fiona Grady: Griffin's friend, met him while they were both working in Africa, runs an animal park in Florida, exotic animal supplier for the Boys of the Bayou Gone Wild.

Fletcher Landry: Married to Jordan. Zeke and Zander's older brother. (Heavy Petting)

Griffin Foster: wildlife veterinarian, Donovan's brother, in love with Charlie Landry. (Otterly Irresistible)

Henry McCaffery: little brother of friends from Iowa. (the Hot Cakes series)

Jane Kemper: friend from Iowa, engaged to Dax. (Forking Around, the Hot Cakes series)

Jillian (Jill) Morris: wildlife veterinarian, specializing in penguins, in love with Zeke. (Flipping Love You)

Jordan Benoit: Fletcher's wife, educational director for Boys of the Bayou Gone Wild. (Heavy Petting)

Josh Landry: Sawyer and Kennedy's brother, cousin to Charlie, Owen, Zeke, etc., partner in Boys of the Bayou, married to Tori. (My Best Friend's Mardi Gras Wedding)

Juliet Dawson Landry: married to Sawyer, lawyer. (Beauty and the Bayou)

Kenney Landry-Baxter: Josh and Sawyer's sister, married to Bennett, Mayor of Autre. (Crazy Rich Cajuns)

Knox: city manager, friends with Fletcher, Mitch, Zeke and Zander, etc., works with Kennedy.

Leo Landry: Grandfather of Landry clan, married to Ellie, founded Boys of the Bayou, ran it with his best friend, Danny Allain (deceased), until he sold it to his grandsons

Louis LeClaire: Naomi and Michael's dad.

Maddie Allain Landry: married to Owen, partner in Boys of the Bayou, Cora's granddaughter. (Sweet Home Louisiana).

Michael LeClaire: Naomi's brother, family friend. Town fire chief and paramedic.

Mitch Landry: cousin to Charlie, Fletcher, Zeke, Owen, Sawyer, etc., works for Boys of the Bayou, handyman, dating Paige Asher. (Four Weddings and a Swamp Boat Tour)

Monique LeClaire: Naomi and Michael's mother. Andre's grandmother. Landry family friend.

Naomi LeClaire: friend of the family, grew up in Autre, high school friend of Charlie and Jordan.

Oliver Caprinelli: friend from Iowa, married to Piper, part-owner in Fluke, Inc/ Warriors of Easton. Writer of the video game and several bestselling children's books and paranormal romances. (from the Hot Cakes series)

Owen Landry: Cousin to Sawyer, Charlie, Zeke, etc., partner in Boys of the Bayou, married to Maddie. (Sweet Home Louisiana)

Paige Asher: dating Mitch, from Appleby, Iowa. (Four Weddings and a Swamp Boat Tour)

Piper Caprinelli: Friend from Iowa, married to Oliver. (from the Hot Cakes series)

Sawyer Landry: Josh and Kennedy's brother, cousin to Owen, Charlie, Zeke, etc., majority partner in Boys of the Bayou, married to Juliet. (Beauty and the Bayou)

Tori Kramer Landry: married to Josh, veterinarian, Griffin's friend and business partner. (My Best Friend's Mardi Gras Wedding)

Zander (Alexander) Landry: town cop, Brothers Fletcher and Zeke (twin), cousin to rest.

Zeke (Ezekiel) Landry: Brothers Fletcher and Zander (twin), cousin to the rest. Owns local construction company (also works as family accountant). Engaged to and father of Jill's baby. (Flipping Love You)

ABOUT THE BOOK

What's a girl to do when faced with a hurricane, her celebrity crush, and a power outage in their shelter?

Keep her damned feelings to herself. And her panties on...

Naomi LeClaire is just a small-town girl who loves her quiet, simple life.

Donovan Foster is a sexy, charming, wildlife rescuing internet sensation who loves the spotlight.

What do these opposites have in common?

Only an impossible-to-resist chemistry that, when they're stuck together in a storm becomes, well, impossible to resist.

But the aftermath of the storm gives them something else in common—a rescue mission to help victims.
Oh, and a heat-of-the-moment kiss caught on camera by the local paparazzi. Not to mention an offer for a reality TV show

documenting them falling in love while saving animals from crazy, dangerous situations.

Wow, that escalated quickly.

This should be the last thing Naomi is willing to do. But he's leaving in two months for his next job, so what's the worst that could happen?

He's either going to be her greatest adventure. Or this wild whirlwind romance will blow over faster than a Gulf Coast hurricane.

All she can really do is hold on tight . . . and hope her heart isn't left in shambles.

1

S he really shouldn't fall for a guy with a death wish.

Naomi LeClaire sighed as she stopped her truck in the middle of the road. She didn't dare pull over to the side. The rain pounding down could wash away the ground on either side of the road in minutes. But it wasn't like there was any other traffic out here in this storm so taking up the center of the road wasn't really a problem.

Thank God this road was paved at least. It wasn't unusual for Donovan to go out on dirt roads and even on not-really-roads-at-all when he was doing rescue and recovery missions for injured wildlife.

She peered through the rain that was pelting her wind-shield so hard her wipers could barely keep up.

He was lying *on* the road in front of her truck. Next to the body of a dead bear.

She shook her head.

A few months ago she would have been alarmed to pull up and find a man lying in the road next to a dead animal.

Today...she'd been expecting this. Or something like it at least.

Of course, a few months ago—i.e., before Donovan Foster had showed up in her tiny hometown of Autre, Louisiana—*she* wouldn't have been out driving around while a hurricane was making landfall two hundred miles east of them.

She really shouldn't fall for a guy who loved action and adventure and chaos and who either thought he was invincible or didn't really care if today was his last one on earth.

But Donovan was out here because there were three orphaned black bear cubs that needed rescuing and he would, of course, not go anywhere until they were all found and taken back to his rehabilitation center.

Or until someone convinced him that *his* well-being was just as important as theirs.

Naomi shut the truck off and reached up to pull her hair back. She wore her hair in cornrows mostly lately, keeping it back off her face and from getting tangled being outside in the wind and weather, doing God-knew-what-might-come-up with Donovan. Now she gathered the long, black braids that fell to her shoulder blades into a bunch and tied them together. Then she got out of the truck.

She was drenched within seconds.

Dammit.

She really shouldn't fall for a guy who was the reason that over the past few months she'd ended up with a favorite outfit stained with something-she-didn't-want-to-talk-about, an infected cut on her hand, and a lost shoe. Not lost in the sense that it was ruined and couldn't be cleaned or repaired. It was just *lost*. Never to be found.

All things considered, she *really* shouldn't fall for Donovan Foster.

The fact that he was outgoing, and charming, and that the crazy risks he took were to save wounded and threatened wildlife didn't help though.

The hard muscles, contagious smile, deep green eyes, quick

sense of humor, and hard, rippling, bunching, often-naked muscles—had she mentioned those?—also didn't help.

Needless to say, she was now wearing much more practical clothes and footwear when she hung out with him. And gloves. Tough, no-way-am-I-bleeding-after-this work gloves.

But right now she wanted those hard, sun-bronzed muscles intact and *inside* where they'd be safe. Along with the rest of him, of course.

She marched across the thirty feet that separated them. Though the effect was definitely less impressive because she had to lean into the wind.

She stopped beside where he was lying. He was completely still, his eyes shut, but she knew he wasn't dead. Or she was *pretty* sure. He'd apparently texted Zander, the town cop, just twenty minutes ago with his location.

Naomi planted her hands on her hips. "What in God's name do you think you're doing?"

He opened one eye, then lifted a hand to block the rain.

"Get off the ground, Donovan."

She had to raise her voice to be heard over the rain and wind. But that was okay. She was mad and more than a little concerned. This man needed to get his fine ass in his truck and head back to town *now*. He wasn't stupid or crazy, but he definitely didn't take care of himself and he took far too many risks and that bothered her. A lot.

Because, whether she *should* or not, she *had* fallen for him.

She didn't want him to lose any fingers wrestling alligators —especially before he'd even had a chance to use those fingers on her in any fun, dirty ways. She didn't want him cracking his head open jumping on and off moving airboats. And she really didn't want him getting washed away by the rain bands of a hurricane. They weren't on the dirty side of Hurricane Clare but that didn't mean it was a nice, pleasant, no-problem day on the bayou.

"Have I drowned? Did something hit me in the head?" he asked, squinting up at her.

"It better have, because if I drove out here to find you lying in the middle of the road in a hurricane on purpose, *I'm* going to hit you in the head."

She didn't mean it. Well, she didn't mean it completely. She had expected to find him doing something to make her heart rate kick up and her grit her teeth. But right after she smacked him, she'd want to hug him.

Put simply, Donovan Foster drove her crazy.

She wanted him to leave. Not just the rain-soaked roadway, but the town. The county. The *state* of Louisiana.

Well, that or she wanted him to stay forever. But if he did that, he needed to get a normal, boring job.

Oh, and fall in love with her too.

Maybe he could be an accountant. Or maybe he could teach science at the high school. He had both a biology and an ecology degree. Or, if he really *had* to work with animals, maybe he could just help feed the alpacas at the local petting zoo. Or keep helping with the penguins their friend Jill cared for.

There were options. Safe, normal options. That didn't involve him potentially dying every few weeks.

Donovan blew out a breath and sat up. "I'm doing it on purpose." He held up a hand. "For a very good reason," he added quickly.

"Yeah, bear cubs," she said. "I heard. You need to get your ass in the truck and get back to town."

Donovan had been in Autre for seven months now. Naomi knew that was longer than he'd stayed in one place in years and she kept expecting him to get antsy to move on. He'd traveled the world as a wildlife rescue and rehabilitation expert who'd eventually landed a show on the *Go Wild* network and then another show that had streamed online for the past couple of years. She found him exciting and educational and yeah, okay, hot. Very, very hot.

But now that she *knew* him, she wanted him to get the hell out of here. She felt like she'd been waiting for the other shoe to drop for months. Because she actually wanted him to stay forever.

See? Crazy.

"What are *you* doing out here?" he asked, looking her up and down. "You should be back in town at Ellie's with everyone else, where it's safe."

She was sure she looked...bedraggled. At best. Because of *him*. She gave him an oh-you-did-not-just-say-that look. "Get in the truck, Donovan."

She *never* fell for guys like this. Not. Ever. And for it to be a guy who didn't get worked up about breaking bones or bleeding, who routinely got within striking distance of teeth and claws that could kill him, and who seemed to think that things like gravity didn't apply to him, really made her nuts.

"There's one more cub," he said.

She looked around. This road wasn't well-traveled even in nice weather. It was definitely a backroad. Both sides of the road sloped at a steep incline of dirt and shrubbery. There were trees on both sides as well. How the hell was he going to find a bear cub that didn't want to be found in this storm? She focused on him again. "So you're lying next to a dead bear trying to get the cub to come to you?"

"Yep."

God, he was brave. And his heart for animals was so huge. She'd only known him for seven months but knew that the idea of an orphaned bear cub out here in this storm alone would be killing him.

It was impossible for her to *not* want him. And to not want to shake him and say, "*You* shouldn't be out here alone either."

And to not want to smack him. And wrap him up in a blanket and feed him. And kiss him.

Donovan was also an orphan. His parents had died when he was sixteen. His only family was his older brother Griffin, who was in love with one of Naomi's best friends, Charlotte. Which was how she knew about their parents and that the guys only had each other now. And that they hadn't been especially close for a long time.

Dammit. "You're nuts, you know that?" she asked, crouching next to him.

"I've heard that a time or two." He gave her a wry smile. "Just a few more minutes. These cubs have been on their own a couple days. He's gonna know to find shelter and food, but he's young. He's gonna come back to his mom. It's bad enough that he's out here alone. But with the storm, we may never find him again."

"But—" Naomi started to protest.

"Go look in the back of my truck," he interrupted.

She glanced at his truck, then back to him. He gave her a nod.

She already knew what she was going to see in the back of his big black Ford Raptor. But she blew out a breath and headed over to the truck.

The truck bed had a cover on it that she needed to fold back. Inside was a live trap with two black bear cubs that were about four months old. Big brown, scared eyes peered up at her from where they were huddled together in the back. Donovan had put fluffy towels down on the floor of the trap and they had nestled into them.

Naomi felt her heart melt. They were little and terrified and probably starving.

She felt her throat tighten. Thank God for Donovan. Not only that he knew *how* to capture them but also that he cared enough to do it. And yeah, now she was going to help him find their brother or sister.

She put the truck cover back in place and headed back for Donovan, who was still sitting in the middle of the road. "Fine. Have you seen him at least?"

Donovan grinned and Naomi felt her breath catch in her chest.

And he just had to be gorgeous too? Really? He couldn't *just* be an animal and ecology activist? He couldn't *just* have big muscles? He couldn't *just* have a tragic backstory? He couldn't *just* have fascinating stories about his world travels? He couldn't *just* be funny and charming and optimistic and kind of a ham when there were cameras around? No, he also had to be stop-her-in-her-tracks gorgeous when he grinned. Which he did a lot.

"Yeah, caught a glimpse. He ran off that way." Donovan pointed to the west as he got to his feet.

"What happened to the mom?"

"Hit by a vehicle, it seems."

"These poor babies."

"I know."

She met his gaze and bit her tongue on, *God, you look good wet.* She swallowed before saying, "It's really not safe out here for you either. At least you got two of the cubs. I know it's heart-breaking to think about leaving him behind, but come on. *Your* safety is important too."

He just looked at her for a long moment. Clearly he was processing what she was saying.

Naomi was struck, as she often was, by the fact that he really was thinking about what she'd said. He didn't do that with anyone else. No one else *insisted* on telling him to be careful and to take his time and to slow down. But when she did, he seemed to listen. She liked that.

He looked around. "Fuck."

She reached out and put a hand on his shoulder. His skin was hot even through the wet cotton of his shirt. "I know. But you need to be safe too. And if something happens to you, who's going to take care of the other two bears?"

Of course, *she'd* do what she could. And there were people back in Autre that would be able to care for the bears—Griffin, for one. His partner, Tori, and their friend, Jill, were both vets as well. But no one had the experience and expertise that Donovan did.

It took a second, but finally he nodded. "Okay." Then he frowned at her. "Hey, what are *you* doing out here by yourself?"

She lifted a brow. "I'm not by myself. I'm with you."

"You didn't have to come."

"Someone did," she said firmly. "And with everything going on in town, everybody else is crazy busy."

His frown deepened. "Okay, let's go."

Wait. Was he suddenly worried about *her*? That's how it seemed.

Naomi felt a warmth curl through her belly. That was nice. She was absolutely capable of taking care of herself—and a multitude of other people—but having someone feeling protective of her, especially a rugged, outdoorsy adrenaline junkie who put his whole self into being a savior every day, was pretty sexy.

Donovan reached for her arm, but out of the corner of her eye, Naomi saw a flash of something black. She looked to her right and, sure enough, that was fur.

She pointed. "Donovan, there!"

He glanced over, then took off without a word, jumping down the embankment and sliding about two feet before getting his boots under him.

The bear cub darted away from Donovan, but it was disoriented in the storm and weak from trying to survive without its mom. That would work in Donovan's favor.

Donovan dodged around a tree and ducked under a branch and Naomi lost sight of them. She moved closer to the edge of the embankment... just in time to see a blob of black come barreling toward her.

On pure instinct, she crouched, her arms shot out, and the bear cub ran right into her chest. She wrapped her arms around it, hugging it close.

The bear wiggled but she immediately started talking to him softly.

"Okay, there you go. Shh. It's okay, baby. I've got you. You're okay now."

Donovan came up over the crest of the roadside ditch, but pulled up short.

Naomi hunched her shoulders, trying to keep the rain from pelting the cub. He was still wiggling, but he wasn't fighting. Either he was too weak, he was resigned to his fate, or he sensed safety. Whatever it was, she'd take it. She pivoted, heading for the back of Donovan's truck.

With long strides, he met them there without a word and opened the back of the truck, then the crate that held the cub's brother and sister. Donovan's big, capable hands helped get the cub into the cage and the animal immediately moved to huddle with the others.

Holy. Crap.

She'd just caught and held a baby *bear*. A real, live, *wild* bear cub. She hugged her arms against her body.

Donovan replaced the top of the truck bed, then turned toward her, but she quickly pivoted away.

She wanted so badly to throw herself into his arms.

She knew it was a combination of adrenaline, and relief, and an itchiness to get the hell out of here and get them all to safety, and a pulsing desire for this man.

But she also knew once she was in his arms, she wouldn't want to leave.

She headed for her truck.

"You want to ride back with me?" Donovan called over the wind and rain.

She paused with her hand on her door and shook her head. "I have to get the truck back."

That was true. She couldn't just leave it out here. But also, she needed some space from this guy. Every time she witnessed a rescue she felt this combination of emotions.

What Donovan did for a living was amazing. And important. She'd been watching him on television and the internet for a couple of years now. She respected him and was a fan. Of the on screen Donovan. Hell, she'd given fifty percent of the money to build his rehabilitation center here in Autre. She believed in what he did.

But she *wanted* him. On a very personal level. She wanted him to be safe and happy and...hers.

Over the past couple of months the feeling of being torn in half had grown stronger and stronger. She loved what Donovan *did*. But...she also loved Donovan. And those feelings fought for dominance in her heart.

"Be safe," he called.

She sucked in a quick breath. And then worked to keep from showing her shock at those two little words he'd never said to her before.

She had to clear her throat and was grateful for the wind and rain to cover her reaction. "Oh, if I get blown off the road and into the Gulf, I will absolutely appear to Gracie Trahan so she can give you a message from me," she retorted.

The little girl had lost her dad and claimed that she communicated with his ghost—and others. No one had any reason to not believe her. Even Donovan, who'd just met her a few months ago.

Yeah, him being good with kids was just another reason for Naomi to want him.

She groaned—also covered by the storm, thank God. She didn't need *anything* more added to that list.

"Let's *definitely* not have that happen," he called back. "Grace doesn't need to learn all those bad words at such a young age."

Ha. Well, he knew Naomi well enough to know she'd be cussing him out if she came back to haunt him. Naomi shot him a grin and then climbed up into her truck.

They made their way back to Autre slowly. He'd only been about five miles out of town, but those five miles took forever. The rain and wind made things precarious and Donovan navigated the roads more carefully than she'd ever seen him drive. By the time they finally pulled up next to the rehabilitation center that Boys of the Bayou Gone Wild had constructed, Naomi made herself take a deep breath and unclench her hands from the wheel.

She grabbed her backpack purse, hiking it up over both shoulders, and then got out. She sloshed through the puddles to meet Donovan at the back of his truck.

"You didn't have to come over here with me," he told her.

"You've got three bears and two hands. Figured you might need some help." She took the other end of the crate.

He didn't argue with her and she was grateful. She really did want to be here with him. To make sure he was okay and didn't try to head back out into the storm for any reason. And because...as much as she sometimes wished it wasn't true, she liked being with him. A lot.

When they got to the door of the building, Donovan yanked it open and she ducked inside. They set the crate down and Donovan struggled against the wind to shut the door behind them.

Finally it thudded shut, blocking out the storm.

The building was very basic, but it had been built by Landrys, so was incredibly sturdy. The Landry boys, with Zeke in the lead and Mitch as his right-hand man, knew what they were doing when they put buildings up that had to withstand the weather of southern Louisiana. The rehab center had a concrete floor, steel and wood walls, and a high ceiling. There were windows up near the rafters, but most of the light came from electric lights positioned throughout the building.

There were pens and kennels of all sizes to house the various animals that Donovan brought in for rehabilitation. Each one had a door that opened to an outside pen as well. Of course, today, all of those doors were not just closed but had been secured with additional plywood.

There were also some interior play and exercise rooms and Donovan had an examination room and an office in the building as well.

Naomi had been here a number of times. She'd somehow ended up as the head videographer for the Boys of the Bayou Gone Wild. They put their videos up on the animal park's website and other social media pages. She'd filmed Donovan here working with the animals several times over the past few months.

She hadn't intended to get involved with the park beyond her anonymous donations, but she hadn't been able to stay away. Her best friends Charlotte—Charlie to her family and friends—and Jordan, were running the animal park and sanctuary for rescued domestic animals like donkeys, horses, dogs, and even a couple of camels. Naomi suspected the guys—Griffin, Charlie's boyfriend, and Fletcher, Jordan's husband, as well as Owen, Josh, and Sawyer, the Landrys who actually *owned* Boys of the Bayou Gone Wild—realized the girls were slowly transforming their simple petting zoo into a full-blown animal park. But as big and rugged and protective as the Landry men were on the outside, when it came to the women they loved, and the women their women called friends—not to mention cute animals in need—they were all big, sweet, jelly donuts.

It was hilarious.

Naomi had known them all most of her life. Her family was close to all the Landrys and seeing the rough and tumble boys who had raised hell on the bayou since they'd been old enough to walk and talk getting all soft and squishy over women and animals was something she was delighted to witness.

Donovan headed for the examination room with the cubs and Naomi followed.

He set the crate on the large exam table, then crossed to the cupboards to pull out two towels. He tossed one to Naomi.

"I've got extra clothes here," he said as he wiped his face and then ran the towel over his hair. "Never know when I'm going to get dirty or bloody or both."

She smiled. "I'm sure that's true."

"Want a t-shirt? Maybe some shorts that have a drawstring would work? We do have a washer and dryer. We have to launder blankets and towels and rags all the time. We can throw our stuff in."

"Yeah, that'd be great." She was definitely feeling uncomfortable in the wet clothes that were now clinging and cold. Her socks were squishing inside her boots and even her bra and panties were wet.

Donovan ducked out of the room and Naomi toweled off as best she could.

She knew Donovan had everything he needed here. There was a locker room with a shower. There was a microwave, coffeepot, and small fridge in his office along with a couch she knew he crashed on often. He spent a lot of nights up here when he had an especially sick or hurt animal in his care.

Yes, she knew *a lot* about his habits. Because Charlie talked about him a lot because Griffin talked about him to Charlie a lot.

And because Naomi asked about him a lot.

She worried.

Yes, she was in love with him too. But he didn't know that. *No one* knew that. She'd barely admitted it to herself. But she also worried about him. Donovan was not just an adrenaline junkie who took crazy risks. He also seemed...restless. Like he needed something but wasn't sure what it was.

She suspected it was family. Roots. Home. A place to belong.

He'd been wandering since his parents had died suddenly when he was a teen. But she saw him now in Autre with his brother, and the Landry family, and *her* family. He loved it here. She could tell.

She really wanted him to want to stay.

Kind of.

At least when he wasn't wrestling alligators and making her question his sanity.

He came back a few minutes later, dressed in a pair of loose gray athletic pants and a dark green t-shirt. His feet were bare.

Naomi felt her stomach muscles—and muscles lower—clench.

She'd seen him without a shirt on a number of times. He had a *very* nice chest and amazing abs. He also had a really hot tiger tattoo that wrapped from the middle of his back to the middle of his stomach.

But there was something about him in simple sweat pants and a t-shirt that made her want to step forward, press her face against his neck, and just breathe him in.

She was losing it.

"These might work." He handed over another t-shirt and a pair of shorts. "Locker room's third door on the right."

She took the clothes and nodded. "Be right back."

In the locker room, she stripped out of her cold, wet clothes. All of them. Every piece of clothing she'd had on was soaked. Standing naked in front of the huge mirror, she shivered. She was cold, for sure. But that wasn't why her nipples were beading and her skin was covered in goosebumps.

It was because Donovan was only a few feet away and they were stuck in here together. Alone. And because the dirty dreams she'd been having about him had been getting more frequent. And more graphic.

And because...dammit...yeah, she was in love with him.

This wasn't just an infatuation anymore. It had started that way. She'd known who he was from his TV show. She'd thought he was hot. It had been a pretty simple celebrity crush. But then it had morphed into more. He'd become a friend.

And now...he was going to break her heart.

She pulled the shirt on over her head. It was white and the front was covered with the Boys of the Bayou Gone Wild logo with the otter face in the middle. It hit her at mid-thigh and in spite of the brown otter and the teal circle surrounding him, her nipples were still prominent behind the soft cotton.

She took a deep breath.

Her bra and panties were too wet to put back on. She should just go out there without anything on under this shirt. She should just walk up to Donovan, look him right in the eye, and say, "I want you."

Naomi pressed her lips together. This was the perfect opportunity. She'd be an idiot not to take advantage of it.

But in the end, she reached into her backpack and pulled out a pair of panties.

Yes, she had an extra pair of panties in her backpack purse. She always had everything she needed in her bag. Her friends and family teased her about it, but they had all—literally every single one of them—benefitted from the fact that she was always prepared for any situation and her bag always had anything anyone needed in it.

She wiggled into the panties, then gathered up her wet clothes and headed back to the exam room.

She stepped into the room, added her wet clothes to the pile of Donovan's, and said, "The shorts didn't really work. Even with the drawstring."

Okay, she hadn't even tried. It was a white lie.

And when Donovan's gaze dropped to her bare legs and he swallowed hard and had to clear his throat before he spoke, she didn't feel bad about that little fib at all.

2

"Wha—What do you mean?"

But Donovan knew exactly what she meant.

Naomi LeClaire was naked underneath that shirt. And she was most definitely within touching distance.

"But the shirt's really long," she said, glancing down. "So I'm just good like this."

Like this. Meaning without shorts. Or, obviously, her jeans. Or anything else.

He was *not* going to ask if she was wearing panties.

He was *not*.

"How can I help?" she asked, moving in next to him as he examined the second cub for any abrasions, cuts, or other injuries.

She smelled amazing. How could she smell amazing? They'd just been outside in a rainstorm. She'd been holding a bear. A muddy baby bear.

"Uh. Just. Um..." He sounded like a dumbass.

But the woman he was already mostly gone for was now standing next to him, practically naked, smelling amazing, after helping him rescue a baby bear during a near-hurricane.

She looked up at him.

Her brown eyes, a warm chestnut color, were so gorgeous. He wanted to cup her face and just stare at her. He wanted to run his hands over her cheeks and down her neck and over her shoulders. Then he wanted to bring her up against him. He wanted to cup her gorgeous ass and press her close.

His gaze dropped to her mouth. He definitely wanted to taste her lips. He'd seen them berry colored, a pinkish color, and crimson red. And yeah, he was just realizing how obsessed he was with her lips. He'd been cataloging her lipstick shades. Apparently. But today she wasn't wearing any lipstick or gloss. And God, he wanted to kiss her.

"Donovan?"

Did she sound breathless? Surely not.

"Yeah," he finally managed. "Yeah. We, um, need to get them fed."

Baby bears. Baby bears that needed care. Specifically food and water. Right now.

He needed to focus.

He moved around the table to the cabinets, pulling out the ingredients to mix up the food—similar to baby cereal—they'd try first. If that didn't work, they might have to bottle feed the cubs.

Two of the cubs took the cereal right away. The third, the one Naomi had caught, was less inclined.

"We'll have to give him a bottle."

"Can I do it?" she asked eagerly.

Donovan laughed. "Sure. Let's get them settled in the pen."

Donovan prepped the bottle and they moved the cubs to one of the pens in the main portion of the building. Naomi propped up against the wall and Donovan gave her a blanket, the bear, and the bottle. The cub gratefully started nursing.

She looked up at him. "Well, this is good, right?"

It was very good, because the blanket was covering her legs

and the flash of white panties he'd seen when she'd gotten down on the floor.

"Yep. For now. He needs the calories. But we don't want him getting dependent on us."

She nodded and looked down at the animal. "You think they've been on their own for two days?"

"Probably about that."

"Poor babies."

He just watched them for a moment. She looked so beautiful like this. She should look like a mess, shouldn't she? Just having been out in a rainstorm? Her hair still wet? Wearing his clothes while hers dried? But no. She looked soft and happy, if slightly amazed to be holding a baby bear. And...she definitely wasn't wearing a bra. The shirt was big on her and fell off one shoulder, but now with the bear on her lap, it pulled more tightly against her breasts and her nipples were obviously hard and there was nothing between them and the soft cotton.

Donovan cleared his throat. "I'll be back with more supplies."

He took his time putting their clothes into the washing machine, texting his brother and Zander about where he and Naomi were and that they were fine, and gathering supplies for the bear pen.

But nothing was going to actually work to get the image of the sexiest and most amazing woman he knew, holding a baby bear, out of his mind.

Finally, he returned to the pen with bedding and toys for the cubs. They were babies. They'd need things to explore and to play with as they gained strength and learned to climb and forage on their own.

They scampered to the far corner as he rolled the first car tire into the enclosure. It would provide something for them to explore and climb on.

Naomi got to her feet and Donovan didn't look away fast enough to avoid the flash of panties he got.

Or maybe he didn't really try that hard.

Naomi joined him as he made a few trips from the supply room, adding two more car tires for climbing, a plastic barrel with the bottom cut off for the cubs to explore, and a large plastic igloo they could turn into a den. He'd add some logs and branches as well when he could get back outside.

"So, now we need a plan here," Naomi told him, surveying the pen. "There's a big storm brewing and you need a plan for not just the bears, but all the other animals that you're housing here. And for *yourself*."

"I've just got a beaver and a wolf. And they're doing fine right now. Plenty of supplies. I checked in and they're restless— I'm sure sensing the storm—but they're safe."

"Okay, good. So now that these guys are settled, you can come up to Ellie's."

Part of him wanted to go up to Ellie's. The way these people always came together pulled at him and made him want to be a part of it every time. But he wasn't *really* a part of it. He was a visitor here. Oh, they made him feel included. Definitely. He felt accepted here in a way he never had anywhere else he'd traveled in all the years since he'd left home. And it was *very* tempting to settle in. To let it all wrap around him and make him feel like never packing a suitcase again.

And if he hadn't gotten the offer to go to the Galapagos Islands to help shoot and narrate a documentary in two months, he might just head up to Ellie's, let her dish him up a huge bowl of gumbo, and get cozy with the rest of them during this storm.

He'd listen to their crazy, fifty-percent-true-fifty-percent-pure-bullshit stories, wallow in their genuine affection for one another—and even for him—and the sense of camaraderie that comforted everyone, even during a big storm. It was a feeling that made everyone certain that, even when the world outside was out-of-control and could make a horrible fucking mess of everything they loved, they'd all pull together to clean it up when it was over and make it right again.

But the job offer *had* come, so he should stay down here and not get any more attached to these people and this place that he might be—*probably* would be—leaving soon with the hopes that this documentary would then lead to even bigger things.

Okay, so he'd told the producers, "Probably," when they'd asked him for an answer. No, he hadn't given them a definite commitment. He'd asked them to let him think about it.

He'd never done that before. A job offer that included traveling to an exotic, faraway place to do work that would benefit animals and educate humans? He always jumped at that. This offer should have been a no-brainer. He knew the foundation funding the documentary had gotten his name from Jillian Morris, the veterinarian and expert on Galapagos penguins who was living and working right here in Autre. He was grateful. He should have been ecstatic.

Instead, he'd said, "Probably. Let me think about it."

He was *probably* an idiot.

"I'll just stay here till the storm blows over," he told Naomi. "So I'm on site for anything."

She sighed. "Of course."

"I stay here a lot," he told her. "Part of the job is to be on site for any needs."

"I know."

"The rollaway bed I have here is actually pretty comfortable." He crashed on the couch in his office for naps and short periods but if he was spending the whole night, he pulled out the bed that folded up and rolled easily into the storeroom.

"Did you actually sleep on the ground and camp out as much as they made it seem on your show?" she asked.

"Maybe not quite as much as they made it seem," he admitted. "But I've definitely slept in lots of tents and on cots and in rundown cabins and in my truck many, many times."

"Fine," she said, handing him the empty bottle.

"Fine? That I stay out here?"

"You probably should. Unlike the other animals in the park, your animals are hurt. You probably should be here in case something crazy happens and you can't get back to them or if they get spooked and hurt themselves or something."

"How bad is the storm supposed to be?"

"You're from the Midwest, right? I assume you've been through tornadoes?"

"Several."

"So kind of like that. But bigger. And with lots more water."

He sighed. Tornadoes could make a hell of a mess.

"The eye of the storm is supposedly going to hit quite a bit east of here. But we could have a lot of water. And these damn storms can shift. So nothing's for sure until it's sure."

"Okay, then let's get you back up to your family."

He turned and stepped out of the pen, holding it open for her. She stepped out and he closed it behind her, turning the latch.

She shook her head. "My family is fine. There's lots of them and they're all together. Plus they're with the Landrys up at Ellie's. They don't need me. And Michael is out doing his fire chief and paramedic thing. If anyone needs anything medical, he's the one they're going to call, not me."

"But you've got duct tape and super glue in your purse," he teased.

Naomi always had whatever anyone needed in her purse, it seemed. She could magically pull out anything from ibuprofen to a hair tie to duct tape to a fork. He'd seen all of those come from her bag at one time or another.

She gave him a half smile. "And Cora's got all of her potions and creams in the back room."

True enough. He leaned in. Yep, she definitely smelled amazing. "Are you offering to stay out here with me?"

Why would she do that?

"Donovan, the storm is no joke. But *you* are the greatest risk to *your* health and safety."

He gave a soft laugh. That wasn't entirely inaccurate. He was an adrenaline junkie. Unapologetic. He lived life hard and fully. He might die young, but he wasn't gonna die with any regrets.

"You're afraid I'm going to go back out there in this storm?"

"God only knows what idea you might get in your head," she said with a nod.

"Well, I do have food and water out here. And blankets and all of that. Phone. Internet. As long as they don't go out. But I've only got the one rollaway and the sofa."

Naomi lifted her chin. "You don't think I can handle a rollaway?"

"Naomi LeClaire, I think you can handle just about anything." He meant that with everything in him.

She seemed pleased by that response.

Just then a loud boom sounded overhead and the lights flickered and went off.

"Well... dammit," Donovan said.

He pulled his phone from his pocket, swiping his thumb over the screen and lighting the immediate area with a soft glow.

"Guess that rules out watching any Netflix while we wait it out."

"Guess so," Naomi agreed.

"So, maybe—"

Naomi suddenly stepped close, took hold of his shirt in

both hands, and pulled him in. "I'm really glad you didn't die out there rescuing those bears," she said softly against his lips.

Then she kissed him.

He was shocked. Actually shocked.

They were friends.

She was too good for him.

And she knew it.

She thought he was a dumbass.

But he was programmed to think quickly on his feet.

So kissing this woman back, very, very thoroughly, commenced exactly two and a half seconds later.

One of his hands fisted in the material of the t-shirt at her lower back and his other hand cupped the side of her head, pulling her up against him more fully.

One of them moaned.

No, *she* moaned.

He *growled*.

It was low and from the back of his throat, but it was definitely a growl and it meant *fuck yes.*

He turned her and walked her back until her butt pressed into the side of the pen where the bear cubs were playing. There were wooden beams holding the chain-link together, but it wasn't firm enough. Seemingly for either of them. He tried to press closer, but the fencing gave a little with the force. He needed a solid surface behind her. Frustrated, Donovan lifted his head.

At some point during the moments he'd been caught up in her, the emergency lights, nestled high in the corners of the ceiling, had kicked on and the building was now lit by a brighter, though still muted glow.

He was grateful for those lights, not because it was going to make his *job* easier as they were intended, but because they allowed him to look into Naomi LeClaire's face.

And see desire. Pure, honest, obvious desire.

He stared down at her, breathing fast. "What is this?" The question sounded harsher than he meant for it to, but his blood was pumping hard and his entire body was screaming at him to strip the shirt off of her, lay her out on the floor, and claim her.

Yeah, he spent a lot of time around animals.

Literally.

She ran her tongue over her lips. "Do you remember the day you jumped from one moving air boat to another to take a baby gray wolf away from those people who had trapped her?"

"I do."

"Do you remember that night?"

"That night you showed up on my porch with an absolutely amazing orange rum cake."

"Gateau a l'orange," she said with a nod. "And what did I tell you?"

"You said you were trying to give me a reason to live. That if I tasted your grandmother's food, I would have at least one more really good reason to stay healthy enough to chew and swallow."

He gave her a slow half grin as he thought about how he'd felt seeing her standing on the porch with a covered cake plate. She'd been wearing cut off denim shorts and a simple, white tank top. She'd looked hot as fuck.

But he'd been shocked by the softer feeling that had accompanied seeing her there. It had felt amazing to have someone care enough to bring him cake. It was stupid actually.

He'd also been shocked by the intensity with which he'd wanted to press her up against the side of the house and kiss the hell out of her. Not because of the short shorts and the long, smooth legs, and the way her curves had filled the denim out, but because of the cake.

Well, the cake and the look in her eyes when she'd handed it to him.

There had been affection there. True I-want-you-to-know-I-care affection.

That had grabbed him in the chest and made him want her in a way he hadn't wanted a woman before.

So, instead of pushing her up against the side of the house, he'd kissed her cheek. Yeah, he might have lingered a bit. But damn, she really did smell good all the time.

"And I thought it worked. But then, a couple months later, you wrestled an alligator. You *literally* jumped on its back and held its mouth shut."

"I did that to save a penguin," Donovan felt compelled to point out.

One of the penguins had gotten away from the little parade they'd done as an enrichment activity. And he had quickly found himself being stalked by a gator. Donovan had tossed a net over the bird from several feet away and hauled him up into a tree out of the gator's reach but, before he could get the alligator out of the way, two others had joined him. The penguin—and Zeke, who had climbed up to calm the bird and eventually bring him down—had dangled over the three alligators for several minutes while Donovan and Zander had subdued and removed the reptiles.

Naomi acknowledged that with a tip of her head. "Still, I was worried about you not having both hands and all ten fingers intact afterward, so I brought you some of my grandmother's griot."

The griot—a Haitian dish with marinated meat that was served with rice and pikliz, a pickled vegetable relish—had been incredible.

"And you told me you were hoping it would make me want to keep all of my fingers so that I could continue to easily use forks and spoons."

She gave him a little smile. "And to live to see another meal."

It had made him hungry, but not for fried pork.

He'd wanted to press her against the side of the house and kiss the hell out of her again. While also hiking up the skirt on the pretty little yellow sundress she'd been wearing. Badly. He'd *badly* wanted to hike that skirt up.

He'd kissed her cheek again instead. But that time he'd dragged the back of his knuckles over her cheek before leaning in to press his lips to her sweet skin. And he'd *absolutely* lingered that time.

He'd also fully memorized the little breathy sigh she'd given when he'd done it. That tiny reaction from her had been enough to send heat straight to his gut and resisting the urge to press her against the house had been nearly impossible.

But he had. Naomi LeClaire was amazing. Sharp. Classy. Sweet. Funny. Composed.

Did all of that make seeing her muddy and windblown and mussed even hotter?

Yes, it fucking did.

It also made him acutely aware of the fact that muddy, windblown, and mussed was not her norm and that she was not someone who should be expected to do any of that on a regular basis.

He was.

He was muddy, windblown, messy, and sweaty, even bloody at times.

They were a major mismatch.

But dammit, if she was going to bring him cake and let him get inside her personal space, he was going to enjoy it.

"So what's that got to do with this?" he asked, his gaze dropping to her mouth.

"After finding you outside during a hurricane rescuing bears, I realized maybe the food hasn't been enough. I thought perhaps you needed something more to make you happy to be alive."

"A kiss from one of the most amazing women I know?" He shook his head, meeting her eyes again. "Definitely happy to be alive at the moment. But feeding me amazing food and kissing me after I've done something dangerous isn't exactly a *negative* consequence, you know. Maybe it's *encouraging* me."

"Well, then I need to give you a demonstration of why having all ten of your fingers is a really good thing." *Her* ten fingers curled into the back of his neck where she'd been holding on as she'd lifted on tiptoe, trying to press closer to him.

"I actually know a guy who lost his index and middle finger when working with a shark in the—"

Suddenly her hand was covering his mouth. "Nope," she said simply.

But the guy hadn't lost the fingers *to* the shark. It had been an accident with some equipment on the boat. That could happen to anyone. "But—" Donovan started, his response muffled behind her palm.

"I'm sure you do. I'm sure he's a great guy. I'm sure he makes things work with those eight fingers and so would you. *But—*" She moved her hand and then took one of his and ran it down the side of her body, over the outer curve of her breast, to her ass. "You've got all ten at the moment and I want them *all* on me."

Donovan grinned and squeezed her ass. "Okay, you've got a point. Kinda wishing I had twelve right now, in fact."

She shook her head but was smiling. She lifted up and put her mouth against his again.

He used his all-fingers-intact hand on her ass to bring her up against him more fully as he kissed her, dragging his tongue along her lower lip before dipping inside to sweep over the inside of her lip and then against her tongue. That lip tasted absolutely as good as he'd imagined all these weeks and feeling her tongue against his, hungry and sweet, sent heat throbbing through his cock.

"I really hope *this* is better than my grandma's cake," she said softly as she pulled back.

"This is..." He took a deep breath. "Everything."

Her eyes were hot. "Then don't stop."

Damn. That sounded like the best thing that anyone had ever said to him. But he had to be *crystal* clear here. This wasn't just some random woman he'd been flirting with in a local bar. This was Naomi.

She was a friend. But she was so much more than that.

He respected her. Admired her. *Liked* her. He also respected, admired, and liked her family. He knew her brother very well. He'd talked to her grandfather several times.

They also had a lot of friends in common.

Donovan hadn't had a group of friends like the group he now had in Autre in...ever. On purpose. He'd kept himself from forming close bonds with people after his parents had died. The only person he'd let close was his brother Griffin, and Donovan didn't spend a lot of time in the same place as Griffin. Also on purpose. It was a lot harder to disappoint people if they weren't around every single day.

But Donovan had screwed up seven months ago.

He'd been so intrigued by the idea of Griffin being sucked into a big Cajun family and falling in love with not just a sassy southern girl, but also a family of otters and a pen full of alpacas, that Donovan had decided to stop by and see it all for himself.

And he hadn't left.

He kept meaning to. He kept telling himself he would soon.

But dammit, Autre, Louisiana, and the Landry family and this petting-zoo-turned-animal-park seemed to have some magical forcefield around it or something. It let you in, but getting back out was nearly impossible.

Not that he'd tried very hard.

And this woman, with the big, brown eyes, and the sweet skin, and the I-want-them-all-over-me lips was definitely one of the reasons.

This was all why he'd told the documentary producers he had to think about the job offer.

Dammit.

"Tell me what you want. *Exactly*." His voice was rough, but he *needed* this spelled out.

She swallowed. Then nodded. "You."

"You can have whatever you want of me."

Her pupils dilated and her lips parted. "All of you."

His fist tightened where it was holding her shirt at her lower back. "Nae," he said, his voice gruff and low. "Spell it out."

She gave a soft laugh. "You'll take every other risk there is, but *this* you're going to be careful about?"

His fist tightened in her shirt again and he brought her close, pressing her against his aching fly. "Yes," he said simply.

Her smile died. "Okay." He felt her fingers slide from the back of his neck to the sides of his head. She held his face between her hands and looked him directly in the eye. "Donovan, I want you. All of you. Hot. Hard. Naked. Under me. In me."

He felt his heart slamming against his chest so hard it almost hurt.

"Okay, then there's something you need to know," he managed. He *had* to tell her he might be leaving.

Dammit, he *was* leaving. Right? Now he had a concrete reason. Before it had been easier to stay because there hadn't been something specific to move on to. But to not take this job would be stupid.

And Naomi deserved to know before anything really happened between them.

She pressed her lips together, studying his face. She was obviously hesitant. Finally she nodded. "Okay."

"I got a job offer. To film a documentary in the Galapagos Islands."

She took a few seconds to process that. "You would be amazing for that."

"Thank you." And then she had to go and say things that made him *like* her even more.

"When?"

"I leave in two months."

She swallowed. "I knew you weren't staying indefinitely, Donovan."

He felt his heart knock against his ribs again. That was fair. He didn't stay. Anywhere. "So, I'll understand if you don't want to go any further here."

Her fingers pressed into his jaw. "That's all the more reason *to* do this. I'm running out of chances," she said huskily.

Heat, sharp and swift, sliced through him. He pulled in a breath through his nose, certain that his desire was clear as he stared at her. "You have one more second to take that back." His voice sounded like a growl now.

"Not going to happen."

Okay then. He cupped her ass with both hands and lifted. She gave a little gasp, but wrapped both legs and arms around him. He kissed her as he carried her across the twenty feet of concrete flooring to the nearest solid wall.

He could barely hear the storm outside through the walls of the building, but the rain pounded on the roof and he could see flashes of lightning through the high windows. The emergency lights were enough to keep him from tripping over anything though. And would allow him to see at least some of Naomi.

Not enough.

He wouldn't get enough of that unless he had fluorescent bulbs and a king-sized bed.

He put her against the wall, and they both moaned as he was finally able to press his cock against the soft spot between her thighs. Her legs tightened around him and she arched her back, as if trying to get closer.

He kissed her deeply, then dragged his mouth over her jaw and down the side of her throat. She tipped her head back, her fingers digging into his shoulders.

"Donovan," she gasped.

"God, you taste amazing. You smell amazing. You feel so fucking good," he muttered against her skin as he kissed and licked and sucked along her throat to her collarbone.

"Donovan," she said again.

"Lose the shirt, Nae," he said gruffly. He needed her as naked as he could get her, but if he let go of his hold to strip her, she'd slide to the floor.

"I—" Then she seemed to give up whatever protest she'd started because she reached down between them and started to pull the shirt up.

Donovan leaned back slightly to let her wiggle the cotton up her torso and yeah, he definitely wished he had more light.

She got the shirt up over her head, pulled it loose from her hair, and tossed it on the floor beside them.

"Damn," Donovan said appreciatively.

She was magnificent. All ten of his fingers were itching to cup and tease those sweet, dark nipples.

She rested her forearms on his shoulders. "Now what?"

"I—"

Fuck, he couldn't even touch her in this position. Not the way he wanted to. This position was for when they were both already naked and hot and ready and it was time to sink deep.

"There's a couch just on the other side of this wall," she said with a little knowing grin.

There was. His office was *right there*. What the *fuck* was he doing?

"I'm a dumbass."

She just laughed as he shifted back and walked them into his office. He sank down onto the sofa that sat against the wall they'd just been leaning on.

Definite dumbass. But all of those thoughts flew from his mind as Naomi's body settled fully against his and she leaned in to kiss him.

His hands now free, he ran them from the curve of her ass up her now naked back and under her long hair. He pulled on the tie in her hair.

"Want these loose," he told her gruffly.

"Yeah?"

"You look like a fucking goddess," he said honestly.

Donovan lifted a hand and took the end of a braid between his thumb and index finger. As he toyed with the silky twisted strand, the back of his finger brushed over her breast, just above her nipple.

She sucked in a breath and shifted in his lap.

He watched her nipple draw tighter and felt her fingers curl into his chest.

He looked up at her.

She was watching him, breathing fast. She wet her lips. "We're going to need a condom."

He huffed out a surprised breath. Well, if things hadn't been crystal clear before, now they were. "Glad to hear it."

"Do you have one in here?"

He brushed his finger back and forth across her breast, loving the silky feel of her hair and her skin. Nearly as much as he loved her sharp intake of air.

"Do I have condoms in my office at the animal rehabilitation center?" He shook his head. "No, I don't."

"I'm actually glad to hear that," she admitted. "Very glad you don't have use for those here on a regular basis."

"But that might be a problem right now."

She swallowed. "I have some in my purse."

He grinned. "Of course you do. You have everything in that purse."

She lifted a shoulder. "I'm very good at anticipating needs. But my purse is in the exam room."

He appreciated that about her, but he wasn't so sure that he loved the idea that she routinely needed to have condoms within reach. "I'm not going to think about you packing your purse with condoms just in case."

"That's only been happening since you got to town."

Heat, surprise, and pleasure stabbed him in the gut. "That right? How long was I in town before you put the first ones in there?"

"About a week."

"It took a week for you to decide you wanted to sleep with me?"

She grinned. "A week to decide that I might act on it."

He ran his finger back and forth again, loving the way her breath caught and her nipple tightened. "It's been seven months, Nae."

She nodded. "Way past time."

"I'm getting your purse." He started to shift her to the side so he could stand and retrieve the bag.

She pressed against his chest. "No, I'll go."

"You're naked."

"Not totally," she said with a mischievous smile. "And I want you right here when I get back." She pushed back off his lap, then stood looking down at him for a moment.

Goddess. It was absolutely the only word that came to mind at that moment. She stood in front of him, unabashedly naked except for the tiny white silk panties she still wore. Her breasts were round and high, with hard, dark centers. Her long legs and bare feet with the berry-colored toenail polish that matched his favorite of her lip colors all added to the picture of a confident, sexy-as-fuck woman who was finally going to be his. Even if it was for a brief fling during a storm.

"Will you take your shirt off?"

He didn't hesitate to reach for the bottom of the t-shirt. He stripped it off, wadding it slightly, and threw it toward his desk where it landed in a heap on the floor.

"Ooh, yes," she said appreciatively. "Now stretch your arms out over the back of the couch."

Amused and slightly puzzled, he did as she asked.

He felt completely on display and objectified. And he loved it.

If Naomi wanted to look at him like this, if this did something for her, he was all in. In fact, he was going to feel cocky about this for weeks.

She nodded, as if pleased. "Yeah, that's how I pictured it."

He was sitting in the middle of the couch, his arms stretched out over the back, shirtless, lounging in sweatpants, the front of the sweatpants quite obviously tented with a big, hard erection. He hadn't put underwear on when he'd changed clothes. Most of the time when he was in need of a change of clothes, it was because his outer layer had gotten muddy or bloody. He didn't often need a change of underwear.

"You pictured *this*?" he asked.

"Oh, I pictured a lot of things."

He liked that. He fucking liked that a lot.

"I'm going to need to hear about this," he told her, his voice rough as lust surged through him. "I want to hear every one of your fantasies."

"All of them?" she asked, tipping her head. "Or just the ones that involve you?"

Sassy. It wasn't that he was shocked that Naomi could be sassy. She was a Louisiana girl. More specifically, an Autre girl. He'd been around when she'd been hanging out with her brother and his friends. And her friends. Sassy was in the water around here. But Naomi was the quiet, cool, composed one of the group. Most of the time. Sassy was unusual.

He really liked it on her.

He narrowed his eyes and lowered his voice. "We'll start with the ones specifically about me. Then we'll move on to the other ones. And I intend to make those all about me as well."

Her eyes widened as did her smile, as if he'd given a very good answer. "Okay, Wild Thing, I'll take you up on that."

He gave a choked laugh. "Wild Thing?"

She gave him another smile that was absolutely full of sass. "Yeah." Her gaze tracked over him from his face, down his naked chest, over his abs, lingered on the front of his sweatpants, moved down to his bare feet and back up. "If you're going to be out there risking your fingers and neck, Wild Thing definitely fits."

Then she pivoted on her heel and left the room.

Donovan blew out a breath.

Goddess. Absolutely.

But a sassy, sexy-as-fuck, totally-in-control, had-him-wrapped-around-her-little-finger, carried-condoms-in-her-purse-just-for-him goddess.

She was even better than he'd realized.

3

Naomi hurried through the dimly lit building to the exam room, grabbed her purse, and headed back for Donovan's office.

Donovan Foster was lounging, shirtless, on the couch, waiting for her to return.

This day was going very well.

In spite of the hurricane battering the coast a couple hundred miles away.

In spite of the fact that she'd been drenched, muddy, and freezing earlier.

In spite of the fact that the man she was mostly in love with had risked his life again today.

In spite of the fact that that man was leaving in two months.

She had to stop and make herself breathe again with that thought.

She'd known it was coming. She'd been shocked it had taken him this long to go. She *had* to stop letting that reality make her heart ache.

And she had to get back in there to him and enjoy every damned minute she had left with him.

She stepped back into the office and took in the sight of Donovan, his tanned skin stretched over his hard muscles, his lightly haired chest, his sixpack abs, and that gloriously hard cock behind the soft cotton of his sweatpants all for her.

Yes, today was going very well.

She reached into her purse, dug into the pocket where she knew she'd tucked condoms, pulled two out, and tossed the purse toward Donovan's desk. She didn't see where it landed. She didn't care.

She climbed back into his lap.

"Now where were we?"

"You are about to put those hands and that sassy mouth all over me," Donovan told her, his voice husky.

She felt her eyes go wide. Donovan was flirtatious. That was like a default mode for him. But charming and on-camera flirtatious was different than sexy flirtatious.

She wasn't sure she'd seen sexy flirtatious before.

She really liked it.

"Was I?"

He kept his arms stretched out over the back of the couch and the idea of putting her hands and mouth all over him seemed excellent.

"Really think you were," he said, making no move to change his position.

As much as she wanted him touching her, the idea of having Donovan Foster stretched out, all to herself, letting her do whatever she wanted was far too tempting.

She thought for a second, then tucked the condoms in the front of her panties so she wouldn't lose track of them.

His eyes followed her motion.

"That's not how those work."

"I need both hands free."

She started with her hands holding his face and leaning in to press her lips against his.

She loved kissing him. She kissed him softly at first then ran her tongue over his bottom lip. He opened with a groan, and she stroked her tongue in along his. He kissed her back, but still didn't move his hands. It was interesting how she was holding his face, yet it felt like he was taking over the kiss.

Heat licked down her body and settled between her legs as his tongue moved against hers and she could swear that she felt the strokes as if he was applying them to her clit.

She ran her hands from his face and down the sides of his neck to his shoulders, massaging the hard muscles there and stroking down the length of his arms. She even relished the size of his thick wrists and the rougher texture of the skin on his hands as she ran her palms over the backs of his hands and then under so they were palm to palm. He curled his fingers into hers briefly and she felt a strange warmth at the seemingly affectionate gesture.

Then she ran her hands up the underside of his arms to his chest and then down over his ribs to his abs. His muscles bunched under her touch and she finally pulled back from the kiss. She watched as her fingertips traced over the tiger tattoo that covered the left half of his abdomen from just below the curve of his pec muscle to the delicious V that dove into the waistband of his sweatpants.

"I love this," she said, her voice breathless.

"I love you loving it."

She lifted her eyes to his. The usual green had deepened to near black with his desire and she loved the surge of empowerment she felt knowing she was affecting him. She shifted to put her lips against his collarbone, then dragged her mouth down over his chest to his breastbone and down the center of his abs until she got to the tiger's head. She licked over the swirling lines that made up the tiger's head, then body. She followed the ink with her lips and tongue, pulling the front of his pants down to trace over the front leg and paw that ended just above his pubic bone.

She looked up. Donovan's jaw was tight and his hands were gripping the back of the couch tightly. He was holding himself still, clearly trying not to move much.

But she really wanted to know what would happen if he moved.

"Are you okay?"

"And you thought all of those times when I was out facing down wild animals was dangerous," he said, his voice low and husky, sending tingles of awareness down her spine. "Your mouth on me is coming closer to killing me than anything ever has."

She gave him a smile that she was sure looked completely wicked. And she didn't care.

"Should I apologize?"

"As long as I don't have to apologize for what's going to happen if you keep going."

She shook her head slowly. "You don't have to apologize for anything, Donovan. I completely trust you."

Hearing her say that did something to Donovan. He couldn't have described it. Certainly he could have chalked that up to the fact that a gorgeous woman was now kneeling between his knees, half-naked, and was reaching for the front of his pants.

But he knew on some level, it also had to do with the fact that Naomi LeClaire was an amazing person and to have gained her trust meant something. She had a huge family and lots of friends, and they were the best people he'd ever met. She didn't need anyone else in her life. She didn't need to open herself up to anyone. She had everyone she needed. To get close to her meant something.

But as she pulled down the front of his sweatpants and gave a happy little hum at the discovery that he had no underwear on, Donovan realized that the universe at large and humankind —at least the male portion—would certainly forgive him for not being able to analyze his thoughts and emotions any further at the moment.

She tugged the sweatpants past the edge of the couch cushion and let them fall around his ankles. Then she ran her hands up the backs of his calves then to the front of his thighs before she wrapped her fist around the length of his cock.

He felt like lightning bolts were streaking through his gut and up his spine. Donovan groaned. "*Naomi.*"

She lifted her gaze from his cock to his face. "God, I want this so much."

He wasn't sure she could've said anything hotter at that moment.

"You need to take your panties off and give me one of those condoms."

"Not yet."

He wanted to protest and insist that she get up here where he could worship her, but she squeezed him then and stroked and his brain short-circuited.

It had been a while since he'd had someone else's hand around his cock.

He had a few offers since coming to Autre and in the first month or two he'd taken a couple of girls up on those offers. He'd traveled extensively and knew that his pseudo-celebrity status got him extra attention. So he hadn't been without female company when he wanted it over the years.

But after his first couple of months in Autre, the casual hookups with local girls had suddenly seemed strange. He didn't want to get serious with anyone here and he'd caught on, somewhere deep in his psyche, that he wasn't going to be moving on from this place as quickly as usual.

And if he had delved even deeper into the psyche—which was a place he did not go often or intentionally—he knew he would've found that this woman had a lot to do with the fact that those other hookups had lost their appeal.

Naomi stroked her hands up and down the length of his cock and Donovan again could only think the word *goddess*. Her touch was heaven.

"Nae," he managed to grind out. "Need you."

She nodded and leaned forward.

A split second too late, Donovan realized that she mistook his meaning.

Not that he was complaining. Her lips wrapped around his head and she swirled her tongue over the tip before taking him deeper. She gave him a slight suck, then another lick. Instinctively, Donovan's hand went to her head and he took a hold of the braids at the nape of her neck. For just a second, he fought between pressing her closer and pulling her off.

But before he had to make that choice, she lifted her head. "You okay?"

He shook his head. "Need you naked."

Her eyes widened. "I'm good right here."

"Naomi." His voice was deep and firm. "Naked. Now."

She looked from his face to the cock she still held in both hands, then back to his face. She seemed to make a decision. It was the right one.

Because if she had not gotten to her feet on her own, Donovan knew he was a half a second away from grabbing her, pulling her into his lap, and ripping those sweet white panties off of her gorgeous body.

She pushed back on her heels, then straightened. With her gaze locked on his she hooked her thumbs in the top of her panties and pushed them to the floor. The two condoms fell with them. She stepped out of the scrap of white silk and bent to pick one packet up.

Donovan drank in the sight of her bare body. She was perfect from head to toe. Sweet curves and smooth skin and an almost regal air as she stepped between his knees and handed him a condom. He took it from her, ripped it open, and rolled it down his length as she watched.

The lights were certainly not as bright as he would've liked, but they could both see everything that was going on. He loved the lack of shyness and awkwardness. In the time he'd known her, Naomi had met everything she encountered straight-on with a composure that he not only admired but was very drawn to. Composure was not something Donovan had a lot of in his life.

When he had the condom in place, she put a knee on the cushion beside him, braced her hand on his shoulder, and brought her other knee up, straddling his lap. She paused and he realized that she was waiting for him to position his cock so she could sink down onto it.

Fuck, that was hot.

But it wasn't quite time for that. He hadn't teased her nearly enough. He hadn't had his hands and mouth on her. Yet.

"You waiting for something, goddess?"

"Goddess?"

"Oh, you know you're worthy of worship."

She was positioned so that she was looking down at him from a couple of inches. She gave him a small smile. "I was just on my knees in front of *you*."

He nodded. "Exactly. But this is where you belong." He put his hands on her waist and brought her forward so that one nipple was right in front of his mouth. "I've got some definite homage to pay."

He took her nipple between his lips, kissing it lightly, then giving it a flick with his tongue. Her hands gripped his shoulders and he licked over the tight center before drawing it in for a long suck.

She gave a soft moan and he did it again, loving the way her grip tightened on him.

He lifted a hand to the other side teasing that nipple as well, plucking and squeezing until she was shifting restlessly over his lap. Switching his mouth to that breast, he ran his hand down her side to her hip where he squeezed before bringing his palm around to cup between her legs. She was hot and wet and she shifted against his hand impatiently.

He glided back and forth, pressing against her clit with the heel of his hand and feeling her grind against it. He kept up the pressure, letting her show him the rhythm she liked as he drew on her nipple, adding a slight nip.

She gasped his name and the sound sent another bolt of electric heat to his cock. He slipped his middle finger into her pussy and felt her muscles immediately clench around him.

"Yes, Donovan."

"Tell me what you need, Nae."

God, he wanted to hear her telling him exactly what he could do for her. Exactly how he could be everything she wanted and needed.

"More. Just... More." He withdrew his finger then pumped it in again. Judging by the way her muscles tightened around him, he figured that was the right thing to do. He did it again, and again, thrusting deep and curling so that he could hit her G-spot. She pressed against him and moved her knees wider. He leaned back so he could look up into her face. She took a shuddering breath and met his eyes. He loved the way she blatantly made eye contact. He slipped another thick finger in. "So fucking tight," he said.

"It's been a while," she told him, breathlessly.

He loved that. It was very primitive of him, he acknowledged, but he didn't want to think about her being with anyone else. He'd known for a while that she didn't date extensively and that she not only didn't have a boyfriend, but hadn't for a while.

Yeah, he'd asked. And he'd put up with Charlie's knowing smile when he'd done it. He didn't care. Knowing more about Naomi was worth his almost-sister-in-law's nosiness. He hadn't expected to be here with Naomi, but he did like knowing there was no other man in this position with her either.

"But there's a little more worshiping I want to do," he told her, moving his hand slightly to circle his thumb over her clit.

She sucked in a breath. "If it involves me riding you on this couch until neither of us can move for an hour or so, I'm in."

Fuck, he was never going to get over hearing the classy, cool Naomi talk dirty to him. "You're not going anywhere until I feel this sweet pussy around my cock," he promised, circling her clit and pumping his fingers deep. "But there's one thing before that."

"What—"

Before she even finished the question, Donovan grasped her hips with both hands and lifted her so that the pussy he was now obsessed with was in front of his mouth. "Knee up on the back of the couch, Nae," he instructed.

She hesitated. He pinched her ass.

"Let me worship you properly. "

She seemed to recover from her shock or whatever had made her pause. She leaned in and put her left knee up on the back of the couch next to his ear. With his big hands splayed on her ass, he brought her forward and put his mouth on the sweetest pussy he'd ever tasted.

He licked and she gasped, bracing her hand on the wall behind the couch.

He licked and sucked, dipping his tongue into her sweet heat, and then sucking again, loving the feel of her legs trembling and her soft gasps and moans.

In particular, he loved hearing his name from her lips.

"Oh my God, Donovan, I'm going to come like this."

Best thing he'd ever heard. "Damn right you are." He pressed her closer to his mouth and ate her with purpose. Like a man starving. But he was starving for *her* pleasure, to be the one to push her over the edge, to make her desperate and satisfied at the same time.

"Donovan! Donovan!"

The next second she tipped over the edge, coming with a cry and slumping forward to rest her forehead on the wall.

With his hands on her hips, he slid her down his body until their lips met and he kissed her hungrily. He hoped she liked the taste of her on his tongue because it was the most delicious thing he'd ever had in his mouth.

She pulled back after several long moments and stared at him. "Holy crap."

"And I'm not done with you yet." He gripped her hips and shifted her back. He took his cock in one hand, then lifted her with his other, positioning himself at her entrance. "Take me, Nae."

Her hands went to his shoulders and again their gazes locked as she lowered herself on him.

Fresh off her first orgasm, he slid into her with ease.

They groaned as she settled on him fully. She pulled in a long, shaky breath. "God." She was looking at where they were joined.

He reached up and tipped her chin so he could look her in the eye. "So much better than orange cake. Very glad to be alive."

She gave him a grin and there was that sassiness around the edges again as she started moving. She lifted and lowered herself on his shaft and each stroke sent waves of heat and lust coursing through him.

This woman was amazing and her fucking him was the

hottest thing that had ever happened to him. He had to sit back and let her take the lead. He actually leaned back, stretched his arms across the back of the couch again, and just let her move.

Her eyes flashed with heat and she braced her hands flat on his chest, picking up the pace, swiveling her hips as she took him, her breasts bouncing, her head thrown back.

Goddess.

He fought to stay still.

"Donovan," she said breathlessly after a few minutes of just moving. "This is so, so good."

He unlocked his tight jaw. "You have no fucking idea."

"But I need more."

His eyes snapped from where she was taking him over and over to her face. "What do you need? Anything."

"I don't know. Something. You."

He gripped the couch. "You have me. All of me."

"Will you..."

"Yes," he answered without needing to hear her whole question.

She smiled, realizing that. "Your desk. One of my fantasies is your desk. Me bent over it. You behind me."

Donovan froze. And again had to consciously relax his grip. "Nae," he said carefully. "We can definitely do that. Sometime. Not today."

She frowned and stopped moving. "Why not?"

"Because I'll hurt you." He told her honestly. "I'm wound tight and have wanted you for too long. This is already killing me. You can't ask me to put you in that position and not fuck you so hard that you end up bruised."

Her eyes widened, but not with any kind of fear or intimidation. She looked completely turned on. Donovan groaned.

"But I trust you," she told him.

"Then trust me when I say no. Not today."

"Okay then... What else?"

Fuck. This woman was everything he wanted and more. More than he'd expected. More than he would've dared imagine.

"You want it from behind?"

She nodded. "It's one of my favorite positions."

Well, fuck. Without thinking it through any further, he shifted, grabbing her waist and turning her body so that she was on her hands and knees on the couch cushion. She gave a shiver and he knew that it was lust and anticipation, not fear.

He moved in behind her. He ran a big hand up and down her back and over the curve of her gorgeous ass.

"Damn, every time I think I know the extent of your goddess-ness, you take it up a notch."

She looked at him over her shoulder with a naughty smile. Her breasts bounced as she wiggled her ass at him. "Show me, Wild Thing."

He gave a short laugh, then squeezed her ass again. "Hang on for the hardest, best worship of your life."

He entered her with a long, hard thrust.

She moaned and he gripped her hips firmly, giving in and taking over.

She met his next stroke and he quickly picked up the pace, thrusting deep and fast until he felt his climax building rapidly.

He reached around for her clit, needing to bring her along, but her fingers were already there, circling her clit as she met his strokes.

"Fuck, Nae," he forced out between gritted teeth.

"Oh, Donovan."

"I need you—"

Then she cried out and clamped down on him as she came, slumping forward, her hips angled upward. He gripped her tighter as he pumped into her faster and harder until lightning streaked through his balls, hot and bright, as he emptied inside her.

They stayed like that, breathing hard, not moving, not speaking for several seconds. Maybe even minutes.

But finally, Donovan withdrew, and Naomi sprawled face-first onto the couch cushion. He chuckled as he pushed up off the couch and dealt with the condom.

He snagged his pants from the floor and pulled them on, then scooped her up, settling onto the cushion with her in his lap.

"I'm still naked," she said, her voice almost sleepy. But she curled into him as his arms wrapped around her.

"Yep." He toyed with the end of one of her braids that lay on her shoulder.

"I should get some clothes."

"You being naked will save us time after I catch my breath."

She looked up at him, one brow arched. "Oh, yeah?"

He stroked his hand down her arm. "Now that I've got you here? Unless you tell me you're done, I'm going to enjoy every damned minute until this storm blows over."

She seemed unsure what to say to that. For just a second his chest tightened. Maybe she was going to tell him she was done. Maybe she'd just needed an itch scratched and now she was good.

But she reached up, cupped the back of his head, and brought him down for a long, deep kiss.

He had just let his hands start wandering, intent on exploring every inch of her, when he heard his phone start ringing.

Then the sound of a phone chiming with a text joined it. He assumed that was her phone.

He lifted his head and met her eyes.

"They're wondering about us," she said.

"They" could be any number of people, but it would certainly be someone who would be very interested in Donovan and Naomi being naked together.

"Yeah. Can we ignore them?" he asked, dragged the tip of his finger along her collarbone, watching the goosebumps break out and her nipples tighten.

She gave a little shiver. "If we do, they'll worry and possibly come down here."

Yeah, they knew a lot of really great people who would be concerned and willing to brave the weather to check on them. Assholes.

"But if we answer they might try to talk us into coming up there. Or tell us the storm is letting up."

She smiled. "Yeah, they might."

He ran his hand up and down her arm again. "And I'm not sure I'm ready to be done with this."

"The storm will blow over eventually."

Did that mean she thought whatever this was between them would blow over too? He supposed that was possible. "Yeah, I guess."

It was strange. When he'd walked into this building, he hadn't expected any of this to happen and now here he was, wanting it to never end.

His phone started ringing again. Another text message came across Naomi's.

She sighed. "We should at least see who it is."

"Impatient bastards. I told them that we got up here fine and that we were going to stay with the bears."

She nodded. "I told them the same."

They looked at one another. Naomi was the first to frown.

"Do you think it's actually a problem?"

It really could be. Everyone they loved was hunkering down for a storm. Yeah, they were just up the road but they didn't know what was happening outside these walls.

"Shit," was all Donovan could say.

Naomi pushed off his lap and grabbed the t-shirt she'd been wearing before, pulling it on over her head and covering up.

Donovan took a moment to appreciate that he'd seen that body naked and to mourn having it clothed again. Then they both went for their phones.

"Mine's Michael," Naomi said. "He's with the family at Ellie's but he's heading out to Mobile soon." Naomi's thumbs started moving over the phone screen, typing in her answer to her brother.

"Mobile?" Donovan asked.

"Yeah. They must have gotten hit hard. He often goes out to help with clean-ups and recoveries after hurricanes and other disasters." She was still typing.

"That's cool." Donovan checked his missed calls. "Fiona is calling me."

Naomi looked up. "Really? She's not in Autre, is she?"

"I don't think so. I wasn't aware she had plans to be here anyway."

Donovan had met Fiona Grady through Griffin. Fiona and Griffin had spent time together in Zambia before Griffin had returned to the States after their parents' death.

Fiona now ran an animal park in Florida, but she had been visiting Autre regularly since Griffin had moved here. She was the one who had been bringing a variety of animals to the ever-growing animal park. All of the animals she brought were from rescue situations or were otherwise unable to be kept in a typical zoo or returned to the wild. They had lemurs, a sloth, porcupines, flamingos, and even donkeys and camels, thanks to Fiona.

Her animal park in Florida was actually more of an animal sanctuary. They did have some animals on display, including her most popular exhibit—a herd of five giraffes—but many of her animals were there because of past abusive or traumatic situations and were not for the public to interact with.

Donovan liked Fiona immensely. Everyone seemed to like Fiona immensely. She hardly gave you an option. She was pushy as hell—and energetic as hell—but she had a way about her that wrapped around you like a hug and caught you up in whatever she was excited about at the time. And before you knew it, you were in on any plan or scheme she had going. The best thing about Fiona, though, was her huge heart. Because even after you figured out that she had talked you into something you normally would've said no to, you realized it was a fantastic idea and you were happy she'd brought you along.

Of course, Donovan never had trouble with regrets when it came to animals. Fiona never had to talk him into anything. In fact, they were a fantastic team.

He tapped his phone to open the voicemail and listened to Fiona's messages.

"What's going on?" Naomi asked after he disconnected.

"Fiona wants me to come to Alabama too. The hurricane is hitting one area in particular especially hard and she's getting people together to do some animal rescues."

"What kind of animal rescues?"

"After natural disasters, there are always animals displaced who have been separated from their families or left behind when people have evacuated."

Naomi frowned. "Pets? Like cats and dogs?"

Donovan nodded. "Yes, in part. Of course, wild animals can be displaced during natural disasters as well. Their habitats are turned upside down and they can have trouble finding shelter and food. There are often babies separated from mothers or sometimes orphaned after a big storm like this. Fiona spent some time in Puerto Rico after Hurricane Maria helping rescue cats and dogs, as well as looking out for wild animals in the area. She's told me some amazing stories."

Naomi was taking all of this in. "So she wants you to meet her down there and help with the rescue and recovery efforts for the animals?"

Donovan shrugged. "Yeah. Sounds like it."

"What about the bears and the other animals here?"

"The wolf and beaver are doing well. And Griffin, and Tori and Jill can easily handle keeping an eye on them. The bears aren't injured. They need monitoring with their feeding and general health status over the next few days, but Griffin can handle that."

"Will Griffin bottle feed the one cub?" Naomi asked.

Donovan grinned. "He will. He'll pretend to be all put out by it, but he'll love it."

"How long do you think you'll be gone?"

Donovan finally focused on Naomi rather than letting his mind spin about all of the animals that were possibly suffering at the moment because of Hurricane Clare. Naomi looked worried and a little anxious. He took a step closer to her and reached up to cup her cheek. "Think you'll miss me?"

She nodded. "Even before what you just did to me. And after that? Absolutely."

Heat raced through him and he grinned. "Very glad to hear I made an impression."

"I'm very glad you finally made that impression too."

He leaned in and kissed her. "I'll be back. This is just a quick trip to Alabama. I'm not staying down there."

She nodded and took a breath.

He studied her face. "But you're worried about me."

She sighed. "Donovan, I'm always worried about you. Add in flood waters, downed power lines and trees, people in trouble, *animals* in trouble... yeah, I'm worried."

He thought about his next question for a couple of seconds, but it didn't take him long to decide that he definitely wanted to ask. "Want to go with me?"

Her eyes widened. "Really?"

"Well, it's up to you. I don't know if you feel like you can be gone for a few days, maybe a week. But if you want to come to

Alabama with me and help me rescue animals, I'd love to have you."

The expression he'd been hoping to see crossed her face—wary excitement.

When she was out with him filming his rescue activities for Boys of the Bayou Gone Wild, it seemed Naomi was always trying to find a balance between being careful and thoughtful about what they were doing and her obvious excitement. She really had a huge heart for the animals and it never took her long to get on board with whatever was going on. She always jumped in to help however she could and he knew that, even though she took far more precautions than he did, she felt the jolt of adrenaline when they were in the thick of things.

Finally, she nodded. "I hate the idea of pets out there lost and scared and alone."

He grinned. He knew she also hated the idea of *him* out there without a babysitter. "Exactly. We'll go down and help them reunite with their families."

She nodded. "That sounds great. When do we leave?"

He gave a soft chuckle. "As soon as things blow past, I suppose."

She glanced down at her phone. "Michael said it's already lightening up."

Donovan sighed. "Damn."

She looked up. "What?"

"I was hoping for a little more time with you in here. This might be the first time I've ever been less than one thousand percent excited to get right on the road to a rescue mission."

She gave him a smile that was part hot and part incredibly pleased. She put her hand against his cheek. "I think that's the highest compliment you could possibly pay me, Donovan Foster."

He turned his face and kissed the center of her palm. "Well, I have no idea what our accommodations might be in Alabama.

There won't be hotel rooms available. We might be putting an air mattress on the floor at somebody's house or at an animal shelter or we might have to just put it in the truck bed, but I'm very happy to snuggle up with you. This just might not be the most romantic trip I could take you on."

"Just promise that you'll keep all your fingers attached so you can use them on me when we get back here and I'll be fine."

He kissed each of *her* fingertips before letting go of her. "Deal."

"Maybe we have another minute," she said, lifting up on tiptoe.

He pulled her in close and their lips met. It only took a second for the kiss to turn hot and dirty and he started walking her back toward his desk. Bending her over it had been her idea after all...

The lights flickered on just then.

And both of their phones started ringing.

They froze. Then groaned. Then pulled apart.

She looked up at him. "Dammit," she said softly.

"Yeah." He kissed her again, but quickly and softly. "I think our time is up." He'd never regretted six words more.

She nodded. "I guess so."

He wanted to assure her it wasn't for good. But he wasn't sure what this was. He'd love to keep seeing her. He'd very much love to keep doing what they'd just done. But did he want to date her? More? He needed to make a decision about that because this was *Naomi*. She was important to everyone who was important to him.

And the things that made them total opposites were still true. They were a very good fit sexually, obviously, and he was more than thrilled to have learned that, but that didn't mean she would put up with him when his pants were on.

Still, the idea of having her with him in Alabama was nice.

This was the kind of work that he wanted to do. He knew that the rescues he'd done in the past mattered. His TV show had mattered. He'd educated a lot of people and he'd definitely brought awareness to multiple endangered species as well as natural disasters and environmental and ecologic issues that people needed to know more about. He was proud of the work he'd done. But he felt a nagging desire to do more.

The typical human didn't run into koalas that needed rescued from wildfires. Typical human beings did, however, encounter things that affected the environment around them every single day. He knew there was a way for him to use his platform in a bigger, more impactful way. He just didn't know exactly what that looked like yet.

But going to Alabama and getting his hands dirty helping find animals and reconnect them with their families, felt like something direct and important that he could do right now and having Naomi with him while he did it, seemed like an amazing way to combine two of his biggest passions.

As much as he wanted to strip her down, he resisted and instead placed a quick kiss on her lips and they stepped apart.

Naomi looked at her phone again and, with a sigh, Donovan pulled on his shirt, and rounded his desk to settle in at his computer.

While Donovan video chatted with Fiona on his laptop, Naomi started the dryer again to finish their clothes and then showered. Donovan showered after she did and within the hour they were ready to leave the building. They decided to take their separate trucks and headed for Ellie's.

The rain had let up and the wind had died down some, but there was water running everywhere and they had to maneuver around tree branches and other rubble. At one point, a large branch and two lawn chairs were blocking all but the narrowest of paths along the one muddy edge of the road.

Donovan stopped and dragged the branch out of the way

and tossed the chairs into the ditch. People would start venturing out and there would be chainsaws and more trucks to help remove debris, but at least that would open up the roadway for now.

When they arrived at Ellie's, they had to park down the street. Dozens of people had gathered to ride out the storm and clearly not many had left yet.

Donovan knew the urge to hold her hand as they walked toward the building was weird. Yes, they'd had sex, but that didn't necessarily change anything, except now he had more fuel for his late-night fantasies when he was alone. At least they had this trip to Alabama to figure out how things were going to be between them from here.

It was a two-hour drive and then they'd have several days there together. They'd be busy, of course, but spending time doing that kind of disaster relief work had a way of bringing people closer and there would be at least a little time alone here and there. He intended to take advantage of that.

It only took three minutes inside Ellie's to realize none of this was going to go according to plan.

4

It was weird that she had the urge to hold Donovan's hand while they walked from their trucks up to Ellie's. Yes, they'd had sex, but they weren't dating now. He wasn't her boyfriend. Nothing had really changed. Except that now, she had more fuel for her late-night fantasies when she was alone with her vibrator.

They were, apparently, going to spend the next several days together on a rescue and cleanup mission in Alabama, which might have meant that they could figure out what came next for them.

But she knew better than to think that was how this was going to go.

Kennedy, one of the Landry granddaughters—who also happened to be the mayor of Autre—was standing on a chair with a clipboard, clearly leading the meeting.

She was wearing her typical fitted black t-shirt with black shorts and black combat boots. The short-sleeved shirt and short shorts showed off her pale skin and the tattoos that swirled up the outside of her entire left leg and left arm. Naomi had known Kennedy all through high school as she was leaving beauty pageants and getting into her goth look so she knew that the tattoo actually extended up the side of her torso as well.

Her long black hair was pulled up into a high ponytail, so the dark red tips brushed her shoulders. Her eyes were made-up with dark liner and shadow and her lips were a deep crimson. The piercings that lined the entire curve of one ear, her nose, and the newest one in her right eyebrow all glinted in the light as she moved.

"There you guys are." Michael met them partway across the room, a few feet from where the majority of the group was clustered around the big tables at the back of Ellie's. It was where the Landry family gathered for meals and for any kind of big family meeting. "We're right in the middle of planning. Need to know where you fit in."

"I'm going to Alabama with Donovan," Naomi told her brother. "Fiona called for his help with finding and rescuing displaced animals."

"Fiona called you?"

This came from Knox. He was the city manager and Kennedy's right hand man. He was also a good friend of the Landrys. Though the animal park had been giving him progressively more severe headaches as it grew and the crowds of people coming to see the animal park got bigger. Some of his headaches also seemed to come from the bubbly, petite brunette who brought the exotic animals to the animal park though.

Donovan nodded. "She often goes to the sites of natural disasters and works on locating and rescuing displaced animals. She's recruiting volunteers for this effort and called me just a little bit ago."

Knox frowned. "She *often* goes to these things?"

"Very often." This answer came from Griffin, who joined them. "She was in Houston after Harvey and Puerto Rico after Maria."

Knox suddenly pivoted on his heel, pulling his phone from his pocket, leaving them without even a muttered excuse.

Naomi wondered if he was calling Fiona. Everyone else that he might need to talk to at the moment was in this room. But there was something going on with him and the animal activist. No one knew what it was, exactly—they seemed to alternate between flirting and annoying the hell out of each other—but Jill, Zeke's fiancée, had said the last time Fiona was in town delivering the flamingos, donkeys, and camels, Fiona and Knox had decided to go out for ice cream. Just the two of them.

Nobody thought they'd actually gone out for ice cream.

Or at least, not *only* ice cream.

"Damn, Harvey and Maria were back to back," Donovan said, clearly unconcerned about Knox's sudden departure.

Naomi nodded. "Funny to think Fiona was down there when all these guys were in Houston too."

"What guys?" Donovan asked.

"Josh, Owen, Sawyer, Leo, and Ellie are all part of the Cajun Navy," Naomi told him.

"The Cajun Navy?" Donovan repeated.

"You've heard about them on the news with past hurricane coverage, haven't you? They're a group of volunteers here in Louisiana who all have boats and equipment that enable them to go into flooded areas and help with rescues. The Boys of the Bayou obviously have boats and the skill and experience to use them. When they heard about a local group of guys heading to Houston after Harvey, they joined in. They were there for about a week helping get people and animals out of their homes and to safety."

"Why am I not surprised that these guys all jump in to help like that?" Griffin asked, looking around the room with clear affection mixed with exasperation. It was a common expression for him to wear when it came to his girlfriend's family.

Naomi nodded. "They're definitely not the types to sit on

the sidelines when things need done." She smiled at the brothers standing in front of her. "Kind of like you guys."

Neither commented on that.

"Leo and Ellie go too?" Donovan asked.

"Leo and Ellie can maneuver boats as well if not better than their grandsons."

No one could argue with that. It was possible that Griffin and Donovan hadn't seen Ellie or Leo in a boat, but the grandmother and grandfather of the Landry crew were not people anyone would underestimate after knowing them for even an hour.

"Okay, so Knox will obviously take over city operations," Kennedy said, her voice rising to be heard over the crowd.

"So pretty much what he always does anyway," Owen, one of her cousins, called out.

Kennedy simply raised one of her middle fingers to him and went on, "He'll be coordinating what clean-up needs done, though, thankfully, we escaped anything major. I'll be over helping Maddie with some of the boat tours while Owen and Sawyer are in Alabama." Kennedy wrote something on her clipboard. "Paige will cover the front office. Rosalie will be coming in to help Cora in the kitchen while Ellie is gone."

Donovan glanced at Naomi and she gave him a smile. She wasn't surprised to hear that her grandmother would be helping out at Ellie's. Rosalie had been a friend of Ellie's and Cora's since they were all little girls and was as good a cook as either of the bar owners. She couldn't stand for as long as Cora and Ellie needed to most days, but Rosalie would enjoy a few days of cooking for the town and helping her friends out.

"Mitch will head to Alabama with Sawyer and Owen so, Zeke, you'll have to fill in for anything that people usually call Mitch for," Kennedy said, reading from her clipboard.

"No can do, Madam Mayor," Zeke said. "I'm goin' to 'Bama too."

"You sure you don't need to stay here for when Jill, your very-pregnant-with-twins fiancée, gets back from her business trip?" Sawyer asked with an eyebrow up.

"Yeah, maybe the two of us should hang back now that we're dads," Josh said from where he was standing with his wife Tori, holding their baby girl, Ella.

Tori looked up at him with surprise. "Don't be ridiculous." She reached for Ella, taking her from Josh. "You're going to Alabama. Those people need more help than we do. Jill and I —and everyone else here—will be fine. We got lucky and just got a bunch of rain. Next time, though, it might be us that needs people showing up to help."

Josh looked down at her, his love and pride showing clearly. He leaned over and kissed the top of her head. "Love you, Iowa."

She smiled. "I know."

Naomi sucked in a little breath watching them. They were so clearly in love it made her chest ache. God, she wanted someone to look at her, to know her, to *get her*, the way those two did one another.

"Jill will be fine too," Zeke said. "If she was here, she'd be tellin' me to go." He pushed back and stretched to his feet. "You all know that."

People around the room nodded. Jill was even more independent than Tori was and Naomi knew that one of the things Jill loved most about Zeke was the way he jumped in to help and support the people around him no matter what.

"Well, good thing *I'll* still be here," Zander said. "Somebody's got to stay back to take care of the womenfolk."

"No gumbo for a week for that one," Ellie called to him.

Zander smirked at her. "Rosalie's going to be here. I'm gonna have griot and Rosalie's sos pwa nwa here all week."

Owen groaned. "Hey, no fair. Maybe I should stay behind."

Zander shook his head and leaned back in his chair. "Nah,

Griffin, Bennett, Knox, and I've got this. We're good. You really should go to Alabama."

"Sos pwa nwa?" Donovan asked Naomi.

She grinned. "Black bean soup. My grandma's is the best."

Any of these guys could show up at her grandmother's house any day and be fed all of their favorite Haitian dishes and they knew it. But Rosalie would love having them gushing over her food and coming back for seconds and proclaiming that her griot was just as good if not better than Ellie's gumbo.

"Well, I won't be here," Bennett Baxter, Kennedy's husband, said. "I'm going to Alabama to help too."

Owen and Sawyer both snorted and Kennedy rolled her eyes.

"And how does having a millionaire philanthropist politician along help anybody?" Zeke asked.

"Oh, you know that Bennett loves everything having to do with the boats and all the big equipment," Maddie said, smiling at Bennett. They had been friends prior to Bennett coming to Autre and Maddie was the reason he'd bought into Boys of the Bayou in the first place. And how he'd met Kennedy, the love of his life.

"I'm going to *help*. Not just because of all the boats," Bennett said.

They *all* rolled their eyes at that.

Naomi laughed. Bennett really was a millionaire philanthropist politician who was also a scientist and climate activist. But he was like a little kid around airboats.

"Just please don't let him die," Kennedy said. "And don't kill him if he gets to be annoying. I still need him for a few things."

"Yeah, like being the only person who can put up with you on an ongoing basis," Owen said.

Kennedy nodded. "Pretty much. And his *very* big..." She looked around the room, then grinned. "Credit score."

Everyone laughed, including Bennett.

"So you're going to go be a big hero and save people from the hurricane, huh?" Paige asked Mitch.

"Absolutely. Because I know how fast you can get out of your clothes when you think I've been an especially good guy," he told her with a grin.

Paige suddenly jumped up and Mitch caught her as she wrapped her arms and legs around him and planted a huge kiss on his mouth. "Every time I think you can't get any hotter, something happens and I realize that I never had a prayer resisting you," she told him, after she let him up for air.

He squeezed her ass and laughed. "Told you so. And if you're not careful, I'm going to think you're on the verge of finally asking me to marry you."

"Oh, don't worry, Bayou," Paige told him. "When I'm ready, you'll know. *Everybody* will know."

"Okay, okay," Kennedy said, raising her voice again. "Lord, it's like herding cats in here. So, Michael's going down to join the other first responders and J.D. is gonna cover emergencies for him while he's gone."

"J.D.?" Donovan asked Naomi.

"He's the new firefighter. He was up with Engine twenty-nine in New Orleans with Caleb and James." The two firefighters had become friends of everyone down here since Josh had bartended at one of their favorite bars. "They recommended him when Michael said he needed more help down here."

Kennedy turned and faced Donovan and Naomi. "And you two are meeting up with Fiona, is that right?"

Donovan nodded. "The animals we have over at the rehab center should be fine with Griffin, Tori, and Jill checking in on them."

Kennedy nodded and gave them all a very pleased smile. "Okay, then, let's go kick some ass."

Everyone started moving around, talking, gathering their

things, and making more specific plans within their own little groups.

Griffin turned to Donovan. "Any specific instructions?"

Donovan nodded. "You want to meet me down there in a little bit? There are three black bear cubs that just came in."

"Yeah, I heard something about those," Griffin said dryly.

"They're healthy. They should do well," Donovan said.

Griffin clapped him on the shoulder. "Now they're with you, I have no doubt."

If Naomi hadn't been studying him closely, as she so often was, she would've missed the flash of surprise and then pleasure that crossed Donovan's face with Griffin's compliment.

"Okay, well I'm going to talk to Michael and everyone and get caught up on everything with the family. Then I'll go home and pack," she said to Donovan. "When do you want to leave?"

"First thing in the morning?"

She nodded. "I'll be ready."

He hesitated and Griffin took the hint. He squeezed Donovan's shoulder, then said, "Be safe, you two. I'm proud of you."

He moved off and again, Naomi saw the flash of emotion on Donovan's face before he focused on her.

"Well, with all these people coming along, I guess you don't need to pack your skimpiest negligee," he said.

She laughed. "You said we might be on an air mattress in the back of your pickup. I wasn't going to be packing any lingerie."

"Yeah, like I said, this might not be a real romantic trip."

She shook her head. "That's not what this is about. But I'm happy to be going along. I've heard the stories about the Cajun Navy for years. I've always been so impressed with what they do and have always wanted to go along and see it up close."

"Well, it will be an adventure."

She nodded happily. "Yeah. I think I'm ready for one of those."

"And maybe when we get back, I could take you out for dinner?"

Oh, wow. She hadn't been expecting that. He wanted to go out? For dinner? Like a date?

That seemed like it should be an automatic no. He was leaving. Why do things that would make her miss him even more when he was gone?

The reality of that—that he actually really was finally leaving Autre—slammed into her again and she had to force air into her lungs the next second. Dammit. She'd known it would happen eventually. Why did it feel so damned bad?

Okay, he was *leaving*. So this date idea, like the time together during the storm, was a do-it-now-because-you-won't-have-another-chance.

She was sure all her emotions, from the surprise at the invitation to the holy-shit-I'm-going-to-miss-him showed on her face, so she quickly smiled. "I'd like that. But—"

"But?"

"Can we keep it under wraps a little? And what happened during the storm? It's not that I'm embarrassed or anything," she said quickly.

She didn't exactly want to discuss her sex life with her grandmother, but she also wasn't ashamed of her attraction to Donovan. Her family loved him. But some things just needed to be private. Especially when the thing wasn't going to turn into anything long-lasting.

"You and I both have a pretty big crowd of spectators to our lives. A big crowd who will be disappointed when you leave, not to mention if they think I'm broken-hearted over it."

Donovan moved until he was standing directly in front of her, blocking out the rest of the room. "I'm not very good at hiding what I think and feel about things."

And that pretty much summarized the biggest way they were different.

He lived life big and loud and had no trouble letting everyone know what he thought about everything all the time. He not only let people know when he was excited, happy, pissed off, or worried—he often did it on camera.

Dating Donovan Foster would not be a quiet, calm, easy-going thing.

And quiet, calm, and easy-going was Naomi's goal in life.

"Yeah," she finally said. "I know."

He studied her for a few seconds without saying anything. For a moment, she thought he was going to lean in and kiss her.

"Hey, Donovan! Griffin!" Charlie called as she came toward them from the other side of the room.

Donovan finally just gave Naomi a wink, before turning toward Charlie. "What's up?" he asked as Griffin joined them.

"Jordan's on the phone," Charlie said, holding up her cell. "She and Fletcher headed down to the petting zoo barn. The goats are going crazy. She wants you two to come down."

The two brothers looked at one another. Donovan with a grin. Griffin with an eye roll.

"We can do that," Donovan agreed.

"Wait, what's going on?" A pretty woman, who looked to be in her late twenties, wearing jeans and a button-up white shirt, with her long blond hair in a ponytail, pushed through the crowd.

"The goats all love Griffin and Donovan," Charlie told her with a grin. "They're all worked up from the storm—I guess part of the roof lost a few shingles and some rain came in—and Jordan's hoping Griffin and Donovan can comfort them and calm them down."

The woman laughed. "That's so cute. Can we tag along?"

Naomi noticed the man who came to stand behind the woman was carrying a camera. The kind a TV news station would use. Naomi gave Charlie a questioning look, but her friend was nodding and escorting the man and woman, along with Donovan and Griffin, to the door.

"Of course. It would be a great piece. Just make sure you have Donovan talk all about it. He's a little more..." Charlie gave her boyfriend a glance.

Griffin just lifted a brow.

Charlie laughed. "Chatty."

"Of course," the woman agreed. "We love talking to Donovan."

The four of them started in the direction of the barn and Naomi followed Charlie outside.

"What's that all about?" she asked.

"That's Rachel Oporto and her cameraman, Tom. She's with Channel Three out of New Orleans," Charlie said. "She's done a few pieces on the animal park in the past and I pitched her the idea of covering how we prepare for a storm with all the animals. She's a big fan of ours—and Fletcher and Griffin and Donovan's," Charlie added with a grin, "and she thought it was a great idea, so came down to do the story and ended up riding out the storm with all of us at Ellie's."

"So she got some behind-the-scenes stuff too?" Naomi asked with a laugh.

Charlie nodded excitedly. "I mean, she's covered us before and interviewed Jill and Griffin about the animals and Jordan about her program with the alpacas and the kids, but this was really fun because she learned about how the whole family gets involved with the animal park and how it all started with the otters and Gus. And she's *really* excited about everyone going to be a part of the Cajun Navy. She's heading to Alabama tomorrow with y'all. She's going to cover what the locals do down there specifically."

As always, Naomi marveled at Charlie's energy and enthusiasm. She was always thinking about and working on ways to get the word out about the animal park and the work they did here and she had no problem calling people up and giving them a hundred reasons they should be interested in Autre and the Boys of the Bayou Gone Wild.

"That's awesome. They deserve the attention," Naomi said sincerely.

"You know it kills me a little bit that I have Zoey At the Zoo right here beside me and I can't use her as a spokeswoman for *my* zoo, right?" Charlie asked, giving Naomi a little hip bump and then a side-arm hug.

Naomi's time on the television show was a well-kept secret in Autre. Very well-kept. And she appreciated it. She'd spent six years as the star of the family sitcom *Zoey At the Zoo*. From ages eight to fourteen. Then she'd left acting behind completely. She'd gone from celebrity to wallflower, easily and happily.

She was grateful *Zoey* had made her enough money—and that her parents had saved and invested wisely and that there were still royalties coming in—that she didn't *have* to work and could be there for her family, especially after her brother had become a single dad when Naomi was only seventeen. As a fire-fighter, where a 'normal' schedule was definitely anything but regular, having Naomi's help with Andre had been the only way Michael could handle it all. Her savings and continuing resid-uals also gave her the ability to do things like volunteer for causes she believed in, help her grandparents, and support projects that were important to her friends. Like petting zoos that suddenly turned into animal parks. Just for instance.

But she was very grateful that everyone in Autre not only accepted that she was done with acting, but helped her protect her anonymity. It had been eleven years now and in all that time, no one had slipped and spilled her secret. It was remark-able, really.

"It's truly a testament to our friendship and how much you love me that you never pressure me about that and haven't outed me yet," Naomi said with a laugh.

Charlie looked appalled. "I would *never*."

"I know that," Naomi said.

"And I'm so thankful for your donations. You know that too, I hope," Charlie said, sincerely.

"Of course, I do."

"Jason Young's big donation helped us so much and Jill's penguins are well funded, but who knew all these animals would cost so much to keep?"

Naomi laughed. She would think *most* people would assume running an animal park took a bit of money. But Charlie Landry was the type of person to put an idea into motion and *then* figure out the details. And it always worked out for her.

"Not to mention the way you've gotten involved with the videos," Charlie went on. "The stuff you shoot is so much better than anything the rest of us could do. That is all amazing. I promise not to bring *Zoey* up again. Besides—" She grinned. "Now we've got Donovan Foster, who is always happy to be on camera, to handle the media interviews."

So Donovan hadn't told Charlie and Griffin about the Galapagos Islands job? That was interesting. Naomi wondered why not. But it wasn't her news to tell.

"Yep, one thing you can always count on is Donovan wanting to be the star," Naomi said, with a little pang in the left side of her chest.

Would she love it if he'd be happy feeding alpacas for a living? Or driving swamp boat tours up and down the bayou? Or even just doing videos and commercials for Boys of the Bayou Gone Wild? Absolutely. But, that wasn't his dream.

She really shouldn't have fallen for a guy who wanted to change the world.

The Autre branch of the Cajun Navy was scheduled to roll out at six a.m. the next morning. Donovan pulled up in front of Naomi's house at five-fifty a.m. exactly.

She met him at the bottom of her porch steps.

"You're bringing a whole trailer?"

The trailer hooked to the back of his pickup was small but she hadn't realized he'd be hauling anything at all.

The rest of the Autre gang were, of course, pulling trailers that held their boats. They were in the four pickups waiting for them along her street.

Michael was in his pickup with Zeke and Mitch. The two Landry boys would go wherever they were needed, but would most likely join the other Landrys in the boats while Michael joined other official first responders.

Ellie and Leo were behind Michael, pulling their motorized fishing boat with their pickup. Josh and Owen were in the next pickup with one of the airboats on the trailer behind them and Sawyer had Bennett with him pulling one of the larger airboats.

The various sizes of boats would be helpful when they got to Alabama. The bigger tour boat would hold more people, but the smaller boats would be able to get into tighter spaces.

The airboats in particular would be helpful in the flood waters since none of their parts were below the bottom of the boat, unlike the motorboats. The airboats skimmed over the surface of the water and so could maneuver over shallower waters than many of the fishing boats.

Naomi felt a surge of pride. She loved that she knew people who were happy to get up at the crack of dawn and head out to help strangers. She was excited to be a part of it.

This was an adventure for her. It was nothing compared to what Donovan typically did, traveling the world, saving wildlife. But she didn't get outside of Autre much. Certainly not much outside of their parish. She was happy here. She'd had her taste of the big, wide world. She'd traveled. She'd been to fancy parties. She'd rubbed elbows with famous people. Now she only needed to travel as far as downtown Autre to get what she needed. The people she wanted to get close enough to rub elbows with all gathered at Ellie's bar. And the only stars she needed to see were in the gorgeous, clear Louisiana night sky.

Still, this trip, with these people, and what they were going to do, gave her a little thrill. It was a devastating situation, of course. That part wasn't thrilling. But being able to help, being able to *do* something that would matter, that was bigger than her usual day, felt good.

"Didn't have enough room in the truck bed for everything," Donovan told her as he stored her bag behind the truck seat with his.

Naomi checked out the back of Donovan's Raptor as he stowed her bag. He had a lot of equipment in the back of his truck as well, but it wasn't the tools the Landrys had packed or the first-aid supplies in Michael's truck.

"Wow, where did you get all of this?"

He slammed the door and joined her. "Made some calls around the area. Lots of people happy to donate or loan supplies and equipment."

He had a number of animal crates of various sizes, harnesses and leashes, blankets, pads, and dog beds, along with bags and cans of food of all kinds.

"That's impressive."

"The trailer is full too. More food, water, crates, plastic tarps. All kinds of stuff." He held out a hand and helped her up onto the seat. She didn't miss the gentlemanly gesture. "Was on the phone with Fiona and then Monica. She runs the biggest pet shelter in that area. Told me some of the supplies they could never have enough of."

"Like a humane society shelter?"

He shook his head. "This is an emergency shelter. They can't shelter animals with people, even in emergencies like this, but it's imperative they set up a separate emergency shelter for the animals too. Did you know that in Katrina forty-four percent of the people who didn't evacuate said no because they didn't want to leave pets behind?"

Naomi's eyes widened. "Wow. That's incredible. They wouldn't let them bring them even in that situation?"

"Couldn't. It poses a safety risk to the other humans. People are allergic. Animals can get aggressive when they're under stress or around strangers. There can be a lot of problems. It's hard enough having that many humans all sheltering together in an emergency. Add in animals and it's a risk for everyone. Even the animals. So there need to be shelters for them too. Usually very close by. That's what Monica has set up down there."

Naomi nodded. "That makes sense. And they need additional staff and supplies."

"For sure. The animals' owners are mostly in charge of coming in and caring for their own pets so that helps with the staffing situation, but they do need experienced animal handlers and can never have enough supplies."

"Are you going there then? To help at the shelter?"

"I'm going wherever I need to go. I'm probably better out doing rescues, but we can do a little bit of everything, I figure."

We. She liked that. She'd also do whatever needed done. She could help at a shelter—animal or human—but she kind of wanted to stick with Donovan.

Which was selfish. She needed to think about the people who needed her in Alabama, not her I-want-to-watch-him-being-a-hero obsession with Donovan Foster.

"And don't worry, I made sure to throw the air mattress back there," he said with a grin and a wink.

She didn't respond. Because her answer would have been *thank God*.

She knew they weren't going to be having sex while in Alabama. This wasn't a sexy, romantic trip. They'd likely never be totally alone and even if they were, they were going to be exhausted. If not sweaty and dirty. She had no idea what the shower situation would be like down there.

But she wanted to cuddle up with him at night.

Even sweaty and dirty.

And that told her everything she needed to know about how gone she was over Donovan.

He rounded the front of the truck and got behind the wheel, pulling out onto the road behind the last pickup in the caravan.

"So how do these animal rescues usually go?" Naomi asked. "How do you find the animals and get them back to their owners?"

"Usually a local group will have set up some kind of hotline or possibly a website or Facebook page where people can report their animals missing or report that they had to leave pets behind. They can give the animals' names and descriptions and so on," Donovan said. "There will also be people patrolling residential areas where animals might have either been left behind or might have escaped when the storm got bad and not be able to get home. There could be animals trapped in debris. There could be animals who left home during the storm, sheltered somewhere else, then came back but can't find their humans. There's a lot of different scenarios."

Naomi felt her heart ache thinking about it all. How scared the animals would be. How heartbreaking a decision it would be for the humans to have to leave a pet behind.

"And then you capture them and take them to a central location and then put the word out?" Naomi asked.

He shrugged. "Pretty much. We'll make sure they're fed,

check them for injuries. There will be local vets around volunteering, I'm sure. Griffin threw in some general antibiotics and bandaging supplies and a few other things we might need for triage too."

"What should I be prepared for?" Naomi asked, feeling her stomach tighten. She led a sheltered life, she'd admit. On purpose. She'd been out in the world as a kid, growing up in the public eye. She'd had enough of it and when she'd come home to Autre, she'd hunkered down. But she could admit that she'd maybe hunkered down too much. She hadn't felt like she was missing out on anything. At least, not until lately.

But now she was on her way to do something bigger than she'd done before. Because of Donovan. While this exact same adventure was tiny compared to his usual.

"There will be some hard things to see. There will no doubt be some animals that didn't make it. There will be some that were abandoned, some we're never going to be able to reunite. But there will be adoption groups on the ground as well. Hopefully a lot of those animals will find new homes."

Naomi nodded and looked out the windshield.

She'd been through a couple of hurricanes, but they had been category twos or lower. She had of course seen the news and heard stories from Harvey and Maria as well as other hurricanes over the years, but she had never been directly involved in any of the rescue and recovery work. She'd stuck close to home, made sure her family and friends were okay.

Her brother hadn't gotten far from home either. But Michael responded to fires and car accidents and medical calls and took care of the town and surrounding area.

She took care of the people in her immediate circle.

Even though Michael had a great reason for staying close—his son, Andre—he still cast his net wider than Naomi did. She took caring for others seriously. She was the one with the purse that always had a magical fix in it—duct tape, super glue, pain reliever, stain remover—and she loved being the one people could depend on for good, reasonable advice...and duct tape... but she didn't open that purse for people outside her closest friends and family.

Now, though, she was on the road to another state, a new city, to help strangers. And she was excited. Apprehensive too because she had no idea if she'd be any good at this. But she wanted to be there.

And it was because of Donovan.

She wouldn't be going if Donovan wasn't a hot, charming, walking-talking package of trouble-waiting-to-happen who she wanted to keep an eye on.

But whatever had gotten her into the truck, she was excited about what was ahead.

She cast a glance at the man next to her. Yes, he was her biggest worry. She was mildly concerned about the others from Autre. This wasn't going to be an easy, totally safe situation. But the Landrys knew their way around water and storms like this. Her brother was a trained firefighter and paramedic. He'd seen lots of hard things and in been in the midst of disasters before. Donovan was certainly brave and had the physical stamina and strength to be a lot of help in a situation like this, but she wondered about his experience and judgment.

"So what happened that made you not want to have your family and friends involved in your dating relationships?"

Her eyes widened as he glanced over and met her eyes.

"How do you know I don't have my family and friends involved in my dating relationships?"

He gave her a *really?* look. "Because I know your family and friends. And I asked about your past boyfriends."

She was surprised. "You did? Why not just ask me?"

"Because you weren't there. I was a little drunk, your brother was there, and it...came up."

She gave a soft snort. "Oh really? What did you ask? What did he say?"

"Just asked if you were seeing anyone." He glanced over. "This was a couple months ago." He focused on the road again. "Michael said he didn't think so. I asked if you'd ever been really serious with anyone. He said he didn't think so. I asked why he didn't know for sure and he said that you just never introduce anyone you date to anyone in your immediate circle. That you keep it all pretty separate."

She did. After spending eight years in the public eye, having everything from what she was wearing to her moods analyzed for teen magazines and blogs, she'd become a very private person.

"We're going to do this before I even have coffee?" she asked.

She knew he wouldn't let it go. Donovan seemed easy-going and laid back and for the most part, he was very good at rolling with the punches. He thought quick on his feet and was able to adjust to any situation in a blink, it seemed. But he also had an intensity about him. He was passionate about the work he did, and the animals he rescued, and she sensed that his intensity could easily be focused on other things that became important to him.

He gave her a grin and reached for one of two paper cups nestled in the cup holders in the center console that she hadn't noticed before now. He handed it over. "You're right. My apologies."

She shivered a little bit as she took a sip of coffee. Being the focus of that kind of ardent attention could be exhilarating. And overwhelming.

As the coffee—the perfect blend of hazelnut syrup and cream in a medium roast—hit her tastebuds, she looked over at him. "You know how I take my coffee?"

He lifted his own cup and took a sip. Then nodded. "We've been drinking coffee together for months."

She studied him as she took another sip. She couldn't remember a time when he had actually gotten coffee for her or anyone else, but it was possible it had happened. Or maybe he'd just listened to her give her order to someone else. Or maybe he'd asked someone how she took her coffee. Like he'd asked her brother about her romantic relationships. She sighed.

"Well, thank you. It's perfect."

"You're welcome." He paused and took another sip of his coffee, his attention seemingly on the highway. But not even a minute passed before he asked, "Have you drunk enough to tell me about your romantic past now?"

"There has to be something else we can talk about."

He pretended to think about that for a moment. Then shook his head. "Sorry. Nothing else interesting. At least not that interesting."

"You want to know all about my romantic past? Really?"

"Really," he shifted on his seat. "More than I would've expected actually."

"What does that mean?"

"I don't usually get that interested in other people's stuff. I mean, we all have stuff. We all have pasts and things that we'd rather not dig up. Certainly not with people that we like and admire and want to like and admire us. So generally, I let pasts be pasts."

She appreciated the fact that she could sit angled on her seat and watch him while he had to focus on driving.

"So why are you digging into *my* past?"

He nodded, not taking his eyes off the road this time. "That's the question."

"Do you have a good answer?"

"I have *an* answer. I'm not sure it's good."

"You mean you don't think it's accurate?"

"I mean, I think that it's…" He took a deep breath. "Complicated. And I'm not sure that making things complicated is a good thing."

She was intrigued. And she shouldn't be. Because being intrigued was also complicated.

Having a crush on this guy had been fun. It had also been simple.

When he'd first come to town, it had been fun to run into him and have the butterflies kick up in her stomach as if she was a teenager again. It was fun to hear her friends talk about him and to lean in to catch little details she didn't know. It was fun to be involved in filming his latest adventure and rescue. But as she got to know him and her feelings had changed from a crush to something a lot more adult and a lot more real, it had gotten less fun. It had gotten more… yeah, complicated.

Crushes were supposed to be from a distance. Crushes were something you got over. Yes, it was a little ridiculous for a twenty-five-year-old woman to have a crush in the first place. But that was the point. Crushes weren't really real.

Donovan Foster had become very real to her.

And that was definitely complicated.

She took another long draw of her coffee. It really was good. And the caffeine was starting to kick in. Which probably should've made her thoughts more clear.

He looked over at her when she didn't reply. "I've tried to resist getting interested in you. I have. But it's not working."

She knew delving into all of this was probably a bad idea, but Naomi still felt her heart flip in her chest.

"You try to not get interested in people on purpose?"

Maybe she could turn the tables here. Maybe she could get him talking about himself and he would forget to talk about her.

And, in spite of her best efforts, she was interested in him.

She'd sensed from the beginning that he didn't know what to do with big groups of people who were interested in him and his life. Or maybe just big groups of people in general.

Because of her stupid thirteen-year-old-girl-esque crush, she always paid a lot of attention to Donovan when he was around. The Landrys and LeClaires could be a lot, especially when all put together, and he always seemed a little befuddled by the big group of people. Even more so when they automatically included him in things and paid attention to details like that he preferred the extra spicy hot sauce and his coffee extra strong.

She was sure he'd expected to blend into the crowd. That's probably what most people expected. Then, he'd seemed a little uncomfortable with the attention he was getting.

At first, that had struck her as odd. He was, without question, an attention whore. But it was a different kind of attention that he seemed to crave. He loved the camera. He loved the action. He loved showing people the great outdoors and wildlife. He liked being a minor celebrity.

When people wanted to know how *he* was—not how the gray wolf he was rehabilitating was or how the release of the owl had gone—he seemed to get awkward. As if he wasn't used to people asking, or caring, about *him*. Only what he did.

But over the months he'd been in town, she'd seen him opening up to it. He brightened whenever Ellie and Leo greeted him when he came into Ellie's. He smiled bigger when he made someone laugh. He actually told stories that had nothing to do with animal rescues. He especially softened whenever Ellie put a hand on his shoulder, or gave him a hug, or filled up his bowl of gumbo with a second helping without asking.

Ellie Landry had a way about her. She made you feel loved and accepted without ever actually saying those words. Of course, she'd bluntly say the words too if she thought you needed to hear them.

Just like she'd bluntly say, "Stop being an ass," or, "Well, that was a really stupid decision," if she thought *that* was what you needed to hear.

The only person who made a bigger difference in Donovan's demeanor than Ellie was his brother, Griffin. Donovan was twenty-five years old but clearly his older brother's praise and opinion still mattered immensely to him.

Naomi wondered if Griffin even realized it.

"Okay," Donovan said, when several more seconds had ticked by without her saying anything. "So I want to know about your past, maybe I should tell you something about mine first."

Naomi felt her heart do a double flip at that. Donovan was going to open up and share? See, this was where it got dangerous.

She wanted to know more about him. But the more she knew about him, the more she would care. The more she cared, the harder it would be to keep her distance. The closer she got, the harder it would be to say goodbye to him when it came time for him to leave.

Still, she was only human, and the guy she had stupidly fallen for wanted to tell her personal things about himself. "Okay," she finally said.

"After my parents died, I spiraled," he said, launching right into the story. "I decided I didn't want to be sad anymore and so I did everything I could to numb the pain and keep things superficial. I started partying. Hard. Lots of drinking, even dabbling in some drugs. I broke things off with all of my friends and started running around with a new crowd. I didn't care about any of them, which was exactly the way I wanted it, and they didn't care about me. I just didn't want to feel anything anymore. I worked especially hard to distance myself from Griffin."

Naomi was riveted. Just those few lines and she was fully

invested here. "That makes sense. That was a horrible thing to have to go through at any age. But especially as a teenager."

His grip on the steering wheel tightened. "Yeah. I have all kinds of excuses. But none of those really matter. It's the consequences. I hurt a lot of people and I knew it at the time. I just convinced myself I didn't care. I figured it was better for them than having to be around a sad, pathetic guy who had decided that life wasn't fair and everything sucked and bad things happened to good people no matter what you did."

"You were just a kid."

"Yeah. But I kept doing it. For four years. I drank and partied and kept myself from getting close to anyone. Because of all that, my brother had to give up all of his plans. He came home from Africa right after they died. He was my legal guardian. But I'm sure he planned to go back as soon as I turned eighteen. And he should have been able to." Donovan swallowed hard, his eyes glued to the road. "But instead, because I was a mess, he had to stay."

"But he went on to vet school. And he loves that," Naomi offered.

"Yeah, eventually. On my schedule. Once I kind of got my shit together. But everything in Griffin's life for a few years there was all about me. He stayed close and went to school near where I did. And then one night I ended up in the ER with alcohol poisoning."

Donovan swallowed again and squeezed the steering wheel, his knuckles turning white.

"A cop actually found me passed out in my car. I'd pulled over, somehow, before I blacked out. Thank God." He took a shaky breath. "But I was driving. What the fuck I was thinking I have no idea. I don't remember any of it. And of course, I had no friends to give a shit, so when I walked out of wherever I was and got in my car, no one cared."

Donovan blew out a breath and was quiet for a few seconds. Naomi just sat, processing it all. She felt like crying.

Donovan could have died. She could have lost him before she even knew him. It was the strangest thing to feel a sense of anger and *loss* in that moment. He was here with her, healthy and alive and fine. But for a moment, she felt a stab of grief.

"He had to sit by my bed and hope that the only family he had left didn't die," Donovan finally went on, his voice rough. "Of course, if I had, it would have been self-inflicted, which was way worse and far more selfish than what happened to our parents. When I woke up in the hospital room and saw him sleeping in the chair next to my bed, I realized that I couldn't keep doing it. He'd given everything up for me and I was completely wasting it. I realized that I wasn't afraid to die, but I was afraid to die in a pathetic, selfish way that would hurt my brother even more and leave him not just sad but also angry.

"So I decided to clean things up and do something mean-ingful with my life. I decided to do that with animals because they were so important to him. And it keeps us close, gives us a reason to communicate and to run into each other and work together once in a while. But I'm also able to stay out of his way. I let him go his direction and do his thing. And I've worked my ass off to do my thing and prove to him that I'm okay and that he can not only stop worrying about me, but he can be proud of me and know that his coming back and being there for me turned into something good."

Naomi knew her eyes were as wide as they could go. She wasn't sure that she had breathed in the past several seconds. Certainly not deeply. She hadn't blinked or swallowed. She hadn't wanted to miss a single word of Donovan's story.

Her heart was hammering hard in her chest and her palms itched to reach out and touch him.

He was wounded. She hadn't expected that. He was such a happy person. Optimistic, constantly excited and on the go, passionate and driven, a focused advocate and activist. He was so charming and funny and approachable. But underneath all of that was a guy who was trying to make amends. Who had regrets and who had made some big mistakes.

How the hell was she supposed to resist him *now*?

He glanced over. "You okay?"

She shook her head, trying to figure out what word she wanted to use. "You... just complicated things."

5

Donovan felt as if his heart was slamming against his rib cage. Dammit. Of course he'd complicated things. His past was complicated. And pathetic and sad and full of screwups.

Naomi LeClaire was not the kind of woman a guy dumped that kind of stuff on. But she needed to know.

He was still in Autre because of her. At some point in the past twenty-four hours, he'd realized that. Of course, it had been happening slowly. He'd been in this town for seven months accidentally. But it was probably the moment when she'd come to stand over him on the highway, with the rain pounding down, and asked him what in God's name he thought he was doing, he realized that he was still in Autre because of her.

So she needed to know all of this grimy, dirty, not-pretty stuff from his past.

"Sorry," he said simply, meaning it. "I wanted you to know. Not just because I want you to, but because..." He shook his head. "I guess I don't even know."

"I like that."

He looked over at her. "You like what?"

"I like that you're not confident and cocky all the time. I like that you just spilled your guts and you didn't need to. I like that we can be complicated together."

He hadn't been expecting that. He sat up a little straighter. "Yeah?"

"Yeah. And... I don't get it either. I do not like complicated. I don't like messy. I've had that and I want easy and simple now."

"So I just fucked everything up by telling you I'm not easy and simple at all."

She nodded. "That *should* be true."

"But?" He looked over. She hadn't said "but". He sensed one though.

"I guess it's kind of like how you dress."

"The way I *dress*?"

She nodded. "Yeah. When you wear a button-down shirt and roll the sleeves up to your elbows when you come up to Ellie's, you look so hot. Or like yesterday at the rehab center when you'd just gotten out of the shower and were wearing sweatpants and a t-shirt and you were fresh and clean and looking casual, I, obviously, wanted to climb in your lap and do dirty things to you."

Donovan had to shift on his seat as heat shot through him at the memory. Damn, he didn't remember a woman ever affecting him the way Naomi did. She could just casually mention something like that and he was instantly hot and hard.

"But," Naomi went on. "I think that you're most attractive to me when you are out in the wild, dirty, sweaty and muddy and —bloody—" She sighed. "Even bloody. And it's not because that makes you more tough or rugged or anything. It's because that's when you're happiest. You're smiling and confident and it's so clearly exactly where you should be."

His chest felt tight as he tried to take a deep breath. "Dammit, girl," he said, his voice rough.

"What?"

"You say stuff to me like that while I'm driving and can't reach over and pull you into my lap and kiss you?"

She was quiet for a second, as if he'd surprised her. "Yeah, damn," she finally agreed. "I can say it all again later."

"If we have even two seconds together I'll have you do that." He shot her a hot look.

They didn't say anything for a long moment. Then she took a deep breath. "Okay, I guess it's my turn then."

Donovan gripped the steering wheel tighter again.

He really wanted to know everything about her, but in particular the fact that she dated in secret intrigued him. And concerned him. If something bad happened to her in the past with another guy, he wasn't sure what he'd do.

He'd learned better coping mechanisms and had grown up and become more rational as an adult, but there was a primitive part of him that still roared to life when innocent and vulnerable beings were threatened. He knew that would be one hundred times stronger if he found out someone had hurt Naomi.

The woman sitting next to him right now had gotten under his skin and into his heart despite his best efforts to keep those walls up high.

"Have you ever heard of *Zoey At the Zoo?*"

He thought for a moment. It sounded vaguely familiar. "It was a kid's show, right?"

"Yes. Kind of. It was a family sitcom. Prime time. It ended about eleven years ago. It was a show about a family that owned a zoo and Zoey, their daughter, grew up there. Her friends were animals and zookeepers and there was a lot of education about the animals and their natural habitats and how we needed to protect them. There were also messages about how Zoey didn't fit in with other kids, but about how kids needed to be confident about the things they loved and doing the right thing and how they would find acceptance from the right people when they did that."

"Okay." Donovan was following so far and again, it all sounded familiar-ish.

She lifted her shoulder. "I'm Zoey. Was Zoey."

He frowned and glanced over. "What do you mean?"

"I was the star of the show. From age eight to fourteen."

Donovan processed that. Slowly. She was Zoey. The girl on the show. That meant... "You were on TV?"

"Yeah. For six and a half years."

"Like network TV?"

"Yes."

That was...wow. Not even close to what he'd thought she was going to tell him today. "How did I not know that? Does everyone else know? Why didn't you tell me?"

"Some know. Not *everyone*. But yeah, most. We don't talk about it because it doesn't matter anymore. After I retired, I came back to Louisiana and gave it all up. Everybody in Autre protects me and my identity. For a while I had private security that kept people from finding me. Now, though, it's been long enough that people don't really look. If anyone comes to town and tries to find me, everyone just pretends they have no idea where I am."

Donovan shook his head. That was...something. He wasn't sure what. "Even with all the tourists in and out of Autre, no one's ever recognized you?"

"They have. Or they think they have, but I just say, 'oh, I get that a lot' or, if they ask someone else if it's me, they lie and say no."

That didn't surprise him. These people absolutely protected each other. "Wait..." His mind was turning. "When we went out to the bar in Bad with everyone shortly after I'd gotten to Autre, and Charlie asked if I was just flirting with you or if I really didn't know who you were—this is what she was referring to, right?"

Naomi laughed softly. "Yes."

"I was going on about my show and how I could sign autographs as a fundraiser and you were sittin' there, way more famous than me." He laughed. "God, everyone must have thought I was such an ass."

She grinned. "No, they didn't."

"But you *are* more famous than me."

"Maybe at one time..."

"You definitely are."

"Maybe to a very specific demographic."

He gave her a look. "You are. Just accept it."

"Well, I don't *want* to be, so now you have to help keep the secret too."

He nodded and put one hand over his heart. "Absolutely."

"Thanks."

"Okay, so what's that got to do with your dating habits though?" Now he *definitely* wanted to know everything about her. This woman was even more fascinating than he'd thought and he was already pretty fucking enamored.

She blew out a breath. "We're back to that?"

"We never really left that."

She rolled her eyes, but said, "Well, for one thing, I spent six plus years in the public eye—some of my formative years as a young teen—and it made me just want to be a lot more private after it was over."

"Okay. That's fair." He could understand that. He didn't feel that way, but he hadn't been in front of the camera until he was an adult and had a lot of say in what happened and what got put out there for the public to see.

"And a personal relationship with a boy was one of the reasons I retired."

He looked over at her quickly. "What happened?" Yeah, see, he was definitely ready to punch someone on her behalf.

"Nothing bad," she said quickly, evidently reading his expression. Or the growl in his voice.

"Then what?"

"One of my co-stars, Liam, was sixteen. We played best friends on the show. No one ever made a big deal out of that or said anything. Until...we were photographed hugging at my fourteenth birthday party. Suddenly the media started wondering—on the pages of their magazines and blogs, of course—if we were more than friends. Then fans got in on it, wanting it to be true, 'shipping' us," she said, using air quotes. "My mother, who was my representative, paid attention to all of that and the moment she saw it, she demanded the show's PR people put a stop to the rumors. But they hemmed and hawed about it because the producers thought it was good for ratings. Then our agents came to us with a proposal—play boyfriend and girlfriend on and off the show. They even offered to increase our salaries."

Donovan looked over at her. He was sure his face showed everything he was feeling. Outrage, shock, and yes, the urge to punch someone. "You were *fourteen*."

She nodded. "My mother said, 'No way in *hell*,' and when they pressed again, she told them I was quitting. I left the show and *Zoey At the Zoo* ended."

"Wow, just like that?"

"Yeah. My mom doesn't play around. There was no way she was going to let her fourteen-year-old daughter have a boyfriend or even let people *think* she had a boyfriend. That just wasn't going to happen."

Donovan stared at the road, processing all of it. That she'd been famous. That she'd been famous so young. That she wasn't now. Just how kickass Monique LeClaire really was.

He already really liked Naomi's mother, though he'd only met her a couple of times, but she'd reminded him very much of her daughter—confident, cool, and not afraid to tell you exactly what she thought. But she'd pulled her daughter out of Hollywood at the first whiff of something inappropriate. That was awesome.

"And I was really happy to come home," Naomi went on. "I was tired of being away from all my family other than my mom. And being away from my friends here. I'd come home for breaks and hang out with Jordan and Kennedy, and Charlie if it was summer or Christmas-time, and I just wanted to be like them. I wanted to be normal. To put on clothes without anyone writing a social media post about it. To order lunch without a blog talking about it. So when all of that blew up just because of a hug between friends, I realized I didn't want to be living my life for everyone to see anymore. I just wanted to have a quiet, simple, private life."

"In Autre?" he asked, teasing. And still processing.

She laughed. "Well, that's a different kind of attention and meddling."

He nodded. She was right. The involved-in-everything-you-do in Autre came from genuine, well-intentioned interest and love.

"So you're okay?" He looked over at her.

She gave him a sincere smile. "I'm very okay. Just...private."

"I get it."

"Thank you."

They were quiet for a several seconds. Then Donovan blew out a breath and shook his head. "I can't believe you're famous."

She shrugged. "More like pseudo-famous now. With certain people I would be famous, but it's been a long time. But, partially because of that, and partially because I just like keeping things private, I decided a romantic relationship should be just between the two people who are in it until it's really clear what the relationship is going to be and that it's going to last. There's no reason to bring other people into it if it's not going to turn in into anything serious."

That point hit home. Hard. He wasn't sticking around. There was no reason to get all of their friends and family involved in something that they already knew wasn't going to last, right? "So when was the last time you introduced a guy to your parents? As a boyfriend?"

She gave him a look, and he glanced over and met her eyes.

"What?" he asked.

"The way you phrased that, makes me think you believe I've introduced guys to my family without telling them they're boyfriends."

He nodded. "Have you?"

She clearly was thinking about how to answer that. "Yes," she finally admitted. "A couple of times. I had a couple of guys hang out at Ellie's just to see how everyone reacted to them without knowing that I was dating them."

Donovan felt a surge of satisfaction that he'd guessed that about her. Maybe he knew her better than she thought he did. "So you just pretended not to know the guy while he was there?"

She shrugged. "Yeah. I wanted to get everyone's unbiased opinion and reaction."

"And how'd it go?" She wasn't with either of them now, so it must not have been great. Donovan liked that more than he should.

"My family and friends really liked one of them. One they didn't."

"And did you break up with the one they didn't?"

She grinned. "I was going to, but he broke up with me first."

Donovan laughed. "Dumbass. Why'd he break up with you?"

"Apparently, the Landrys and LeClaires together can be kind of overwhelming."

Donovan nodded. "He's not wrong."

"No, he wasn't. And it was good that he found that out. And it was great because then my family wasn't hurt by thinking I was introducing them to someone important and then having him bail."

Donovan nodded. "I get it. It makes sense. What happened with the guy that they liked?"

"We dated for a while. I introduced him to them. It was a very normal relationship."

"But you're not still together," Donovan pointed out. "Something must've happened."

That was definitely a stab of jealousy he was feeling. It was an unusual emotion for him and he wasn't quite sure what to do with it. It was ridiculous for one thing. He and Naomi had, clearly, not known one another when she'd been dating this guy. Donovan had no claim on her. He had no reason to be jealous. But the idea of Naomi LeClaire with any other man rubbed him the wrong way.

"He got a great job and wanted to move to South Carolina and I didn't."

Well, that made sense. There were lots of reasons that relationships ended. At least Donovan assumed so. His always ended because he was moving on. Or because they never really started in the first place.

"And he was the only one who you were ever that serious with?"

She nodded. "I date, but I'm picky. And not very many of them get to the point where I want to bring them to Autre."

Donovan thought about that as he drove for a couple more minutes.

"Are you interested in traveling at all?" he finally asked. He was maybe not as surprised by the question as she was, but he was plenty surprised.

He not only never put down roots for long, he never traveled with anyone. On his shows he had, of course, had his crew. But it had been a job to them and when the show ended, or even when they were on hiatus, they all went home to spouses or significant others.

"I've done some traveling," she said. "But I'm very happy here in Autre now. I'm a homebody."

He nodded. They weren't just talking about if they enjoyed travel or what other parts of the world they might want to see. He was asking her whether, if they dated, there was any chance she would come with him.

And she was saying no.

"Do you plan to do more traveling?" she asked. "After this next job?"

He nodded. "I think so. I don't have any plans right now. But I want to do something... important. I feel like I've built enough of a platform that with this added exposure I can do something more. I just have to figure out what that is."

She didn't say anything to that. And he didn't have anything more to add.

They really liked each other. They had amazing sex. But it seemed that was all this was destined to be.

Maybe dinner out wasn't such a great idea after all.

Because even just sitting next to her in a pickup made him never want to leave her.

Taking her out on a date would be stupid.

In any other circumstance, he would be a guy that she'd never take home to meet her family.

He was lucky he already knew them.

Because all those other dumbasses were missing out.

F orty minutes later, they pulled into a mall parking lot to meet up with the rest of the volunteers heading into Mobile.

Sure, the Cajun Navy seemed like just a group of people with boats and some time on their hands, but it quickly became clear that they were so much more than that.

Already they were organizing into smaller groups and dividing up the city. There were people taking calls from inside the city with more specific details about where help was needed and what kind of numbers they were looking at.

"We are fortunate that the mayor and city council members are completely on board with having us here," a man with a bullhorn standing on the back of the truck told the gathered group. "Sometimes we are told that we're in the way and we're not needed in these situations. FEMA is on the way and there are other government organizations here. The Red Cross is already on the ground. But we are definitely welcome. Don't worry about that. We've got all of the communications set up. And if you will all just log into the apps and make sure our command centers have your phone numbers, we should be able to get everybody out quickly."

Donovan and Naomi were standing with the Landrys and Michael.

"Damn, this is impressive," Donovan commented.

Sawyer nodded and tucked his hands into his back pockets. "It hasn't always been this organized. They definitely haven't always had all of the communications and texts set up like this. When it first started out, it was just a bunch of guys with boats trying their best. But it's definitely become a more organized group over the years. We've even been doing some training drills here and there. They really want to be effective, and they want to show the communities that they know what they're doing."

"They really got in trouble for coming in to help?" Naomi asked.

"They have. Lots of times it's the local government people not wanting to get shown up," Owen said with a frown. "And at times it's been FEMA themselves or even National Guard. Everybody comes in and tries to help with good intentions, but there's just something that sometimes rubs people the wrong way when it comes to civilians."

"Which is bullshit, of course," Mitch added. "Nobody takes care of each other as well as neighbors and people who have been through the same stuff themselves. Even if we haven't been hit by a bad hurricane, we all know it could happen anytime."

"And those other groups have a lot more going on," Sawyer said, looking around. "The people who show up here with their boats are just normal people. We're here for one reason—to help the victims. All we're doing is getting them to safety. We're not the ones trying to help them with financial situations, or worrying about staffing medical tents, or having to worry about reuniting family members who have gotten separated. Those are beyond us. There're other groups who are way better at all of that. We just show up with boats and give people rides."

Naomi shook her head. "What you guys are doing here is huge. Don't underestimate it. If it wasn't for you going in and pulling people out of their flooded homes, they wouldn't need medical tents and organizations helping them reunite. The only people who need to be reunited with family are the ones who live through this."

Sawyer met her gaze, gave her a grin, then a nod. "You're right. What we're doing here is important. And we believe in it. *And* you're doin' it too this time."

She grinned back at him. Damn right she was.

"Yep, if those egotistical assholes like the paramedics try to turn us back—we'll just tell them to go to hell," Owen said.

They all looked at Michael and chuckled. Michael rolled his eyes.

"Yeah, y'all are huge heroes. And I mean that. But you do realize there's time for everything. Sometimes civilians, even the ones with the best intentions, do get in the way of professionals trying to do their jobs."

Zeke clapped his friend on the back. "We know. And we know that if we don't watch ourselves and use our heads, *we* might be the ones needing your services and that doesn't help anybody either."

Michael narrowed his eyes and looked at Zeke. "Wow, are you being sarcastic or has your pending fatherhood made you mature a little?"

Zeke shook his head and shrugged. "Hell if I know. It's not sarcastic, so maybe I've actually grown up."

Owen put a hand over his chest and gasped. "Holy shit. The day Zeke Landry becomes responsible is the day the entire fabric of the universe shifts."

"Shit, you're right," Zeke said looking mildly concerned. "Fuck it. Let's go be big heroes and do something amazing to get our gorgeous mugs on the news."

"That's better," Owen said. "Damn, for a second there, I was worried."

Michael sighed heavily. "You don't have to *bleed* to be on the news. Just remember that."

"I don't know...pretty boy Donovan sure bled a lot on his TV show," Owen said.

Donovan just shrugged when they all looked over at him. "It wasn't on purpose."

"Still, bet it got you a lot of pussy," Owen said.

Ellie smacked him on the back of his head. Owen rubbed the spot. But didn't apologize.

Donovan cast a glance at Naomi. Then realized he shouldn't look at Naomi since nothing was supposed to be going on there. Which meant she shouldn't care about any past pussy in his life. Which meant he shouldn't worry about her being upset about the past pussy in his life.

Because yeah, for some reason the bleeding *had* gotten him plenty of...that.

"It was because he always took his shirt off."

Everyone looked at Naomi now.

"Oh yeah?" Owen asked.

She lifted a shoulder. "Every time he bled on his show, it was somewhere that required him to take his shirt off. Conveniently." She shot him a look that said she knew that was no coincidence. "The women weren't interested in the blood. Trust me."

Was he the only one who noted the way she said that? That *trust me* sent a lick of fire through his gut. And she was definitely looking at him as if picturing him with his shirt off. And now he was absolutely imagining *her* with her shirt off.

"Well, that's not gonna be any kind of problem," Owen said, looking at Zeke. "I have to take my shirt off down on the docks all the time. I figure I'll have a camera crew following me around pretty quick."

And apparently no one was going to mention the fact that Naomi had commented on Donovan being shirtless being a big draw to his show. And to his off-camera fan club.

Because, in typical Landry fashion, Owen and Zeke were now one-upping each other.

Zeke scoffed. "You think *you're* gonna get more attention than me? Is that what you're sayin'? Please. You're old and I do construction. You just drive boats and fish all day."

"I'm *old*? I'm what, three years older than you? Fuck off. And I don't fish all day." Owen started to reach for the hem of his shirt.

"No fucking way," Leo broke in before anyone stripped anything off in the middle of the mall parking lot. "Put your dicks and the tape measure away. You're both super hot and I'm sure the news crews will be all over you." He looked at both of his grandsons. "As long as *I* don't take my shirt off."

Three full beats passed before anyone responded, but everyone snorted at the same time.

"Jesus," Owen said. "Speaking of *old*."

"Fuck off," Leo said with a grin. "Landrys just get better with age."

"I can attest," Ellie said.

"Tell you what, boys," Leo said. "Twenty bucks says I'm the first one to get an oh-thank-you-you're-my-hero kiss."

Owen considered that. "On the cheek or on the mouth?"

Leo shook his head. "Either."

"Male or female?" Zeke asked.

Leo lifted a brow. Then seemed to consider the question. "Either."

Owen took that in. "Any particular age range?"

Leo laughed. "Nope."

Owen stuck out his hand. "Deal."

Zeke looked at everybody else. "We're gonna be on separate boats. So we'll need witnesses."

Josh grinned and nodded. "Oh, trust me, I will definitely be telling the story of the open mouth kiss Owen gets from the seventy-five-year-old man he rescues from a rooftop."

"Yeah, maybe we should make it forty bucks," Owen said, thinking about Josh's comment.

Zeke nodded. "Agreed."

"Wow," Naomi commented to Ellie. "I'll never get over how competitive your grandsons are."

"I'll never get over how slow they are," Ellie said nodding.

Naomi laughed. "Slow? What?"

"They have never, in their lives, out-witted Leo Landry at

anything. He's got something up his sleeve that will ensure he wins this even before he puts the bet out there."

"You're saying Leo cheats?" Donovan asked.

"For a chance to win money *and* knock two of his cocky grandsons down a peg or two? For sure," Ellie said. "But Leo could charm the devil himself into letting Leo throw a crawfish boil in hell and the next thing you know, Lucifer is begging to be invited on the next fishing weekend. There's no way Leo's not getting that first kiss and the forty bucks."

"They really don't realize he always wins?" Naomi asked.

"Oh, sure they do." Ellie gave Naomi and Donovan a grin. "But it gets them working harder and having fun and I suspect they realize that too and that's why they keep falling for it."

Donovan laughed, taking it all in. He loved this family. Fifty percent of anything any of them said was bullshit and you had to be around them for a day or two to figure out which half was which. But underneath all the joking, teasing, and inappropriate humor, were hearts of gold.

They had each other's backs. No matter what. And, as was evidenced by them standing in a parking lot on their way to Mobile to help a bunch of strangers, they had the backs of people in need around them as well.

He felt a strange camaraderie with them in this moment. He'd felt flickerings of it with his crew when they'd been out on wildlife rescues. He'd always felt safe and knew the people around him would jump in to help with any especially precarious situations.

But there hadn't been as much of a feeling of brotherhood. There hadn't been the joking and teasing and the feeling that these people knew everything about you and loved you in spite of it all.

He thought about Griffin. He and Griffin had been far enough apart in age that they hadn't spent a lot of time together after Griffin hit junior high. Then Griffin had headed off to Africa as soon as he'd graduated high school, while Donovan was still at home. They'd never fought or not gotten along, but they just hadn't been especially close. Then when Griffin had come home, it had been in the midst of tragedy.

And then Donovan had made Griffin's life especially hard.

He knew his hanging out in Autre for the past seven months had been in part because being with his brother again had been so great. Griffin had always been wound tightly. It had gotten him fired from two different jobs at zoos. But Donovan had been surprised by how happy his brother was when Donovan had stopped through Autre the first time. He didn't know if Griffin would ever actually be what he would call laid back, but there was a contentment in Griffin now that he'd never seen before.

Donovan knew very well that that had to do with Charlie, the love of Griffin's life. But he knew it was more than that too. It was all the Landrys, the animal park that Griffin hadn't thought he wanted but was now his passion, and really, the entire town of Autre.

Griffin had found the place where he belonged.

Donovan's chest was tight and it took him a minute to realize that Naomi was standing in front of him, saying his name.

He focused on her. "Sorry. What?"

"I was asking if you're ready to go?" She narrowed her eyes, studying his face. "But now I'm asking if you're okay?"

He suddenly wanted so badly to take her face in his hands and press a kiss to her lips.

When he was with Naomi he felt a contentment that he had to assume was a lot of what Griffin felt when he was with Charlie.

And that was weird.

Donovan had been looking for it and to find it in this tiny

town in Louisiana that he hadn't even intended to ever visit, not to mention stay in, was bizarre.

Plus, they just laid out all the reasons why things couldn't work out between them.

Autre was a great place filled with great people. This woman was amazing. But to have her he'd have to give up his plans to do something bigger with his career.

Wouldn't he?

He looked around the parking lot.

These people were doing important things. Just down the road from Autre as a matter of fact.

Fortunately, hurricanes didn't blow through on a daily basis, so this kind of work wasn't any kind of regular occurrence, but it was definitely important.

He looked at her again and managed a smile. "I'm okay. Just thinking about how huge this is. Kind of amazing."

She nodded. "It really is. I'm glad you're here. Thanks for asking me to come."

"Really glad you said yes."

They just looked at each other for a long moment. Finally, she swallowed, and said, "This might be better than dinner."

"Yeah? Because nobody knows we're together?"

She looked almost sad for a moment. "That's not what I was thinking. I think it's better because I've been to dinner with other men. I've never done something like this. And I don't think I would do something like this with anyone else."

That hit him hard. It was a big deal that he got to help out this way, but it was awesome if he had somehow inspired someone else to do it as well.

"That doesn't make me want to buy you dinner any less, goddess," he told her.

He didn't have to try to drop his voice lower and softer to avoid being overheard. It seemed that his voice naturally did that when he spoke to her.

He saw a flicker of emotion in her eyes at the use of the endearment.

"Well, I suppose we'll have to eat later. I have a feeling that even if that turns out to just be a sandwich, it'll be the best sandwich I've ever had," she said quietly.

"Dammit, girl, you say things like that when I'm standing in the middle of a bunch of people you don't want to know about us, so I can't kiss you the way I want to right now."

She nodded and dragged her tongue over her lower lip. "Dammit is right."

But he shouldn't kiss her at all. Not even if they were alone. Because he was leaving.

"Okay, let's head out," Sawyer said. "Next stop, Mobile. We're heading over to the southwest part of town. There'll be somebody there to meet us who will help us get the boats in the water and direct us where to start."

"I think we'll head over there with you," Donovan said, making himself focus on the task at hand instead of Naomi.

He'd gotten a voicemail from Fiona while they'd been driving and he'd listened right after they'd parked. "Fiona won't be to town until later on this evening. They've got an emergency animal shelter set up, so they're hoping to have a few rescue boats that are willing to pick up animals and get them to the shelter. Knowing there's somewhere safe for their pets could help convince some of these people to actually leave their houses."

"Absolutely," Sawyer said. "You and Naomi have all the details?"

"I can fill her in."

"Great. Owen and I will each take one of you on our boats. They're big enough we can fit some crates and carriers on them."

"We'll need to bring some food and supplies too," Donovan

said. "We might need to coax some animals out and there might be some injuries."

"Fine," Sawyer agreed.

Donovan glanced at Naomi. "You okay with this?"

She looked a little nervous, but she nodded. "Yes. If that's what needs done, I'm in."

Yeah, it was impossible not to be crazy about this woman.

6

She really shouldn't fall for a guy who could convince her to balance on the side of an airboat, jump across four feet of flood waters to a rooftop, then climb through a tiny window into someone's attic.

The owner's cat, who had escaped when the humans had finally realized they needed to abandon their house, was supposedly hiding out in that attic. They'd notified the animal shelter who had passed the word to Donovan. Their airboat was full of people they'd picked up from five blocks over—including two dogs—but Sawyer had agreed to head this direction to check the house for the cat.

Now Naomi was climbing over the slippery shingles of a house and trying not to think about how devastating this all was. This family had lost everything. The water reached up to the roof of their porch. There was hope there were things on the second floor that could be salvaged but furniture, food, and mementos from the first floor were gone.

Naomi blocked that out as she held onto the eaves of the house and made her way to the attic window.

"You couldn't have fallen in love with that welder from Bad, could you?" she muttered to herself. "Or that architect from New Orleans? Or that firefighter Caleb introduced you to? He was a *firefighter*, Naomi. Sure, he does risky things for a living, but he wouldn't have *you* climbing into burning buildings."

Donovan wasn't right beside her, actually telling her to do this, of course. He was in the other Landry airboat about three houses away. But she was doing this because this was what he would have done and it was why she was here. She wanted to help. She was here to help Donovan *rescue animals* specifically.

And she was the only one on the boat small enough to climb through the attic window.

The cat better be up here.

The owners were assuming Mr. Paws had stayed in the house. It was probably a fair assumption. Their house was, literally, surrounded by water. The cat would have had to swim to get anywhere else.

"What did you say?"

Naomi glanced over at Bennett, who had accompanied her out of the boat and onto the roof. "Oh nothing, just talking to myself."

He gritted his teeth as he inched along the slippery rooftop behind her. "Okay, good."

She got to the window. The owners had told her that it would be unlocked and it should be no problem for her to get inside. She started to pull it up and found it stuck, however. "Dammit."

"Here, let me try." Bennett moved in beside her and let go of the eaves overhead to grab onto the lower part of the window. One of his shoes slipped and he cursed. "Motherfucker."

Bennett pried on the window for a couple of minutes and

finally got it to budge slightly. Together they shoved it upward. They got it about three-fourths of the way up.

Bennett eyed the opening. "Think you can slide through there?"

Naomi pressed a hand to her belly. "Makes me wish I had laid off Ellie's bread pudding a little bit."

Bennett chuckled. "I think you'll be okay." He grabbed a flashlight from the toolbelt he had hooked around his waist. He shone it through the window. "There's not much of a drop on the other side, and it looks like it's clear below the window."

Naomi wet her lips and nodded. "Just keep the light shining there, okay?"

"You bet."

She put her hands on the windowsill, gripping it tightly. Then leaned in and very ungracefully slid through. She braced her fall with her hands on the other side feeling a twinge in one wrist. "Dammit."

"You okay?" Bennett asked.

"Yeah. I didn't practice my landings."

She heard him chuckle, then he handed the flashlight through the window to her and took another out of his toolbelt and shone it through the opening.

Naomi got to her feet, flashing the light around the attic. It was a very typical attic. It had boxes and trunks and lots of dust and cobwebs.

"Mr. Paws?" she asked. Her fall to the window had probably startled the feline, making the chances of finding him even more difficult. The only things she had going for her were that the attic was relatively small, he didn't have many other places to go, and he was probably hungry.

"I don't see him. We're probably going to have to convince him to come out."

"Here you go," Bennett said, handing a small sandwich bag of cat food through the window.

Naomi set the flashlight on a box to her right so it would shine into the room and opened the bag.

"Here, kitty, kitty, kitty," she called softly. She shook some of the food out onto the floor. "Come on, kitty. Come on, Mr. Paws. I won't hurt you."

She backed up away from the food and settled in to wait, giving the animal some space to come out on its own. Of course, capturing it and getting it out of the house would be the next step, but locating the animal was obviously where they had to start.

Naomi backed up to the wall and leaned in to wait.

But it wasn't long before she heard a scratching sound and then saw a cardboard box in the corner to her right shift.

She straightened away from the wall. Donovan had also reminded her that house cats tended to be a lot more friendly and generally calm around humans. It was a much different situation than trying to catch feral cats or wild animals.

Mr. Paws was ten years old and generally friendly with even guests and visitors, all of which made the situation seem like it would be an easier capture.

A moment later, a large gray and black cat came waddling out from the shadows.

"He's coming out already," Naomi told Bennett. "

"That was easy," Bennett commented.

Thank God. She would love to think that her first attempt would be a success. She not only would like to have this turn out for the family, but she wouldn't mind showing Donovan that she could handle this. She wasn't going to think too hard about wanting to impress Donovan Foster.

The animal crept closer and Naomi worked on holding very still. She was going to give it a chance to eat a little bit, but she was going to have to be prepared to scoop the cat up and hand it out to the window to Bennett.

Mr. Paws was reportedly declawed so she wasn't worried

about being scratched, but he was a big guy and if he put up a fight, he might be difficult to hang onto.

"Hi, kitt —" Then she gasped.

"What's wrong?" Bennett asked.

Naomi backed up quickly, right into the wall. "Um... This isn't Mr. Paws."

Bennett leaned down, peering through the window. "What do you mean?"

"Bennett, this is a raccoon."

"*What?*"

"This is a raccoon, not a cat."

"Well...shit."

The raccoon, however, didn't seem bothered by Naomi. In fact, it seemed to be enjoying the cat food. It ate quickly and searched the area for more. Naomi reached into the bag she still held and tossed more onto the floor. The raccoon followed the scattered food, eating it quickly as well.

"Bennett, can you get another animal carrier."

"What? Why?"

"To put the raccoon in."

"Seriously? You're going to capture the raccoon?"

"Well, it's trapped too. There's nowhere for it to go either and it's obviously hungry. I'm sure it came up here because it was higher ground. We can't just leave it here."

"I..."

She heard Bennett blow out a breath.

"Yeah. Okay. Hang on."

Naomi dumped the rest of the food onto the floor for the raccoon. Then she heard more scratching. She sucked in a breath. She reached for the flashlight, shining it over in the direction the raccoon had come from.

Three smaller, clearly *baby* raccoons made their way out from behind the stack of boxes in the far corner.

"Holy crap," she muttered.

She watched the little raccoon family finish off the cat food as she waited for Bennett to return. It was several minutes. But he finally appeared outside of the window with one of the medium-sized carriers.

It wouldn't fit through the window.

"I'm going to have to pick this raccoon up," she said. Not so much a question for Bennett as a realization out loud for herself.

"Guess so." Bennett passed a pair of work gloves through the window to her.

She sighed. "Well, all four of them actually."

"Four?"

"There are three babies too."

There was a pause, then Bennett said, "Of course there are."

"Is there a towel or something in the carrier?" she asked.

She remembered watching Donovan rescue a possum that had gotten caught in a barrel. He had to cut one end of the barrel off and then he'd covered the possum's head with a towel. It had kept the possum from panicking when it saw a human coming for him. It had also given Donovan something to wrap around the animal so as it wiggled it couldn't scratch or bite.

Oh, God, this raccoon could scratch or bite her.

Naomi looked down at her bare arms. It was hot and muggy down here. It would have never occurred to her to wear long sleeves.

"Here you go." Bennett passed a bath towel through the window.

Naomi assumed the babies would be easier to handle than the larger raccoon but they might be harder to capture. Still, she thought, starting with the mother was maybe the way to go.

In truth, she had no idea what she was doing. But she had to do her best. She was the only one here, so this was her job now. She had to help these animals if she could.

She approached slowly and quietly. The raccoon was still eating, which helped. When she was close enough, she tossed the towel over the raccoon, careful to get it over its head. Then she quickly scooped underneath the animal, wrapping the towel around it. It definitely wiggled and tried to get away. She quickly crossed to the window and shoved it into the carrier. Her heart was pounding and her mouth was dry as adrenaline pumped through her system.

Bennett closed the door on the carrier and Naomi stepped back, breathing hard.

"Okay. There we go." The raccoon had already worked its way out of the towel and was chittering angrily.

"I know," she told the animal. "I know. But we're helping. I promise. I'm going to get your babies and we'll get you someplace safe."

She understood why Griffin talked to the otters all the time at Boys of the Bayou Gone Wild. It was an affectionate joke that the grumpy vet spilled his guts to his furry friends more easily than to humans, but it was impossible for Naomi to *not* respond to the raccoon's clear fear and displeasure.

She turned back to find the babies had scattered. Awesome.

It took her nearly twenty minutes, but she finally found all three of the babies, scooped them up and got them into the carrier with their mother without letting any of the previously captured animals back out. Somehow.

Bennett was a huge help and she had no idea how he kept his footing on the slippery roof, while also managing a heavy, shifting crate full of animals.

Trying to catch her breath and calm her racing heartbeat, Naomi stood by the window.

The people on the air boat were probably getting antsy since they'd been at this house for nearly forty minutes now.

And she still hadn't rescued the owner's cat. The entire reason for this stop.

She turned back to the attic. Dammit. Mr. Paws wasn't here? Now what were they going to do?

Just then, there was a soft thump as if something had jumped from a height. A moment later, a fluffy gray cat came strolling out from the shadows.

And yes, this time she was sure it was a cat.

She propped her hands on her hips. "Well, it's nice to see you, Mr. Paws."

No doubt the cat had gotten up somewhere high to avoid interacting with the raccoons.

The cat gave a soft *meow* and sniffed around on the floor where the cat food had previously been.

Naomi laughed. "Sorry, buddy, you have to get on the boat if you want some food now. Your roommates ate all I had."

The cat approached and rubbed against her legs. Clearly, she didn't have to worry about bribing this one. She leaned over and scooped him up. The cat settled in against her chest and started purring. "Well, I'm happy to see you too." She turned back to the window. "Need that other carrier after all."

Donovan had told them that cats were going to be safer in carriers even if they were house pets and seemed docile. It would be easy for them to get spooked on the airboats and no one wanted cats going overboard. Dogs could, of course, be kept on leashes, but cats were a different story.

Bennett looked at her and Mr. Paws and chuckled. "I knew this would be interesting, but I didn't quite expect this."

When Sawyer pulled their boat into the main drop off location to let their passengers off, Donovan, Owen, and Mitch were letting off a family with three dogs.

Donovan caught Naomi's eye and gave her a big grin. She returned it with a wave. But they didn't have a chance to talk. They were all handed more addresses where people were waiting to be rescued.

Over the course of the next several hours, it felt as if they'd traveled every street in Mobile. About ninety percent of the people they ran across agreed to get on the boat. The ones who decided to stay behind were given contact information for if they changed their minds and bottled water, batteries, and other supplies.

Naomi didn't feel quite the same rush of desire and affection that she felt for Donovan in his heroic moments, but watching Sawyer, Bennett, and Zeke carrying little kids and older people from their porches to the waiting airboats made her heart feel full in a different way. The guys all worked to make the people laugh, reassured them everything was going to be okay, and distracted the kids with alligator and otter toys that Maddie and Kennedy must have stored on the boats from the Boys of the Bayou gift shop.

She'd been surrounded by these good people all her life and, while she'd always known it, seeing them in action like this, outside of Autre, outside of *their* comfort zones, was a great reminder that she was lucky to know them.

Their lives on the bayou might seem small and simple, but the truth was, they interacted with people every single day from all walks of life. Sawyer took tourists out on the bayou every day. Zeke did construction and worked to make houses into homes. Bennett was a climate activist and politician. Yes, that meant he spent a lot of time trying to convince other people to think *his* ideas were good, but that took a lot of listening too.

They were all naturals at this and at the end of the day, Naomi was exhausted, but she felt like she'd really been a part of something important.

Nearly twelve hours after first putting their boats into the water, they gathered in the parking lot of a grocery store with a good portion of the other volunteers.

They all debriefed about the rescues they'd done that day

and about what was waiting for them the next day. A few boats planned to go out even tonight. There were a lot of people who were hesitant to evacuate during daylight hours, but once the sun went down they got a little more willing to leave their dark, powerless homes.

A couple of local church groups were providing food for the volunteers and the Landry crew stood around the back of Sawyer's pickup, eating and chatting.

Naomi sensed Donovan as he came up behind her before she saw him.

"How was your day?"

She turned and smiled at him. "Amazing."

He looked her up and down, his gaze hot. She knew she was a mess. So was he. And it didn't matter at all. He looked rugged and capable and competent and she wanted to grab him by his amazing biceps, pull him in, and kiss him.

"I heard you had to climb in a window to get someone's cat," he said, one corner of his mouth tipping up as if he was amused and impressed at the same time.

She spread her arms. "I do what I have to do. And I didn't just get a cat."

"No?"

Bennett overheard them talking. He chuckled. "Leave it to Naomi to walk out of a single cat rescue with four additional animals."

Donovan was clearly surprised. "Were there other cats sheltering up there?"

"A mama raccoon and three babies," Bennett told him. "And Naomi barely blinked."

Naomi shook her head. "Oh, I blinked. And backed up. And almost panicked."

"Almost?" Donovan mouth curved more fully. "Did you guys have a live trap on the boat?"

"We just put her in the cat carrier," Naomi said.

"How did you get it in there?"

"Queen Bad Ass here just picked the thing up and shoved it in there."

Donovan suddenly frowned. "Wait. You just picked it up?"

"Well, I threw a towel over it first."

"But then you just picked it up?" He seemed concerned suddenly.

"I didn't have a choice. The cat carrier wouldn't fit through the window."

Suddenly Donovan grabbed her hands and started turning them over and running his hand up and down her arms from her fingertips to her shoulders.

"Donovan, what are you doing?"

"It didn't bite or scratch you, did it? They can carry rabies and canine distemper. They can be really nasty when they are cornered."

"Stop it." She tugged her hands from his grip. "It was too confused and hungry to be aggressive. It all happened really fast for both of us." She held up her hands with her palms out. "Michael already checked me out. No scratches or bites. I was wearing gloves and used the towel. I'm fine."

Donovan just stood staring at her for a long moment. Then he said, "Come with me."

She tipped her head. "Where?"

"I need more lemonade."

She narrowed her eyes. She didn't really want to be yelled at. She was fine. In retrospect, she could have possibly done something different with the raccoons, but she honestly didn't know what. She supposed she could've waited for Donovan and sent him back over to the house. But the animals had needed to be rescued. They'd been trapped and hungry. There had been *babies*. She'd done what she needed to do in the moment. She shook her head. "I'm good."

"Just come with me."

His jaw was tight and she could tell he was upset. Well, too bad. They were all taking some risks out here. She wasn't special. She didn't need to be treated with kid gloves or left in the boat when important things needed done.

"The stand with the lemonade is right there." She pointed to the tent about thirty feet away. "I'll wait here for you."

Bennett had turned away to talk to someone else and Donovan leaned in close to her ear. "Come with me or I'll throw you over my shoulder and carry you over there and that will *definitely* get everybody talking."

Her breath caught in her chest and her eyes widened. "You wouldn't."

"Fucking dare me."

She had never heard Donovan talk like that. Certainly not to her. But she wasn't sure she had heard him talk that way to anyone. Yes, he definitely got intense at times, but he never got angry.

Studying his face, she realized he wasn't exactly angry, though. He was...wound up. Still, she decided not to see if he was kidding about the over-the-shoulder thing.

"Fine."

They walked together to the tent where huge vats of iced tea and lemonade and ice water were set up on long folding tables. But they didn't stop in front of the tables.

Donovan grabbed her wrist and tugged her around to the opposite side of the tent. Out of view of the Landrys and her brother.

He turned to face her.

"Look, Donovan, you can't be mad. I did what I had to do and I'm not sorry. I was as safe as I could be and you, of anyone, should know that sometimes we have to take some risks to get this stuff done."

He stepped forward, took her face in his hands, and covered her mouth with his.

She sank into the kiss immediately. She wasn't an idiot. He was worked up and there was a lot of adrenaline pumping for both of them, but Donovan was kissing her. She was going to pour all of her mixed-up emotions into this too and enjoy it for a few seconds.

He finally lifted his head. "I'm not mad." His voice was husky as he looked into her eyes.

"You're not?"

"I was...worried. I guess feeling protective. But I'm also—" He broke off, shaking his head as if he couldn't figure out what words to use.

"You're also what?"

"I just *like* you so fucking much."

That took a second to sink in, but when it did, Naomi laughed. She understood exactly what he was feeling. "I worry about you and like you so fucking much too."

"And I really just need space to do this." He sealed his mouth over hers again.

D onovan was amazed by the intensity of emotions rolling through him.

And he wasn't sure he could have named any of the feelings specifically.

He was just...worked up.

Naomi seemed to be too. She was arching close, her fingers digging into his upper arms, her mouth open, her tongue dueling with his as if she was trying as hard to drink him in as he was her.

"Oh, excuse me!"

They broke apart as a woman came around the edge of the tent.

"I'm really sorry to interrupt."

It was Rachel, the reporter who had been following the Autre crew around all day.

"Hi, Rachel. You're not. It's fine," Naomi managed, stepping back from Donovan and running a hand down the front of her clothes.

That was funny. Her clothes were dirty and wrinkled and it had nothing to do with what they'd just been doing.

It had everything to do with her being fucking amazing and jumping in today to save animals. Even wild animals. Without thinking for a second that it might not be safe for her.

He was rubbing off on her.

He wasn't sure that was a good thing. But he definitely felt pride mixed in with everything else swirling through him.

She really was a goddess.

"I'll leave you alone, though," Rachel said, backing up. "Sorry, again."

Rachel slipped around the corner of the tent, leaving Donovan and Naomi alone. But they were both now very aware of the fact that they weren't completely alone and they probably shouldn't have been doing what they'd just been doing.

No, actually they *definitely* shouldn't have been doing what they'd just been doing. They needed to stop kissing. Not just because they might be seen, although that was certainly a consideration. But because the more they kissed, the harder it was to not fall for this woman.

She'd made it clear she was not looking for that. And he should have been just as adamant about that.

"I'm glad you had a good day," he finally said.

"I really did. This is all amazing."

"And I'm not surprised that you just jumped in and did what needed doing."

"It's exactly what you would've done."

He nodded. "But I have more experience than you do."

"And how did you get that experience? By doing the stuff. Donovan, I'm fine. If I had been bitten or scratched, Michael would've taken care of it. If I had needed more attention than that, we would have taken care of it. Sawyer and Bennett and Zeke were looking out for me."

He drew in a breath. He knew that. The guys she was with would've definitely taken care of anything that would've happened. Maybe that was what was bothering him. He wanted to be the one there, taking care of anything that happened. He wanted to be the one she was handing the raccoon off to.

And that was ridiculous.

"You worry about me. Why can't I worry about you?"

"Because I let people take care of me when I need them."

Her words hit him in the gut. She not only had a good point, but she knew him. Before they'd even shared their backstories. She'd figured out that he didn't let people fuss over him.

"Griffin gave up a lot and spent a lot of time taking care of me. I try to be self-sufficient now."

She lifted a hand to his face and ran her palm down his cheek. "Self-sufficient and totally alone are not the same thing."

He turned his face and pressed a kiss into the center of her palm before her hand dropped away. "I'm getting that."

She gave him a pleased smile.

"So they said one of the high schools has running water and they're opening it up so that volunteers can shower there," he said. "Then there are various places around town that are letting people set up cots and air mattresses. But I'm thinking about the air mattress in the back of my truck tonight. I have a cover over the top and room for one more."

He could tell she was tempted, but she slowly shook her head. "My brother is taking me over to the next town's firehouse. They're offering showers there too and they have an extra cot. I figured maybe it was better if we didn't cuddle up in the back of your truck tonight."

"I smell that bad, huh?"

She laughed. "No, but this group will definitely notice where the two of us sleep."

She really was adamant about keeping every little bit of her private life private.

"Okay, but maybe we can work on the same boat tomorrow."

She shook her head. "They need an experienced animal handler on each boat. Putting us together would mean one boat would go without."

He groaned. "You're an experienced animal handler now, huh?"

"Tell me I'm not."

He still shuddered to think that she could have been bitten by a rabid raccoon, but he did love her sassiness.

They walked together around the corner of the tent and Donovan again had to resist the urge to take her hand as if they were boyfriend and girlfriend.

"Hi again." Rachel was waiting in front of the tent.

Naomi and Donovan drew to a stop. "Hey," Donovan said.

"I know this is probably really annoying," Rachel said, clearly addressing Donovan. "But I was wondering if you'd be okay with me asking you about the big rescue from earlier."

Naomi looked at him, one eyebrow up. "Big rescue?"

He shook his head. "It wasn't that big."

"There was a little boy on a rooftop who was holding a puppy and wouldn't leave without his dog. There was also a power line down in front of the house, making it impossible to get a boat close," Rachel explained. "Donovan jumped into the water, swam to the rooftop with an inflatable pineapple, got the little boy and the puppy onto the pineapple, and swam back to the boat."

"An inflatable pineapple?" Naomi asked.

He shrugged. "One of the other families we rescued had it. Came in really handy."

Naomi turned to face him more fully, crossing her arms. "And there were downed power lines?"

"It was a little boy and a puppy."

"And you were mad at me about a raccoon?"

He gave her one of the I-am-really-cute-and-charming smiles he'd perfected over the years. "You really fucking like me, remember?"

"So I got the video from one of the guys on your boat," Rachel pressed. "But how about an interview?"

"Actually, we were just—"

Naomi jumped in. "Of course he'll do an interview about how important evacuating is and how many people are out here working hard to help keep everyone safe." She turned to him. "Any time you have a chance to be on camera to make a case for a good cause, you should do it. You're amazing at it." She sighed almost as if she wished it wasn't true.

He grinned. He knew that his attention seeking seemed to be just that, at times, but he knew that Naomi saw deeper than that. He loved how she seemed to understand him.

He looked at Rachel. "Okay, fine, I'm happy to talk for a few minutes. Do you mind if I grab a shower first?"

Naomi jumped in again. "Oh no, do it like this."

He looked at her again. "Really?"

She rolled her eyes. "I've already told you that you're hot all the time, but you look especially good when you're dirty and rumpled and fresh off doing what you do best."

He couldn't help himself. He leaned in a little closer. "But I wasn't just doing what I do *best*."

Her eyes widened as if she couldn't believe he just said that. "Rescues. I meant rescues, Donovan."

"But you said *best*."

She shook her head. "Go do your interview. Be charming and rugged, and amazing. I'll see you tomorrow."

It took everything in him not to lean over and kiss her, and as he watched her walk away, he was fairly certain that even though he hadn't, anyone watching them knew that that was exactly what was on his mind.

7

The next morning, they were all back in the grocery store parking lot and loading up, doing inventory of their supplies, and waiting for a list of addresses to check first thing. Apparently, the boats last night had brought in an additional six families and they were feeling good about the remaining number of people still in the houses.

"Morning, everyone." The Autre group all turned to find that Fiona had finally joined them.

She gave the members of the group hugs one by one, coming to stand in front of Donovan last.

"About time you got here," he told her, enfolding her in a big bear hug.

She let him go, laughing. "Well, I had to plan to be gone from my animal park a little longer than I'd expected."

"Oh yeah? What's going on?"

"Well, a big growly city manager in Louisiana seems to think I need to report to Autre before heading back to Florida after this."

Donovan narrowed his eyes. "Knox wants you to come to Autre?"

She nodded. "He says it's because I shouldn't just send this new animal back to Autre with you without coming to be sure everything is settled. But I think he's been worried about me."

"You've been talking to Knox?"

"Yeah." And that was all she said.

"You and Knox have been talking? Regularly?"

The petite brunette lifted one shoulder. "Yeah. I mean when he calls it's always to bitch about something. But I think it's really just an excuse to flirt with me."

"Knox. Autre city manager. Big guy. Doesn't smile much. Perpetually annoyed. Calls you regularly to flirt."

Fiona looked up at him, squinting. "Did you hit your head on something yesterday? Why are you acting slow?"

"I didn't realize something was going on between you and Knox."

Fiona laughed. "Where have you been?"

"So there *is* something going on with you?"

"We flirt. I keep him on his toes. And he likes to complain about that. Though apparently he found out from someone"— She gave Donovan a look that said she completely blamed him —"that I routinely show up to hurricane disaster sites to do animal rescues. He was concerned about that."

"You do."

"Yeah."

"I didn't realize that was a secret. And Griffin actually confirmed that."

"It's not a secret. But who knew that Knox would be all protective and concerned and sweet."

"*Knox* was sweet?" Donovan asked. "I don't believe that for a second."

Fiona laughed. "Well, not typical sweet. Knox sweet."

Donovan studied the woman. He didn't know Fiona well but what he did know was that she was spirited and incredibly independent and had her own ideas about how just about everything should go. She didn't seem like the type that the growly city manager, who also always thought *he* knew exactly how everything should go, would want to take on.

Of course they lived about seven hundred miles apart. Maybe that made it easier to keep it to just flirtation and nothing more.

Donovan looked over to where Naomi was finishing up a breakfast sandwich, also supplied by the church group from last night, and coffee with her brother and Sawyer.

When he left Autre, could they keep up a long-distance relationship? He'd never expect a woman to sit around and just wait for him to drop by and visit. Still, he liked the idea of being able to just call her up and chat and flirt when he started to miss her.

He thought about that. *When* he started to miss her? He'd be calling her every day.

He looked at Fiona. "How often do you hear from Knox?"

"Every few days. And sometimes it's really stupid stuff." She didn't seem annoyed at all, though.

"You ever call or text him first?"

"Of course. It's really hard to annoy a guy if you never call or text him."

Donovan shook his head. Fiona was a handful. If Knox wanted to take that on, he was a brave man.

"So anyway I came over to talk to you about this new animal."

"The new animal you're bringing to Autre?"

"Actually, *you're* bringing this one."

"I am?" Donovan straightened.

"Yeah, I know a guy here in Alabama. Jeff and I've worked on a couple rescues before. But this is a little unusual. And I need *your* help in particular."

Donovan perked up. "Is it a big cat?" Everyone knew that Donovan's true love, if he really had to pick, were big cats.

Tigers and lions in particular. He'd worked with several different kinds over the years. His rescues of bobcats and lynx and even a jaguar had been some of the highlights of his career.

"Well..."

"It is." Donovan's heart started racing. "What's going on?"

"Okay, there is a tiger. And a zebra," she said. "And they're being rescued, in the sense we're taking possession of them and moving them. But there's an animal that's actually *stuck* and needs someone to get it out. I figured since I have an experienced rescuer right here, I should take advantage of that."

Donovan processed all of that as quickly as he could. Wow, there was a tiger. But he focused on the *stuck* part. "What's stuck? And where?"

"A harbor seal pup. He's stuck in his swimming pool."

He hadn't been expecting that. "Seriously?"

Fiona nodded. "There's an animal park about twenty miles outside of town. It's sketchy to say the least. But in addition to having a questionable status to start with, now it's been totally wiped out with this hurricane. We're re-homing several of the animals in Autre. Zeke is finally getting his zebra." She shot a grin over in the direction of the youngest Landry grandson.

Donovan grinned too. Zeke was a bigger fan of penguins now that Jill had brought her colony to Autre, but he'd been hoping for zebras ever since they'd started the animal park.

"But the guy also had a seal. No one's really sure where he got it and no one knew that he had it. He's also not talking. But anyway, the pool collapsed in the storm *on top* of the seal. It can breathe but can't move around much, and they think it has a significant gash on one flipper and they're not sure what else. It has been without food and water since yesterday."

Donovan made up his mind in about two seconds. "Let's go." Donovan grabbed her arm and started for his truck. "We're standing around here talking about Knox when we should be there trying to get that seal out?"

"Relax," Fiona replied, nearly jogging to keep up with his long strides. "They're up there now breaking up the side of the pool to get him out."

He stopped and frowned down at her. "Who is?"

"Some guys." She shrugged. "Obviously power tools are in short supply around here with *lots* of people needing things cut and broken up, but these guys had the right equipment to cut through the metal and plastic."

"No. Have them stop. We need to get there and assess the situation. They can't just go cutting into it. And we need to be there as soon as they get the seal free. We need to be ready to treat whatever injuries he has and then get him back to Griffin immediately."

Fiona didn't argue. But she did tug free of his grip. "I'm bringing my truck," she said, gesturing to the gigantic purple truck she drove all the time. It had a trailer hooked on the back. "Jeff and I will load the other animals and head to Autre. I'm texting the directions to you right now so that you can go find the seal. Then you head straight to Louisiana."

Donovan looked around. "Just leave all these guys?"

Fiona followed his gaze. "These guys are fine, Donovan."

Donovan's eyes landed on Naomi. He was bringing her with him. He knew that she was enjoying this and felt like she was doing some good here. He didn't want to take her away from that. But he could really use her with him on the road. It was only a two hour drive, but it was always better to have another pair of hands when dealing with an injured animal.

He strode toward the group. "Hey, I have an injured animal emergency. I'm heading over to help them rescue it and then taking it back to Autre. I could use someone along with me."

Naomi straightened. "What kind of animal?"

"Harbor seal."

Everyone's eyes went wide.

Donovan nodded. "Long story. Some guy had it and shouldn't have. But now it's injured and needs a new home."

"Go," Sawyer said with a nod. "We're good here."

"Who's going to build an enclosure?" Zeke asked, looking at Mitch.

"We'll keep it at the rehab facility for now," Donovan said. "It's not going to need a lot of space for a bit."

"We'll get started as soon as we get back," Zeke said.

"No problem," Mitch said. "We'll discuss plans on our way home."

Donovan looked at the group. They just did what needed to be done. They met challenges head-on, backed each other up, and jumped in with their whole hearts. Being included in this group was a huge compliment.

"I'll have a better idea of what we need by the time you get back," he told them.

"That animal needs you a lot more than we do right now," Owen said. "Go do your big superstar Noah thing. We'll stick around here and play with our airboats for a little longer. We'll meet you back home."

"Superstar Noah thing?" Naomi asked.

"Yeah," Owen said. "Noah was the first one to save all the animals. Sure, he just loaded them up on a boat and floated around until the flood went down. What Donovan does is a lot bigger deal than that. I mean"—Owen looked up at the sky —"like, don't tell Noah and the big guy I said that. I'm not saying what he did wasn't important."

They all laughed.

Mitch clapped Owen on the shoulder. "Yeah, I think we're all okay with you puttin' Donovan in the same category as Noah from the Bible."

Donovan shook his head. These people were half crazy. And still their admiration and support for what he did meant more to him than he ever would've imagined.

"Yeah, we'll see you back home," Sawyer said. "You better get going."

Home. He liked the sound of that. It sounded right. Which was strange. He wasn't from Autre and he wasn't planning on staying. So nothing about the town should've felt like home.

But it did.

"I'm coming with you," Naomi said.

Thank God. Donovan gave her a smile. "You sure?"

"Who knows what kind of trouble you can get into on your own with a harbor seal between here and Louisiana," she said with a smile that definitely had touches of affection in it.

"Louisiana is like two hours from here." Owen said.

"Naomi is going with Donovan," Ellie told him.

"I'm just saying, he's not going that far away."

"Naomi is going with Donovan," Ellie repeated.

"But who's gonna save the raccoons today then?" Owen asked.

Ellie put her hands on her hips and looked at Owen. "I guess maybe you have to be the raccoon rescuer today. Maybe a raccoon will kiss you since Leo got the forty bucks yesterday."

Owen sighed. "I swear he set that up somehow."

Donovan stifled a laugh. He didn't know if that was true, but he'd heard all about the gorgeous, thirty-something woman with the broken leg Leo had carried from her house and who had rewarded him with a not-at-all-quick-peck-on-the-lips for his heroism yesterday.

"Yeah, well, my big muscles make it hard for me to climb in through windows," Owen said, flexing some of those big muscles.

"You sure it's not all the extra helpings of biscuits and gravy?" Ellie asked him.

"You wound me, El. You truly wound me," Owen said, putting a hand over his heart, but ruining his fake pain with a grin.

Ellie didn't look at all apologetic.

"Okay, fine, but I want the floating pineapple today," Owen said. "Apparently that's how you get on the news."

Donovan and Naomi just let that go. They headed for Donovan's truck.

"Donovan! Naomi!"

They stopped and turned as Rachel, the reporter, came rushing up.

"We heard about you going to rescue a seal! Can we tag along?"

Donovan thought about what Naomi had said last night. When he had the chance to go on camera for a good cause he should take it. This was an opportunity to talk about all of the exotic animals kept as pets that shouldn't be. "Absolutely."

"Wonderful!" Rachel turned and motioned to her cameraman. "I was hoping to talk you into letting us follow you around on your rescues today anyway. This is even more exciting!"

"Well, I'll be honest with you," Donovan told her. "I prefer rescues to *not* be exciting. I like it when they're routine and they go according to plan and everything works out."

"Oh, of course," Rachel gushed. "But just that there is a seal and you're going to be saving it makes this not-your-usual-day."

"It's very safe to say that every day with Donovan is not your usual day," Naomi said dryly.

Donovan opened his mouth to ask if that was a good thing or bad, but thought better of it. For one thing, he wasn't sure he wanted to know. For another, he thought maybe he already did know. Naomi liked her life just as it was. Which was pretty... yeah, usual.

"Aw, that's sweet," Rachel said. "How long have you two been together?"

Naomi straightened and Donovan winced.

"What? Oh, we're—" Naomi said.

"Oh." Rachel frowned. "It's just, last night when I

interrupted—"

"We're really good friends," Donovan jumped in. "We've been working closely together for a few months. I was really proud of Naomi yesterday but was also worried when I heard about the amazing rescue *she* pulled off. The adrenaline and the emotions and the moment just kind of caught up to us." He gave Rachel a smile and a shrug. "Plus, she's gorgeous. You can't blame me for wanting to kiss her, right?"

Rachel looked back and forth between them. She slowly shook her head. "No. I can't blame you. You guys definitely have a lot of chemistry."

Naomi and Donovan exchanged a look and then smiled.

"Like he said, we're good friends and yes, there's an attraction," Naomi said. "But we don't want to mess that up."

And she didn't want it out in public. Donovan could almost hear those words tacked on to the end of her sentence.

Rachel nodded. "Okay, sorry to assume."

"No problem. But we need to get going now. Naomi is going to come retrieve the seal with me and then we're heading back to Autre," Donovan said. "So you can definitely tag along and think of any other questions you've got for me. We're going to want to get on the road with this animal as soon as possible."

"You've got it." Rachel turned to her cameraman and they started for their vehicle. "We'll be right behind you."

When she was out of earshot, Donovan blew out a breath and looked at Naomi. "That was close."

"Well, we do have chemistry. That's why we have to watch what we do and say."

He nodded. "I get it. I just wish it was different."

She gave him a small smile that had a touch of sadness to it. "Me too."

The words *I don't have to go to the Galapagos* were right on the tip of his tongue, but he bit the words back before they came out. Barely.

On their way out of Mobile to the animal park that didn't even have a name, Naomi looked up what she could find on her phone.

"It looks like a guy who has just been collecting exotic animals. He has occasionally charged admission to school groups and other people to come look at the animals and it sounds like he had some issues with authorities on a few occasions. It looks like at some point they tried to shut him down completely and maybe they believed that they had?" She looked over at Donovan. "Even the information on the internet is pretty nonspecific."

Donovan was scowling at the road in front of them. He was following Fiona's grape purple pickup and the trailer she was pulling. Rachel and her cameraman were in another truck behind him.

Rachel had certainly been fine with the change of plans. Naomi was sure that rescuing a harbor seal and a zebra would make a better story than just hauling typical cats and dogs out of houses, but it didn't hurt that Donovan was extremely good-looking and had clearly charmed the reporter.

And was Naomi feeling a tiny stab of jealousy? Yeah, she was. One that wasn't so tiny, actually. And she wasn't happy about it. She and Donovan had agreed that it was a bad idea to pursue a relationship. She had given up any rights to being jealous. Still, that didn't mean she wanted to watch a beautiful, perky blonde fawning over him all day.

Still, the work Donovan did with animal rescues was important. And if they could shine a light on some shady business practices and why not just anyone should get to own exotic animals, whether they called their business an animal park or not, this would be a great story. Apparently this guy had been around for a while, and Naomi suddenly wanted to know why no one had done a story on him owning these animals before this.

"There's some speculation in a couple of these articles that the man who owns the animals has a friend in the mayor's office," Naomi said. "I suppose it's possible he knows someone who convinced the authorities to look the other way. Or who promised to make sure he was on the up and up."

"Fuckers," Donovan said. "This kind of stuff happens more often than people would think. Everyone thinks they should get to be special. If they have the money they can do whatever they want. God only knows where he got these animals. And it doesn't sound like he's been doing a great job taking care of them."

"Well, we're here now. Fiona seems determined to take the animals away."

"And making a news story out of it locally could help. Shaming him in the community might keep him from getting any more animals," Donovan commented, glancing in his rearview mirror at the truck behind them.

Naomi rolled her eyes, but he wasn't wrong. As long as Rachel didn't focus only on the exciting rescue of the seal and Donovan's tight ass in all of her shots.

Now that Fiona was aware of this guy, it would be a lot harder for him to fly under the radar too. Naomi didn't know quite how Fiona had developed all of her contacts but her network was impressive. She'd already called a friend at the Animal Legal Defense Fund and she apparently knew people at the ASPCA as well.

One of these days Naomi and Charlie and Jordan were going to have to get Fiona liquored up on Leo's moonshine and get her to spill some of her secrets. Naomi wasn't sure why she thought Fiona had secrets—other than whatever was going on with her and Knox—but she was convinced that Fiona had some very interesting stories.

They pulled off the highway onto a dirt road and drove for several miles before turning into a driveway and rolling up to a huge house that looked like a very typical southern antebellum mansion.

"Well, that explains some of it," Donovan said dryly, throwing the truck into park.

She knew exactly what he meant. This guy obviously had money.

"Rich assholes. These guys get bored and decide that fancy cars and yachts and airplanes aren't the most interesting toys they can have. They decide living animals, actual living beings, are something they should own."

Naomi reached over and squeezed his forearm. He looked over and when their eyes met, she gave him a soft smile.

"But we're here now. We're going to take these animals home with us. They're going to be okay."

Donovan took a deep breath and nodded. "You're right."

"I'm glad you're here. And Fiona. These animals obviously need you."

"There are more animals in Mobile that need us too," Donovan said. "And if this asshole hadn't decided that he needed to have exotics and then wasn't able to care for them, we could be there helping people get their family pets to safety. That's important too."

Naomi felt her heart flip a little at that. Donovan had done some of the most exciting things in some of the interesting places in the world with really cool animals. But he cared just as much about cats and dogs.

"But yesterday you were able to show everybody else how to handle those animals. You gave them the supplies and equipment they needed. Now, Mitch and Zeke and Sawyer and Bennett can save those animals. You're just one guy, but because of you, now all these other guys can do even more work and save even more animals."

He looked at her for a long moment. "Dammit, girl."

She smiled. "What?"

"You say stuff like that when we're just pullin' up to save a zebra and a seal and I can't drag you over here and show you just what that means to me."

She gave a soft laugh. "I'd tell you that I would keep that in mind for later, but we really have to stop doing that."

"Yeah, I know."

But as they sat just looking at each other, it didn't feel like either of them *really* knew that.

Thankfully, they were interrupted before either of them made the move to kiss the other.

Fiona banged on the front of Donovan's truck. "Come on, let's go!"

It turned out Jeff was an Alabama Conservation Enforcement Officer and had called the sheriff and a couple of deputies who pulled in just then.

The owner of the animals wasn't happy to see them, but he also didn't put up a fight. For one thing, he clearly knew that he was in the wrong and that messing with Jeff and the sheriff wasn't going to end well. Or maybe he took a look at Fiona and realized that messing with *her* wasn't going to end well.

The other issue was that the harbor seal truly was stuck in the pool behind the man's house.

It looked like he had constructed a normal swimming pool that even a human could use. However, it was above ground and the hurricane winds had collapsed one side and the seal was stuck under the debris.

The water had rushed out when the side caved in, giving the animal air to breathe, but unable to move or escape.

"So you just left all the animals outside while the hurricane came through?" Donovan asked.

The guy didn't answer.

He'd probably been instructed by his lawyer not to.

There were a couple of guys with power tools taking the pool apart and moving the debris off of the animal as they went.

Donovan stalked over to them. "Stop! You guys gotta hold up!" he yelled over the whine of the saws.

The men shut them off. One pushed his safety glasses up. "What's the problem?"

"You can't see what you're doing. You can't just keep cutting straight through. You might hit the seal."

"Man, we've got a lot of shit to do today. If you don't want us here, we've got other places to be."

"Just give me a fucking minute," Donovan muttered, frustrated. Jesus, they were just going to keep cutting and hope they didn't hit the *live animal* underneath?

He got on the ground and crept under the crumpled metal frame as far as he could go. He felt Naomi crouch just behind him.

The seal was about three feet away. It started wiggling when it saw him.

"Shhhh, baby, you're okay now," he told it.

The seal didn't believe him, of course.

"How is he?" Naomi asked.

"Fuck," Donovan swore. Then he took a breath. "Okay. He's breathing and moving, but he's clearly weak. He's probably been fighting to get loose for hours. He's terrified and one flipper is obviously bleeding. It's also possible there are internal injuries or injuries on the other side or underneath that I can't see."

Donovan turned onto his back and slid out partway.

"There's really no choice," he told her grimly. "We just have to get as much of the debris off him as quickly as possible so I can get him out."

Naomi nodded. "We're here now," she said, reassuringly. "We'll get him out."

He nodded, then looked up at the men with the tools. "Okay, keep going."

"You gonna move?" the one with a huge metal cutter asked him.

Donovan shook his head. "You're getting down close to him. I'm going to stay under here and brace this piece so it won't fall on him." He put his hand on a metal bar. "And I'll try to block any falling debris from hitting him.

"The falling debris is gonna hit you then," one of the guys pointed out.

"I'll be all right."

"Donovan," Naomi said.

She had that look on her face. The one that said she was worried about him and also that he was being a dumb ass.

"I don't have a choice, Nae," he said. "I need to be under here or they might hit him."

"They might hit you."

"But I can tell them if they get too close to me. I can signal or yell out."

"Oh for fuck's sake," Naomi muttered. "Don't do anything for a minute," she told everyone. Then she got to her feet and stomped back toward the front of the house.

Donovan assumed that she had some kind of plan and he knew from experience that it would be a good one. So he just laid his head down and studied the seal. "You're in good hands now. I know it may not seem that way right at the moment, but I promise we're the best for you. We're getting you out of here and taking you over to Louisiana."

"Here, at least get this over the top of you and as much over the seal as you can." Naomi knelt beside him with a thick blanket a moment later. "Then you need to come up with some hand signals in case they can't hear you over the noise of the tools."

"This is going to be hotter than hell," Donovan said. But it was a good idea. It would keep the debris from falling on him and nicking and scratching him.

"Well, hopefully they'll go fast. I'll buy you a cold beer after," she said dryly. "Cover yourself up with the blanket, Donovan. And put this on." She handed him a hard hat.

He laughed. "Seriously?"

"Well, your abs and ass are some of my favorite parts and I'd like to keep them protected, but it's probably best that you have your head covered when there's falling metal pieces and power tools whizzing around near your skull."

He grinned at her and put the hat on.

"How's that?"

"You look hot. And a little dumb."

"So pretty normal," he joked.

She simply sighed and nodded.

"How about this? You lie where you can see me and the workers. Then if they can't hear me, you can give them signals when they get too close," Donovan told her.

She looked from him to the workers and back. Then she surveyed the immediate area. She nodded. "Okay, fine." She looked up at the men. "You need to watch me. This will mean stop." She held up her palm in a typical stop signal. "This will mean slow down and take it easy." She wiggled her hand back and forth.

The guys nodded and Naomi settled onto her belly on the dirt a couple feet from Donovan and out from under the pool.

She was mostly out of the range of any flying debris, but he did feel compelled to say, "Look out that nothing hits you."

She nodded. "But if I get hurt doing this, you're going to be the one to kiss it all better."

He felt a stab of heat along with the becoming-more-common swirl of God-I-like-her. "Oh, trust me, nobody else is going to be kissing you better."

She chuckled and shook her head. "See, we have to stop this."

He nodded. "We do. You need to knock it off."

She nodded. "I know."

He pulled the blanket up over his head. "Okay, let's get this over with."

Naomi looked up at the workers and gave them a thumbs up.

F ifteen minutes later they had cut through the rest of the debris and Donovan had freed the seal.

"There you go, buddy," he cooed softly. He wrapped a clean towel around the seal, stood with it, turned, and handed it over to Naomi.

Her eyes went wide as he slid the animal into her arms. "Really?"

"Just carry it over to the truck. I'm right behind you."

She knew that he was trying to hide the gash on his upper arm from her. She suspected he was going to clean that up quickly before joining her at the truck. But she was so awestruck by the baby seal in her arms that she couldn't even tell him she knew about his injury.

A few minutes later, they nestled the seal in a towel-lined plastic tub. Donovan gave it some water and it drank greedily. He cleaned the bloody flipper and bandaged it and then inspected it for any other injuries. There were just a few general scrapes, thankfully, though he was still concerned about bruises and internal injuries.

"Okay, we need to hit the road and get back to Autre. We

don't have any food for him and we need Griffin to take a look."

Naomi, still slightly stunned from everything that had happened, simply nodded. "Whatever you say."

She took in the sight of him again, rumpled and dirty, but now scowling. She was used to him looking excited and happy. Especially when a rescue had gone as well as this one had. But he was clearly upset about the animal's condition and worried about getting it somewhere he could actually provide care.

Impulsively, she reached out, grabbed the front of his shirt and pulled him in, kissing him quickly.

His hands went to her hips instantly and he pulled her up against him, kissing her back. It was almost as if he had been anticipating it. It seemed that kissing had become their new emotional outlet. And there were plenty of emotions swirling around at the moment.

The kiss went on longer than she'd intended, but she finally let him go. They had things they needed to do and they couldn't get distracted. But she smiled up at him as he looked at her questioningly.

"What was that for?"

"I just really fucking like you."

He gave her a quick smile. "I'm really fucking glad."

They stepped apart and went opposite ways around the truck to their respective doors. They were climbing up when Fiona came stomping over, clearly angry.

"We have to get these animals out of here. They're in terrible condition. I hate that it's two hours but there's not really a better option than just taking them straight to Autre."

Donovan nodded. "I agree a thousand percent. I'll call ahead and everything will be ready when we get there. Between Griffin, Jill, and Tori they'll be ready for us."

Fiona nodded. "I'm right behind you."

They pulled out onto the highway and Naomi dialed Griffin's number. The call connected over the truck's speakers.

"Donovan, how's it going?" Griffin answered.

"We're heading home. We have some rescue animals we're bringing back to Autre."

"Cats and dogs?"

"A zebra, a harbor seal pup, and a tiger."

There was a long pause on Griffin's end of the phone. "A *tiger*?"

"Yep. He's a mixed breed, I think. About two years old. I think he's been in captivity all his life."

"No shit."

Donovan chuckled. "No shit. Asshole rich guy running an under-the-radar animal park on the outskirts. Got hit hard by the hurricane and now the animals need to be re-homed. But these are in pretty bad shape. He's on his way to the police station and Fiona, Naomi, and I are headed back to Autre."

"We'll be ready for you when you get here."

Naomi was watching Donovan and she caught the small smile on his face. "Thanks. Not at all what I expected when I came down here, but feels good to be able to do something."

"Since I got to Louisiana, I've kind of stopped expecting things to go the way I expect them to," Griffin said.

"Good advice, big brother."

They disconnected and Naomi sat for a few moments before she said, "Griffin's really proud of you, you know."

Donovan glanced over at her. "I'd like to think so."

"It's really obvious, Donovan."

"I'm really proud of him too."

She thought for a moment if she should say what was on the tip of her tongue and finally she decided there was no harm. "Your parents would've been proud of both of you."

He didn't respond right away, but finally he nodded. "I think you're probably right."

"I don't know how it would be possible for them *not* to be. Any parent would want to know that their child grew up to be so big hearted and brave and willing to put themselves out there to make things better for other lives."

He was quiet for a moment.

"I think Griffin and I have both always focused on the animals because they're easier than people."

Naomi was surprised at his insight. "Animals are definitely easier than people. That makes sense. Especially after what you guys went through. You dealt with a tragedy that most kids never have to face at the ages you were. And it's made a complicated relationship between the two of you."

"Yeah, I hadn't thought about it for a long time, but it seems clear that we both needed an outlet, a way to care about something in a way to make a difference, but it seemed easier and more straightforward to pour it all into animals."

"But doing that together gave you a bond."

He nodded."

"It matters a lot. The animals need you. What you and Griffin both do is special."

He looked away from the road and met her eyes for just a moment before focusing in front of the truck again. "Thanks for caring if I had a hard hat on today."

She studied him. He couldn't even show up as a volunteer at a mass disaster with hundreds of other volunteers and rescue personnel without being recognized and put on camera. But no one had thought to cover him up with a blanket or hand him a hard hat when he'd been right underneath a power saw.

Maybe he didn't have a death wish. Maybe he just didn't have anyone looking out for him. And maybe he didn't know he deserved that.

Before she could respond, her phone rang again. It was Jill. Which was for the best. Because she really might have blurted out that not only did he deserve to have someone looking out for him, but it should definitely be her, because she was madly in love with him.

8

The drive back to Autre was spent coordinating with everyone about the condition of the animals, the supplies and equipment needed, and how they were going to keep a tiger and a zebra in the animal park together.

Donovan was grateful for something to concentrate on other than how Naomi LeClaire seemed able to see straight into his head. And his heart.

Whether it was a hard hat or hearing that his work mattered or a hot, sweet kiss, she always came up with exactly what he needed in every moment.

He didn't even know what he needed in a lot of moments.

Griffin was the only other person who had cared what Donovan needed in a very long time and Donovan had worked hard to make sure Griffin thought he didn't need anything.

With Naomi, it was incredible. And addictive.

And she wanted to just be friends. Non-kissing friends.

Something else to focus on was definitely welcome.

Once they pulled into Autre it was all hands on deck and the zebra was quickly settled in the barn with the donkeys, camels, and horses.

Tori checked him out right away. He was underweight, his hooves were in terrible shape, and he was definitely traumatized by the storm, but she reported he'd be fine with proper nutrition and TLC.

The tiger was put into a pen at the rehabilitation facility. He, too, was malnourished and Griffin decided to wait a few days to get him fed and rehydrated before doing a more thorough physical exam under sedation. But the big cat seemed mostly unconcerned with his new surroundings and being with humans, which told them that he had been more of a pet than even an exhibit animal. A fact that was confirmed when they realized he'd been declawed.

"That motherfucker," was Griffin's opinion about the human or humans who had done that.

Donovan agreed whole-heartedly.

Donovan helped Griffin clean and tend the wound and examine the seal for additional injuries. There were a few scrapes and abrasions, but in general the pup seemed in good physical shape, other than also being slightly underweight.

"That bastard didn't know anything about taking care of these animals," Griffin said with obvious disgust.

"That or he just didn't give a shit," Donovan said.

"Then why do it?" Griffin asked. "Why go to the trouble of getting exotic animals and building pens and pools if you don't really bother to do it correctly or really care?"

"Because they can," Donovan said. His anger matched his brother's. "There aren't enough laws and regulations around it."

Griffin nodded unnecessarily. They were on the same page here. Some brothers bonded over sports, some over family issues, some over business. Griffin and Donovan bonded over wanting to save the world. The animal world anyway. They'd ranted and raved together about this topic and many other animal welfare issues over the years.

"Wow, he's beautiful," Charlie said as she joined Griffin and Donovan outside the tiger pen.

"He is," Griffin said. "Other than the fact that he's severely underweight, his coat is dull, and his footpads are cracked from living on a hard packed dirt surface, and they fucking declawed him."

Charlie looked up at him. Donovan could see she was worried about Griffin.

Griffin got very protective of all animals, but he had a special affinity for tigers. In fact he'd been fired over the way humans handled tigers at the National Zoo in DC, which had led him to the tiny town that he now called home.

"You can't drive to Alabama to confront this guy," Charlie told him.

"He's lucky he's in police custody," Griffin said, watching the tiger.

Charlie moved in close to him and ran her hand up and down his back soothingly. Griffin wrapped his arm around her waist and tucked her close to his side. Donovan watched his brother draw in a deep breath and let it out, clearly relaxing under Charlie's touch.

Damn, Donovan loved them together.

Charlie was bright and bubbly and optimistic and had a way of always pushing Griffin a little further than he wanted to go when it came to the animal park. Hell, she even pushed him when it came to displays of affection and being involved with family events.

But his brother was...blossoming. That wasn't a very manly term for it, but it was accurate. Griffin had lightened up and opened up since being in Autre, and Donovan knew that it was directly because of Charlie's influence.

"What are we going to do with him?" Charlie asked. "Do you think you'll want to rehabilitate him and give him to a zoo?

I guess it's not like we can just release him into the wild once he's strong and healthy again."

"Yeah. Even if tigers were indigenous to Louisiana," Griffin said dryly, giving her a little smile, "this guy's never lived in the wild. He was raised in captivity. I doubt he'd even do very well in a zoo. I think he's been hand fed."

"That's incredible," Charlie said, shaking her head. "To think some guy just had him in his backyard."

"There are more tigers in captivity in the U.S. than are living in the wild in the entire world," Griffin said.

Charlie looked up at him quickly. "What? Really?"

He nodded. "There are estimated to be a little over three thousand wild tigers in the world, but about five thousand in captivity just in the U.S."

"*What?*" Charlie was clearly shocked.

And hell, that *was* a shocking statistic.

Donovan shook his head. "And we all know the number in captivity is even higher than that. That estimate is dependent upon decent people reporting and we know a lot of these people aren't decent."

Charlie swallowed and looked at the tiger again with sad eyes.

"There was a really famous case right here in Louisiana," Griffin said. "A tiger was kept in a cage at a truck stop for nearly seventeen years. Animal rights activists fought to free him for years, but the owner didn't care. Called them terrorists, cozied up to lawmakers to get his way. The animal died in captivity."

Charlie looked like she was going to cry. "Wow. I'm so glad you found this one."

"I don't know if this guy in Alabama has owned this cat since he was a baby or if he's been passed around, but either way he's a lot better off with us." Donovan looked at Griffin. "I'm not just saying this because I love big cats. I think he should stay here."

Griffin looked at him over the top of Charlie's head. "He's going to take a lot more care than the alpacas."

Donovan nodded. "I know. I feel like we're up to it."

"We?" Griffin asked. "Are you including yourself in that? Like if we had a tiger, you might stick around?"

Donovan blew out a breath. He focused back on the tiger. It wasn't just the idea of having a tiger here. It was everything. The work they did here mattered. Whether they were rescuing a tiger or a donkey, all the animals deserved to be cared for and he loved doing it with these people. In all his travels around the world working with animal advocacy groups, he'd never felt as much a part of the team as he did here.

Finally, he said, "I don't know. I...have a job offer. In the Galapagos Islands. A documentary."

Griffin turned to face him more fully.

"That sounds perfect for you."

Donovan nodded. "Yeah. It would be."

Griffin nodded. "I'm really proud of the work you do, Donovan. Wherever you do it."

Donovan felt his throat tighten. "Thanks." That was really all he'd ever wanted—to make Griffin feel like his sacrifices for Donovan had been worthwhile.

"But, if the park is going to keep growing like this, we could really use some extra help. I mean, obviously, some days it's just somebody to help feed the animals and check in on them and do some enclosure repairs and things like that, but there are definitely times when having a rehab expert on staff would be really helpful," Griffin said. "Plus, the work you're doing here with the animals that you rehabilitate and release is really awesome. It's not like there won't be a continued need for that. So, think about it."

Donovan felt emotion tighten his chest. Stay here with Griffin? And Naomi? "Yeah, you're right."

"Will it be enough for you?" Charlie asked. "Exciting

enough? I mean, we can't guarantee tigers and seals every day." She grinned.

"Yeah, but beavers and black bears are cool," Donovan said. "And honestly, even rescuing the cats and dogs yesterday felt damned good."

Griffin suddenly gave him a big smile and Donovan knew that at his age and maturity level he shouldn't care so much about his brother approving of him, but he did, dammit.

"We would love to have you stay," Griffin said. "Working with you these last few months has been really amazing. You're great at what you do, Donovan. If you want to stay here in Autre, we're all for it."

Charlie was nodding enthusiastically. "Really. It would be so great to have you here and have the family all together all the time."

For a second, Donovan was unable to take a deep breath. He and Griffin hadn't had a family in a long time. The two of them had tried as best they could, but they hadn't been that good at rebuilding after their parents died. They'd just barely hung on. But now here in Autre, it felt like maybe they had a chance at truly being a family again.

Finally he managed to nod. He cleared his throat. "Okay, I will definitely give it some thought." He glanced at the tiger, blinking rapidly. "And I'll look into the paperwork for this big guy."

"While you're at it, might as well ask about having harbor seals too. I don't think that guy's gonna be able to go back into the wild," Griffin said.

"No?" Donovan frowned. "We'll have to take him back up the coast somewhere." Harbor seals weren't found in the Gulf. "But once he's strong enough to swim and hunt you don't think he can go back out?"

"I think he's blind in one eye. Maybe both," Griffin told him.

"Really?"

Griffin nodded. "We'll watch him. Test him. But yeah, I think maybe so. It's possibly why the guy was able to buy him? Or maybe an injury caused it. Either way, if he's blind, he'll be at risk in the wild."

Donovan nodded. "Damn." He looked at Charlie. "Think Zeke and Mitch can build a permanent seal enclosure?"

She grinned. "I'm sure of it."

"Do we have funds for that?" Running an animal park, especially one that kept growing, wasn't cheap.

"We have a donor who seems to always know when we need something," Charlie said with a sly smile. "I'm not worried."

"Wait, we do?" Donovan asked. "For real?"

Charlie shrugged. "Yep. That's how we built this place." She gestured to indicate the rehab facility.

"I thought Jason Young's donation built this."

"It did some of it, but we ran low before it was done. This person found out and we had a donation within a couple of days."

"And we really have no idea who it is?"

Charlie tipped her head. "I think you do know who it is."

Donovan started to shake his head, but froze. It clicked into place a second later. "Nae."

Charlie nodded.

He wasn't sure he would have put it together if she hadn't told him about being a TV star. He wouldn't have realized she had that kind of money. But it made complete sense. "Wow. I'm..."

"She won't want you to make a big deal out of it," Charlie said. "She knows what you're doing with the money. She's seen it up close, obviously. That's enough. She knows you're thankful."

He nodded. That sounded like Naomi for sure. "I get it."

"Oh my gosh, this is great!" Charlie suddenly skipped

forward and grabbed Donovan in a big hug, squeezing him tightly. "I'm so happy you're thinking about staying."

Donovan hugged her back, feeling his throat tighten. He'd never had a sister. Griffin was his only sibling, but now he had an almost sister-in-law who was impossible not to love. And she came with an entire crazy family.

And don't forget the extended family.

The LeClaires.

Naomi's family.

The goddess.

They were going to need to have a talk. If he stayed, that would change everything.

N aomi wouldn't admit it to anyone, but she'd been watching the door anxiously waiting for Donovan to step into Ellie's. When he did, she'd expected to feel relieved and happy. She always felt those two things when she saw him.

This time though she felt like her heart flipped so hard she got a little lightheaded and her entire body got warm.

Dammit, girl, get a grip.

It was the sex. It had to be that she'd had sex with him, right?

But a second later she realized that wasn't it.

It was how happy he looked.

He had showered and changed clothes and he looked ridiculously hot in his jeans and navy blue t-shirt. And *that* was about the sex. Jeans and t-shirts were nothing new. Knowing full well what was inside those jeans and that t-shirt was, however.

But mostly she noticed that he looked happy. *Incredibly* happy. He was with Griffin and Charlie and was grinning and laughing and then, to make the I'm-flushed-and-dizzy feeling worse, he caught her eye and gave her a wink.

A stupid wink and she was all aflutter. What the hell?

It was too crowded and loud for anyone to have noticed the wink, thankfully. Or for her to respond to it in any way, fortunately.

Sawyer, Bennett, Mitch, and Zeke were back, having headed home from Alabama after a final massive sweep of Mobile had turned up no additional needs for evacuations. They'd rolled into town about thirty minutes ago and had all just stored their things, showered, and headed straight to Ellie's for food.

They were all gathered around the table and Rosalie was helping Cora and Ellie bring out platters and bowls full of gumbo, fried plantains, pikliz, macaroni au gratin, grilled fish, and the black mushroom rice, diri djon djon.

Unfortunately, or possibly fortunately, there was no seat right next to Naomi, so Donovan was four chairs down on her left. Naomi was next to Jordan who wanted to know every detail about her time with the Cajun Navy and the big seal rescue.

Apparently, the seal rescue had made it on the news already down in Alabama and the clip had been shared on YouTube for all the world to see. Everyone in Autre had already seen it.

"Oh my God, you both looked amazing," Paige told them. "I immediately called home and told everyone to look at the clip and that I know you both. I can't believe we now have a seal, a tiger, and a zebra. I can't believe this is where I live."

"It's about fucking time we have a zebra," Zeke said. "I built that barn and pen months ago."

Jill looked at him. "Zebras can be real dicks, you know."

"I've heard. But real dicks will fit right in around here," Zeke said.

He plucked the last of the fried plantains from the plate right in front of Zander.

"Yeah, no kidding." Zander looked at his twin. "I thought

you guys were going to be gone for a few more days. I barely had a chance to stuff myself full of Rosalie's food without you all sitting around hogging it."

"Yeah, well, *we* were actually doing stuff that would work up an appetite," Owen told him. "We weren't just sittin' around up here, tellin' fishin' tall tales and being doted on by the *sweet* grandmas of Autre."

"I suppose that means I'm not one of the sweet ones, since I was with you in Alabama?" Ellie asked, leaning in to set another bowl of pikliz on the table.

Owen took a big bite of Rosalie's macaroni and cheese that was a Haitian specialty and so far beyond regular mac and cheese it almost didn't count. He chewed and nodded. "Pretty much."

Ellie looked relieved as she turned to Tori and took baby Ella into her arms. She smiled at the baby and started swaying with her as the little girl gazed up at her. "Thank God. I thought maybe I was gettin' soft."

Owen snorted. "Don't let that sappy, sweet smile fool ya, Ella," he told his niece. "Just wait 'til you carry a puppy in here and ask her if you can feed it some scraps, then you'll see how mean she gets. To you *and* the puppy."

"That 'puppy' was a baby alligator," Ellie told him. "And 'it' was *six* of them. And you put them down in the center of the bar in the middle of the lunch crowd."

"I was like two! I didn't know the difference!" Owen said, grinning widely.

"You were eight and did it on a dare from Josh," Ellie told him. She looked down at Ella. "All you need to know is that I always know everything that's going on and you'll never get away with anything." Then she cuddled the baby closer and made her way over to the bar to show her off to people she wasn't related to.

"I'll have you know, Knox and Josh and I had been cleaning

this whole town up while you were all galivanting over state lines," Zander said. "Being good citizens right here at home and all that."

Naomi laughed at that. She knew very well that Zander, Knox, and Josh would have been right beside the rest of them in Alabama if they could have been.

"I'll give that to Josh," Owen said. "But you and Knox are *paid* to be good citizens. Our tax money at work." He popped another bite of cheesy macaroni into his mouth.

"Now, now," Rosalie set a fresh plate of fried plantains down right in front of Zander. "No need to fight over the food. There's plenty."

Naomi took in her grandmother's happy glow. She loved cooking for the family and she considered all of these people part of her circle too.

Naomi loved this part of her life. Where she just sat back and watched everyone interacting and listened to all of them being crazy and loud and loving and fun.

"I have all the paperwork ready for you guys," Fiona said, coming in through the back door, waving a stack of papers. "I also have a friend who is going to rush it all through for you. The animals are all good to stay here if you want them. That asshole is actually going to be doing jail time too." She looked thrilled by that.

"We definitely want them," Charlie said.

"Fuck yeah, we want them," Zeke agreed.

"I need to talk to you," Knox said, stretching to his feet.

Fiona looked up at him. "All of these animals have been rescued and need a new home. All the paperwork and licensing will be in place."

"Not about the animals."

She frowned at him. "You sound grumpy."

"I always sound grumpy."

"Well not *always*," she told him with a tone that caught everyone's attention.

Suddenly the entire table was quiet and watching and listening to them. Owen even put down his fork and Zeke didn't even notice that Zander took a plantain off Zeke's plate.

Knox cleared his throat. "We need to talk," he repeated. "In private."

Several eyebrows went up around the table.

"In a bit. I need to go over some details with these guys."

"That can wait." Knox wrapped his big hand around her upper arm and started tugging her toward the front door.

"Knox," Fiona protested, though she made no move to shrug out of his hold. "I was going to come over later."

Yeah, everyone made note of *that* too.

Naomi shot Jill, Jordan, then Charlie a look.

Their eyes were all wide. And *very* interested.

Knox stopped walking, then frowned down at her.

Instead of saying anything, however, he leaned over, wrapped a big arm around her waist and picked her up. He was over a foot taller than she was, so her feet dangled several inches off the ground as he carried her toward the front door.

She just sighed and waved to everyone. "I guess we'll talk about the permits later."

There were several beats of silence after the door closed behind them.

Finally Owen let out a long, "Daaaa-yum."

Fletcher coughed. "Should we...someone...go rescue her?"

Zeke looked around the table. "I'm thinking since we haven't heard any howls of pain from the parking lot indicating that she's ripped his balls off, she's okay with what just happened?"

Charlie looked confused but she nodded. "She definitely seemed okay."

Jill was the only one who didn't look shocked. She sipped

from her sweet tea, then said smugly, "Told you they didn't just go out for ice cream when she brought us the flamingos."

Sawyer shook his head. "Maybe we don't want the details."

"Oh, I *really* want the details," Zeke said.

"Same," Zander agreed.

"I think—" Owen started.

But he was cut off by a loud, "Hello, Autre, Louisiana!"

They all pivoted again toward the front door.

A small crowd of tourists had just come through the door. But they looked completely at ease having the attention of every person inside Ellie's trained on them.

"Dax!"

Suddenly Paige was up and out of her chair and running across the room.

Mitch was also up, grinning widely, and making his way toward the group.

"Who the hell—" Sawyer started.

"Holy shit." Owen turned to Zeke and Zander. "Is that Oliver Caprinelli?"

"It looks like him," Zander agreed, pivoting on his seat to get a better look.

"Paige knows him," Zeke said. "He lives in her hometown now. He's married to one of her best friends."

"That's definitely him," Jordan said. "And that's Dax Marshall."

"Who is Oliver Caprinelli?" Sawyer asked.

Zeke and Zander both turned to stare at him at the same time.

Sawyer frowned at them. "What?"

"He is only the creator and writer of the world's *best* video game," Zeke told him.

Zander nodded. "You've never heard of Warriors of Easton?"

Sawyer gave him a look. "No. Because I'm a grown man."

"Whatever. It is the most fun you can have on your couch by yourself."

"Not sure that tagline is one they'll appreciate."

"Actually, that is one of their taglines," Zander told him. "And the dude's a millionaire. I'm guessing he knows a little bit more about it than you do."

"So this videogame guy is a celebrity to you?" Sawyer said.

"He's a celebrity to a lot of people. He's got a huge online following and practically gets mobbed at Comic-Con," Zander told him.

"You know. Between Jason Young being from just the next town over, and Donovan Foster working here, and now this videogame guy visiting, there's a lot of famous people hanging out in Autre," Jill commented.

"Well, pseudo-famous," Owen said. "Except for Jason Young. He's legit famous." He shot Fletcher a grin.

Even though Fletcher and Jordan had been married for a few months now, it still never got old for Fletcher's brothers and cousins to give him shit about Jordan's ex being a country music mega-star.

"Yeah, just imagine what I've got going for me to have stolen her away from him," Fletcher said, cracking his knuckles and linking his fingers behind his head.

Jordan patted his chest as they all laughed at that.

"Jordan, love! I'm here!"

Jordan looked across the bar and waved. She grinned at Fletcher. "Gotta go."

She crossed the room and was enfolded in a huge hug by one of the very good looking, apparently pseudo-famous, millionaires who had just breezed into Ellie's.

Owen looked at Fletcher. "You were saying?"

Fletcher sighed. "Jordan and Dax have an alpaca obsession in common."

"I thought he was into videogames," Sawyer said.

"He also owns the nursing home back in Iowa," Fletcher said watching Jordan and Dax laugh and chat a few feet away. "He's been using alpacas as therapy animals with the older population in a lot of the same ways Jordan's been using the alpacas with kids. Paige introduced them online and they've been chatting about their programs."

"Geez, man, he's good looking, rich, created a kickass videogame, and also loves alpacas. I'd be worried," Owen told his cousin.

Fletcher rolled his eyes. "Sure, if good looks, charm, shared interests, and tons of money are the way to get women."

They all laughed. Naomi knew that Fletcher wasn't a bit worried about losing Jordan to Dax Marshall or anyone else. Still, she felt inclined to say, "I think you're safe. Dax is happily married to the gorgeous redhead right there."

The guys all looked over.

"Damn," Zander said. "I've seen photos of her with him online, but she's even more gorgeous in person."

"I've heard him say in interviews that she's the one that keeps him grounded. She's not into the whole fame and fortune thing," Zeke said. "They actually seem like really awesome people."

Naomi leaned in and rested her chin on her hand. "Aw, you guys get to meet your celebrity crushes."

Zeke and Zander, two of the most rugged, confident, Cajun bullshitters she knew, both pivoted—Zeke to look more fully at the room behind them, Zander to look forward at the table.

"Hey, that's true," Zeke said, obviously comfortable enough in his masculinity to have a crush on another man. Or two.

"Crush is a little extreme," Zander said right on the heels of Zeke's comment. Clearly Zander was not quite as comfortable.

Naomi laughed and looked over at Donovan. He was sitting back and enjoying the craziness the way she so often did. But he gave her another wink when she caught his eye.

Zeke and Zander looked at one another.

"It's not a *crush*," Zander insisted. "We like their game. We're...fans."

"It's more than that for me," Zeke declared. "I want to become their best friend, or, if I can't do that, I want to get them drunk, get some inappropriate photos that I can use as blackmail, and use those to get all the new game releases early and back stage passes to all future Comic-Cons."

Naomi looked at Jill. Who simply rolled her eyes and rested her hands on her very pregnant belly. She had definitely gotten more laid back since she and Zeke had gotten together and found out they were bringing two more Landrys into the world. That was a very good thing. Mini Zekes running around, pushing limits and living loud, were going to be a handful. Especially with big Zeke still running around pushing limits and living loud.

And no, they didn't know if the twin babies were boys or girls or one of each—or if they did, they weren't telling the family yet—but no one doubted that even Zeke Landry's daughters would be charming, delightful trouble.

"You've really given this a lot of thought considering they just walked in here five minutes ago," Naomi said to Zeke.

"It's not a brand new plan. Paige and Mitch know them well. I knew I'd get my chance," Zeke told her, tipping back his glass of tea.

"Spoken like a true stalker," Zander said. "And as a law enforcement officer, I should probably pretend I didn't hear you say any of those things."

"I've got witnesses that you did, big brother," Zeke told his older-by-only-two-minutes twin. "So now you're complicit. Plus we're identical twins. I'm not above committing a crime and pretending to be you. You might as well go all in."

Zander groaned, clearly believing Zeke would impersonate him. "Define all-in."

"Well, that's the beauty of this plan," Zeke said with a grin. "They're down here for vacation, right? They want the real Louisiana experience. Who better to give that to them than two born-and-bred Cajun boys who know all about havin' *fun* Louisiana style? As part of that, we give them a boys' night out in New Orleans, starting at Trahan's Tavern," Zeke said of the very popular bar in the French Quarter owned by some of the Landry boys' best friends. "I figure there are two directions that can go. The next morning we're either their best friends or we've got plenty of drunk blackmail photos."

Zander sighed. But he didn't say no.

Naomi looked at Jill.

"You can't end up in jail. At least not for more than a night," Jill told her fiancé.

Zeke leaned over and rubbed her belly. "Oh, I'm not leaving you a single mom, Kansas. No worries."

"I'm more worried about not having you around to do my laundry and make me grilled cheese," she told him.

"Doesn't Elizabeth still do a lot of you all's laundry?" Owen asked.

It was not at all a secret that Zeke, as baby of the family, had been spoiled by his mother and still let her do his laundry as much as possible.

"That is true," Jill said, looking at Zeke thoughtfully. "She's never made me grilled cheese but I'm certain she could handle it."

"She makes amazing grilled cheese," Fletcher confirmed.

"Well, then, go do whatever dumb thing you want in New Orleans," Jill told Zeke. "I guess I'm good."

He laughed, put a big hand on the back of her neck and pulled her in close. He whispered something in her ear that made her blush, then kissed her soundly.

"Right?" he asked when he'd leaned back again.

Jill cleared her throat. "Right."

"Thought so." He looked very pleased with himself.

Naomi could only imagine what he'd reminded Jill only he could do for her. And it made her shoot another glance in Donovan's direction. He was watching her. That fact sent tingles racing through her and she shifted on her chair.

So she wanted him whispering naughty things in her ear. Big shock.

The intensity with which she wanted the intimacy that Zeke and Jill and all the other couples had was a bit of a surprise though.

She cleared her throat and focused on the conversation again.

"Okay, you, me, Dax, and Oliver tonight," Zeke said to Zander. He glanced around the table. "And whoever else wants to come."

"I'm in," Owen said quickly.

"What are we gonna talk to Dax Marshall and Oliver Caprinelli about?" Zander asked. "We live in a tiny town in Louisiana. You do construction. I'm a cop. They're multimillionaire game designers."

"They live in a tiny town in *Iowa*," Zeke said. "Iowa's got nothing on Louisiana."

"Excuse me," Paige interrupted.

Zeke and Zander had to pivot to look at her. She'd just come over to the table from greeting her friends from up north. They were getting settled around a big table a few feet away and Ellie and Cora were already there with sweet tea and Hurricanes.

Paige planted her hands on her hips. "Are you disparaging my home state? With me standing right here?"

"In our defense, we didn't know you were standing right there," Zeke told her.

"Well, I was going to introduce you to the two guys who made the videogame that almost got Zander fired, but if you're going to talk shit about Iowa, I'm not doing you any favors."

"That video game almost got you *fired*?" Sawyer asked Zander.

"Just because I lost track of time," Zander said, shifting on his chair. "And Knox is just super anal about me showing up places on the dot."

"You mean he thinks you, as the town cop, should show up places when you're supposed to?" Sawyer asked dryly. "Yeah, he's such an unreasonable asshole."

"Well I made it. Barely. But I still made it."

"Was that the day that you made a bunch of kids leave the docks when they were down there just hanging out?" Owen asked.

"They were smoking pot and annoying the neighbors."

"You parking your car down there so you could catch a nap doesn't make *you* a *neighbor* exactly," Owen said.

"Was that the same day you ended up with ducks in your squad car?" Sawyer asked.

Paige's eyes went wide. "How'd ducks get in your squad car?"

"Those same kids put them in there," Zeke said. "He'd fallen asleep and was so dead to the world, he didn't hear a thing. He woke up to a duck sitting in his lap."

"Stupid things crapped all over my car," Zander muttered.

"Funniest fucking thing I've ever seen was Zander driving down the road with three ducks in the back of his squad car as if he'd arrested them," Owen said, laughing out loud now.

"Even Knox got in on the jokes about how Zander was getting his ducks in a line-up rather than in a row," Zeke added.

"And that was because you were up all night playing that stupid game?" Sawyer asked.

Paige was pressing her hand over her mouth to keep from laughing out loud.

"I hate you all," Zander informed them.

"But you still play that videogame?" Naomi asked. "It's obviously caused you some trouble."

Zander leaned in, his expression solemn, meeting her eyes directly. "I am not overstating it when I say that it is the best videogame ever created, and the most fun I have had on my couch in at least two years."

"*By yourself*," Owen said. "That's an important part of that tagline. It's the most fun you've had *by yourself* on your couch in at least two years."

Zander looked over at him. "I said what I said."

Owen practically snorted his sweet tea out of his nose.

Sawyer shook his head. "You've been spending time with the wrong women."

Zander sat back in his chair. "Talk to me after you play the game."

"Holy shit, we're going to hire you guys for our next commercial."

Zeke's and Zander's backs both went ramrod straight. Then they turned slowly and looked up at Dax Marshall and Oliver Caprinelli.

9

"**D**amn, no kidding," Dax agreed with Ollie.

Zander groaned and slumped in his seat.

"How much of that did you hear?" Zeke asked them.

"Enough to know that we definitely want to advertise that our game is so good that it almost gets grown men fired. Even cops," Dax said with a grin.

Zander looked mortified.

Naomi pressed her lips together to keep from laughing. Zander never looked mortified.

"Dax Marshall, Ollie Caprinelli," Paige said. "Your biggest fans are named Zeke and Zander Landry. They're Fletcher's brothers."

Dax extended a hand and shook Zeke's hand first. "Thanks for letting us crash your party. Jane couldn't stay away any longer from her favorite wedding planner." He moved his hand for Zander to shake and Sawyer had to nudge Zander so that the cop would extend his hand.

Naomi almost choked on her laughter as she met Paige's eyes. Paige just shook her head.

"Well, your game is awesome and it's a thrill to meet you," Zeke told them.

"Glad to hear it," Dax said. "We'd love to talk more about what you like and don't like. We get a lot of our in-person feedback from ten-year-old boys and a seventy-something woman. It'd be great to pick your brains."

"A seventy-something woman?" Zeke asked.

Dax looked behind him. "Didi is one of our biggest fans and a Fifth Level Master Enchantress at this point." He motioned with his chin toward the older woman with the snowy white hair sitting with the rest of the Iowa gang.

"Of course, she got to be fifth level because she made me put that in just for her," Ollie said.

Zeke laughed. "You do that for people?"

"Special people," Ollie said with a smile.

Zeke looked at Zander. "We are *definitely* taking them to New Orleans."

"Did you tell them about the alpacas?" A little boy, who had to be one of the ten-year-olds Dax had referenced, squeezed in between Dax and Ollie.

"Haven't gotten there yet, buddy," Dax told him. "Everyone, this is Henry. He's Cam and Zoe's little brother, Didi's best friend, and is a member of the creative development team for Warriors of Easton."

"Hey, Didi!" Henry called. "Come here! We're talking about the Armageddon Alpacas!"

Didi perked right up and excused herself from the conversation she was in. She came over to the table and Mitch got up to give her his seat. She gave him a smile and slid in next to where Henry was standing. He put a hand on her shoulder in a familiar and sweet gesture.

"We don't call them Armageddon Alpacas," Dax said.

"We should," Didi told him.

"But they don't bring on Armageddon," Dax said. "It doesn't make sense."

"They do for the dragons," Henry said.

"They do?" Zeke asked.

Apparently having some kind of radar for fellow Warriors of Easton fans, the boy focused on Zeke and Zander. "Picture this. They're alpacas. That shoot lasers out of their eyeballs." His tone and expression were completely serious. "They can take down even the small and medium dragons one on one. If the dragons are in flight, they just *die*. And then fall from the sky and smash everything under them."

"So it's important to take them out when they're over a nest of other dragons," Didi said.

"Exactly," Henry agreed. "Armageddon."

Dax rolled his eyes.

"Or..." Zeke leaned in the way Henry had. "The Alpacalypse."

Henry's eyes got wide and he nodded slowly. "Yessss."

Dax laughed at that and even Zander chuckled.

"Have you met our alpacas yet?" Zander asked. "One of them is named Alpacalypse."

"That's amazing!" Henry looked up at Ollie. "Take a note of that."

Ollie tapped his temple. "Got it right here."

"And—" Henry leaned in as if to impart a very closely guarded secret. "A herd of them can take down even the large dragons."

And that was finally what snapped Zander out of his starstruck stupor. He leaned in. "How do they turn the lasers on?"

"They blink."

"How do they turn them off?"

"They blink again," Henry said as if that should be obvious.

"Was that your idea?"

"Totally," Henry said proudly.

Zander looked impressed. "How did you get this gig?"

"Mostly by being brilliant and adorable."

Everyone laughed.

Zander nodded as if that made complete sense. "Any tips on how I could maybe get in on this?"

Henry regarded him. "You don't seem very adorable."

Naomi, Jordan, Paige, and Jill all snorted.

"Oh, he is," Didi assured Henry.

"Really?" Henry didn't look convinced.

Zander, however, gave Didi a grin and Naomi had to admit that while 'adorable' wasn't quite the right word, she understood why he didn't sleep alone unless he wanted to. It was definitely, in part, the uniform. It was also the bad boy turned good guy protector thing. But his long hair, tattoos, green eyes, and big, solid build did not hurt.

Zander shrugged and told Henry, "I think I'm kind of past the point where I can change my level of adorableness. What else can I use to get in good with the bosses?"

Henry thought about it. "Dax really likes candy."

Dax laughed. "True."

"You think they'd like it if we took them to New Orleans and showed them around?" Zeke asked Henry.

"For sure! Can me and Didi come?"

Paige shook her head. "Not tonight, but we'll make a trip up there while you're here."

Zander tapped Henry's arm, regaining his attention. "So what else you got in the works for Warriors?"

"Ollie's going to hang out and study the penguins so he can add robot penguins," Henry said.

"Was that your idea?" Zander asked.

"Nah. That was Dax."

"I want to hear *your* ideas," Zander told him.

Henry looked pleased, but then Didi leaned in and whispered in Henry's ear. Henry nodded and narrowed his eyes at Zander. "Well, what kind of milkshakes do you have here?"

Zander lifted a brow. "What are you willing to give up for a good milkshake?"

Henry looked at Didi and she nodded. "My ideas for the rain swords."

"Rain swords? How do those work?" Zander asked.

Didi leaned in and whispered to him again. "I really can't say any more about it," Henry told him. "At least not without some *encouragement*."

Zander looked like he was fighting a smile. "Encouragement in the form of ice cream, chocolate syrup, and whipped cream?"

"Don't forget the sprinkles," Didi said.

Zander looked up at Dax and Ollie. They were just grinning. "He knows how to negotiate?"

"Oh, that all comes from the girls. Including Didi," Dax said.

Zander focused on Henry again, then looked at Didi. "Are you two gamblers, by chance?"

Henry and Didi exchanged a look. "We've dabbled," Henry said.

The corner of Zander's mouth quirked. "Okay. How about this—I give you something I think is even better than a milkshake. If you agree, you tell me all about the rain swords *and* you listen to my idea about the snake shields."

Henry's eyes widened. "Snake shields?"

Zander nodded. "But if you like the idea, you have to pitch it to Dax and Ollie and tell them it's from both of us."

"What are you giving me—"

Didi poked him.

"Us. What are you giving *us* instead of milkshakes?" Henry asked.

"You ever had pecan pie?" Zander asked.

"No," Henry said.

"Oh, yes," Didi answered. She looked at Henry. "It's good. You'll like it."

"Yep," Zander told him. "Buckle up, buddy. You're about to forget all about ice cream and sprinkles."

Zander stood and helped Didi to her feet, then escorted her and Henry to the bar. He introduced them to Leo and Armand and then helped them up onto the high stools next to the men, before taking the stool to Didi's left himself.

Naomi turned to Jill. Jill's eyes were wide. Then she looked up at Paige. Paige nodded in silent understanding.

"Wow," Jill said.

"Very wow," Paige agreed.

"Right?" Naomi asked.

"What?" Zeke asked.

"I've never seen Zander like that," Naomi said. "I mean, he's great with Andre and the kids from New Orleans, but that was..."

"Sexy as fuck," Jill said.

Zeke scoffed and shook his head. "Nah, you're projecting. He looks like me and you've got all those hormones whooshing around. You're just confused."

Jill laughed. "Okay." She looked at Ollie. "You're going to add penguins to the videogame?"

"Of course we are. Despite what he says, Henry is totally into that," Dax said. He looked at Ollie. "Of course, Oliver's the writer. But I have no doubt he'll figure out a way."

"I've already got the penguins worked in," Ollie said. "That kid's gonna take over our whole company someday."

"Sounds like Stella. She's the daughter of one of the guys you're going to meet in New Orleans. She is determined to take over the whole Boys of the Bayou operation one of these days," Zeke said.

"We should introduce them," Ollie said. "Henry doesn't have many kids who can keep up with him."

"Oh, Miss Stella will be able to keep up with him. She might scare him off of Louisiana girls permanently, though," Sawyer said.

"You hope so," Paige told him. "You love being Stella's big favorite, but one of these days some guy's going to come along and steal her heart from you, Sawyer."

Sawyer stretched his arms out across the backs of the chairs on either side of him. "They'll have to get through me first."

This Stella-Sawyer dynamic was hilarious and sweet. Stella had developed a crush on Sawyer as a little girl, but it had had a lot to do with his airboats and alligators. Now that she was older, she still had her sights set on those boats and gators but was determined to be Sawyer's boss when she got older. Sawyer was more like an uncle to her and he felt protective.

"Okay, that's about enough craziness for me," Jill said, pushing her chair back and standing.

Zeke reached out for her, almost instinctively it seemed. He rested his hand on her hip. "Want me to take you home?"

She shook her head. "You and the boys go ahead and have a good time. I'm just going home to take a nap and then I need to head up to see the penguins. I'm fine. You go show these guys what a good time Louisiana can be."

"Call me if you need anything," Zeke told her.

"Of course." She leaned over and gave him a quick kiss.

Naomi grabbed the opportunity. She loved all of these people, and the addition of the group from Iowa was definitely fun and interesting, but she'd had a couple of big days in Alabama and now all of this was making her long for about an hour of peace and quiet on her back porch all alone.

She stood as well. "I'll give you a ride. I'm ready to head out too."

She couldn't help but glance at Donovan. He gave her a

look. And for some reason, she interpreted it as him asking if he could or should walk her out to her car.

He was so sweet. And yes, she wanted him to. But that was unnecessary and probably a bad idea. It was broad daylight and the place was packed with family, friends, and friends of friends. It wasn't as if they could even sneak a quick kiss.

Nor should they. No more quick kisses. Or long kisses.

She shook her head and he just gave her a grin.

She was actually hoping that he would accompany the guys to play Warriors of Easton and then head to New Orleans. She would love for him to feel the same camaraderie and have him be included in this group of guy friends. She knew all of the Autre guys liked him a lot and all he had to do was ask to tag along.

"Donovan, you should head up to New Orleans with them. You've only been to Trahan's a couple times, haven't you?" she asked.

So much for letting it all run its natural course.

He lifted a brow as if he knew that she was trying to set him up on a play date. "I've been there couple of times. Great place. Awesome food, though nothing like Ellie's."

Zeke turned to look at him. "You want to come? I thought maybe you had a bunch to do with the animals, but if not you should absolutely come with us. This is gonna be great."

"I've got a really good camera on my phone," Donovan said.

Zeke nodded. "You're totally coming. And I apologize in advance for the arrest record you may come home with."

Donovan smirked at him. "It wouldn't be the first."

"I like you, Foster," Zeke said. "I really like you."

Naomi and Jill made it to the front of the restaurant before they heard Jordan and Charlie calling after them. Naomi turned back and waited for the other women to join them.

"Where are you guys headed?" Charlie asked.

"To take a nap," Jill said.

Naomi nodded. "We both need a little alone time. This group is a lot on a normal day and then you add all of that fun noise from up north and we just need a break."

Jordan laughed. "Dax is definitely a big personality. I can't wait to go over the alpaca program with him tomorrow. But it looks like the guys are planning a whole thing today. I'll walk out with you."

"I'm coming too," Charlie said. "I wanted to see how things went in Alabama."

The four women walked out to the parking lot and stopped next to Naomi's truck.

"Yes, tell us all about Alabama," Jordan said.

"There's not that much to tell that you haven't already heard," Naomi said. "You heard about all the rescues. All the guys were amazing. My rescuing the raccoons was kind of ridiculous, but also kind of cool. The seal and tiger and zebra rescue was, of course, amazing."

Charlie flipped her hand, waving all of that away. "Yeah, yeah. All of that is great. But what about you and Donovan?"

"What about me and Donovan?" Naomi hedged.

Charlie propped a hand on her hip. "You're crazy about him. You just spent time down in Alabama together. What did you talk about? What did you do?" She dropped her voice and gave Naomi a sly smile. "Where did you sleep last night?"

Naomi crossed her arms. "Well, I told him about *Zoey*."

Charlie and Jordan both gasped.

"That's huge!" Charlie said.

"It is. And he told me about his problems right after his mom and dad died."

Charlie nodded. She, of course, knew that story.

"And we talked about how we couldn't be a couple. And I slept at the firehouse where Michael slept."

Charlie groaned. "Come on. You've wanted him since he

first set foot in this town. You're telling me you totally wasted that time alone together?"

Naomi stubbornly lifted her chin. "Being stuck together during the storm was a once-in-a-lifetime fantasy and we need to go back to being friends now. I had a great time in Alabama learning about the rescues and—"

"Wait, being stuck during the storm was a *fantasy*?" Jordan broke in. She peered closely at Naomi. "You have to go *back* to being just friends? What exactly happened between you two during the hurricane?"

Naomi wet her lips and then made a huge mistake—she dropped her gaze. With these women, she had to be confident and composed all the time so that they didn't get a read on her emotions. These women had known her for a long time. It was hard to keep a secret from them.

Charlie gasped and pointed a finger at Naomi's nose. "Something did happen! Tell us!"

"You know I don't talk about this stuff. This is private. And it's not going to happen again. It was just a spur of the moment, we're-stuck-together-in-stormy-weather-without-pants-on thing." But she immediately groaned as their eyes widened. Dammit, she had to be more careful.

Jordan and Charlie both took a step forward. Naomi straightened her spine, but she knew she wasn't going to get out of this.

"I need to get Jill home. She is crazy pregnant and can't be standing around on her feet this long."

Jill shook her head. "Oh, I'm fine. You didn't have pants on?"

Naomi groaned. If they were pulling Jill into their gossiping, all hope was lost.

"Okay, I kissed him. Are you happy?"

"Very," Charlie said.

"And then...tell us about the no pants thing," Jordan said.

Naomi blew out a breath. "We got all wet and muddy

rescuing the bears. So we changed into some extra clothes he had and threw our stuff in the washing machine. The clothes were too big for me, so all I wore was a long t-shirt."

Charlie gave her a little knowing grin. "Sure, that was why you were only wearing a long t-shirt and panties."

Naomi ignored that. "So then I kissed him, because I was trying to convince him that I really care about him not accidentally or intentionally killing himself on one of these rescue missions. And then one thing led to another."

"Oh no, you're not getting away with just 'one thing led to another'," Charlie told her. "Details."

For some reason, in that moment, looking at the three women who she counted as her closest friends, all of her bravado rushed from her body with her next breath and Naomi said, "What happened next was the best sex of my life."

Jordan, Charlie, and Jill all gasped at the same time.

"You slept together!" Jordan said. "Oh my God, Naomi, that's *awesome.*"

It really had been awesome. It had been *so good.* In fact, she was afraid she was never going to get over it.

"It was awesome," she agreed. "But..."

The other women all fell silent. Naomi took a deep breath. "He's not staying in Autre, you guys. Nothing is going to happen with us long-term."

"He's not?" Charlie asked, frowning. "How do you know?"

This wasn't her news to tell, so she simply shrugged. "Donovan isn't the type to put down roots. He's always roamed and wandered. It's what makes him happy. I think he's getting restless to get going again."

"But," Jordan protested. "Then you *really* have to tell him how you feel. He has to know if he stays, he can have you."

"I don't want to be the reason that he stays here if that's not what he wants," Naomi said, meaning it with everything in her. "I want him to have everything he really needs to be happy."

Charlie gave her a soft smile. "Well, I hope you realize you are officially in love with him."

"It's not love. I like him *a lot*. He's a great guy. And he's very hot. And the sex was really, really good." But she knew she was in love as surely as she knew that if Donovan went to the Galapagos Islands, he'd do an incredible job and it would lead to even bigger things and he wouldn't be coming back to Autre.

Charlie reached out and squeezed her arm. "Wanting the other person to be happy, even if that will take them away from you? Wanting them to be happy, even if that makes you a little miserable? Being willing to give them up so that they can have what they want? You're in love."

"Okay, I need to go," Naomi told her friends abruptly, turning for her truck. "I really just need some time and space."

Charlie Landry didn't understand having time alone and space, but she leaned in and gave Naomi a quick hug as Jordan gave her a smile that was full of affection.

Naomi took Jill home and dropped her off, then headed home, poured a lemonade, and settled onto the big swing on her back porch.

She started the swing swaying, took a sip, and looked out over her backyard.

It was so quiet here. Peaceful.

It had been such an easy place to hide away for all these years.

She'd been safe here. Escaping the public eye had actually been easier than she'd expected.

Of course, her family and friends and community circling her and acting as a forcefield had been a part of that initially, but by refusing to do *any* public appearances or interviews, not even making any social media posts, interest in her life had died off quickly.

She'd been happy with her very quiet, predictable, safe, anonymous life. Well, anonymous to the outside world anyway.

Then Donovan Foster had barged in.

She was now doing crazy things. Her heart had beat harder because of him—physically and emotionally—than it ever had in her life. She was feeling breathless...also literally and figuratively. She was taking chances. She was feeling exhilarated.

And she was on camera again.

No one had "recognized" her yet. She was Naomi LeClaire when she was named at all. Most of her appearances were on the Boys of the Bayou Gone Wild website and Facebook page. That was a relatively small audience of course—though it was growing—and she was simply Naomi there. No one cared about her past life. Donovan and the animals were front and center, as they should be.

Still, he'd pulled her back on camera. Something she'd sworn she'd never do again.

And now, she'd been on the news in Alabama and the local Louisiana station had picked the story up as well. She'd just been in the background during the seal rescue, really. He'd handed the animal over to her and the camera had followed as she'd carried it to the truck and held it as Donovan examined it, but Donovan and Fiona had done the talking. Naomi had been there, though. In front of a much bigger audience. Because of Donovan.

And she'd felt...proud. Proud and passionate about what they were doing. Proud of *him*.

With him in the Galapagos Islands, she wouldn't be jumping off of airboats onto roofs, or handling black bears, or showing up on the news. But with him in the Galapagos Islands, she'd most definitely be a little heartbroken.

She really shouldn't have fallen for a guy who was so damned amazing.

10

Naomi managed to relax and eat a nice quiet dinner with her family, and even go to sleep early and only dream of Donovan rather than lying awake thinking about him.

But she didn't sleep very late the next morning.

Her phone was ringing by 7 AM.

She fumbled for the phone and lifted it to her ear, still lying in bed. "Michael?" she mumbled. "What's going on? Are you okay?"

"Yeah," her brother answered. "Exhausted. But doing well, mostly. I'll probably be heading home in a couple of days."

"Great. I hope you're taking care of yourself, along with all the people."

"Of course. But I'm calling to see how you are?"

Naomi pushed herself up in bed and forced her eyes open. "I'm fine. Slept well last night. Little sore but mostly feeling like I'm recovered."

"I wasn't talking physically," Michael said. "I mean, how are you doing with the internet stuff?"

Naomi ran her hand over her face. "Internet stuff? What are you talking about?"

"The video on YouTube that's getting so much attention?" Michael asked. "I can imagine that's not exactly how you expected that to go."

"The video," Naomi repeated, her brain still waking up. "From the seal rescue?"

The news had only shown a short clip of video with their story during their primetime broadcast, but Rachel had said something about posting a longer segment online.

"Well, yes. There is definitely more about the seal rescue. And the tiger and zebra," Michael said. "But there's plenty of you on there too."

"Me? When was I helping Donovan?"

Michael chuckled in her ear. "I can see why he might have considered that 'helpful'."

She frowned. "What are you talking about? It seems like you know something I don't know."

"Well, apparently you haven't seen the video I have. I wouldn't have found it on my own. My friends down here brought it to me. They were wondering how I felt about my friend kissing my sister like that for all the world to see."

"All the world? It was a local news channel."

"It's on the internet, Naomi. That basically makes it worldwide."

Then his words actually sank in. "Wait... the video is of us *kissing*?"

"Yeah. I didn't know that you and Donovan were seeing each other."

Of course he hadn't known that. Because she'd kept that from him. On purpose. But there was *video* of her and Donovan kissing? On the internet? She was now wide awake. She swung her legs over the side of her bed. "Where were we? In the video?"

"You don't remember where you were when you and Donovan were kissing?" Michael asked.

"There was maybe more than one kiss, Michael," she snapped. "That's not important."

Naomi headed into her bathroom, shedding her clothes as she went, determined to jump in the shower and then go find... someone. She wasn't even sure who to look for exactly. Probably Rachel. This had to be video from her following Donovan around.

"It's by his truck. After the seal rescue."

Oh. When she'd grabbed him. Huh. She hadn't realized Rachel and Tom had been right there with the camera. Of course, they'd been everywhere Donovan had been. So that was probably on Naomi. "So...how is it?" she asked hesitantly.

"It's a really passionate kiss between two people who obviously like each other a lot. Not that one of them told her brother that they liked each other a lot. But it's nothing to be embarrassed about."

"I'm not *embarrassed*. It's just not something we were going to make public. He's...not staying. It's not going to turn into anything. And the news shouldn't be able to just splash that all over the place without telling us."

"Listen, everybody watching the video loved it," Michael said. "It's a *kiss*. No one's naked or anything. You're making people happy. They're super complimentary of the work that you're doing and they think it's awesome that you're together. Seems like just a bunch of good stuff, Nae."

She took a deep breath.

Her older brother was protective of her to an extent, but he also knew that she was a strong, independent, intelligent woman and didn't really need his protection in most cases. And this was, apparently, a case where he didn't think she needed to be protected.

"Okay," she finally said. "Thank you. I appreciate the warning. I'm going to... figure this out."

"Look at the video. Talk to Donovan. It's so much better than you're imagining, I'm sure," Michael said.

"Okay. I'll talk to you later."

They disconnected and Naomi stood, staring at her phone.

She didn't want to watch the video.

But she kind of did.

Michael had said it was a passionate kiss between two people who obviously liked each other. And it had a lot of comments.

She wanted to see the comments.

Or did she?

She pulled up the website and typed in Donovan Foster. Sure enough, the video was right at the top. The headline read *Sealed With A Kiss!* And it had over a hundred thousand views.

Holding her breath, Naomi hit the play button.

It wasn't just a video of their kiss. It was a montage of video clips with Rachel narrating over the top. The clips included Naomi on the airboat with Sawyer, crawling through the attic window, and handing the rescued raccoons over to the volunteers at the drop-off point.

How the hell had they gotten those videos? Clearly someone on the airboat had shot them. It hadn't been Bennett or Sawyer, since they'd both shown up in the clips. It could have been Zeke though. He'd probably done it for the Gone Wild website. Had Rachel seen them and asked to include them?

There were also clips of Donovan's rescue of the little boy and his puppy on the pineapple floaty and him carrying a St. Bernard through waist deep water to his waiting family. Those had also, clearly, been shot on a phone by someone on the boat with him.

It wouldn't have surprised Naomi if Charlie had put a bug in someone's ear about getting some video for the Gone Wild website, actually, now that she thought about it.

And, of course, there was footage of Donovan under the pool, bracing the metal beam as the power tools cut through the thick plastic directly over his head. That had definitely been filmed by Rachel's cameraman. There was also the final image of him handing the seal off to Naomi and of her holding the seal while Donovan examined it.

And then, right there at the end, was the shot of her grabbing the front of his shirt and pulling him in for the kiss.

He came willingly of course. His hands went to her hips and he deepened the kiss almost immediately.

She rewound just that portion of the video and rewatched it.

Twice.

Yeah, that was a hot kiss.

Naomi felt warmer and her lips tingled remembering it.

Wow. The world was watching that.

And they did look damn good together.

She started to push the replay button again but stopped herself. Still...she scrolled through the comments.

Oh, people really did like them. Her eyes rounded as she read.

They liked all of it, actually. The rescues, the animals being reunited with their humans, the baby seal's cuteness. They were also concerned about the flooding, asking about where and how to donate, outraged over the ownership and treatment of the animals, and even talking about protests. People were linking to organizations that were helping flood victims as well as groups that were fighting to protect animals. One guy had even listed the numbers and email addresses of Alabama elected officials so people could contact them and demand changes in legislation.

There were two comments that noted she looked a lot like Naomi Williams from *Zoey At the Zoo* and saying they'd loved that show and wondered what she was up to. She tried to ignore those.

And then there was the kiss. That clip was definitely getting the most comments.

She shook her head. More than a cute baby seal? Come on.

But it was right there in black and white. Well, and some orange in the fire emojis and red in the heart emojis. And a few GIFs of people fanning themselves or dumping water over their heads to cool off.

Naomi set her phone on the counter. She thought about it all as she started taking out her braids. Then as she gathered her hair up under her shower cap. Then as she stepped into the shower. And the entire time she went through her shower routine.

It was really not cool that someone had captured that private moment on film and had broadcast it to the world. It was also silly that anyone cared about that she and Donovan had kissed. They should care about the animals and the people who were suffering from the hurricane, not Naomi and Donovan making out. Didn't these people have any sense of priorities? This was crazy.

Then again...it really wasn't. She knew how this worked. People loved to watch other people's lives. The more dramatic the better. People ate up moments of happiness and humanity in the midst of chaos and misery. They'd been watching a video about animals being rescued from flood waters and abusive humans and that had been uplifting, but then to hit them with a surprise moment of hot romance like a big old "and they lived happily ever after" at the end? Of course, they were watching and rewatching and responding.

So this wasn't a *bad* thing. This was a normal thing. Okay, normal-ish.

The story was a good one. Donovan was saving animals and she was kissing him. There was nothing *scandalous* about that.

If more people figured out who Donovan Foster was and got interested in the work he was doing, and the animal park where he was doing it, that could only be a good thing. And it seemed there were a lot of other good things coming from this as well—donations and protests and letters.

Okay, so a bunch of people had seen her kiss Donovan. So what? If she *didn't* want to kiss him—and take every chance she had to do so—*that* would be a lot crazier than anything on that video.

Yeah. That was absolutely true.

By the time she was rinsing off and reaching for a towel, Naomi had decided she was fine with people knowing she had amazing taste in men.

And that Donovan Foster wanted to kiss her back.

Damn right, he did.

And as she stepped out of the shower, she reached for the play button on the video one more time.

But just before she could hit it, her phone lit up with a text.

From Donovan.

She opened it immediately.

Donovan: *Hey, you coming to Ellie's this morning?*

Naomi: *I was on my way over there in a little bit.*

Donovan: *Good. Need you.*

Her heart flipped even as heat swirled through her lower belly.

Donovan sent another message before she could reply.

Donovan: *Rachel's here. She's talking TV show. With me. Animal rescues and rehab. Here. You need to come tell me it's a terrible idea. Because it sounds kind of awesome.*

Naomi had to re-read his message three times. A TV show? About Donovan's rescues and rehab? He'd already done that. His show had been very popular, but could he do it again? Maybe. And what he was doing here in Autre was a little different. This was everyday wildlife, not dolphins and elephants. Though they did now have a tiger...

Naomi shook her head. It was a crazy idea.

Maybe Rachel was just talking about a segment on the news. That would make more sense. And Donovan would be amazing at that too.

Honestly, Donovan would be amazing at anything that involved animals and cameras.

A segment on the news, even if it was a regular thing, was a lot smaller scale that what he'd done previously, but he'd said that it sounded "kind of awesome" to him.

Naomi definitely wanted to hear more about this. Because there was one very important word in his message that she couldn't ignore.

Here.

Whatever they were talking about would be *here* and that meant Donovan would stay. At least a little longer.

Suddenly her heart was flipping and her stomach was swooping again. Donovan didn't need her right now in a sexy way. He needed her as a stand-in, pseudo-agent.

She could definitely help him with this. Because this could mean that Donovan, the man she was madly in love with, the man she knew she wanted more than anything, could stay here with her.

She'd do whatever she needed to do to make that happen.

D onovan was *always* happy to see Naomi.

But when he was sitting in Ellie's at eight forty-five in the morning, trying to concentrate on a meeting with two people who were telling him things that sounded too good to be true, on only three hours of sleep, Donovan felt a healthy dose of relief along with his usual God-she's-gorgeous-and-I'm-so-glad-she's-here.

She'd help him sort all of this out. She was smart and practical and always knew what he needed. He lifted his coffee cup to his lips for the thirty-eighth time that morning already and cursed Zeke and Zander Landry. Then he added a few choice words for Gabe and Logan Trahan as well who had been mixing the drinks for Zeke, Zander, Owen, Dax, and Ollie.

Donovan had been the designated driver and herding three drunk Cajuns and two drunk millionaires through the French Quarter had taken more time, more curse words, and had caused a far bigger headache than it should have.

"Coffee, Naomi?" Ellie called from the bar.

"Please," she answered with a smile. But her gaze was back on him immediately as she bee-lined for his table.

She was dressed in a yellow top that left her shoulders bare and faded blue jeans. Her hair was down and natural today and she wore no make-up, though her lips were his very favorite berry color.

But her expression was wary as she approached. And noticed who he was sitting with.

Yeah, she'd probably seen the video by now.

He braced himself.

Rachel greeted Naomi with a bubbly, "Oh, hi! I'm so glad you're here!" from right across the table.

Donovan grimaced as his brain asked *why can't we just go to sleep again?*

Well initially he'd gotten up because the animals needed him.

But now there was no way he was going to be able to sleep even if he did head home. His brain, as sleep deprived as it was, was spinning.

Rachel was in town with her boyfriend, Brent, to pitch Donovan an idea. For a TV show. A fucking reality TV show.

About his wildlife rescues and rehabilitation. Shot right here in Autre.

It was probably a terrible idea, but it was truly beyond him at the moment to figure out why.

Naomi's arrival made him all the more certain that she really was a goddess. Or his guardian angel. He needed her calm, rational thinking right now. She would absolutely tell him why this idea sucked.

"Good morning, everyone," Naomi said. She pulled out a chair at their table and sat.

"You have perfect timing," Rachel told her. "We were just about to get into the details."

Naomi looked from Rachel to Donovan and then back. "Details?"

"I'm sorry, I'm jumping way ahead," Rachel said. "Naomi LeClaire, this is my boyfriend Brent Meyer. He just graduated with a degree in media arts production. He'd like to produce TV shows and documentaries. He's looking for projects and asked me to keep an eye out for amazing people doing amazing things in this area that might make a great story. He's heard me talk about Boys of the Bayou Gone Wild before and so, of course, I told him all about the big animal rescue the other day and he's now seen the footage we shot."

Naomi's eyes narrowed. "Yes, it seems a lot of people have seen the footage."

Rachel nodded excitedly. "I know. Isn't it great? We cannot believe how that has blown up."

"So you did put that montage together?"

"We did." Rachel gave her a big grin. "That's just a tiny bit of what Brent can do. We saw some of the clips on the Gone Wild website and asked if we could use them. We put it together with some of my footage and uploaded it. In exchange for letting us borrow their videos, we offered to share it with Gone Wild. And now, we want to do something more. Even before we saw the response we thought it could be great. But now? This definitely has the makings of something special."

Naomi frowned. "Something more? Like what?"

"Think reality TV show," Brent said.

Naomi's eyes narrowed. "Donovan's already done that."

"That's what makes it even more enticing," Brent told her. He leaned in, resting his forearms on the table and clasping his hands. "Donovan Foster, TV reality star, internet sensation, world traveler, wildlife adventurer, has now settled down in small-town Louisiana to try to make a normal life. But excitement finds him even here. In what looks like a typical backyard to the rest of us, on Main Street USA, in a muddy bayou... Donovan finds adventure."

Brent's eyes were practically sparkling.

Damn, Donovan's head hurt.

"My plan is to get enough footage to put together three mock episodes. We'll have a focus group that will look at what we're putting together and give us input and reactions. We'll also be sharing clips here and there, along with still photos and behind-the-scenes bits on social media. All of that together will be packaged into a presentation to two potential major investors. One is the uncle of a friend of mine, Jonathan Anders. The other is a friend of his. Jonathan, however, is the one we have to win over. If he decides to invest, his friend will too. If Jonathan gives us the financial backing, that, combined with bringing in a lead who has some reality TV history and a big social media following"—He gave Donovan a grin—"will make a great project to shop around to the streaming networks."

"Um..." was the best Donovan could do.

But it seemed they didn't need a reaction from him.

"And of course, there's you," Rachel said, looking at Naomi. "Everybody loves a bad boy who's been tamed by true love."

Donovan looked at Naomi quickly, "I didn't tell her that."

Naomi had made it clear—very clear—how she felt about people being privy to her personal life. Even if they *were* dating —and they seemed to have come to the conclusion that that wasn't going to happen—she would hate that video being online. She would doubly hate the idea of putting *more* content like that online.

"I know you didn't," Naomi said, not looking away from Rachel. She seemed thoughtful. "We told you in Alabama that we were just friends."

"But you have a *ton* of chemistry," Rachel said. "I witnessed it in one kiss and now the world's seen it in another. You can't argue with those comments and reactions."

Donovan braced himself for Naomi's reaction.

But instead of leaning in and pointing her finger at Rachel, or slapping a hand down on the table, or springing to her feet, Naomi sat back in her chair, crossed her arms, crossed her legs, and asked, "What are you thinking?"

Donovan felt his eyes widen.

"Because there won't be seal and tiger rescues every day," Rachel said. "We really play up the romance angle. The idea that he's given up all the world travels and major excitement for the adventure of falling in love, is gold." Rachel leaned in, clearly sensing that she had a small window in which to deliver this pitch. "Women absolutely swoon over the rugged, alpha guy turning his life upside down for the woman he falls for, right?"

"We're not a couple," Donovan interjected. He had to, didn't he? Naomi didn't want this and had gotten dragged into it because of a spur-of-the-moment kiss caught on camera.

But Naomi was nodding. "There's no question that romance sells."

"Absolutely," Rachel agreed. "Look at all the reality TV that's *entirely* about people falling in love. A bunch of women get together to compete for one eligible guy. People who agree to show up and get married to someone they've never even met before. Hell, the Dating Game started forever ago. And even the scripted TV shows have a romantic subplot or at least some will-they-won't-they tension."

"You're absolutely right," Naomi said.

She was? Donovan didn't watch a lot of TV and he should probably defer to Naomi here but he was surprised by her calm, almost contemplative, reaction.

"*And*," Rachel went on, "the kiss was the most replayed and commented on part of that video. People love you two together. Donovan and his confidence and compassion, and you learning as you go, being willing to jump in even with your inexperience are absolutely captivating, but then when you're together... whew!" Rachel fanned her face. "The way you look at each other and protect each other and work together is absolutely addictive. I saw it even before the kiss. Then when I saw that, I couldn't wait to call Brent."

"She showed me the kiss just from her phone," Brent said. "Even that way it was clear it would sell."

"That was *private*," Donovan felt the need to say.

This was...weird. And that he felt weird about it was also weird. He'd never cared that people watched him falling on his ass, getting pooped on by a multitude of animals, screwing up and getting bitten and stung. But hearing that people might tune in to watch Naomi do... well, anything...felt strange. He felt protective. He didn't like the idea of people watching her potentially fall or struggle or fail, but he also really didn't like that she might be put in the position of doing something she just didn't want to do.

Rachel looked at him and nodded, then sat back in her chair, folding her arms. "Yes. I know. I get it. People would be witnessing some private moments, for sure. But they will be very invested in the two of you. Your chemistry will definitely get people tuning in to see your relationship develop. I'd be willing to bet your audience will grow with every single episode."

"But we're not developing a relationship," Donovan said. "Not beyond our friendship. Yeah, there's chemistry, but that kiss was just...impulsive. We were happy the rescue had been a success. It was taken out of context."

He looked at Naomi. Who didn't say anything. Shouldn't she be protesting this too? It was mostly his fault the kiss had been filmed. Rachel wouldn't have even been there with her camera if she hadn't recognized him the night before and wanted to follow him around. But *Naomi* had kissed *him*. Of course he'd been all in, but this wasn't *entirely* his fault. Why was he the only one arguing here?

Rachel didn't even glance at him. She was studying Naomi. "Well then..." Rachel asked, "can you fake it?"

Donovan frowned. He watched Naomi. Who, even after five seconds ticked by, still hadn't said *absolutely not*.

He blew out a breath. "We aren't going to—"

"Donovan, can I talk to you for minute? Alone?" Naomi asked.

He snapped his mouth shut. What the hell was going on?

Well, there was one way to find out. "Definitely."

He got up and followed her to the door. As they walked through the bar, he noticed a table of women watching them and whispering. There were four of them, clearly tourists, and they seemed excited to see him and Naomi together.

They'd probably seen the video too.

He was pretty sure the whole town had seen it by now.

Great. That, plus Rachel now insisting they should do a reality show where they kissed even more, meant that the chances were pretty good that Naomi was going to yell.

They stepped outside and rounded the corner of the building.

"Listen, I'm really sorry," Donovan said as soon as they were alone. "I didn't know they were filming us when we kissed. I swear."

"I believe you." She paused. "But it's really good."

"It...is?"

"The whole video is really good. But especially the kiss."

The kiss *was* really good. He'd watched it more than once. "It's sexy as hell," he agreed.

She gave him a little smile and his gut tightened. The kiss had been really hot. On video and in reality.

"And the work we did in Alabama was important."

"Definitely," he agreed.

"And everyone who's seen the video is really enthusiastic about it."

"Yes." The comments on the video were definitely excited. About them, but about the animals and the clean-up effort too. People wanted to get involved.

"So...I think we should do it."

"Do what?" Donovan asked.

"The show. I think they should follow us around and film you doing your thing. We've been doing it on the Gone Wild website anyway, and this will be a bigger production. They'll be able to get more footage and distribute it more widely. Potentially anyway," she added. "This is what you wanted. More reach. A bigger platform."

It would be all of that. "But they want you to be my girlfriend on the show."

She nodded. "I think we should do that too. Rachel's right that it will pull in a bigger audience."

Donovan studied her face. She seemed serious about this. "But you don't want to have a public relationship."

She nodded. "I know I said that."

"But that's exactly what this would be."

"I know."

"So why would you do this?"

"Because this would mean you could stay here."

Donovan couldn't breathe for a moment.

"I know that I'm going to sacrifice some of my privacy for this. I get that. But...I'm willing to do that if it means you could stay," she said, her voice a little husky, but her gaze steady. "I was a kid before. Being in the public eye was really overwhelming. Not being able to address the rumors myself and not being in control of what was going on around me made it an easier choice to just stop doing it all together. My mother was right to pull me out of there. It was a lie. They wanted to use me. But I'm a grown woman now. And this, between us, isn't a lie. And you won't use me. And I won't let Brent and Rachel or anyone else use me."

Donovan forced oxygen into his lungs but found he had no words.

She was willing to do this for him. For them. So they could be together. And he could stay in Autre. With Griffin. With the Landrys...

"If you want to do it, of course," she added. He still hadn't spoken.

"I...do. I want to do it."

Her smile was bright. "Good. Then it's a go."

What he *really* wanted to do was to push her up against the side of Ellie's and kiss the hell out of her.

So he did.

He backed her up, cupped her face, and covered her mouth.

She melted into him just like all the other times. This was their preferred outlet for their emotions and he was totally on board.

When he finally lifted his head, she smiled up at him.

"We'll definitely need to throw some of this in on camera," she said.

"How could I say no to that?"

"It could be fun."

He stepped back, giving her a little room to breathe. "I have no doubt about that."

She grinned. "This will be so good."

"You really think so?" Again, he didn't watch a lot of TV. Was this really what people went for?

"Oh, for sure. They'll see you teaching me about rescuing and rehabilitating animals and they'll learn too. But they'll be watching in hopes of catching more kissing."

"All I heard was that I get to kiss you some more."

She wet her lips as her gaze dropped to his mouth. "I think that's a must do. We'll definitely mix romance, flirting, chemistry, and action-adventure. We'll rescue animals and educate people all while letting them hope we're falling in love. It can't miss."

Falling in love.

Those words hit Donovan in the gut. He was already there.

Donovan decided to focus on the part he did understand—he was going to get to keep kissing Naomi and he didn't have to hide it now.

He started to reach for her to do just that, but just then he heard someone shout, "Goat Bingo!" from the front of the building.

He pulled back and sighed. Goat bingo meant that the goats from the petting zoo had gotten out again and Benny, the border collie, had rounded them up somewhere. Somewhere that wasn't the barn.

Benny was a great herding dog, though Donovan suspected she thought she was a goat. Or she was in love with one of the goats or something. She belonged to Jordan and Fletcher, but she cried if they tried to keep her at home overnight rather than letting her sleep in the barn. The only problem with her goat herding was that she just didn't bring them back to the barn, she simply got them into the nearest building. Whatever building that might be. They'd been found in the school gymnasium, several people's kitchens, the Methodist church, and even Ellie's bar.

It had become a game in town. Literally. Ellie had printed up bingo cards and whenever someone saw the goats somewhere, they marked the location off on their card. When they got bingo, they brought the card to Ellie's. The first one to show up got a beer and fried pickles. And no, in spite of several suggestions, Ellie wasn't interested in making those fried goat cheese balls instead, no matter how funny they all thought that would be.

"Looks like I need to go," Donovan said.

On cue, a phone vibrated in his pocket.

It wasn't his regular phone, though. This was the Goat Phone. The phone that Knox had jokingly gotten Donovan when he'd agreed to be the main goatherder in town. The number was only used to report goat sightings.

He pulled the phone from his back pocket and looked at the screen, then grinned at Naomi. "They're at the hair salon."

11

Naomi laughed. "I'll come with you. We should bring Rachel and Brent. They can film."

"This isn't exactly an animal rescue." It was definitely more of a human rescue... *from* goats.

"No, but people will think it's charming and quirky and funny."

Without even thinking too hard, Donovan could name at least ten people who didn't find the goats any of those things, but he shrugged. "You're the expert."

They headed back into Ellie's.

"We're in," Naomi announced.

Rachel's eyes went wide. "Really? For all of it?"

"Yes. We'll talk specifics later, but generally, we're in. Internet sensation, wildlife rescuer Donovan Foster having small town adventures in Louisiana is a go."

"And falling in love with his... assistant? Side kick? Girl next door?" Rachel wrinkled her nose. "Which of those fits?"

Naomi took a deep breath. "Actually..." She glanced at Donovan, then back to Rachel and Brent. "I have an even bigger hook."

Brent lifted a brow. "Okay."

"Internet sensation and reality TV star showing sitcom child star what it's like to work with real, untrained wild animals."

Rachel shook her head. "I don't follow."

"Are you familiar with *Zoey At the Zoo*?" Naomi asked.

Rachel frowned. Then her frown deepened. Then it deepened some more. Then suddenly she gasped and sat back with her hand over her mouth.

"What about *Zoey At the Zoo*?" Brent asked. He looked from Naomi to Rachel and back.

"She's Zoey!" Rachel said, dropping her hand. "Oh my God, you're Naomi Williams?"

"That was my stage name," Naomi said.

"Wait, *you* are Zoey?" Brent asked.

"Yep."

Naomi gave him a weak smile and Donovan felt trepidation slide through his gut.

"So you've got experience with wild animals too," Brent said.

"Well, yes, but they were highly trained and had handlers with them all the time. It's completely different from what Donovan does. That could be an interesting twist too," Naomi said.

Rachel was already nodding enthusiastically. "Yes. I love it. Definitely." She turned to Brent. "We have *two* stars now. Jonathan will love that."

"But she hasn't been on TV in years." He looked up at Naomi. "Right?"

"Right. Well, reruns. And it's streaming now."

"Women our age will *love* this," Rachel insisted. "*Zoey At the Zoo* was *huge*. These women will totally tune in to see her with real wild animals. And to watch her with a hot wildlife rescuer! Oh my God, yes. And they'll have their kids watch for the animal stuff. This is so good." Rachel was nearly vibrating with excitement.

"Okay, great. Well, we've got our first small-town animal call," Naomi said. "Wanted to see if you want to tag along."

"Oh, yes!" Rachel bounced up out of her seat.

Ten minutes later they were all heading to downtown Autre. Just as Naomi had predicted, Rachel had even used the terms 'charming' *and* 'quirky'.

It definitely seemed that Naomi knew what she was talking about.

She really was *famous*. He hadn't ever watched her show that he could remember. He hadn't been into TV much as a kid either. He preferred being outside, running around, getting dirty, and playing sports. But her show had been big enough that he'd been aware of it.

He was definitely going to be binging *Zoey At the Zoo* soon.

D onovan and Naomi walked into I'm Gonna Dye and greeted Rory and Lennon, the two women who owned the salon.

There were three other women in the chairs in various states of makeover, along with the goats and Benny.

Rory turned away from Nancy Bollier and set a hand on her hip. "I made the mistake of propping the door open while I was sweeping the floor."

Donovan winced, then gave her a grin. "Looks like you followed through on your threat."

"Threat?" Naomi asked, but she was staring at the goats who were all corralled into one corner. They were making a lot of noise but they weren't going anywhere. Benny was making sure of that.

"The last time they came in here, Rory told them if they showed up again, they were getting the full treatment."

"So you dyed their hair and put the hair bows in?" Rachel asked.

Rory shrugged. "I figured they came back for a reason. I painted Benny's nails too."

Sure enough, the collie had bright pink toenails that matched the bright pink bow that was clipped on the top of her head.

The dog looked perfectly happy about the situation. She cocked her head and looked up at Donovan with what he could've sworn was a grin.

"Anyway, this will make it easier to tell them apart," Lennon said. "They're color-coded."

She handed Naomi a piece of paper. Donovan leaned over to look. Each of the goats had a streak of colored hair dye that ran from the top of their head down their snout or down the back of their neck. Three of them had hair bows and two had bows around their tails.

"Oh my God, this is hilarious," Rachel said.

Rory shook her head, her own blond hair with the pink tips swishing back and forth over her back. "The thing is, I don't think it was any kind of deterrent to keep them from coming back. They all seemed to enjoy it."

Donovan laughed. "You weren't trying to deter them. They're gonna be walkin' around town like little billboards."

Rory laughed. "Unfortunately not too many people here in Autre are in the market for neon green hair." She pointed at Happy, who had a neon green stripe down her neck and a matching bow on her tail.

"Well, you know that Charlie is now going to have you dye them all for Halloween or something," Naomi said.

"Oh my God, that would be great. Maybe we can even dress

them each up as a different character. The kids can come in and say, 'I want the Sugar', and I'll give them ten percent off."

Naomi shook her head. "I'll tell Charlie to call you."

"Okay, guys, time to head back to the barn," Donovan told them all. "Benny, come." The collie immediately came to Donovan, heeling like a perfectly well-trained dog.

The goats all looked over and decided they'd had enough spa treatment for the day and followed their favorite canine to the door and out onto the Main Street sidewalk. As if exiting a hair salon with hair bows in was a normal, everyday occurrence for them.

And Brent got it all on camera.

They got the goats back to the barn and Rachel beamed at them.

"That was adorable. Definitely can work this into the whole small-town theme."

Naomi cast a glance at Donovan. He didn't seem particularly complimented.

"So what else is on your agenda for today?" Brent asked.

"We just work on care of the animals we've already got and wait on any rescue calls that come in," Donovan said. "It's pretty fly by the seat of our pants. We never know for sure what's going to come in."

Brent nodded. "We get that. We know that we're going to have to shoot a lot of footage and that there will be some downtime."

Donovan shrugged. "You can just tag along today and we'll see what happens."

Naomi was trying to read him. She knew that he was tired and a little hung over. But he was less enthusiastic about this than she had expected.

"Why don't we take you out to the rehab facility? There are some animals out there now. Just before we headed to Alabama, Donovan rescued three black bear cubs."

Brent perked up a bit at that. "Oh, that would be great. You could talk us through that rescue and what's involved in caring for them."

Rachel nodded her agreement. "And can we get some follow-up on the seal, tiger, and zebra? My station would love that too."

"Yeah," Donovan agreed. "But maybe we should get some paperwork taken care of? I assume you've got some contracts and things we should all be signing?"

Brent and Rachel exchanged a look. "Well, nothing's official until we get Jonathan on board," Brent said.

"Right. But we should lay out how all of this initial stuff is going to go, right?"

"Sure. We can do that."

"Great. Then after that, I'll take you out to meet the other rescue animals that have been here a little longer," Donovan said.

"Oh, what else do you have?" Rachel asked.

"We have some rescued camels, donkeys, and horses. They were pulled off the farm where they had been neglected for some time. But they're doing great now."

Rachel's face fell. "Oh. Just donkeys and horses?"

"And camels," Donovan repeated.

"Do you have any before footage or photos?" Brent asked. "Like what they looked like when they first showed up?"

"I do," Naomi said. "I do all the videography for Boys of the Bayou Gone Wild. There's probably some stuff on a website and I'm sure I have some footage we didn't use."

Brent turned to her. "That would be great if I could look at some of the stuff that you have. Including the penguin rescue."

Naomi smiled at him. "Oh, I've definitely got that. You won't see that anywhere else. Penguins and alligators don't run into one another very often."

Brent chuckled. "I'm sure that's true. I saw the video on the Gone Wild website. We'll need to pull that down, by the way."

Donovan scowled. "Why is that?"

"We'll obviously want the footage we have to be exclusive. We'll want people to tune in to see it from us."

"But you didn't shoot that rescue," Donovan said.

"No, but it's a hell of a video. You got on the back of an alligator, man," Brent said. "That was kickass. And there was a penguin there too. I mean, that's gold."

"It's already been up for a while," Donovan told him. "Too late to be exclusive."

"Hey, no offense. I know a lot of people have seen it on your site. But there's a much bigger audience of people who haven't. Who will see it if *we* put it up."

Donovan drew himself up straighter. "So you're not going to want us to put stuff up on the website anymore? Naomi isn't going to be recording things?"

"She can record the usual. Any of the normal feeding and care activities of the petting zoo and animal park animals. I suppose even just the general care of the penguins is fine." Brent glanced at Rachel as if gauging her reaction as well. "I guess we're just going to want to keep the actual *rescue* activities exclusive. And any of the hands-on, intensive rehabilitation activities we do on camera, we'll want to keep under wraps."

"So we can show me feeding penguins and alpacas, but not my work with the tiger or the seal?" Donovan clarified.

Brent grinned. "Exactly. Or any future work rescues."

"How about the donkeys and horses?" Donovan asked. "Those were rescues and we're still rehabilitating them. Animals don't just magically get better and never have another issue. Are you gonna want footage of them?"

Brent shook his head, clearly missing the harsher under-tone of Donovan's question.

"You know if those are just horses and donkeys, you guys can feel free to film those all you want. We'll do the more interesting ones."

Naomi grabbed Donovan's forearms as he took a step forward. "Okay, I think we'll head out to the rehab center and you guys can follow along behind us," she said.

Donovan gave her little frown and she just squeezed his arm reassuringly.

Rachel also seemed oblivious to the fact that Brent was pissing Donovan off. She nodded quickly. "That would be great. We'll chat a little bit on our way out there about what we're looking for from the footage. Maybe we could get the bears outside and do a little restaging of the rescue."

"Restaging?" Naomi asked. Okay, now she might have to get involved.

Up until now she understood what Brent and Rachel were going for. She didn't love the idea of pulling the videos down from the website either. She understood why that irritated Donovan. All of those videos had helped make the park's website popular which had made people want to visit the park when they were in Louisiana. It had been great for the park's business, which had been great with the Landrys, which in turn made both Naomi and Donovan very happy.

The animals that were staying in the park, now including the tiger, seal, and zebra were technically the Landrys'. Not Donovan's.

They were going to have to discuss all of this with Sawyer, Maddie, Owen, Josh, and Bennett. Though Naomi was certain she could pitch it to the partners as ultimately a very good thing for Boys of the Bayou and for Autre in general.

She also knew that Brent and Rachel were figuring this out

as they went along as well. They were all going to have to work together for this.

But the idea of taking the rescued animals back out into a situation where they could potentially be traumatized again, or even lost if they ran off into the woods, seemed unnecessarily risky.

"It would be so great to get the bear rescue on film. Unless you recorded it," Brent said to her.

"Well, we—"

"We were rescuing them in the middle of a fucking hurricane," Donovan said. "No, she didn't get it on video. She shouldn't have even been out there herself."

Brent shrugged. "Okay, then maybe we can set it up again."

"You're going to plan another hurricane? Find another bear? Set up—"

"That won't work," Naomi broke in, again squeezing Donovan's arm. "We can't take the cubs back out into the woods. They'll run off and they're not ready to be out there on their own yet."

"Okay." Brent looked crestfallen. "That would've been an amazing rescue to film. Be sure you call us any time something comes up from now on. If there's no way for us to get there, be sure *you* get it," he told Naomi.

Donovan actually leaned toward him and Naomi had to squeeze his arm harder. "Great," she told him.

"Not if it's dangerous," Donovan said. "If it's something where she's putting herself into a bad situation, she's not going to be filming."

Brent shook his head. "We need exciting footage for this, Donovan."

"I thought this was about an adventurer who's *settling down*."

"Sure, but nobody's going to tune in to watch a guy feeding

horses. Lots of people can see that right outside their own houses."

"And that's kind of the point," Donovan said. "We're trying to teach people about the things that are happening in their own backyards. Things like animal neglect and injured and orphaned wildlife. Most people don't run into koalas and dolphins every day. But lots of people run across raccoons and horses and donkeys that need help."

"Look," Brent said, his tone turning placating. "I get where you're coming from and I respect it. But we're trying to pitch a show. You know how this works. Once we get the show picked up and on air, we can go a little softer."

"You think saving donkeys and raccoons is softer?"

Brent narrowed his eyes, studying Donovan. "Don't you?"

"What's that supposed to mean?"

"You've made your name doing the big, wild, exciting rescues with big, wild, exciting animals."

Naomi could feel the tension vibrating through Donovan. His arm was tensed under her hold and she couldn't look away from the mix of emotions on his face.

She felt like she should intervene here. Somehow play peacemaker, say something composed and calming. But she wasn't sure what that was. She agreed with both men. She completely understood where Donovan was coming from, of course. She did believe in all of these animal rescues.

But she understood Brent's side as well. They had to give people something to keep them coming back and to entertain them and excite them.

And honestly, she couldn't believe that Donovan Foster was insisting that the rescues of domestic horses and donkeys and a family of raccoons was as big as when he'd rescued an elephant from poachers in Kenya or even the rescue of a penguin from an alligator.

But...that wasn't true. Even as she thought it, she realized that the man standing next to her right now was a different guy than the Donovan Foster who had come to Autre almost a year ago.

He'd changed. Right in front of her eyes. And she hadn't really noticed. He'd become...softer. She didn't doubt that he'd always cared about all of the animals, but over the year he'd been here, and without the big camera delivering him a huge audience all the time, he'd become more content with the smaller things.

Maybe it had helped him focus more on the actual work he was doing. Or the people he was doing it with. Or the animals he was doing it for. She wasn't sure, but he'd definitely been happy while he'd been in Autre and there hadn't been an audience of millions watching him.

And now he was offended by the idea that someone would think rescuing donkeys wasn't important.

"How about this," she finally said. "This is all new to all of us. We just decided to do this. Brent and Rachel, why don't you guys take the rest of the day and talk through your plans. Donovan and I will do the same. We'll also run all of this past everyone else. This really is all about Boys of the Bayou Gone Wild. I know they'll be supportive and they certainly trust Donovan, but they need to know what's going on. Let's just take the rest of the day and get our plans in order."

Donovan relaxed slightly under her hand and she did what she had been fighting the urge to do for some time—she slid her hand down his arm to his hand and linked their fingers together. She felt him look down at her and then the little squeeze he gave her hand.

Brent nodded and looked at Rachel. "Okay, that's probably a good idea. We'll all regroup and meet up again tomorrow." He turned to Donovan. "I think we can make something really great here."

Donovan gave him a simple nod.

Brent and Rachel headed for their vehicle.

When they'd driven off, Donovan turned to Naomi.

"This might be a horrible idea."

She nodded. "Yeah, it might be. But I think we need to try."

"Do you?"

His question was sincere and she knew her opinion really mattered to him.

So she gave the question of couple of seconds of thought. But that was all she needed. This could be good for all of them.

She nodded. "Yes."

"Okay then." That was his simple answer. He was just going to trust her that this was all going to be fine.

And that meant that she was going to do whatever she could to make it fine.

Somehow.

F or the next four days, nothing exciting happened with any animal rescues.

Brent and Rachel had come to the rehab facility and Donovan had done a great job talking them through the status of the seal, tiger, and zebra as well as the rehabilitation that was in front of them and the prognosis for all three. He also made sure to point out the fact that they would all likely be staying with Boys of the Bayou Gone Wild permanently.

He also introduced them to the bear cubs and they got some great footage of the bears playing and Donovan handling them all for examinations and feedings.

On the fifth day, as Brent and Rachel reluctantly watched Donovan interact with the donkeys over at the sanctuary barn, a call did come in for a rescue. Finally.

"We've got a trapped heron," Donovan said, striding across the field toward the fence line where Naomi, Rachel, and Brent were watching him work with one of the more skittish of the donkeys. "We need to get out on the bayou."

Brent and Rachel looked like little kids who had just been told they were going to the candy store.

"A heron?" Rachel said.

"Awesome," Brent said.

Donovan shot him a look as he came through the gate.

Brent held up his hands. "Not that it's trapped. But this should be some great footage. Getting out on one of the boats will be awesome."

Donovan let it go. He knew that he was being hard on the guy. He couldn't completely explain it. Brent had been rubbing him the wrong way since they'd met but he needed to lighten up.

The guy was offering him a TV show, for God's sake. Okay, not really. The TV show was a very big maybe. Brent was offering to record a bunch of footage, put it together, and pitch it to people who might, possibly, maybe decide to make it into a TV show. Still, Donovan should be flattered, at least, and excited. He'd been looking for something bigger, and this seemed perfect. This should be exactly what he was looking for. But it seemed that everything Brent and Rachel wanted to talk about and focus on annoyed him.

Which made no sense. He understood why they were looking for exciting footage. He really did. But it annoyed the fuck out of him that they thought the donkeys were boring. They were some of the sweetest animals and their recovery had been awesome to see.

He'd gone soft.

And the only thing that surprised him about that was that he didn't mind.

Donovan glanced over at the woman sitting next to him.

He hadn't *really* touched her in days. Not the way he wanted to. The way he *needed* to. And he was hungry for her.

They'd flirted for the camera. He'd caught her when she'd slipped on the edge of the penguin pool yesterday. But he'd known that was coming because they'd scripted it. They'd almost kissed when they'd put the baby seal in the big plastic pool and he'd happily made a lap around the edge. But again, that had been scripted.

He didn't want his interactions with her scripted. He wanted every smile, touch, and word to be real. He *definitely* wanted to back her up against the door in his office and kiss the hell out of her. And more. So much more. Without a single other person around.

Donovan gripped the steering wheel tightly and worked on keeping his mouth shut. She was doing all of this for him. And if this show actually got picked up by someone, he could stay in Autre. So he needed to adjust his damned attitude.

They pulled up to the docks a minute later.

Driving an airboat had been new when he'd first come to Louisiana, but now it felt as natural as driving his truck. Within minutes they were out on the water and he pulled his phone out to check the coordinates he'd been given.

He saw the bird immediately as they rounded the bend. It was hanging from a low branch of the tree. Its beak had caught a fishing hook and it had somehow become entangled so that the line was wrapped around its beak several times. Its neck was fully extended, its feet at least a couple inches above the surface of the water. A fisherman had noticed it, but it was hard to tell how long it had been hanging there.

He was worried first about the bird's general condition and how long it had been without food and water, but with its long neck extended the way it was, he was concerned about injury as well. No doubt the bird had flapped and wiggled at first to try to get free, however it now hung motionless.

He killed the engine and they floated closer.

Without the huge fan rotating at the back of the boat, he

pulled his headphones off and jumped from the tall captain's seat.

Naomi came to her feet, tossing her headphones onto her seat. "Oh my God, the poor thing."

As she moved toward the front of the boat, Brent and Rachel seemed to realize that they could remove their ear coverings as well.

"What the hell happened?" Brent asked.

"Fishing line," Donovan said grabbing binoculars to get a closer look. "Lots of fishermen will put lines out and leave them, coming back to check them later. It's always a little bit of a mystery how some of these animals get entangled, but it happens a lot."

The bird barely moved as they drifted closer.

"Fuck," Donovan said. He looked at Naomi. "Can you handle the boat?"

She nodded.

He couldn't help his little smile. This woman had been on the bayou all her life. Well, except for the few years she'd spent in Hollywood. He still had trouble wrapping his head around that and had to remind himself it was real. He had, in fact, taken time to look up some old clips of not just her show, but interviews she'd done, as well as photos and various commercial items from *Zoey At the Zoo*.

She'd been cute as hell, and he knew that if he'd watched the show as a kid, he would've completely had a crush on her.

They drifted closer to the stand of trees where the bird was tangled. Airboats didn't have brakes so they nosed into the reeds and grass near the tree and then Naomi got up on the side of the boat and reached for a branch of a tree to steady the boat.

The bird startled, and fluttered its wings, but was clearly exhausted and didn't put much effort into getting away.

Donovan did take just a second to appreciate the beauty of

the sight before him. Naomi was wearing a dark green tank and khaki shorts with brown ankle boots. Her hair was wild around her shoulders, her muscles tensed as she braced the boat, and she looked every bit the outdoorsy goddess that she'd turned into.

He knew that she hadn't been much for outdoorsy adventures before he'd showed up, and the fact that she was out here with him now like this, made his heart pound and yes, his cock swell.

Hey, he was a guy. And he wanted this woman more than he'd ever wanted another. But it went so much deeper than physical attraction. She was absolutely gorgeous, and she'd already been the best sex of his life, but she was strong, compassionate, brave, sharp, and witty. And she had a way of making him feel cared for and yet respected in a way he never had before. Her admiration and support made him feel humble and cocky at the same time.

He did, however, manage to focus on the task at hand after only a few seconds of lusting after her. He moved in closer to examine the bird.

"This is bizarre," he told his companions. "It looks like the line wrapped around his beak once, but then maybe as he struggled, he somehow rotated, wrapping the line around and around and shortening it as it went?"

"Was he going for a fish that was caught on the line?" Brent asked.

"Probably. That's what happens a lot. We rescue a lot of animals and birds from fishing lines." Donovan knelt and grabbed a utility knife out of the toolbox, extending the blade. "Okay, buddy," he said softly to the bird as he evaluated the situation. "I've got you."

He was vaguely aware that Brent was recording but he didn't worry much about giving the guy a good shot or getting in his way. He cut the line entirely to free the bird from the tree, then pulled the bird down and tucked it under his arm in his lap. He kept its wings folded and secured between his side and arm so the bird wouldn't suddenly take off. The line was still wrapped around its beak, holding it shut and if he flew off, he wouldn't be able to eat and he'd die.

"He's so big," Rachel said, her voice hushed.

Donovan took the knife and started working to cut the line around the bird's beak. Doing it one-handed was difficult, however.

"Here, let me help." Naomi was suddenly kneeling in front of him.

Now they had the bird on the boat with them, she didn't need to hold them in place. She'd let go of the tree and they were drifting down the bayou.

He nodded, grateful for the second pair of hands. She took the knife as he continued to hold the bird.

"Just cut under the edge a little bit to get it loose and we can peel it off," he coached. "We want to use the blade as little as possible in case it would slip."

She nodded her understanding, her gaze intense on her task.

She eased the sharp blade under the edge of the line, working it back and forth gently.

Donovan was stunned to realize the bird wasn't struggling at all. He didn't know if it was just incredibly weak, but he sensed that the bird understood that they were helping. He eased his hold slightly, and sure enough the bird sat quietly.

Naomi finally got enough of the line cut through that Donovan could start untwisting the pieces. It took a few minutes but eventually they got the layers of fishing line unwrapped.

He gently eased his hold and waited to see how the bird moved. It sat for just a minute, not moving at all, and Donovan wondered if it was more injured than he'd first expected. They could certainly take it back to the rehab center and keep it overnight.

But just as he was about to suggest that, the bird suddenly hopped away from him and up onto the edge of the boat. He and Naomi both sat back, watching. The heron rotated his head back and forth, reassuring Donovan that its neck and head were uninjured. Then it spread its massive wings and flapped them up and down.

Donovan grinned and glanced at Naomi, who looked amazed. She returned his smile, but immediately returned her focus to the bird. It sat there for another few seconds, and Donovan was heartened to think that it wasn't in a huge hurry to get away from them.

Then all at once, it spread its wings and took off, soaring across the surface of the water.

Donovan felt a surge of satisfaction and awe as he always did when a wild animal was re-released, healthy and happy. Every time he was able to do this, his decision to go into this line of work was validated again.

Naomi blew out a breath and turned to him. She was still on her knees, sitting back on her heels on the floor of the boat.

"Wow, that was beautiful," she said, her voice soft.

"Yeah, beautiful is a very good word for it." But he didn't just mean the bird.

It hit him that over the past few months, everything about being in Autre and the new contentment that he felt here, even with the less exotic animals, had to do with sharing it with these people, particularly Naomi.

He had loved educating people around the world with his work on the other shows, but they were strangers and he only ever ran into a handful of them in person. Here, it was every day. The Landrys, and Naomi, Michael and Andre, even sharing this with Griffin, put all of his work on a different level.

Suddenly Naomi leaned forward, took his face in her hands, and pressed a kiss to his lips.

"You're amazing," she said against his mouth before leaning back.

He gave her a smile that he was sure was full of emotion that he wasn't supposed to be feeling for her. "Ditto, goddess."

She laughed a happy, contented laugh.

"That really was awesome," Brent said.

"And that kiss. That's what were talking about," Rachel said. "Perfect. All of that was cool. The bird, the rescue, the way the bird flew off, you two at the end. Just amazing."

Naomi's eyes widened slightly as if she'd almost forgotten that Brent and Rachel were there.

And the kiss was on film now too.

That was part of the deal though. Donovan had to remember that. All of this was part of pitching this new show.

He didn't think that Naomi had kissed him for the camera, but if she had, this was what he'd signed up for.

12

The next two days were also very routine. And Donovan was sure Brent and Rachel were bored to tears. But they finally got another call about a deer that was trapped in a fence.

They pulled up along the side of the road with Brent and Rachel in the backseat and it took about ten minutes for Donovan to cut the deer loose from the fence and for it to run off into the woods.

"Well, hopefully something big will happen tomorrow," Brent said, lowering the camera with a sigh.

Donovan looked at him. "That wasn't exciting enough for you?"

"The thing obviously wasn't even hurt."

"You were hoping for it to be hurt?"

"We have yet to take anything back to your rehab center. Even the seal, tiger, and zebra are doing well."

"So, sorry to disappoint you," Donovan said dryly.

"But you're just feeding them and they're just hanging out in their pens," Brent said. "You're not even really working with them.

"I'm waiting for them to get stronger. The zebra and tiger aren't going to need much intervention. We're tending to the wounds on the tiger's paws."

"But we already shot footage of that. We're not going to keep showing the same stuff."

Rachel looked up at Brent. "We just need to be a little patient. We have some time."

"I know. Jonathan was just asking how things are going."

"Did you tell him it's just going to take some time? That things don't happen every day?" Donovan asked.

"Which is something I want to talk to you about," Brent said. "I mean I'm not saying that we should completely stage rescues, but after we talked the other day about the bear cubs, it got me thinking—"

Donovan shook his head. "We are not taking the cubs out to the woods and pretending to rescue them again," Donovan scowled. "That's stupid. They'll run off and then be at risk all over again."

"No, man, I get that. They aren't ready to be out on their own," Brent said. "But we were talking—"

Rachel shook her head. "I told you I didn't think that was a good idea. I don't think he'll go for it."

"Go for what?" Donovan asked. He was fairly certain he was not going to go for it. But for some reason he wanted to hear this stupid idea.

"We were talking about the penguin rescue and how you need to pull it down off of the website. We looked at it, thinking that maybe we could edit it into some of our stuff. But there are several angles of that rescue that could have been shot so much better and that would really add to things," Brent said. He gave Naomi a look. "No offense."

Naomi rolled her eyes. "No offense taken."

"We want real raw footage," Donovan told him. "The point

is, she's there like any visitor to the park would be. She's showing them what they would see if they were there."

Brent nodded. "And that completely works for what you guys are doing. But now we need to take it to a little higher level. So I was thinking we could restage *that* rescue pretty easily. You have the penguins. We could take one down there and get a net—"

"You have to be fucking kidding me," Donovan said. He turned and started walking away.

Brent hurried to catch up with him. "Now, listen. It would be in no danger."

"I assume you'd want the alligators there."

Brent nodded. "Well obviously, that's what makes it exciting."

Donovan stopped and pivoted to face the other man so quickly that Brent almost ran into him. "Those are real alligators. Wild animals. They had every intention of killing that penguin. And they would've attacked me and Zeke as well. We weren't playing around."

Brent, either stupid or completely full of himself, made the mistake of grinning. "It looked like you were having a good time though."

Donovan started to lean in but felt Naomi's hand on his arm.

The thing was, Brent wasn't wrong. There had been times, in the not-so-distant past, when Donovan had put on a show or played up situations he'd been in. Sometimes risking possible injury to himself. But he'd changed. He'd...mellowed. Or something. Autre, and the animals here, and the people here, and *Naomi*, had showed him that there were more important things than getting "like" clicks and comments on videos.

"We're not restaging the penguins rescue," Naomi said calmly but firmly. "And I just got a text that Donovan is needed down at the goat barn."

"Another goat needs rescuing?" Brent asked.

Naomi shrugged. "Yeah." She looked up at Donovan. "One of the goats has his head stuck in a feeder."

Donovan nodded. "Let's go."

He needed some space from Brent and he needed a good dose of those goats. The goats made him happy, dammit. All the animals here made him happy.

He didn't need to wrestle alligators or swim with the dolphins or rescue koalas. He needed to take care of animals that needed to be taken care of. Whether it was Australia or Africa or Autre.

At the petting zoo, it was happy chaos as usual. Naomi saw Donovan visibly take a deep breath when they stepped inside the main gate.

The petting zoo was open and there were visitors milling about, along with goats, potbellied pigs, ducks, and peacocks. The alpacas were in their own areas, but they were only separated from the main barnyard by a simple wooden fence and a few of them were just on the other side of that barrier checking out the commotion. The rabbit pen was to the right, the hedgehogs beside them, and the porcupines just beyond that.

Donovan's grin was big and bright as he looked around and Naomi felt herself smiling in return. She hadn't realized until that moment, but every time she saw Donovan in the petting zoo he was smiling. The multitude of small animals here were far more common than the animals he typically associated with, but he always seemed happy when he was in the ragtag zoo.

He was very rarely called to the petting zoo for any kind of actual emergency. Everything that happened with these animals was handled easily by Griffin or one of the other veterinarians or any of the many Landry boys who were used to being around the menagerie. But Donovan made a point of stopping by to see the animals often and was definitely not above helping with their feeding and general care.

Naomi knew he was happy whenever he was around any animal, but the contrast between things like black bears and potbellied pigs was stark now that Brent and Rachel were there observing.

"Jordan?" Donovan called.

"Over here!" they heard Jordan answer.

They rounded one end of a stall to find Jordan standing with one of the goats between her knees, trying to wrestle a white plastic cylinder off of his head.

She looked up at them with clear relief.

She also had spectators.

"Sleepy got his head stuck in the chicken feeder somehow," Jordan said. She was clearly gritting her teeth. "Griffin's on a call outside of town, Tori has Ella at some play date, and I didn't want Jill down here wrestling goats while she's so big with those twins."

Donovan shook his head, striding forward. "No problem." He grabbed onto the other end of the plastic cylinder and looked into it. "How did you do this, buddy?" he asked the goat.

The goat had gotten his head into the end of the cylinder, but his horns were keeping him from getting back out.

"I tried pulling, I even used vegetable oil to try to grease it," Jordan said. "I think we're gonna have to cut it off. But I definitely need an extra pair of hands for that." She glanced around. "And that would definitely seem less traumatic for all of these people." She lowered her voice. "You know what drama queens these goats are."

Naomi laughed. They definitely were.

Donovan nodded. "We're going to ruin this feeder."

"I'm not worried about that."

Within ten minutes, Donovan had cut through the hard thick plastic and had peeled the cylinder from around the goat's head and neck. The little crowd cheered and the goat bleated—though it was hard to tell if it was "thanks" or "about damned time".

Donovan examined the goat for any abrasions or cuts, but the animal seemed fine, if annoyed at having been manhandled. Jordan patted the goat's rump and it went running off to join its friends.

Donovan straightened and wiped his hands on his jeans, grinning.

Naomi looked over at Brent and Rachel. She realized they hadn't been filming.

Frowning, she crossed to them. "Is everything okay?"

Rachel looked at her. "Sure."

"You didn't film any of that."

Brent snorted. "It was more goats. That wasn't exactly a heart pounding rescue."

He had a point, of course, but Naomi couldn't ignore the flicker of annoyance she felt. She'd seen it in Donovan as well. These animals weren't exotic, and certainly this particular instance had not been at all life-threatening for anyone, but it was still part of the everyday life of taking care of the animals in this small town. "Well, we never know when a situation could turn from seemingly easy and routine into something more dangerous."

They both shrugged. "And you weren't the one helping him," Rachel said. "So we couldn't even build on the relationship angle."

Ah, right. Naomi glanced at Donovan. She was very used to standing back and watching him do his thing, but she was going to have to remember that they were supposed to be flirting and building an on-screen relationship every time they went out together.

Damn, being "on" like this was exhausting. How had she forgotten that?

She swallowed. Okay, she could do this. Getting close to him was no hardship. She had no trouble acting attracted to the guy.

Naomi looked around.

It was general anarchy in the barn. The goats weren't the only animals inside of course. The doors were wide open so animals were wandering—or running at full speed, or meandering, or waddling, or trotting—in and out in all directions. So were the people.

There were some wooden cut-outs of various animals set up sporadically through the barn where kids could pose to get their photos taken. Overhead hung a paper banner that declared it to be Stan the goat's birthday. There were bits of streamers and balloons hanging along the rafters on either side of the banner.

Stan himself was standing off to one side, minding his own business. His actual name was Satan because he could be a real dick. But the Landry ladies had insisted Satan was a mean name and had shortened it to Stan. Which was also more appropriate for a banner hanging in a public space with kids, Naomi supposed.

As Naomi studied the banner and balloons, an idea came to her. That she immediately hated.

But it would work. She knew television. She knew what would play well on the screen.

Okay, she could fix this too-boring-to-even-pull-a-camera-out-for situation. Probably.

She and Donovan were supposed to have talked about what

they were going to script for the relationship portion of the show. They hadn't spent a lot of time doing that, so she was going to have to take the lead here.

They couldn't set up the animal rescues, but they could set up *some* of what happened on camera. And, she reminded herself, it wouldn't be entirely fake. The feelings between them were real enough. The chemistry was real. The circumstances were just going to have to be massaged a little.

"You're going to want to have the cameras on for this next part," she told Brent and Rachel as she started across the barn.

She already hated this idea so much.

It was going to be so stupid. This was completely out of character for her.

But they had to make the show work.

Naomi kept telling herself that as she picked up an abandoned half-empty cup of blue raspberry slushy—which was absolutely not allowed in the animal areas and needed to be picked up anyway—from the top of a wooden barrel and headed for the far darkened corner of the barn.

She had no idea if Donovan noticed. She was hoping he was still in conversation with Jordan and distracted by all of the animals.

This is such a bad idea, this is such a bad idea, this is such a bad idea.

Naomi climbed the built-in wooden ladder that would take her from the ground to the loft overhead where they stored the additional animal feed and other supplies. When she was in the loft, still balancing the half empty blue slushy, she made her way to the wooden beams that crossed over the main part of the barn. She looked down and saw that Brent and Rachel were in fact filming. Donovan, however, was kneeling and talking to a little boy at the moment.

Awesome. Donovan had no idea what Naomi was doing. This was perfect.

There was a streamer caught on a nail on one of the beams. They always did a mass cleanup after events in the barn, of course, but it was too good a prop for her at this moment. Besides, the viewers wouldn't care about *why* she was doing this when they saw the end result.

Holding the blue slushy in one hand and bracing her other hand against the wall she inched out along the rafters until she was directly over Donovan's head. She was only about ten feet in the air. That wasn't enough to get *really* hurt if she fell. Probably.

But the whole idea here was to not get hurt at all. Because Donovan was down there to save her.

Taking a deep breath, she stepped out onto the rafter and leaned over to grab the streamer, loosening it from the nail. But as she bent, she tipped the blue slushy. The melted-yet-still-pretty-cold blue liquid hit Donovan on the shoulder and splashed down the side and front of his shirt.

Jordan gasped, and Donovan leapt to his feet, swearing in spite of the little boy standing next to him.

Oops.

He immediately looked up and at that moment, Naomi grabbed the rafter and pretended to slip so that she was dangling just over his head.

"Naomi!" he yelled.

Everyone in the barn gasped and looked up.

"Donovan!" Naomi cried in a very believable oh-my-god-help-me tone, if she did say so herself.

She couldn't believe she was doing this. She wasn't exactly the damsel in distress type anyway and putting herself into that situation was making her feel like an idiot.

Still, she knew that Brent and Rachel were filming and it was definitely getting the attention she'd intended. This show would mean Donovan would have fulfilling work and could stay in Autre. That was worth feeling foolish. And possibly landing on her ass in front of a crowd of people and a big online audience. But she really hoped it didn't come to that.

"Naomi! What the hell?" Donovan bellowed from below.

"Donovan, I slipped!"

"Are you all right?"

"Yes." She took a deep breath, wincing as she said, "just scared."

"I'm right here," he told her. "I've got you."

"I don't know what to do," she said. What she could do, was drop down to the floor from this height. Though she might sprain an ankle, she would certainly live to tell the tale.

"Just let go, I've got you."

She rolled her eyes. This was going exactly the way she'd intended. She should be a director, not an actor.

"I don't know if I can." She made her voice shake just a little.

"You can do this, I'm right here."

God, he was such a good guy. She really didn't need to set him up like this.

It's for the show, it's for the show, it's for the show.

Naomi took a deep breath, peeled her fingers off of the rafter, and let herself fall.

Sure enough, Donovan caught her in his arms easily.

"I've got you," he told her.

Another collective gasp went up around them.

Well, holy shit. That had been pretty damned chivalrous, she had to admit.

"I'm good. Thank you," Naomi told him, looking up into his face and working to be sure she looked properly adoring.

Jordan was beside them a second later, totally ruining the five seconds of staring into each other's eyes Naomi had planned.

"What the hell were you doing up there?" Jordan demanded.

"There was a streamer stuck up there and I didn't want it to fall and have one of the goats eat it," Naomi said.

"There are still a ton of streamers up there!" Jordan exclaimed.

"This one was loose. I was sure it was going to fall." Naomi frowned, wanting her friend to really look at her and catch on that Naomi had been plotting.

But Jordan was looking at the streamers. "We could have gotten a *ladder*. Or I could have had Mitch climb up there later or something."

"I'm perfectly capable of climbing up there to pull down a streamer," Naomi told her with a frown.

Donovan was still holding her, Naomi noted. She was also aware in her peripheral vision of Brent and Rachel recording the entire exchange.

"Are you capable of that?" Jordan asked her dryly.

Naomi sighed. "I slipped."

"Because you were carrying a blue slushy at the time you were climbing up into the rafters?" Jordan asked her.

"The slushy was sitting on the barrel. Those aren't supposed to be in the animal areas. I didn't want it to spill or have one of the animals find it," Naomi told her.

"Yeah, we wouldn't want that to spill all over the place." Jordan's sarcasm was thick as she pointedly looked at Donovan covered in blue raspberry syrup, then looked down at the floor around them.

Naomi wiggled a little and Donovan finally let her feet swing to the floor though he did let her slide down his body a little slower than was probably necessary. Their eyes met, and for just a moment, she noticed the heat as well as just a flicker of suspicion.

Naomi looked around at the floor, as well as down at her own clothes that were now also covered in slush since being up against Donovan.

"Yeah, we should help clean this up before one of the goats decides to take a taste," she said as she unbuttoned her fitted short-sleeved button up she was wearing and shrugged out of it, leaving her in a spaghetti-strap tank and khaki shorts. She dropped her outer shirt onto the floor to help mop up the blue raspberry.

She realized that shirt was now a loss, but it was worth it when she noticed the way Donovan was taking in the sight of her in the fitted tank.

She was sure that was going to translate well to film as well.

His gaze roamed over her from her face to her waist, lingering on her breasts. Then, with his gaze locked on hers, he reached for the bottom of his shirt and he did exactly as she'd hoped he would. He stripped his shirt off as well and dropped it on the floor.

It was almost as if they'd scripted *this*. He seemed to remember her telling him that viewers liked when he was shirt-less on his show because he didn't appear to be a bit self-conscious as he started to mop up the rest of the blue slushy with his Boys of the Bayou Gone Wild shirt.

She took her time cataloging the hard contours of his shoulders, tanned chest, and abs as well as the tiger tattoo she was so fond of. He seemed to be pausing just for her inspection in fact.

Naomi didn't glance in Brent and Rachel's direction. She had to trust that they knew how to get the right shot. Though she wasn't sure if they were going to focus on her earnest atten-tion or the very hot *object* of her intense study.

Jordan, however, was definitely watching them both. "What the hell is going on? Why are people stripping in my barn?"

Naomi finally pulled her eyes from Donovan and looked at one of her best friends. "What do you mean? We're cleaning up."

"You're standing in the middle of a goat barn, half-naked,

and smelling like blue raspberry after falling from the ceiling. None of this makes any sense."

"It's fine," Naomi told her, widening her eyes in the universal sign for "drop it".

Jordan narrowed her eyes. "Seriously. This isn't normal for you at all. You never get messy and...dangerous like this."

"This wasn't *dangerous*," Naomi said. She tried the knock-it-off look again. "And I get messy."

Jordan shook her head. "You're always the one handing out wet wipes." She looked around. "Where's your purse?"

The magical back-pack purse with everything in it—including wet wipes—was in Donovan's truck. Huh. Naomi had just realized that. Why had she left her purse in Donovan's truck? Did that mean that she felt more capable of handling whatever was going to happen outside of the truck when she was with him...

Okay *that* was crazy. What was she doing getting philosophical like this? This was a staged, last-minute, I-have-to-do-something set-up scenario.

"It's in the truck," Naomi said. "No big deal. I can go get it." Not having it with her didn't mean anything. It was like forty feet away. If someone *needed* a wet wipe she could easily get one.

She avoided looking at the blue raspberry mess. No one *needed* a wet wipe, dammit. Certainly not literally. A wet wipe wouldn't do any good here. But also not metaphorically. Stripping her shirt off was doing a fine job of mopping up the mess. Was it more spontaneous and maybe more risque? Okay *maybe*. She wasn't *naked*. Or even half-naked. But sure, taking her shirt off was not in character. Sure, she *typically* would have pulled out a wet wipe. That would have been in the purse that she would have had *right there with her*. But none of this really *meant* anything.

Probably.

"This is *really* not normal," Jordan said, looking at Naomi as if she thought her friend had possibly been possessed. "You even climbing up that ladder is crazy."

"You're one to talk about crazy," Donovan said teasing. "You went to Vegas with one guy and came home married to another one."

Thank you, Donovan, Naomi thought as he now came to her rescue again, though in a whole new way.

Jordan pressed her lips together as if biting back a retort.

Donovan grinned. "Exactly."

She loved that Donovan got along so well with her friends.

That thought hit her before she could prepare for it. Or avoid it.

But she really did. He'd come into her life and blended seamlessly. No, it hadn't been as a boyfriend but that almost made it better, didn't it? He was a friend first. He was a part of her circle first. The relationship and the love came next...

Dammit. What was she doing?

They *were* in the middle of a goat barn, half-naked, smelling like blue raspberry with a *camera rolling*. This was all a stupid staged oh-aren't-they-cute chance for any viewers to think that they should be a couple. This wasn't supposed to result in anything meaningful. Sure, Donovan without his shirt on caused her some very real lust but this wasn't supposed to be causing her real *feelings*.

Jordan shook her head. "Something is going on."

"It's nothing to worry about," Donovan told her, meeting Naomi's eyes again and giving her a wink.

"Fine," Jordan said. "But surely, by now, you realize that in Autre the word 'secret' is simply another term for 'the evening news'."

Donovan laughed and Naomi felt her stomach flip.

So he was onto her, as was Jordan, clearly. But that didn't

matter. They could all be in on this. It was the people on the other side of the camera that was pointed at them that needed to believe this was real.

Naomi did glance over now. Sure enough, Brent and Rachel were recording.

Obviously some of this was going to need editing. But the stupid scene of her falling into Donovan's arms and then him stripping his shirt off were now on camera. That was the important part.

They finished cleaning up the barn and Jordan called out, "We *will* talk later," after them as they headed out to the trucks.

Naomi just winced. She could let Jordan and the rest of their friends in on the whole fake relationship thing but that wouldn't make climbing into the rafters after a stray streamer and "falling" out of them any less stupid.

She was certain saying it all out loud would make it so much more, in fact.

But Rachel seemed pleased when she said, "We're going to get some lunch and go over some notes and things. Give us a call if anything comes up."

"Will do," Donovan told her.

Donovan and Naomi watched them drive off. But when Naomi started toward his truck, Donovan reached out and caught her wrist, tugging her back and around to face him.

"So you staged all of that."

It was ridiculous to lie to him. "Yeah."

"Because they were bored?"

"Yeah."

"Don't do that again."

She smiled. "We're probably going to have to. But we should sit down and talk about it ahead of time."

"I don't like you taking risks like that."

His tone was gruff and his protectiveness made a ribbon of

pleasure wind through her belly, but she kept her tone light. "Oh, come on, that wasn't that dangerous."

"Then why is my heart still hammering?"

D onovan watched Naomi wet her lips.

And seemingly contemplate an answer to his question. But he thought she actually knew the answer. She was just trying to decide if she should say it out loud.

She should definitely say it out loud.

He moved a little closer. "Naomi? Do you know why my heart is still hammering so hard?"

"Maybe."

Uh-huh. "Is it the same reason that you always get so worried when I do something dangerous?"

"Probably."

"And why is that?" he prompted.

"Because I'm a very kind and caring person."

His lips curled. "Yes, you are. But I don't think that's what it is."

"You're not kind and caring?"

"I am kind and caring. To and for all kinds of people and things. But I've never felt like *this* for anyone else before."

He saw the flicker of emotion in her eyes.

"Really?"

"Really." He stepped even closer. "I think my heart was hammering so hard because watching the woman I'm falling in love with tumble from the ceiling and almost hit the floor was terrifying."

Her eyes widened and her mouth fell open.

He chuckled softly and lifted a finger to her chin, closing her mouth. "You're not *that* surprised."

She swallowed. "I am surprised."

"You can't be. Because what I'm feeling is what you feel when you see me taking risks."

"You think I'm..." She swallowed. "...falling in love with you?"

"I do. That didn't occur to me before, but when we were in Alabama, plenty of people were taking risks just like I do—"

"No one takes risks like you do, Donovan."

"See, it seems that way to you, because you're in love with me."

He really loved saying those words. Because the more he said it, the more *he* believed it. Just as he knew all of his feelings were new and unique to Naomi, he realized the way she acted was only for him.

"No one else was underneath the collapsed swimming pool with power tools coming at his head," she pointed out.

"If I hadn't been there, someone else would've done that."

She opened her mouth as if to respond but then seemed to think about what he'd just said. She frowned. Finally, she admitted, "I don't know if they would've done it exactly like you did. But other people would've tried."

"And you wouldn't have felt the way you did watching it."

"I would've been *concerned*. It probably would've been Fiona crawling under there and I would've been worried," Naomi told him.

"Yes. And, if Jordan had been climbing around in the rafters and fallen, I would've tried to catch her too. But I wouldn't have felt the same flash of holy-shit-I-have-to-do-whatever-I-can-to-make-sure-she's-okay-no-matter-what that I do with you."

She seemed to be mulling that over.

"But that's weird, right?" she finally asked. "That we can worry about other people but not worry about them in the same way that we do each other?"

He ran his thumb along her jaw line, staring into her eyes. He shook his head slowly. "Not weird."

"No? Why?"

"Because you're mine."

She sucked in a little breath. She seemed surprised. But only for a second. Donovan's heart turned over in his chest and thumped hard against his ribs as she slowly nodded.

"Yeah." She took a deep breath and nodded again. "You're mine." She seemed to be testing those words out. But after she said them out loud, she smiled.

Those two words made something inside him crack open. It was almost painful. But it was so fucking good too. It felt as if he'd been trying to keep something together, hold something tight so it wouldn't hurt, and now, with this woman, he couldn't anymore. He had to open it up. And it was a damned relief once it happened.

He moved his hand to the back of her neck and brought her in close.

"That's why ever since you got here, I've had this urge to make sure you're okay," she said, her breath warm on his lips. "Safe and happy and...fed...and just whatever you need. It's like I want everyone else to be okay too, but I have this *need* to actually be the one making it happen for *you*."

Nothing had ever made more sense to him in his life.

"Exactly." He started to lean in, intending to kiss her.

But she added softly, "And it's especially important to me that you, more than anyone else, have all ten of your fingers intact."

His grin was wide just before he sealed his mouth over hers.

Naomi leaned into him immediately, wrapping her arms around his neck and arching closer. His hand settled on her hips, and he drew her up against him. He *needed* her. He'd been too long without touching her and tasting her. He kissed her long and deep. Hungrily. Drinking her in now that he'd realized why he felt all the things he did.

He hadn't had a chance to *really* kiss her since they'd

returned from Alabama. They'd been busy with the animals and having Rachel and Brent following them around.

Now, though, it was just the two of them and he was going to take full advantage.

Lifting his head he asked, "What are you doing the rest of the day?"

"We should probably script what's going to happen with the show."

"What I heard there was that you were going to spend the rest of the day with me."

She smiled. "Yes, that's what I said." She paused. "Do you still have the air mattress in the back of your truck?"

His whole body heated instantly, and he gave a little groan as his fingers curled into her hips. "Yes, I do."

"Excellent answer."

"Naomi."

"Yes, Donovan?"

"I'm in love with you." He needed to say those words out loud very clearly in that moment.

Her eyes widened. "Good."

"Just so you know that."

"I figured the *you're mine* thing implied that, but I like hearing it word for word. By the way," she added. "I'm in love with you too."

His grip on her tightened as his desire intensified and he had to clear his throat before he answered. "Awesome. I just wanted those soft, sweet emotions out there so when I start talking dirty, you know that there's more underneath it."

She gave a little shiver of delight. "Soft, sweet emotions noted and dirty talk highly encouraged."

"Excellent. Then get your gorgeous ass in my truck because I need my face between your legs in the next ten minutes."

She gasped, then laughed, then pushed him back and rounded his truck quickly to climb up into the passenger side.

Feeling an odd combination of lust and happiness, Donovan headed for the driver's side.

As they drove to a spot he knew of down by the bayou, Naomi said, "We really should talk about how we're going to handle our relationship for the show."

"Okay."

She pulled a notebook and pen out of her purse.

Donovan shook his head with a smile. That purse.

"The flirting has been good. But we've always been good at that." She shot him a grin. "And you talking me through what you're doing on the animal rescues and me asking you questions about the animals as we go is great," she said. "It's the perfect way to educate people watching while also building our relationship. We have lots of time together and we're working side by side."

She jotted something down in the notebook. "And then there are the moments when you get to be protective, like when we ran across the snake and you stepped in front of me to deal with it—even though, I totally know how to handle a cottonmouth, thank you very much."

"You shouldn't have to play damsel in distress."

"Oh right now, to get this picked up, it's fine. People love that stuff. As long as we make it light-hearted, and I can point out that I've probably run across more cottonmouths than you have and you just can't help your heroic ways."

She was the least damsel in distress woman he'd ever met. He kind of hated the idea of making it seem that she *needed* him.

She looked over at him. "We should definitely include more moments like the other day when you wiped the mud off my cheek. Those play as really sweet, romantic moments on camera."

"I didn't do that for the camera."

She gave him a soft smile. "I know."

Donovan was listening. He really was. She'd said everything was good so far. She said everything they'd been doing was working. But he was having a hard time keeping his mind from wandering to wishing he had his own place right now.

He would love to take her back to his bedroom and spread her out on his bed and keep her there all day. He'd make her dinner tonight and then they'd cuddle up on the couch and watch a movie later, and then have more sweet, hot sex before falling asleep in one another's arms and spending the night together.

He hadn't done any of that with a woman before. Ever. When he did hook up with women it was for a quick rendezvous only. It was very often in hotel rooms when he was traveling, though occasionally it would be in the woman's apartment or house if she was local.

But he'd never cooked for a woman, and he'd never cuddled on the couch watching a movie. Those were relationship things, and he'd avoided those at all costs.

Now, he wanted them, and he had no way of giving them to Naomi. He was still staying with Griffin and Charlie because his time in Autre had been temporary. Or so he'd thought.

"Don't you think?"

He glanced over at her. He'd missed what she'd just said. He should just say yes. In his experience, it was pretty safe to always say yes to whatever Naomi had come up with, but he decided to be honest with her right now.

"Sorry, I was thinking about how much I wish I had a house where we could spend the rest of the day and night together."

He'd clearly taken her aback.

"Well, as nice as that sounds, it would definitely make it difficult to pretend that this is just the start of a casual, short-term relationship."

He turned onto the narrow dirt road that would lead them down to the water. The ground got marshy long before the actual flowing water of the bayou but there were a few areas of higher ground that looked out over the water that served as great places to watch the sunset. And do some heavy petting, as Ellie Landry would say.

"I don't want this to be casual or short-term," Donovan told her.

"I know. I don't either. So I really want this TV show to go well. To be picked up so you can stay."

He reached across the seat and took her hand lacing her fingers together. "I can stay anyway."

"But I want you to have what you want," Naomi went on. "The show would mean that you could stay and not..."

"Not what?"

She blew out a breath. "Regret it eventually."

He pulled the truck to a stop, threw it into park, and turned to face her. "I am not going to regret being here with you. With everyone. This is the first place I've felt like I actually have a home. I have a family here. I *want* to stay."

"I know." Her voice was thick. "But you have a passion and an incredible ability to educate other people and make them care about things in a way that most people can't. You have to do that. The animals need you to do that. If the show doesn't grab the investors' interest, you *have* to go to the Galapagos Islands. That's a huge opportunity."

He stared at her. He wasn't sure he'd ever had anyone believe in him and push him the way Naomi did. He'd always been pushing himself, driven by a need to make up for Griffin's sacrifices for him.

This felt different.

"Will you—"

The *wait for me if I leave* was interrupted by his phone ringing.

Not the goat phone this time. His real phone. And it was the ringtone for Bailey Wilcox, with Louisiana's Department of

Wildlife and Fisheries. That meant there was a ninety-seven percent chance that she had an animal in need.

Dammit.

"Hold on. We're not done with this."

Naomi simply nodded. She knew that ring tone.

Donovan answered the call. "Hey, Bailey."

"Hey. I've got a bobcat stuck in a tree with burned paws and possible other injuries," she said without preamble.

"*Burned?* How?" He put the phone on speaker and shifted the truck back into drive.

Naomi reached for her seat belt and he took a second to appreciate how she was always willing to just roll with whatever came their way.

"Some stupid teenagers were out here messing around and started a campfire," Bailey said. "It got out of their control and spread."

"Oh, fuck." Donovan turned out onto the main road. "But everything's so wet yet from the storm. Is it bad?"

"Worse than it should be." Bailey sounded pissed. "But yeah, the rain definitely helped. We needed firefighters from New Orleans though because it was too big for just Michael and J.D. alone. It's mostly under control now and we don't think there are too many wildlife issues. Someone spotted the cat just a few minutes ago. He's pretty high up in the tree, but even with binoculars I can see some injuries."

"Okay, on my way."

She gave him the location and he disconnected and looked at Naomi. "Well, you can call Rachel and Brent. At least they'll really like this."

"I didn't even think of them." Naomi pulled out her phone. "So glad to have a silver lining," she muttered.

"Hey." He waited for her to look at him as she lifted the phone to her ear. "You okay?"

"I just hate that this will get them excited, you know? Like they're vultures just sitting around waiting for bad things to happen to animals."

"Yeah."

"But we can definitely use this to make a point about how being irresponsible with campfires can impact wildlife right?"

Sure. That mattered. But he hated it too. "Right."

13

The scene was, of course, chaotic even with the fire already being controlled. There were three fire trucks and two crews along with the Autre ambulance, Zander's car, and several people just curious about what was going on.

"What are you doing here?" Michael asked Naomi when he saw her.

"Donovan was called for a stranded bobcat."

Michael looked at Donovan. "You always have to bring her along?"

Donovan looked at her, then at her brother, and shrugged. "Yeah."

"She needs to film *every* single thing you do?"

Naomi frowned. "I'm not filming. I'm here to help."

"You're not a firefighter or a wildlife expert."

Naomi took a deep breath. Her brother was stressed. And probably pissed. Teenagers had set a fire. That was a bad situation no matter how quickly it had been handled. And it could have been much worse. No doubt he was holding himself back from yelling at the kids, or their parents, or at least stomping over there and making sure Zander yelled at them. Which Zander wouldn't do.

Zander Landry certainly had a temper, but he handled his police work with a laid-back air that almost seemed indifferent at times. That wasn't true, of course, and everyone here knew that, including Michael. But often Zander's more passionate friends and family members wished he'd show a little more emotion.

"Don't worry about me. I'm fine," Naomi told her brother. "You go do your thing."

"Well, it's my job to worry about everyone on the scene," Michael told her crossly. "So unless you're going to go back to the truck and just sit there, I'm going to worry."

"She's very capable, Michael," Donovan said. "She's smart and is here for the right reasons."

"And I'm going to be coming to more of these scenes," Naomi said. "So get used to it."

"I know you think this is exciting to watch, but—"

"I'm getting my wildlife rehabilitation permit. I'm going to be doing this *with* Donovan, not just watching."

"You are?"

Naomi turned to Donovan. She hadn't told him yet, but it seemed like the natural next step. "I am. If you'll write me a letter of recommendation. I need one from a permitted Wildlife Rehabilitator and one from a veterinarian. I figure I've got the vet covered with Tori or Jill or Griffin. I just need you. And to take the course and pass the test. I was going to tell you about it later, but...yeah. I really want to do this."

"Okay." He looked a little stunned.

"Really? You'll write me a recommendation?"

"Sure."

"Okay, dammit. I can't do this right now," Michael said.

"You don't have to do this at all," Naomi told him. "This is happening."

Michael frowned at Donovan. "I blame you for this."

"I'm okay with that."

Naomi felt her stomach flip at the look in Donovan's eyes. It was pride and admiration. She knew that she didn't have to take risks like this for Donovan to like her or want her or even to date her. But the fact that he'd helped her find this passion mattered. And it was a passion they could share. That was a big deal. A few months ago, she would have never believed she'd want to be the one getting dirty and possibly bit, scratched, or stung. She'd always known it was important work, but she'd never thought she could actually do it. Her past work had always been with very safe animals in very controlled environments.

With Donovan, things were not safe. It felt very out of control at times.

And she'd never felt more alive and more fulfilled by her work.

"Hey, Donovan. Hey, Naomi." Caleb Moreau, a firefighter from New Orleans and a friend of the Landry boys, strode toward them.

Naomi smiled at him and James Reynaud, the firefighter beside him. "Hi, guys."

"Hey, Caleb. James." Donovan shook both their hands.

"What are you two doing out here?" James asked. "Join the fire department?"

"There's a cat in a tree and I guess the old stereotype that firefighters get those down isn't true," Donovan said.

Caleb chuckled. "You're kiddin'."

Donovan grinned. "It's a bobcat. Probably trying to get away from the fire. Need to bring him down and treat some burns."

Caleb gave Donovan a look. "No shit."

"Yep." Donovan shrugged.

"I've carried a couple of humans who tried to bite me out of burning buildings, but never a wildcat," James said.

"You've rescued biting humans?" Naomi asked.

"One was high," James said with a nod. "But one was just a mean old man."

Naomi laughed.

"So we're okay to go in? Bailey said the cat was on the west side of everything," Donovan said.

"Yeah, you should be okay. But we can head in that direction with you and check it out," Caleb told him.

"Thanks, man."

Naomi reached out and caught Donovan's arm as he started to follow the two firefighters. "I really hate to say this, but we should probably wait for Brent and Rachel."

Donovan grimaced. "Shit. It's bad enough that we're going to have to deal with going into the fire, but taking two extra people in is a pain in the ass."

"But we're not going *into* the fire," Naomi said. "We're going to wait for the all clear from Caleb and James." She peered at him. "Right, Donovan?"

"We'll wait until it's safe enough for me to go."

"Donovan, you were not going into a still active fire."

"I'm not going to walk through flames, no, but the longer we wait, the better the chance the cat gets down and heads off somewhere on his own and I won't be able to treat him."

Naomi knew he had a point, but her heart was hammering. She hated the idea of him going in if it wasn't entirely safe. "So what's your plan here?"

"I'll tranquilize it first, but I'll have to get close enough to keep it from falling from the tree once it goes under," Donovan said.

She swallowed. Then took a deep breath. "Okay, I'm here to help." She spread her arms. "Show me what to do. I need to learn."

Donovan stopped and looked down at her with a frown. "You wait for Rachel and Brent."

"Hi, guys!"

He sighed and Naomi couldn't help but grin as Rachel and Brent walked up.

"Okay, now what?" she asked.

"I'd rather you didn't come," he told her.

"Too bad."

"I don't like it."

The irony did not escape Naomi. The fact that they'd gone from *her* worrying about *him* and trying to get him to be more careful to him now not liking her doing dangerous things in the name of wildlife rescue, would've been funny if it wasn't annoying. And taking up time.

"Well, if you didn't want me to do this then you shouldn't have shown me how important it is." She stepped around him and started after Caleb and James. "Come on, Brent and Rachel. We've even got hot firefighters for you in this one."

"Awesome," Rachel said.

Yeah, that's what Naomi figured she'd say.

"You coming, Donovan?" Brent asked. "We kind of need you if we're filming for the show."

Naomi heard Donovan's heavy sigh.

"Yeah. I'm coming."

Twenty minutes later, Naomi found herself up in the tree, a few branches below Donovan, extending a long stick with a syringe on the end.

"Okay, I'm going to keep his attention on me, hopefully," Donovan said. "You get that in his flank. I'll be in position to reach him—or catch him—when he starts to relax."

Naomi bit her lip but nodded. The cat was clearly scared and pissed off, feeling cornered, without anywhere to go. Caleb and James were on the ground keeping the cat from feeling safe to jump down. He'd gone about as high in the tree as he could and Naomi and Donovan were blocking his way back down and over to the next biggest branch. That didn't, of course, mean that he wouldn't lunge or take a swipe at the nearest threat—Donovan—though.

But an hour and half later they had the bobcat sedated, down from the tree, and back at the rehab facility. His paws were bandaged and he was comfortable in a pen where he'd stay a few days before being released. The fire was completely out and the teens who had started the whole mess were down at the police station with their parents and Zander.

After all of that, Naomi, Donovan, Rachel, and Brent stood in the middle of the main portion of the rehabilitation facility.

"So...I guess that's it," Naomi said, feeling like there should be a more exciting way to wrap it all up.

"Yeah, I need to get up to the penguin enclosure," Donovan said. "But it's just a regular weighing and feeding. You've already got that footage." He didn't roll his eyes but Naomi could hear the eye roll in his voice.

"Yeah, guess we'll head back to the motel to go over the footage from the fire." Brent and Rachel started for the door.

And Naomi just stood, watching them all go.

She was still amped up from the adrenaline and wanted to *do* something.

But she didn't have anything *to* do.

So she went home to help her grandmother make dinner.

"What is wrong with you, girl?"

Naomi blinked and looked at her grandmother. "What?"

Rosalie moved in beside her at the stove, bumping Naomi out of the way with her hip. "This is poulet aux noix. You've made this a million times. You could do this in your sleep."

Naomi looked at the stove top. Rosalie was right. So what was the problem?

But it quickly became clear that Naomi had screwed the dish up.

She ran a hand over her forehead. "I don't know. Just a lot on my mind. We had a big rescue today. There was a fire. And there are these people in town who are demanding a lot of attention and energy. And..."

"It's that boy."

Naomi lifted her gaze to her grandfather who was sitting at the little table by the window with her nephew, Andre. "What?"

"It's not the animals or the fire or anything else. You handle all kinds of things all the time. You take everything in stride. There's only one thing that could throw a woman like you off kilter," Armand said. He winked. "It's the boy."

Rosalie nodded. "Yes, it's the boy."

"What boy?" Naomi asked, but she knew exactly who they were talking about.

But how did *they* know who they were talking about?

"Donovan," Armand said with a smile. "You're in love with him."

Naomi stared at her grandfather. "What? I am..."

Her first reaction was, of course, to deny it. But she couldn't get the words out.

That was new. She downplayed or flat out kept her relationships from her family all the time. But here, right now in this moment, she couldn't bring herself to deny her feelings for Donovan.

She took a deep breath and nodded. "I am."

Rosalie and Armand shared a smile, then looked at her.

"As you should be. He's wonderful." Rosalie told her.

"How did you know?" Naomi asked her grandfather.

"I know you. I've seen you with him. It's obvious."

"And you kissed him," Andre added with a grin.

"How do you know that?" Naomi asked, planting a hand on her hip.

Rosalie laughed. "Everyone knows. We saw it on the internet. Andre showed me."

Naomi looked at Andre. "You saw the kiss?"

Andre grinned at her. "*Everyone's* seen the kisses, Naomi."

Rosalie made a humming sound. "It was a good kiss, cher."

Naomi sighed. There was no point in denying that. "It was a good kiss." Then she frowned and looked at Andre. "The *kisses*? Do you mean more than one?"

"*Both* of them!" her nephew said, giggling. "The one by his truck—"

"The yummy one," Rosalie interjected.

"And the one by his truck again."

She frowned. "Which one?"

Andre shrugged. "Just today I think."

Naomi straightened quickly. They'd kissed by his truck before they'd driven to the bayou. Before Bailey had called about the bobcat. "There's a video from today? Before the fire?"

"It's just a photo," Andre said. "But yeah, I think today."

Well, where the hell had *that* come from?

"Kissing him is a *very* good idea," Rosalie told her. "Keep doing that."

Okay, it was creepy that there was a photo of them kissing when she'd thought they were alone, but were they *ever* really alone? They'd been outside of Ellie's. In broad daylight. She should have known better.

Naomi sighed. "I think I can do that." She gave her grandmother a grin. "He is a good man. And yes, I am in love with him. He says he feels the same way."

Armand clapped his hands together. "Excellent. Then what are you doing here having dinner with us and not him?"

Naomi suddenly wanted Donovan here. "I'll call him to come over."

She'd only done that once before. The one boyfriend who'd

gotten serious before he decided to take the job out of town had come over one evening to meet her family.

Of course, Donovan already knew them. But it would be symbolic to them and to him if she invited him over to dinner here in her grandmother's house.

"Don't be ridiculous," Rosalie said. "You don't need to share him with us. We know him. He knows my griot. Go. Be with him."

Naomi couldn't believe this. She looked at her grandmother. "You *don't* want him here?"

"Of course I do. On my birthday. On *his* birthday. And Christmas. And Sunday after church. And to play checkers with your grandfather."

"And Warriors of Easton with me!" Andre said.

Naomi smiled even as she rolled her eyes. Andre had become fast friends with Henry McCaffery and now played Henry's favorite video game almost constantly.

"That too," Rosalie agreed. "And when I need heavy boxes down from the attic and Michael's at work. And when there's a family of possums camping out under my front porch. And when he's in need of some doukounou."

"Which will be often," Armand inputted.

"Right," Rosalie said, pointing her spoon at her husband. "But tonight?" she asked Naomi. "No. You need time with him alone."

Naomi's throat had tightened when her grandmother said that Donovan should be here on *his* birthday. Yes. He should. He deserved to have a big family gathering and people who loved him celebrating that. Had he had a birthday party in all the years since his parents had died? Suddenly she needed to know that. And needed to throw him a huge party on his next one.

She studied her grandparents. Her mom and dad would be over for dinner soon. Michael would stop by as well. This was their usual. She'd kept her past boyfriends away from all of this because...it had felt like too much involvement. Too many people getting too many feelings mixed up. But maybe she'd underestimated her family. Maybe she hadn't needed to be quite so stringent about the boundaries between her romantic relationships and her family and friends.

Or maybe Donovan had just changed her perspective on everything.

Or maybe Donovan was just the first that she *actually* wanted involved with the rest of her life.

Because she definitely wanted this *for* Donovan. He'd been alone for so long. He needed to have people in his life, feeling things for him, mixed up in the things he was doing, giving him their opinions—for better or worse—because they cared.

And yes, throwing him parties.

But right now? Yes, she absolutely wanted him to herself. Not because she wanted to keep him away from all of this but because...she wanted him very, very involved in all of this. And she needed to tell him that. While they were naked. After a lot more kissing.

She leaned in and bussed her grandmother's cheek. "Thank you."

"We won't wait up," Rosalie said with a wink.

Naomi gave her a grin and started for the door with a plan for how to actually get alone time with Donovan.

It was a good thing she'd gotten comfortable climbing around on roofs.

Donovan heard the tapping on his window but it took him a second to realize that it wasn't a branch or even a bird. Though why a bird would have been tapping on his window he didn't know.

He got up from the bed where he'd been reclined reading. He pulled back the curtain. Then immediately shoved the window up.

"What the hell are you doing?" he asked Naomi. He removed the screen and reached through the window, wrapping a hand around her upper arm and tugging her inside.

She laughed as she tumbled over the windowsill and up against his chest. "Well, that wasn't much more graceful than when I went through the window in Mobile."

He shook his head and wrapped one arm around her while he reached to push the window back down. "Climbing on roofs is going to be a regular thing now?"

Her hands were flat on his chest, her body pressed against his. She looked up at him. "Maybe," she said, her voice husky.

Donovan certainly didn't do anything to put space between them. "What are you doing here?" he asked.

"I realized that I could come through the front door. It's not like Charlie and Griffin would care if I was up here with you. But I also realized they might want to talk. Or have the four of us sit around and have a beer or something."

"And you don't actually like my brother and his girlfriend?" Donovan asked with a smile.

"I wanted you to myself."

Heat and want kicked him in the gut. "Oh, yeah?"

"You mentioned spreading me out on your bed and keeping me here all night and I haven't been able to think about anything else. I nearly ruined the poulet aux noix tonight."

"I have no idea what that is, but I'm guessing that's a big deal."

"*You* are a big deal."

She wasn't teasing with him tonight. Her eyes and her tone were serious and Donovan felt emotion tighten his chest.

"My family has guessed that I'm in love with you. And they want you to come over for things like birthdays and holidays and to help my grandmother with things from time to time and to play checkers with Armand and video games with Andre."

Donovan felt his throat tighten too and he had to swallow twice before he said, "I'd love that."

A part of him wanted to head over there right this minute. He wanted to eat Rosalie's food and play checkers and hang out with Andre, Armand, and Michael right now.

But a bigger part of him was very aware that, for the first time since the storm, he had Naomi all to himself. No one knew they were here together. They didn't need to be anywhere else. And the door to his bedroom locked.

He ran his hands up and down her back. "You could have called me and asked me to come over."

She nodded. "But turns out, I don't have to keep you a secret to have time alone with you. I just have to say that I want you to myself. They get it."

"And you want time alone with me now?"

"So much that I even snuck over here on foot, cutting through the yards instead of using the sidewalk, and climbed up the tree outside your window and came in through your window so none of our friends would know I was here because I don't want to share you."

Her hands were running up and down his arms and Donovan felt his skin getting tighter and hotter.

"You don't think they would understand alone time? They all love alone time with their significant others."

"They do. But they all also like to *talk*. A lot. They'd have questions and would want to tell us how great it was that we're together and you know what? I already know that. And all of that would take time away from this." She turned him and gave him a little shove.

He sat back on the foot of his bed and she climbed up into his lap, immediately cupping his face and pressing her lips to his in a hot, hungry kiss.

They didn't need a lot of foreplay. They just needed each other. And bare skin.

Donovan slid his hands under the edge of her shirt, taking it up her body.

She pulled back, lifting her arms, so he could strip it over her head. Then she reached back and undid her bra, tossing it away. His gaze on her breasts, he reached over his head and grabbed his shirt between his shoulder blades, pulling it up and off.

Then he took her hips and lifted her, flipping her to her back onto the mattress. He hooked two fingers in the top of her shorts on either side and waited for her to unbutton and unzip them, then, making sure he caught her panties as well, he slid them down her legs and dropped them to the floor.

He shucked his sweatpants and boxers off, then hooked his hands behind her knees and tipped her back.

He settled between her thighs and her "oh, Donovan" was the sweetest thing he'd heard in a long time.

He kissed up the inside of her left thigh as his thumb ran over the outer folds of her pussy. She squirmed and lifted her hips toward his touch.

"You have no idea what it does to me to be able to give you pleasure like this," he told her huskily, running his whisker roughened jaw along her inner thigh.

"I do," she said breathlessly. "I love giving you pleasure too. The idea that someone like you—brave, and strong, and rugged—can be weak for me, is the hottest thing ever."

He placed a kiss on her mound right above her clit. "Oh, I am weak for you, goddess," he told her. "You can bring me to my knees when nothing else will." He demonstrated by hitting the floor and pulling her ass to the edge of the bed.

She reached down and tangled her fingers in his hair. Her nails stroking over his scalp sent electricity racing down his spine.

"Be careful what you confess, Wild Thing," she told him.

More than her touch, the affection in her voice nearly undid him.

"You gonna use it against me?" he asked, kissing his way to the crease where her leg met her pelvis.

"Oh yes," she promised. "I'll use any power I have to keep your mouth and hands on me as often as possible."

"To have my mouth on you, all you have to do is ask." He licked along the outer edge of her pussy.

"Please, Donovan."

She moved her legs farther apart and twisted her fingers slightly in his hair.

"Anything." He lowered his head and gave her a long lick. He dragged his tongue over her sensitive flesh, loving the way she shuddered underneath him, relishing the taste of her on his tongue.

He loved the moan she gave and licked again just to hear it. He circled her clit with the tip of his tongue and then sucked, making her hips buck up off the mattress.

"Donovan! More," she begged.

He licked and sucked again, harder and faster, needing to feel her come. He slipped two fingers into her, rubbing over her G-spot as he flicked over the sweet nub.

She gripped his hair tightly and arched against his mouth, and a moment later came apart for him.

He didn't even wait for her to catch her breath before he crawled up the bed, dragging her to the pillows with him. He kissed her deeply, spearing his fingers into her hair to hold her head still.

He reached for the bedside table, but as his knuckles hit the edge, he wondered what the hell he was doing. He'd never had a woman in this room and had no condoms beside the bed.

"My purse," she said with a breathless laugh.

"I love that fucking purse," he told her, kissing her hard and then leaning over the edge of the bed to grab the bag.

He hauled it up onto the mattress with them and she reached in, shuffling through the contents blindly. He teased her breasts and nipples with his fingers and tongue as she searched for the condom, making her wiggle and gasp.

Finally, she withdrew a foil packet and handed it to him, shoving the bag back off the bed. It hit the floor and he was certain that he heard several items spill out. But Naomi didn't seem to care.

She reached for his cock, stroking her hand up and down. "Hurry."

He ripped it open and sheathed himself in one fluid movement that he was actually quite proud of. Then he braced himself on his elbows on either side of her head. He looked into her eyes. "You're amazing."

"Ditto," she told him with a little smile.

"Seriously. You're incredible. And the idea that you want to be with me like this—actually even just having a cup of coffee with me—humbles me and makes me feel like a fucking king at the same time."

She swallowed hard and pinched his ass. "If you make me cry right now, I'm going to be really upset."

He leaned down and kissed her. "What do you want me to do instead?"

"Love me."

He'd been prepared to hear dirtier words. *Fuck me*, to be specific. But, while hearing this classy woman talk dirty to him always sent a stab of heat through him unlike any other, hearing her say *those* two words, was the end of him.

And the beginning of *them*.

He was never going to be the same person. He was never going to do this with another woman. It was the strangest, most amazing, most important moment of his life.

"Better than anyone else ever has," he promised.

Then he eased into her as she arched up to meet him and they both moaned.

He hesitated for just a moment, absorbing the feel of her, the moment, everything about all of it. Then he started moving.

He thrust deep but slow, wanting to make it all last.

But then his goddess started moving with him. She arched her back, and hooked a leg around his waist, taking him deeper and moaning his name in the way that always undid him.

"Naomi," he groaned roughly.

"Donovan," she answered.

They didn't have to say anything more than that. They kept moving, the pace quickening naturally as the pleasure and the emotions built.

He moved faster, thrusting deeper and harder, until finally they both gasped. Her pussy clenched around him as she came and a moment later, he felt everything in him tighten and then release as he emptied into her with a long groan.

He slumped against her and then rolled to his side, pulling her up against his body. She slung her leg over his hip, one hand resting on his side as he dragged in deep lungfuls of oxygen.

They stayed entwined like that for several long moments. He loved the idea that she didn't have to leave, and that she would be here in the morning when he awakened, but he wasn't ready to let her go even a few inches away yet.

Her breathing slowed and their bodies cooled and eventually she rolled to her back. He took a deep breath and got up to deal with the condom in his attached bathroom. When he returned, she was under the covers and she lifted them for him to join her. He slid in next to her and she snuggled up against his side.

"I want this," he said softly in the quiet room.

"You can have this whenever you want.

"Well, that. For sure." He squeezed her ass. "But also this." He ran his hand up her back.

He felt her shift to look up at him. "I want this too. Assuming you're talking about sleeping with you and getting to run my hands over your naked body whenever I want to."

"That. And...everything."

She shifted again, this time moving away slightly and looking up at him more fully. "Good."

"I'm staying. No Galapagos Islands for sure. I'll give them my final decision tomorrow."

She pressed her lips together. Then nodded. "Okay. Then we'll *make* this show work. We'll give them exactly what they want."

"Ooookay." He frowned. There was something in her tone that made him pause. "What does that mean?"

"Tomorrow we absolutely for sure script out everything that's going to happen on camera. And..."

He shifted back so he could see her more fully. "And?"

"We...figure out a couple of animal rescues."

His frown deepened. "Define 'figure out'."

"Just something basic."

"What are you talking about?"

Naomi took a deep breath and Donovan braced himself. For some reason, he knew he wasn't going to like this.

"We need to stage a couple animal rescues."

He opened his mouth.

"Hear me out," she said quickly. She sat up, clutching the sheet to her breasts. "They want some more exciting footage. I understand where they're coming from. And we *have to* make the show work. So we have to give them what they need."

Donovan pushed himself up too and propped his back against the headboard. He shoved a hand through his hair. "We're not going to stage animal rescues, Nae."

"Listen, it won't be hard. We can reshoot the airboat rescue you did of the gray wolf. It would be so easy. We already have a lot of footage. We'd just add to it a little. We'd get a couple of boats out there so we could get some closer shots of you jumping from one to the other. You could have the wolf you have in rehab on one of the boats and we could get some tighter shots of her too."

"That's not the same wolf."

"I know but—"

"So you want to reshoot the airboat chase and rescue that concerned you so much that you brought me cake to try to talk me out of doing it again?"

She wet her lips, but nodded. "I've learned over these past few weeks that I was probably overreacting. You're a professional. You take risks, but they are calculated risks. You know what you're doing."

He huffed out an unamused laugh. "Well, thank you for that. But we're not staging a rescue just to make the show exciting."

"It's not like it's a lie. You actually did that rescue. And we have actual footage from it. We just need to stage part of it to get some more up close shots and different angles."

"Naomi—"

"And then maybe one other," she said quickly. "We just need a few things for them to piece together to show the investors. Come on, Donovan. You understand that we have to *sell this*. We need this platform to make a difference. But we have to get *on* the platform first."

Donovan just studied her face. He couldn't believe this was the same woman who had brought him food, trying to convince him to not take as many risks. He couldn't deny that seeing her passionate about what he did and wanting to become a bigger part of it was a turn-on, though.

And she had a point. That airboat chase *had* actually happened.

"I'm listening," he finally said.

She sat up straighter. "When you were shooting for the Go Wild Network, some of those rescues were staged, right?"

He shook his head. "Those were all authentic."

"I'm not saying the rescues weren't real, but I know you had to shoot a few of those things more than once."

Again he paused, studying her. She knew television. He kept forgetting that somehow. Finally he nodded. "Okay. All of the rescues were authentic. All of the animals were actually in need. But we might have repeated a couple of the sequences or maneuvers more than once. When it was completely safe to do and didn't threaten the animal's health or that of any of the humans," he added.

She grinned. "I knew it. Sometimes you have to do that to get the right shot. It's just like all of the home renovation shows. It's not like they ever show us the ones that worked out perfectly. We never see the house that comes together with no issues. It's always the one with a terrible mold problem or that was built over some ancient burial ground or something. They only show us the dramatic, exciting ones. That's what keeps people tuning in. They don't want to see the everyday routine stuff."

Donovan reached out and laced his fingers with hers. "But I'm starting to really like the routine everyday stuff."

She gave him a little smile that seemed partly surprised, but also touched. "I'm glad. And me too. But I want you here for the routine everyday stuff all the time. Which means we need the show to work. We need to show the world the exciting parts so we can have the quiet, routine parts to ourselves."

Dammit. She was convincing him.

"Okay. What other rescue are you thinking about?"

She wrinkled her nose as she said, "The penguin rescue."

His answer was swift. "No way."

"Come on. Not only is it very unique and exciting, but we

already have a lot of footage. We can use what we've already shot and just redo a few angles and repeat a few things to get some closer shots. It would be very safe. We could mostly shoot the penguin and the alligator separately."

"But you would have to have the penguin in a net, hanging from a tree."

She swallowed and nodded. "Yeah. But that could be okay, right?"

He shook his head. "You're going to have to convince Jill of that. You really think that's going to happen?"

"I'm just saying that it's unique and exciting, which is what they're looking for and it's something that we could almost fully control."

"Almost," he said. "Key word. We'd be bringing alligators up close, if not to the penguin, to the humans."

She nodded. "I know. It's not perfect but we could manage it, couldn't we?"

"I don't like this."

"Okay, just… think about it. And I'll keep thinking too. I just really…want you to stay. I want this show to go so that you can have what you want, and I really feel like we need to give them something amazing."

"I hear you. But there has to be something else."

"Well, I was also thinking —"

He reached for her, wrapping an arm around her and pulling her over his body so she lay on top of him. He cupped the back of her head and brought her mouth up to his. "Nope, no more talking. No more thinking. This is the first night I've had you all to myself, the first night in this bed, and I don't want to spend it talking about your crazy plans for the TV show."

She wiggled against him and he felt his cock already rising to the occasion.

"Well, you're going to have to come up with a pretty great

way to distract me. I'm very into this idea of making this TV show a huge hit."

He settled both hands on her butt and slid her higher so he could fasten his mouth on a nipple, swirling his tongue around the tip as it stiffened. He plucked at the other and was rewarded by a delicious moan as she ground her hips against his.

"You really want to talk about the TV show?" he asked.

"What TV show?" she asked.

Grinning, he flipped her to her back. "Very good answer."

14

Waking up in Donovan's arms, in his bed the next morning, was heaven.

Naomi stretched with her eyes still shut and grinned as Donovan's arm tightened around her waist. She arched her back, pressing her butt more firmly against his already hard cock.

He nuzzled her neck and said roughly in her ear, "Good morning, goddess."

"Morning."

"I get to go hang out with a tiger, a seal, and three black bears today and I'm not in any hurry to get out of bed."

She laughed softly. "And yes, I happen to know that's the highest compliment you could possibly pay me."

He turned her to her back, leaning over to kiss her. "I'm glad."

They made love slowly and leisurely. Then showered and got dressed—of course she'd brought extra clothes along in her backpack purse—before tiptoeing down the stairs and leaving the house together before Charlie and Griffin stirred.

They headed to Ellie's for breakfast in separate cars, but

Naomi didn't think that anyone would've been particularly scandalized to find them pulling in together. It was very possible her grandparents had noticed something no one else had about her feelings for Donovan, but now she didn't care who knew. Things with her and Donovan were going to work out and their friends and family were absolutely going to be a part of it.

It was incredibly liberating to think about being able to date him publicly.

So this time, when they met at the front bumper of Donovan's truck, Naomi laced her fingers with his and they headed inside hand in hand.

Not that anyone noticed.

Things were already busy at Ellie's and the usual group, plus or minus a few Landrys, was gathered at the back table already deep in debate over something. Of course.

"I think Navy is the best name," Charlie said.

And it looked like Naomi and Donovan had snuck out of the house for no reason. Both Charlie and Griffin were already at breakfast.

Naomi and Donovan exchanged a grin as he held out a chair for her and then took the one next to hers.

"Navy?" Mitch asked. "Why?"

"For the seal?" Charlie said. "Navy Seal? Come on, that's funny."

Mitch rolled his eyes.

"It's Selke," Knox said, setting his coffee cup down.

"Why Silky?" Maddie asked.

"Not Silky. Selke. They're mythological creatures that look like seals," Knox said.

Everyone stared at him. Except Jordan. She laughed and took a drink of her coffee. "I keep telling you, he's a nerd under that long hair and those muscles and tattoos."

"Okay," Kennedy said to her city manager. "Which bear names do you like best?"

"Pollux, Castor, and Ursula, of course," Knox said.

He was sitting back in his chair, one arm hooked over the back, looking mildly bored.

He often acted completely exasperated by this group. Moreso as the animal park grew. But he continued to show up and hang out with them.

Naomi knew deep down he loved the Landrys as much as she did. And felt like he'd been adopted into the family the way everyone who spent even an hour with them did. Knox had been hanging out with the Landrys since high school. He was as much an honorary Landry as anyone.

"What are we talking about?" Donovan asked as Ellie set a plate of biscuits and gravy down in front of him. He gave her an adorable smile. "Thanks, Ellie."

She patted his head. "Toast and eggs, darlin'?" she asked Naomi, setting a glass of orange juice near her elbow.

"Please. With bacon?"

Ellie lifted a brow. "Sure thing."

"And maybe hashbrowns too," Naomi added.

That caught more attention. Naomi definitely usually ate light, especially in the morning. But she was ravenous.

"You go for a run this morning or something?" Zeke asked with a grin that said he knew very well that wasn't what was going on.

"Nope." That was all Naomi was going to give him.

At least, that's how she'd always been in the past about her relationships.

But as she reached for her orange juice, she was suddenly gripped by the desire to be as open and audacious as the rest of these people. At least about what was making her happier—and hungrier—than she'd ever been. Or rather *who*.

"I just didn't realize how many calories all-night-long sex would burn. I would have put a granola bar in my purse or something."

Zander froze with a forkful of eggs right at his mouth. Zeke started coughing as he swallowed his coffee wrong. Mitch dropped the biscuit he was holding. Owen spilled water down the front of his shirt.

Donovan, however, just took a huge bite of his food, chewed, swallowed, and then wiped his mouth, looking around the table at the men who were now staring at him.

"You don't seem shocked," Zander commented.

"Of course not," Donovan said. "This girl earned those hashbrowns. I mean, also throwing in a short stack wouldn't be inappropriate."

All of the men hooted and Naomi had to admit she felt only happiness as she laughed and then chugged two thirds of her orange juice.

This felt good. Teasing like this. Sharing this happy, in-love stuff with these people. Maybe she'd overreacted by keeping her dating life separate from them all in the past too, but at the same time, she couldn't imagine it being like this with anyone other than Donovan.

He reached under the table and squeezed her leg and she realized that he understood what it meant that she'd come out publicly about how they'd spent last night. She gave him a grin.

"Okay, before Zeke regains the ability to speak and says something inappropriate"—Jill interjected, patting her fiancé on the back—"why do *you* get to pick the bear names anyway?" she asked Knox.

"Charlie was dragging her feet about starting a contest to name the new animals on the Gone Wild website, so we started one on the city website instead," Kennedy said.

"I wasn't dragging my feet," Charlie protested. "I didn't

know the animals were staying." She looked at Donovan. "We *still* don't know that the bears are staying for sure." She blew out a breath. "Why did you think the city should have the contest?"

"Because I realized I could put Knox in charge of choosing the winners and personally delivering the stuffed animals to the winners and runners-up," Kennedy said, shooting the city manager a grin.

"You did it just to annoy Knox?" Charlie asked.

"It's revenge," Knox said. "I told Fred Williams he could have an hour with her last week."

They all grimaced. Fred Williams wanted an hour meeting with Kennedy every week. Because he had that many complaints. His main one being the aliens who lived in the woods behind his house having orgies. That they wouldn't invite him to.

"You deserve having to deliver some teddy bears to people around town for that," Mitch told him.

Knox just shrugged. "Some of the entries for the names were really good. And you all end up naming alpacas things like Alpacapella and pigs things like Dumbledore."

"And goats after the Seven Dwarves," Griffin added.

"Exactly," Knox said. "I'm happy to add some decent and creative names to this craziness."

"I personally like the ducks that are named after the Brady Bunch," Charlie said.

"The penguins named after Mr. Popper's Penguins are really the best," Maddie said, looking at Jill.

"So the bears are staying?" Kennedy asked Donovan.

He shook his head. "Not all of them at least. I'm keeping my eye on the little girl. She's not eating and gaining weight as quickly as the other two. But at least two of them are going to be released."

"Well, at least the boys will be together. You can't separate Pollux and Castor," Zander said.

Knox nodded. "Right."

Everyone else just stared at them.

"What are you talking about?" Kennedy asked.

"Pollux and Castor are the twins that Zeus agreed to never separate," Zander said. "So it would be wrong for *us* to separate them."

Kennedy frowned. "*What?*"

"Didn't you pay any attention in school?" Zander asked. He looked at Bennett. "Bet your nerdy smart hubby knows who Pollux and Castor are."

Kennedy turned to her husband. "Do you?"

"Well..." Bennett pushed his glasses up his nose. "You sure you want me to answer? You know what it does to you when I go all brainy."

She leaned in. "Spill it, Baxter."

"Pollux and Castor are two of the stars in the Gemini constellation. They are also characters from Greek mythology," Fletcher answered before Bennett could.

"Hey," Kennedy protested.

Fletcher smirked at her and looped an arm around Jordan. "You're not the only one who loves a guy who got good grades."

Jordan cuddled up to him. "Go on, Professor."

"He teaches third grade," Zander pointed out.

"Well, he's Professor Landry to me," Jordan told Zander. "At least sometimes." She wiggled her eyebrows. "In fact, just the other night—"

Fletcher leaned in and kissed her to shut her up. Then whispered something in her ear that made her blush and laugh.

"Anyway," Bennett said. "Pollux and Castor were twins but one was a demigod and one was human. When the human one,

Castor, was killed, Pollux asked Zeus to give some of his immortality to his brother so he wouldn't die. Zeus agreed and made them into the constellation where they could be together forever."

There was a beat of silence. Then Kennedy said, "He just made them into stars? Instead of letting them live?"

Bennett shrugged. "Yeah."

"That's dumb. Zeus is like the main god, right? Why didn't he just bring the dead one back to life?"

"He...I don't know," Bennett said.

"And why was one part god but the other was all human if they were twins?" she asked.

"I think one of them was his son and one was another guy's son," Fletcher said helpfully.

Kennedy rolled her eyes. "I don't think that's how it works."

"It's Greek mythology," Zander said. "A lot of it falls down if you really dig in."

"*Anyway*," Knox finally broke in. "The names are creative. I like them. I get to decide. So it's Pollux and Castor and Ursula."

"Is Ursula another star in the constellation?" Charlie asked.

"Ursa Major is another constellation all together," Knox said. He paused and then actually smiled. "It's also called the Great Bear."

Charlie grinned. "Oh, I like that."

"Creative as fuck, right?" Knox asked.

"Definitely."

He tipped back the rest of his coffee and pushed back from the table. "Okay, then that's settled. So glad we got the really big business of the day decided." His tone was dry. But then, Knox's tone was often dry.

"So, Fiona headed back to Alabama?" Griffin asked.

Knox froze for just a moment. Naomi wasn't sure anyone would have noticed if they hadn't been looking right at him but there was definitely a second where he seemed caught off guard.

"Yeah," was all Knox said.

"Everything okay then?" Griffin asked. *He* was definitely watching Knox.

Naomi looked from one man to the other, suddenly sensing a tension between them. Griffin and Fiona had been friends long before either of them had set foot in Autre. Was Griffin feeling protective?

"Everything is fine," Knox said. Firmly. Meeting Griffin's gaze directly.

"Would Fiona say the same if I asked her?"

"Does anyone ever really know exactly what Fiona is going to say about anything until she says it?"

That was actually a very fair point.

Griffin blew out a breath. "Dammit. Is she all right?"

"I'd say she's better than she's been in a while, as a matter of fact," Knox said. "But whether or not she'd admit that is another thing altogether."

Then he pivoted on his heel and stalked out of the building.

No one said anything for a few beats. Then Zeke shook his head. "What the fuck is going on with them?"

Jill just patted his back. "It's a good thing you're pretty."

Grinning and feeling lighter than she had in forever, Naomi got up and went to the bar for a refill on her orange juice. She was very parched this morning and she couldn't help but grin to herself when she thought about the reason for her dehydration.

"Well, you seem downright delighted this morning," Ellie said as she came over with the pitcher of juice.

Naomi smiled. "Delighted? I guess that's not inaccurate."

"Delighted is one of my favorite ways to be," Ellie said. "It's about time you had a little of that."

"Delighted is one of your favorite ways to be?" Naomi repeated. "Really? Because you're very practical. Delighted seems like a...flippant word for you."

"Well, sure, I'm practical. That's what makes being delighted so fun when it happens." Ellie filled Naomi's glass, then leaned her elbows on the bar, and studied Naomi. "That's why it looks so good on *you*."

"Because I'm practical?"

Ellie nodded. "Yes, that fits, but I guess I would use the words 'content' and 'steady'."

"Is content the opposite of delighted?" Naomi asked.

"Not exactly. But delighted is another word for excited. And you, my dear, avoid getting excited."

Well, Ellie wasn't wrong.

Still, Naomi frowned. "You make me sound like I'm no fun."

"Do you know other synonyms for excited?" Ellie asked.

"Charmed. Enchanted."

"Yes, and thrilled. Also annoyed, agitated, worked up, disturbed."

Naomi held up her hand. "Okay. So in some ways you think I've avoided being delighted because I would also avoid being...agitated."

Ellie nodded. "Let's be honest..." She glanced over the large table full of her family, mostly her grandchildren, "...there's a very fine line between being delighted and annoyed."

Naomi laughed. "But even when you're agitated, you love it."

Ellie pointed a finger at her. "Bingo. When there's love there, the line between delighted and agitated gets nice and blurry. Like how you feel about Donovan and the crazy shit he does for a living."

Naomi shouldn't have been surprised. "So I guess that means you've also realized that I'm in love?"

Ellie nodded. "I'm just glad *you* finally realized it."

"And you're right, that line really is blurry. The first few times I went out with him and recorded him doing an animal rescue, I was definitely agitated."

"And when did it change to delight?"

"Probably when he saved a baby bunny from a drainage ditch and then kissed it on its head," she said.

Ellie laughed. "You're sure it wasn't the first time he had to take his shirt off?"

Naomi gave her a sly grin. "Well, I definitely wasn't *annoyed* when that happened."

"I knew that rabbit got to you," Donovan said from behind her.

She turned quickly. Then narrowed her eyes. "Did you kiss that bunny to win me over?"

"Of course not. Anyone who's holding a baby bunny and *doesn't* kiss it on the head is an evil, coldhearted, soul-less asshole," he declared. But then he gave her a sexy little smirk. "But I definitely looked over to see your reaction when I did it."

She gave him a playful shove. "Well, I know you didn't let that fox fall asleep in your arms just to win me over, and that was completely adorable too."

"I didn't even know you were around then."

"I—"

"I am so sorry to interrupt, but we have been waiting for a chance to say hello and decided we just needed to come over and introduce ourselves."

Donovan gave Naomi a wink, then turned to face the four women who had approached. "No problem," Donovan said, flashing them one of his best grins. He moved in next to Naomi, looping an arm around her waist.

"My name is Sara," the woman said. She turned to indicate the three women behind her. "These are my best friends, Roni, Kate, and Alexis."

"Hi, ladies," Donovan greeted.

"Nice to meet you," Naomi added.

"We're here for a girls' weekend," Sara said. "We all went through our OB-GYN residency together and now we're here for Alexis's bachelorette party."

"Wow, that's amazing. Congratulations on all of it," Naomi said.

"Very cool," Donovan agreed. "How'd you decide to celebrate down here?"

"I took a swamp boat tour with Owen a couple of years ago and enjoyed it so much, I told these girls that we had to come back," Sara said.

"Owen makes a great impression," Naomi agreed with a grin.

"He does. And the addition of the animal park is so fun," Sara said enthusiastically.

"We *love* the animals," Roni said. "All of them. Though the llamas are my favorites."

"Actually—" Donovan and Naomi both started. Then they grinned at one another and Donovan gestured for her to go ahead.

"They're alpacas," Naomi finished the statement.

"Right, alpacas," Roni said. "They're adorable."

"But even besides the otters and penguins and gumbo and beignets and *everything,* this trip has been even better than we imagined because we get to meet *you,*" Sara said. "Would it be possible for us to get a photo with you?"

"Of course you can," Naomi said, reaching for the phone Sara was holding out as Donovan slipped his arm out from around Naomi's waist. "Here, I'll take it. You all get in there."

"Oh," Sara said, hesitating and glancing at her friends. "Um."

"You're great," Alexis said, jumping in. "We've loved the videos of your animal rescues and everything. And you two are *so* cute together."

"Thanks," Donovan said. But he gave Naomi a puzzled glance.

"But we were hoping for a photo with Naomi," Alexis said.

Naomi was startled. "Me?"

"Oh yes," Kate assured her.

"It's just that we all *loved Zoey At the Zoo*," Alexis said. "I watched it all the time. It was the best. And then when we got here and saw you the other day and Kate said she thought it was you and we started talking and realized we were all huge fans, we were completely starstruck."

"I learned so much about animals from your show," Kate told her. "I especially loved the polar bear and for my birthday one year I asked my parents if I could adopt one. You know those programs where you send in a monthly donation to symbolically adopt a wild animal? And they sent me a stuffed animal and a tote bag and stickers and stuff. I carried that bag around until it fell apart because I was so proud of that."

"Oh, we did that at our local zoo, but we adopted an elephant," Roni said with a big grin.

"My older sister became a veterinarian because of your show," Alexis added.

Naomi was having a hard time swallowing. They'd recognized her? This hadn't happened to her in... years. She'd almost forgotten what it felt like. But these women were so genuine and sweet and Naomi realized that it felt *good*. These women had enjoyed her show. They'd watched faithfully. They'd been influenced by it.

There had definitely been drawbacks to being famous at such a young age. But there had been good things about *Zoey At the Zoo* too.

She finally managed a smile. A genuine, bright smile.

"We're just *huge* Naomi Williams fans. Sorry," Sara told Donovan.

"No offense," Kate said quickly. "We could get a photo with you too."

Donovan chuckled. "No offense taken. I'm very happy to take the picture." He reached for Sara's phone.

The women looped their arms around Naomi and everyone leaned in with big smiles. Donovan took several shots and then handed the camera back to Sara.

Sara pulled the photos up and flipped through them.

"Oh my gosh, these are so good." She looked up at Naomi. "Thank you so much. I'll post a couple on Facebook with our other ones."

"Great. You should tag me."

"Oh I will. I'm so glad you've liked the others."

Naomi paused. "The others?"

"You've seen the others I've tagged you in, right?"

"Your other photos? You've tagged *me*?"

"Of course." Sara opened the Facebook page for Boys of the Bayou Gone Wild on her phone and scrolled down.

Naomi saw a few photos of Sara and her friends along the fence next to the alpacas, one of Kate feeding a lemur, and one of Alexis holding Slothcrates, the sloth.

But then she stopped on one photo in particular. "I love this one," Sara said. "It's so sexy."

Yeah, that photo wasn't of Sara, Kate, Roni, or Alexis. It was of Naomi. And Donovan. Kissing.

It was the one that had been captured next to his truck yesterday without their knowledge.

"*You* took that photo?" Naomi asked.

Sara nodded and smiled. "I wasn't sure if I should just post it, but all of the posts have to be approved by the page administrator, so I guess they liked it too. It's so..." She sighed. "Just swoony."

"We didn't realize anyone had noticed us."

"We've definitely noticed you. You're great together." Alexis gave them both a big smile. "I don't know if it's because we're here for my bachelorette party or what, but the romance around here is palpable. All of the couples around here just seem so crazy about each other. It's like watching one of those reality TV shows where everyone falls in love."

Naomi bit back a sarcastic retort. It was interesting that she and Donovan were supposed to be establishing their relationship on screen for the show, but these women were appreciating their private candid moments more.

She looked at Donovan. There was no question she had very real feelings for him. She shouldn't be surprised that they were obvious to people watching them together.

"Again, thank you so much. This has been a thrill," Sara told her.

"It was really nice to meet you all," Naomi said.

"Stay tuned on our page," Donovan added. "We've got some exciting stuff coming up."

"Oh, absolutely," Kate said. "And we're telling everyone we know."

They moved off back to their table and Naomi turned to Donovan. "Well at least one of our goals for this whole thing is working out. We're definitely attracting more visitors to the animal park's page."

He laughed and slid an arm around her waist, hugging her up against his side. "I'd say a lot more than that is working out."

"And—"

Just then three kids came running into the restaurant.

"Mr. Landry, Mr. Landry!"

Naomi and Donovan spun to watch them head straight for Fletcher.

Naomi didn't know the little boy or one of the little girls, but one of the girls was Sophia Abar. She knew Sophia because Jordan had talked about her all the time when she'd first met the little girl. Sophia had also been in Fletcher's third grade class this past year.

Sophia had been coming to the petting zoo regularly since her father had died last summer and she'd bonded with one of the alpacas. She was one reason Jordan had started the program using animals to help kids deal with both physical and emotional issues. They used the alpacas and even some of the goats and bunnies in everything from physical therapy to grief counseling with trained professionals now.

"Samuel, Katie, Sophia, hi," Fletcher greeted the kids. He pivoted on his seat to face them. "What's up?"

"We need your help!" Samuel said.

"Something bad happened!" Katie added.

Fletcher frowned. "Like what?"

"Come on. We'll show you!" Katie reached out and grabbed Fletcher's hand, pulling.

"Can you tell me here?" Fletcher asked, getting to his feet. He glanced at Zander.

Zander hadn't moved, but he was listening and watching intently.

"No." Samuel looked around the big table full of adults he didn't know. He dropped his voice to a loud whisper. "We'll tell you outside."

Fletcher nodded. "Yeah. Okay."

Jordan frowned. "Can I come?"

"No," Samuel said, shaking his head. "Mr. Landry only."

"Okay." Jordan sat back, obviously trying to look casual. "That's cool."

They all returned to eating, but they were a little quieter, and they kept casting glances toward the front door.

After a few minutes. Jordan said, "That was weird, right?"

"Don't worry, if he's not back in a couple minutes, I'll go check on things," Zander said.

But Zander didn't even have to get out of his seat. Fletcher came back through the door a moment later, striding toward the table with a frown.

"Zander, need you."

Zander shoved his chair back and stood without any more explanation from his older brother than that. Zander definitely came off as laid back and even annoyed at times when duty called, but he actually took his job very seriously and would always step in to do whatever he could. Badge or not.

"Anything you need from any of us?"

Fletcher looked at Donovan. "Might have a dog in trouble."

Donovan stepped forward. "Let's go." That was all he needed to hear.

Naomi also straightened. If Donovan was going on an animal rescue, she wanted to be there with him. Not that he needed her help, especially with Fletcher and Zander there. But she really did want to learn as much as she could from him.

"Do you need any of the rest of us?" Zeke asked.

Zander shook his head. "We'll call if we do." He looked at Fletcher. "What's going on?"

"The kids think there's a dog trapped in someone's yard. I'm thinking it might be a situation like with the seal where it got trapped by some storm debris. But it's Denny Jenkins' place."

Zander scowled and Naomi sighed.

"Does that mean something?" Donovan asked.

"Denny can be kind of an asshole," Zander said.

"And a drunk," Fletcher said. "Sophia lives across the street from Denny. She's heard the dog crying and said she hasn't seen Denny in a couple of days. She got Katie and Samuel to go over with her, but they couldn't get into the backyard."

Zander frowned. "Good. Those kids don't need to be gettin' into other people's yards. Who knows what they might run into."

Fletcher nodded. "I told them the same thing. But I suspect

they did sneak in there and saw the dog in trouble. They're just not wanting to confess they were there."

"And why'd they come get you?" Donovan asked.

"I was their teacher this last year. And I suppose most of their parents are at work right now. Or they didn't want to risk getting grounded for messing around at Denny's."

"And because they knew where to find you," Zeke said with a little chuckle.

"Well, I'm not sorry that it's common knowledge that helpful people can be found at my place," Ellie told them, coming to the table with a coffee pot for refills. "Get going and see what's going on with this dog."

As they passed Rachel and Brent's table, Donovan said, "We got a call for possible rescue."

Rachel straightened. "What is it?"

"A dog. We're actually not sure what's going on, but we're going to go check it out."

Brent slumped back in his chair. "Just a dog? That's okay. We'll pass."

Naomi frowned. "Seriously? Just a dog? What the hell is that?"

Brent looked up, seeming surprised. "The idea is that Donovan is a *wildlife* rescuer. Every other person watching this show will have a dog of their own. That's not exciting."

She put a hand on her hip. "You don't think that them having a dog of their own won't make them even *more* invested in watching us *rescue* one? It's a surefire way of making people care and relate even stronger to what we're doing."

Brent shrugged. "Not interested."

"Then maybe you need to—"

Her reply was cut off by Donovan's low voice in her ear. "Fuck them."

She pulled in a deep breath. He was right. Fuck them.

Brent was a way for her to get this show produced and to do

great things for animals and to keep Donovan here. She didn't have to agree with Brent on everything and she definitely didn't have to respect or like him.

"Fine. Stay here. But I'm right," she told Brent. Then she turned on her heel and walked out of Ellie's.

The kids were standing by Fletcher's truck when they headed across the parking lot.

Fletcher stopped to talk with them. He could be heard saying, "No, you can't come with us. But I promise to let you know what we find."

Then, as Fletcher turned toward Zander's truck, Samuel said, "Come on! We'll go to Sophie's house and watch from across the street."

Fletcher sighed.

Zander was already starting the truck. "You can't keep the kids out of their own front yard."

"I know. As long as they stay across the street and don't come over and try to get involved, it will be fine."

"Well, I trust they'll listen to their teacher, if he tells them to stay out of the way," Zander said, turning out onto the street.

"You'd think so, wouldn't you?" Fletcher said wryly.

"We'll bring my truck in case we need any supplies," Donovan said, pulling his keys from his pocket.

"Meet you there," Zander said with a nod.

Denny lived on the far edge of town.

They pulled up in front of Denny's house, behind Zander. Donovan killed the engine.

"Wait here a second," Zander called. "Let me go check things out."

Fletcher, Donovan, and Naomi stayed by the trucks and watched Zander first go to the front door and knock loudly as well as call out to Denny. There was no answer. He moved to the front living room window and tried to peer inside.

No one came to the door, so he moved around the corner of

the house and tried knocking on the side door. When that also produced no answer, he disappeared around to the back of the house.

"So Denny's not a great guy?" Donovan asked.

"He's kind of a dick," Fletcher said. "Quick temper. Big mouth. Full of himself. I don't know that I think he's an animal abuser, but he's not really that warm, cuddly type either."

A couple minutes later, Zander came back around the house.

He didn't look happy as he approached the truck.

"You want to come check this dog out?" he asked Donovan.

Donovan started forward without word.

Fletcher and Naomi followed. Zander didn't say anything about them *not* accompanying them. Naomi assumed since she was with a law enforcement officer, it wasn't actually trespassing.

"Denny's not answering and there are no vehicles here so I'm going to assume he's not home. The dog looks like he's been here on his own for a little bit," Zander said grimly. He opened the back gate and motioned for them to step through.

The fence around the backyard was high and enclosed a space that was more dirt than grass. There were two old cars and a pickup parked behind the house. There were also several miscellaneous items like old lawn furniture and plastic crates, but it was hard to tell if they'd been tossed around by the recent storm, or by just human carelessness.

Their attention, however, was immediately drawn to the dog that was chained to the front bumper of the truck in the middle of the yard. It was an adult German shepherd. He was dirty and as Donovan started toward him, the animal started barking and growling ferociously.

"Yeah, he's not happy to see us," Zander said. "I really hope if those kids were sneaking in back here that they kept their distance."

"They would have told me if they'd gotten bitten or anything," Fletcher said.

Donovan was scowling deeply. "He's acting like this because he has no idea if we're friend or enemy."

Zander nodded. "He's also not in great shape. His food and water dishes have been knocked over. Hard to tell for how long. And that chain is really short."

Naomi and Fletcher hung back, letting Donovan and Zander take the lead, but it was easy to see, even from a distance, the two metal bowls that were now lying upside down and the chain around the animal's neck that was only about five feet long and seemed to be too tight.

"My God, where has he been sleeping?" Naomi asked, looking around. There was no shelter of any kind. Not a kennel or a doghouse.

"He's probably been going underneath the truck," Fletcher said.

"That doesn't give him protection on all sides," Donovan said, tight, his voice rough.

He was approaching the animal slowly but the growling and barking had intensified.

"You guys just stay back there," he instructed. He dropped to the ground and sat, facing the animal and extending his hand. The dog couldn't reach him yet, but it was definitely a position of submission.

"It's okay, buddy. I know this sucks. I really want to help you. I'm a friend." Donovan's tone was soft and easy as he spoke to the dog.

Naomi was holding her breath and she lifted a hand to cover her mouth as she made herself breathe and stay quiet.

She looked over at Zander. His jaw was tight and he was clearly angry. A quick glance at Fletcher showed a similar expression. She focused back on Donovan. He'd started to scoot forward on his butt, a few inches of the time. He was still talking softly to the dog, his hand extended, trying to show the animal that he was not a threat.

The dog stopped barking, but was still growling low in his throat, and baring his teeth.

"Hey, guys?" Donovan said, keeping his tone nice and even. "I'm going to need somebody to find me some dog food and water."

"On it," Fletcher said quickly. It seemed he was grateful to have something to do to help. He pivoted and started for the gate.

"I'm gonna see if I can track Denny down," Zander said, suddenly, pivoting on his heel and stalking toward the gate as well. "I'll be in my truck."

Naomi stayed right where she was. Donovan might need a hand, and nothing could pull her away from the sight of him inching toward the dog and the dog slowly lowering his head. Even as he continued to growl softly, the dog seemed to sense that Donovan was there to help. Donovan was now within reach and if the dog wanted to take a bite out of him, he definitely could've gotten a finger or two. Instead, Donovan was able to reach out and let the dog sniff his fingers. The dog did, then gave Donovan's hand a lick. Donovan put his hand on the dog's head and stroked softly between its ears. He kept talking but his voice was low enough now that Naomi could barely make out the words.

"Naomi?" Donovan said softly, again keeping his voice steady.

"Yeah?"

"In my truck, I have metal cutters. We need to get this chain off. I've also got an extra long leash. I'm going to need some antibiotic cream and a bandage."

"Of course." Naomi ran to the truck and met Fletcher heading back to the yard with a bag of dog food and a jug of water he'd gotten from the truck.

She returned with all the supplies quickly. The dog was drinking greedily from the bowl they'd filled with water and they waited for him to finish, but now that the dog let Donovan close and had gotten head scratches, it seemed he was accepting of all kinds of help. Donovan was able to remove the chain easily and the dog let Fletcher hold him as Donovan tended to the wound on his neck.

"Okay, fill up the food. I think she's been without any food or water for couple of days." Donovan was stroking the dog's back, not looking at the other humans.

"It's a her?" Fletcher asked.

"Yup. She's probably about four."

Fletcher filled the food bowl and the dog went to it as if she were, literally, starving.

Naomi felt her throat tightening as she watched. "Poor thing."

Donovan just nodded, his jaw tight.

When she was finished, he put the leash around her neck, over the bandage, and then looped the end of it around the bumper of the truck.

"What are you doing?" Naomi asked.

"It's softer and lighter than the chain. It's also a lot longer, so she'll have more room to move."

"But why are you tying her up again? Aren't we taking her with us?"

"We can't," he said shortly. "Not until we determine the circumstances."

"The circumstances? She was tied up with no food or water or shelter. Those are the circumstances. We should be able to take her with us."

Donovan shook his head. "That's not how it works. She had bowls. We don't know what happened here. If we just take her, that's basically stealing."

"But we can't just leave her here!"

"We've improved her situation. We've given her what she needs for now. She's got food and water and we'll clean up the area and construct a makeshift shelter for her. For now. Zander will track down the owner and see what's going on."

Donovan still hadn't looked at anyone but the dog. Naomi reached out and grabbed his arm, squeezing. Finally, his gaze met hers.

"Donovan, you can't be serious. We have to take this dog with us."

"We can't. That's illegal."

"It's illegal to save a dog from abuse and neglect?"

"We're not law enforcement, Naomi, and the abuse and neglect haven't been proven. This could just be a bad circumstance. Which we've corrected."

"Zander's law enforcement."

"And there are procedures for this. He has to take the right steps. She has an owner. We can't just take her away. Unless we have really good reason to believe that she's in danger."

"She's a dog. She's a companion. She depends on humans for her well-being. You risk your life to save wild animals that can, for the most part, fend for themselves, but this animal that needs human intervention is going to be left behind?"

He pulled his arm away from her grip. "Stop it. That's not what I'm saying. We're going to be sure she's taken care of."

"No. You've made a career out of convincing other people to care about animals. So, here I am, *caring*."

His eyes flashed with emotion, then he simply pivoted on his heel and stomped away.

She stared after him. But she didn't say anything else.

Obviously he was emotional about the situation. She knew him. She knew he wouldn't leave this dog behind if he had a choice. He was a certified rehabilitation expert for wildlife and this dog did not fall under wildlife. Okay, so there were rules.

But she didn't like it. This was wrong. There were plenty of rules and laws and procedures and policies that didn't go far enough, or, in some cases, were just flat-out wrong.

Zander rejoined them just then. "Can't fucking get a hold of him."

"Who? Denny?" Fletcher asked.

"Yeah. Apparently he headed out of town for work just after the hurricane. Nobody's heard from him since. He's not answering his phone. I can't track him down."

"So what does that mean for the dog?" Naomi asked.

"I need a little more time. I have to exhaust all the possibilities of finding Denny and getting a decent explanation about this."

"A decent explanation for his animal being neglected and left alone?"

"If I can't find him, or at least talk to him, within the next twenty-four hours, I'll do something."

"Like what?"

Zander blew out a breath. "Naomi, seriously, I need you to back off."

Naomi looked from him to Fletcher, then to where Donovan was pacing several feet away. "Fine."

Without another word, they all worked to clean up the area around the dog of waste and the debris that had blown in from the storm. They constructed a shelter for her using a kennel from Donovan's truck and several pieces of plywood and plastic from around the yard. It was actually a decent looking dog house, by the time they were done.

Naomi was still upset.

She didn't speak to Donovan or Fletcher on the way back to Ellie's and when they got there, she headed for her truck, intending to go straight home.

"Naomi," Donovan called after her as the other two men went inside.

She turned to face him and folded her arms. "I don't want to talk to you right now."

"I know what I'm doing."

"Okay. That doesn't mean I have to agree with it. Or be happy about it."

"You can't be upset with me for following the law."

"I can be upset with you for just about anything, Donovan," Naomi told him. "We're not going to agree on everything all the time. And this is definitely one of those times."

"I just..." He shoved a hand through his hair. "I've *always* felt like I was giving every situation my all. When I'm out in a hurricane rescuing bear cubs. When I'm jumping on the back of an alligator. When I'm climbing a tree just outside the ring of a forest fire. When I'm rescuing a seal. And I thought you believed that too. Even when you think I'm doing something dangerous, you believe in me. Sure, afterward, you try to give me reasons to not take the big risks, but you've always under-stood *why* I do it. I've always pushed because I was willing to sacrifice for a greater good. I was working to be worthy of being given a second chance myself." He swallowed hard. "Then you convinced me that I don't have to take those big risks for what I do to matter. That you knew my heart was always in the right place and that even the routine rescues of goats and raccoons *matter*. And now... I'm doing things safer and more routine and you don't like it." He blew out a frustrated breath. "I thought you knew who I am and that I'm doing what I'm doing for the right reasons no matter how I handle a situation."

Her heart was aching. She felt raw. She *hated* everything about all of this. She hated that the dog was still in that yard. She hated that Donovan was torn up about that. She hated that he thought she was doubting him. And she hated that *he* was doubting *her*.

"Well, *you* taught *me* that sometimes risks are necessary and worth taking," she told him. "And that sometimes I might be the only person who's willing and able to take the risk."

He frowned at that. "I don't know what you're thinking but—"

"Donovan." She shook her head. "I can love you and find you worthy and believe in you, and still not agree with every decision you make. And vice versa. And you're going to have to get okay with that if we're going to make this work."

Then she turned on her heel and stomped to her truck without looking back at him.

15

"Girl, go find your man," Rosalie told Naomi three hours later.

"No."

"Please."

Naomi frowned at her grandmother. "No. I'm mad at him. He needs time to think. And I need some space."

Rosalie shook her head. "Fine, but get out of my kitchen. You just ruined the tablet kokoye."

Naomi looked down at the countertop in front of her. Then blew out a breath. She had been making the dishes that her grandmother had handed down to her in this very kitchen for most of her life. And now, since meeting Donovan Foster, she had nearly ruined two.

She threw down her spoon. "Fine. I...need to go for a drive."

Rosalie narrowed her eyes. "I thought you didn't want to talk to him."

"I don't." That Naomi knew for sure. But there was something that she'd been thinking about constantly. That would make her feel better.

Ten minutes later, she pulled up at Denny's house.

Yeah, okay, it was maybe kind of trespassing. But she could not get the dog's face out of her head. So they couldn't take the dog with them. That didn't mean she couldn't come back over and make sure the dog was okay. The poor thing was tied up here all alone. She could spend a few minutes here with it, keeping it company.

She headed around the side of the house and let herself into the backyard. And immediately drew up short.

The dog was not alone.

Sophia, Samuel, and Katie were there.

The kids sat in a semicircle around the new doghouse and the dog lay in the middle of them, her leash still on. Her chin rested on her front paws and she seemed completely content as two of the kids stroked her head and back as Katie read out loud from the book in her lap.

Naomi felt her heart swell and she pressed a hand over her chest.

"Hey, guys," she called softly so she wouldn't startle anyone.

They all pivoted to look at her. "Oh," Katie said quickly. "We're just...dog sitting."

"Yeah. Denny is Sophia's neighbor. He wouldn't mind."

"Yeah, I pet Brinkley sometimes when she's outside playing," Sophia said.

"The dog's name is Brinkley?"

Sophia nodded.

"And you play with her?"

"Well..." Sophia cast a glance at Samuel.

Samuel shook his head quickly. As if to tell her to be quiet.

"It's okay." Naomi approached the kids and dog. "I know Denny doesn't treat her very well. I want to help. You can be honest."

"Okay, sometimes she gets loose. She runs over to our house. That's when I pet her," Sophia said. "He doesn't let her out very much. He doesn't play with her or walk her or anything."

Yeah, Naomi had suspected as much. She dropped onto the ground with the kids and sat with her legs crisscrossed. She reached out and stroked Brinkley's head. "That's really too bad. She seems like a really nice dog. I don't understand why people don't treat their pets better."

"I know. And we didn't like that she was over here all by herself, so we thought we would come over and keep her company," Katie said.

"I think that's really nice. It's why I'm here too." Naomi withdrew the package of dog treats she'd pilfered from Donovan's truck after the very tense drive back to Ellie's earlier. She handed one to each of the kids. "I'm glad she's got some friends. I hated the idea that she was here by herself."

"I wish I could take her home," Katie said. "But we already have two dogs and my mom said that's enough."

"My mom said I can't have a dog either," Samuel said. "She said I'm enough of a handful all by myself."

Naomi grinned at him.

"And I think that if I took her to my house, Denny might still yell at her sometimes." Sophia looked sad.

Naomi shook her head. "He yells at her?"

Sophia nodded. "He yells at everybody."

Naomi didn't know Denny very well, but she *really* didn't like him.

"What's going to happen tonight when it gets dark?" Samuel asked.

"What do you mean?" Naomi asked.

"She'll still be here all by herself."

"Yeah, but she'll go in her doghouse and sleep. She'll be okay." But, stupidly, Naomi didn't like the idea of Brinkley out here in the dark by herself either.

"We could camp out over here," Katie said.

"My mom won't let me camp out here if there aren't any grown-ups here," Samuel said.

"It would be scary over here," Sophia said.

"Well, it will be scary for Brinkley too," Katie said.

"You'll just have to tell your parents that you're at a friend's house," Katie told Samuel. "If they don't know we're camping here they can't say no."

Naomi closed her eyes. "You guys can't camp over here with Brinkley. She'll be okay."

"You could camp with us," Samuel said. "Then there would be a grown up here."

She was *not* going to take responsibility for three kids overnight. Three kids she didn't know that well anyway. And certainly not to camp in some guy's backyard without his permission. Or even his knowledge. "Not going to happen," Naomi said. "Sorry."

"Then will you come over and be sure she's okay tonight?" Sophia raised big, wide brown eyes to Naomi.

Naomi blew out a breath. What was she supposed to say? She had, after all, showed up here in the middle of the day. And even if Sophia hadn't asked, there was a good chance that Naomi would be lying in bed tonight and thinking about Brinkley over here by herself.

Of course, dogs slept outside by themselves in the dark. But Brinkley was literally here all alone. Who knew how long Denny had been gone? Brinkley might be feeling abandoned. She might be wondering if anyone was ever coming back for her. She clearly was a sweet dog when treated well.

"Will you?" Katie asked. "It would be better if a grown-up checked on her anyway."

Naomi sighed. These kids were good. She wondered if Fletcher was as wrapped around their little fingers as Naomi was now after only five minutes.

Then she laughed to herself. Fletcher Landry was absolutely wrapped around the little kids' fingers and she was sure they knew it.

"Yes, I promise to come over and check on her tonight after dark. So you guys don't have to worry. You don't have to come over here yourselves. I'll make sure Brinkley is all right." She had to come over if for no other reason than to be sure these kids didn't come back.

Katie was clearly the mastermind. Naomi wouldn't have been a bit surprised to find the little girl curled up with the dog alone when she stopped by later.

"Will you bring her a dog toy?" Sophia asked. "I wanted to bring her a toy, but we don't have any in our house."

"Yeah, and all of our dog's toys are kind of chewed up and slobbered on," Katie said.

"I can give you some of my allowance money," Samuel said. "I have a dollar thirty-eight."

They were manipulative, but they were sweet. Naomi nodded again. "Yes, I will also bring her a toy and you don't have to give me any money. You guys have been over here reading her stories. You're being really good friends to her."

"This one is really cool," Samuel said, leaning over and pulling something from out from inside the doghouse. "But I think she needs a soft one to cuddle with tonight." He held up a bright blue plastic toy that was shaped like a bone. Clearly, it was a chew toy for a dog.

Naomi frowned. "Where did that come from?"

The kids shrugged.

"It was here with the blanket when we got here," Samuel said.

That was the first that Naomi had noticed the blanket that was just peeking out from inside the doghouse. That definitely hadn't been here this morning when they'd constructed the makeshift shelter.

But Naomi was pretty sure she knew exactly who had brought the blanket over.

Donovan might not have agreed with her about taking Brinkley home with them today, but clearly he had been concerned about the dog too. He'd taken care of her on-site, cleaning and bandaging her wound as well as making sure she had a proper harness, plenty of room to move, and a shelter, but he'd also come back with a blanket and a toy.

Yeah, she was in love with him. She was really going to have to hope that he would get okay with her not thinking he got things right every second of the day.

"Yeah, I'll bring her something cuddly tonight," Naomi said, her voice a little rough with emotion.

"Good. Can we stay a little longer and finish reading to her?" Katie said.

Naomi nodded. "I think it's fine. Of course, if Denny comes home, you guys get out of here, okay?"

"We can get out through that slot in the fence over there," Sophia said pointing to the far corner of the yard where the fence was missing a board. "He won't even know we were here."

That made Naomi feel better. Of course Denny would know someone had been here when he saw the shelter, new leash, and blanket, but she suspected that Zander had left messages on Denny's phone as well as with a couple of friends at least. She also assumed that Zander would be showing up at Denny's as soon as he had any indication the man was back in town.

"Okay, but don't get into any trouble. You can use this to freshen her water before you leave," Naomi said, setting her bottle of water down next to Samuel. "Then you let me check on her tonight."

"We'll come back tomorrow," Katie said, looking at her two friends.

The other kids nodded.

"Fine, but keep checking to see if Denny is home first,"

Naomi sighed. "Officer Landry is going to be keeping track of this. I promise that we're going to be sure that she is treated well from here on."

It might be true that Zander's hands were somewhat tied when it came to intervening with Denny's ownership, but Naomi was going to stay on top of this and do what she could to pressure Zander to keep an eye on Denny. Was that heavy-handed? Maybe. But the wild animals around Autre were not the only ones that needed a savior, apparently.

Naomi headed home, resisting the urge to call Donovan and tell him how sweet she thought the blanket and dog toy were. He still needed to understand that they were going to disagree from time to time and there would simply be moments when they argued and didn't see eye to eye. If he wanted a woman who was just going to praise him and dote on him and swoon over his heroics...well, she understood why he'd thought that was her initially. But no more. He was an amazing man and she wanted him, for the long-term, for better or worse.

But he had to want her for better or worse too.

By the time the sun went down and Naomi was preparing to go back to check on Brinkley, she was antsy, and restless. It just felt wrong to leave the dog over there by herself. Not so much because she was alone and it was dark, but because Naomi didn't know when Denny might be back. And what might happen to the dog when he did return.

Fletcher had said that he didn't think Denny was abusive, but she wondered if his opinion had changed now that he'd been over to Denny's place and met Brinkley.

She didn't understand why people who didn't want to be pet owners got pets in the first place.

She changed into leggings and a light hoodie and was

pulling on her tennis shoes, preparing to head to Brinkley's when it occurred to her that she was going to have a hard time leaving the dog over there alone, not knowing when Denny might come home.

She paused in the midst of tying one of her shoes. Dammit. The kids couldn't camp out over there. First, they couldn't lie to their parents. Second, they couldn't be over there unsupervised. Third, they really could get in trouble if Denny came home in the night while they were there.

But Naomi could stay over there.

Was it ridiculous to think that she should camp out over at Denny's house to keep Brinkley company?

Maybe.

But she could not shake the pit in her stomach that had settled there when they'd walked into the yard and first seen the dog. She'd been miserable. Scared, hungry, hurting.

No living being should be any of those things, and certainly not when people who could fix it knew about the situation.

Okay so, Zander and Donovan had their hands tied. Zander was law enforcement and had procedures he had to follow. Donovan was a certified wildlife rehabber and also had certain rules he had to follow or risk losing his certification.

But she was neither one. She had more leeway here.

The worst she would be doing was trespassing.

And that was if she got caught.

Before she could think about it any further, Naomi went to her closet and pulled her sleeping bag from the top shelf. She hadn't camped out in years and when she had, it had not been her favorite experience. She wasn't an outdoorsy girl. At least, she hadn't been until Donovan had come into her life. But one thing he'd showed her for certain over the past several weeks, was that sometimes a little discomfort was worth it.

She grabbed a pillow off her bed, stowed a flashlight, bottle of water, and can of bug spray into her backpack, and said a prayer that snakes and other nocturnal things would stay away from a German shepherd.

Denny's house was still dark and there were no additional vehicles parked in the driveway or at the curb. Naomi left her truck two blocks over just in case Denny came home and she had a chance to sneak out without being seen, but she was relieved that the house still seemed unoccupied.

As she let herself in through the gate to Brinkley's yard again, she heard whispers. She froze. Then heard a giggle, more whispers, and the sound of a wooden board slapping against another.

She narrowed her eyes. Apparently, at least two of the kids had decided to come over and check on Brinkley in the dark anyway.

That was it. She definitely needed to stay here overnight. The kids would come back if she didn't. She would feel much worse if their parents found out they had lied, if Denny came home and found them here, or even if one of them ended up with a snake or spider bite from camping out in the yard.

Naomi shuddered. She *really* didn't want to end up with a snake or spider bite. But better her than a ten-year-old.

"Hey, girl," she said softly to the dog as she approached.

Brinkley lifted her head, and Naomi could hear her tail thumping against the side of the kennel.

"You're so sweet," Naomi told her. She sat down next to the dog and stroked her head. "How can anyone just forget about you?"

Brinkley was lying on her new blanket and her food and water dish were both nice and full.

She'd had more visitors today than she probably had in her life, and that made Naomi's heart ache even as she smiled and felt warmer thinking about those humans. Small and large.

"Okay, we're going to have a little slumber party. We'll figure out what to do about everything else tomorrow."

Naomi had just unrolled her sleeping bag and was telling herself that lizards—from geckos to gators—definitely didn't like German shepherds when she heard a rumble.

A rumble that sounded very much like thunder.

She frowned and looked up at the dark sky. No way. It wasn't supposed to rain tonight. Was it?

It was probably a truck rumbling along the road in the distance.

But then she heard it again.

Dammit. No.

She hadn't checked the weather. Which was also very unlike her. She was much more prepared than this typically. But everything in her life had been very topsy-turvy lately. She honestly couldn't remember the last time she had checked the weather. Or the news that wasn't related to a certain hot wildlife rescuer and the other guys of Boys of the Bayou being heroic. And shirtless.

With a sigh she pulled her phone out and opened the app.

Dammit.

Sure enough, rain. And not just rain, a full-blown thunderstorm was headed her way.

She looked at Brinkley. "Well, this isn't exactly awesome."

The dog gave her little *woof*.

Well, now what was she supposed to do? She wasn't really the sleep-outside type in good weather, and she definitely wasn't the type to do it in the rain. She also wasn't about to leave Brinkley out here. Sure, she had a basic shelter now, but it was more for shade from the sun and maybe a light sprinkle rather than an actual storm.

The thunder rumbled overhead again, and a big fat raindrop hit Naomi in the cheek.

Only one solution came to mind. She lifted her phone again and typed out a text.

Meet me at the corner of Maple and Sixth. Wear all black.

She sent the message to the only two people she really could.

A moment later she got back exactly the responses she'd expected.

On my way.

Be there in a second.

I t hadn't even been forty-eight hours, but as Donovan made his way to the big table at the back of Ellie's and saw Naomi having breakfast with the rest of the Landrys and the gang from Iowa, he realized it felt like four months since he'd seen her and talked to her. And touched her.

She was avoiding him. At least it seemed that way. He'd called her about a raccoon rescue yesterday and she'd said she had some other things she needed to take care of. He'd texted and asked if she wanted to come help him with the bear cubs and the baby seal last night and she'd said she was busy.

She'd answered, she just hadn't shown up to be with him. She'd had other things going on that were more important than what he needed. Which was fine. That was normal. Adults had things they had to take care of and sometimes those things needed to be prioritized and he didn't need a babysitter, after all.

But this was the first time since he'd come to Louisiana that she'd felt that was true.

Even Rachel calling and cajoling her about them needing both Naomi and Donovan together in what they were filming for the show wasn't enough to get her to show up.

As he approached the table, she looked up and their eyes met.

He felt the connection streak through him. She even gave him a smile.

She looked a little sad as she turned her attention back to her breakfast and whatever Jill was talking about from across the table, but at least there had been a smile.

Fuck, he missed her.

They needed to talk. He assumed.

He didn't really do this part of relationships. Because his relationships never got to this part.

And he wasn't going to apologize for his actions about the dog. He'd been right about that. It had killed him to leave the dog there like that and it had killed him that she didn't know that, but he'd been right. But he could tell her that he understood what she was feeling and that he appreciated it and explain how they could be on the same side about an issue but just approach the solution differently.

She laughed at something Zeke said and Donovan felt his gut clench.

Or maybe he'd just kiss her.

Or at least he'd start with the kissing. Because he really fucking missed kissing her. He'd realized over the past day and a half that her being mad at him was okay, as long as he could still kiss her. Eventually.

Not just because of the kissing. The kissing was amazing and he'd never get enough. But he knew her kissing him meant more than just...kissing.

He pulled out a chair, gave Ellie a grin as she put cheesy grits and eggs in front of him, and looked around the table.

Naomi spent time with all of these people. They knew her. She took care of them. She laughed with them. She probably got mad at them and maybe even argued with them. But she didn't let any of these guys kiss her. She kept her kissing relationships separate from these closer, warmer, more personal relationships.

Until him.

So yeah, he knew that if they could work together, and argue, and then kiss again, it would really mean something.

She was five seats down on the other side of the huge table with a bunch of loud Cajuns between them, but Donovan leaned in, determined to catch her attention.

"Nae—"

"I want someone arrested!"

Everyone at the table looked over at the man who'd just come storming into the building.

Well, dammit.

"Denny," Zander said, coming up out of his seat. "Where the hell have you been? I've been calling you since Wednesday."

Ah, so this was Denny. The owner of the dog. The dog that Zander had assured him was in someone else's custody when Donovan had inquired about Zander's authority to take possession of the animal after looking up the state laws.

"Three people snuck into my yard two nights ago and stole my dog. I have it on video," Denny said. "And I want you to find them."

Wait, someone had *stolen* the dog?

Donovan's attention immediately went to Naomi.

She swallowed her bite of grits and put her spoon down, wiping her mouth with a napkin. She shot Jordan and Charlie a glance. Both women looked like they were working to keep their composure as well.

Yep, Naomi knew exactly where the dog was. Well... fuck. With a sigh he sat back in his chair, waiting to see how this was going to play out now.

"I been out of town working," Denny told Zander. "I couldn't get back because of the storm. My brother needed my help cleaning up and a goddamn tree fell on my truck and I had to replace the windshield."

"What happened to your phone?" Zander asked him. "You couldn't call me back?"

"Well, believe it or not, you weren't my first priority."

"Well, believe it or not, I'm your first priority now," Zander told him, coming around the end of the table. "I have some questions for you."

"That's just great. I have something to talk to you about too. Three women broke into my backyard and stole my dog."

Zander cast a glance in Naomi's direction.

So Zander suspected her too. Donovan shook his head. But he was torn. He was frustrated with her but the fact that she'd rescued that dog, in spite of everything—in spite of *him*—also turned him on. Sure, he'd love for her to think he always knew best and to just follow his lead. But a gorgeous woman who would risk everything for an animal in need? Yeah, that was always going to do it for him.

Naomi pretended not to notice both Donovan and Zander looking at her. She reached for her purse, pulled out a tube of lipstick and a compact mirror, and started applying it as if she had not a care in the world.

Watching her turning her lips his favorite berry color made Donovan have to shift on his chair to get more comfortable even as he wondered if she had a plan here now that Denny was home and looking for his dog.

"You mean the dog that I've been calling you about since *Wednesday*?" Zander asked. "The dog you left without food or water or shelter when you went out of town?"

"She had water and she can get under the truck. I secured her to the truck so that she would be safe from the storm."

That finally fully pulled Donovan's attention from Naomi.

"Instead of fucking putting her inside your house?" Donovan shoved his chair back and stood. "You have to be kidding." He'd been wound tight ever since he'd gone over to check on the dog and left her a blanket and toy. The sweet thing had wanted love so badly. After leaving there for the second time, he'd gone straight to Zander, demanding to know what he was doing about the situation. Zander had assured him it was being handled and he was getting a warrant that would allow him to take custody of the dog.

But if Naomi had taken the dog, that meant Zander hadn't been in a hurry to get back over there. So Naomi had risked sneaking back over and taking the dog. What if she'd run into Denny? What if he'd been home when she'd gotten there?

"If I left her inside the house, she would've shit all over."

"Which is why you don't leave dogs all alone for days." Donovan advanced on the man. "It's illegal to tie up an animal in inclement weather in Louisiana. Did you know that?"

Zander's arm shot out, his palm flat against Donovan's chest, restraining him. "Hold on."

Donovan glowered at Denny. "And the chain around her neck was too tight and too heavy for her. The wounds that I examined clearly indicated it had been on her longer than just a couple of days."

"Yes, I have that in your report," Zander said, dropping his hand as he apparently decided Donovan wasn't going to go after the other man physically.

At least not at the moment.

"Report? Who the fuck are you?" Denny shot back. "You're not a veterinarian."

"No, but I am." Griffin rose from the table. "And I agree with everything Donovan reported."

Donovan felt a wave of surprise and gratitude and something he couldn't quite name go through him. Griffin hadn't examined the dog. He hadn't even known about the dog until this moment as far as Donovan knew. But his brother had his back.

"She was underweight too. She clearly hasn't been fed

adequately in some time," Donovan added. "She was dirty and she didn't have enough room to move."

"Yes, I know," Zander said. "I—"

Griffin nodded. "I concur."

"*All right!*" Zander put his hands on his hips and faced Denny squarely. "You probably don't want all of this aired out in public though, right, Denny? How about we go downtown and talk about it?"

"Fuck that. Three people snuck into my backyard and took something of mine. I expect you to do something about it. Do I need to go higher?"

"Define 'go higher'," Zander said, with one brow up.

"Would you like to talk to the mayor about it?" Knox asked. "I can set up a meeting."

"She's free right now as a matter of fact," Kennedy said, spreading her arms wide. "What would you like to talk about, Denny?"

"That your cousin isn't doing his damned job."

"You mean our Chief of Police?" Kennedy asked. "Because it sounds to me like he's looking into a report of animal abuse."

"This is all bullshit!" Denny exclaimed. "Someone stole my fucking dog. And I'm going to find out who. If you won't take care of it, then when I figure out who it is, I will."

Zander took a step forward. "Not smart, Denny. If you think you know who did it, you tell me. You're not going to take care of anything on your own."

"Why? You won't do anything."

"Denny, I strongly encourage you—"

"I did it."

Donovan internally groaned as Naomi spoke above the two men.

She pushed her chair back and stood, almost regally, turning to face Denny.

Zander shook his head. "Naomi—"

"You *bitch*."

Denny took a step forward, but Donovan moved in front of him. "I don't think so."

Denny shoved him back. "Get out of my way."

"Not a chance."

Zander grabbed Donovan's shoulder. "Don't."

"I'm just standing here," Donovan told him, his eyes locked on Denny's.

"Where is she?" Denny asked Naomi, leaning around Donovan. "I want her back."

"I'm not—" Naomi started, but suddenly Fiona popped up from her chair, reached out and grabbed her hand, squeezing.

"It was me, actually," Fiona said. "And I'm not saying anything else without my lawyer." She gave Naomi a pointed look.

"But two nights ago you were..." Knox trailed off as Fiona gave him a *shut the hell up* look.

"She was what?" Owen asked, clearly not caring about the legal drama playing out if he could get some gossip.

"Nothing," Knox said shortly.

"You got an alibi for her?" Owen asked with a grin. "*Ooph,*" he suddenly grunted as Maddie's elbow connected with his stomach.

"Focus, babe," she said through gritted teeth.

Owen rubbed his abs. "Yeah, okay."

Then Maddie stood up. "It was me, too," Maddie said.

Owen frowned. "What was you?"

"The dog. I took him."

"Her," Naomi corrected.

"Right." Maddie nodded. "Her. I took her."

"But you—" Owen was cut off by Maddie's elbow again.

"It was me too," Jordan said quickly, getting to her feet.

Fletcher, however, *didn't* act confused by her confession. He just sighed.

Huh.

Charlie stood up next. "It was me too."

"It was me too," Kennedy said standing and crossing her arms.

Denny scowled at the women. "Fucking hell. It wasn't all of you. There were only three people in the video."

"What video?" Zander asked.

"The video from my doorbell. I only saw the front sidewalk though. Nothing in the back."

"Pull it up," Zander said shortly.

Denny pulled his phone from his back pocket and tapped a few buttons. Then he held the phone up for Zander to see.

Zander watched, then sighed. "Okay, let's go downtown. We'll sort through all of this."

He cast a wistful look toward the chair he'd been sitting in. Donovan followed his gaze. A fishing pole was propped against the wall behind the chair Zander had occupied.

Donovan snorted. Poor Zander's fishing trip was going to have to be postponed.

"Are you taking all of them?" Denny asked, gesturing toward the women behind Zander.

Zander pinched the bridge of his nose. "I—"

"Tell these five crazy bitches to stop fucking around," Denny said.

"Six," Paige said, standing and stepping forward.

"What?"

"Six crazy bitches. I did it too."

Mitch didn't even sigh. It was as if he'd been waiting for her to join in.

"Make that eight," Jill said, pushing up from her chair awkwardly with her huge belly. "Unless I count for three."

"Uh, you're seven, babe," Zeke said, actually helping her up from the chair to claim she'd been a part of a posse of dog-nappers.

Donovan felt a smile threatening.

"You be eight, Jill." Ellie came from behind the bar. "I'll be seven."

"El—" Zander started. Then he stopped, blew out a breath, and looked up to the ceiling. As if praying.

"What the fuck are you all doing?" Denny demanded. "You *all* want to go to jail?"

"What we're *doing* is establishing reasonable doubt," Fiona said, one hand on her hip. "You have proof there were three people. But you can't identify any of them. You now have eight people that it *could have been*. But you can't actually prove it was *any* of us."

"This is bullshit," Denny said again.

Zander straightened again and raised his voice. "If everyone would just—"

Donovan heard the scraping of chairs and glanced back. Owen, Fletcher, Sawyer, Mitch, and Zeke were now all on their feet.

"*You?*" Denny asked. He laughed, but there was no humor in his tone. "You fuckers weren't there. That photo is clearly of women."

"You come after one of us, you come after all of us," Fletcher said. "And you might have to put us *all* in a jail cell at first and sort it out later."

"Oh, Jesus," Zander said, running a hand over his face. "That is *not* happening."

"For fuck's sake," he heard Knox mutter. But the big man also shoved his chair back and stood.

Fiona gave him a big, bright smile. He just rolled his eyes.

"Well, okay then."

Jane and Piper, two of the women from Iowa, stood up.

Paige grinned at them and gave Piper, the one standing closest, a little hug.

Piper looked over at Dax and Ollie. "Well? You're not standing up?"

Dax and Ollie were both leaned back in their chairs, watching the whole scenario unfold. Ollie had his long legs stretched out and his coffee mug resting on his belly. Dax had an ankle propped on his opposite knee. They looked completely casual, though definitely entertained.

At Piper's question, they looked at one another, then back at Jane and Piper, and shrugged.

"We're more the we'll-get-the-bail-money types than the share-a-cell types," Dax said.

"And the smuggle-a-shiv-into-jail-in-a-cake types," Ollie added.

"You've both been in jail before," Jane told them, propping a hand on her hip. "Sharing a cell if I remember the story correctly."

"You do," Piper confirmed.

"Well, yeah, but that was..." Ollie looked at Dax.

"A misunderstanding with foreign officials about local laws," Dax said. "There was no bloodshed or stolen property or trespassing."

"Well..." Ollie said. "There was that one time in Rome—"

"That was more of a language barrier issue," Dax said quickly. But he gave his fiancée a big grin.

Jane just rolled her eyes.

Donovan felt all of his anger and worry drain away and he was definitely fighting a smile by the time he looked back at Denny Jenkins.

The guy had come after the wrong bunch of crazy.

He might win in the end. Someone *had* stolen his dog after all. But it was going to be miserably frustrating for him in the meantime. And the fucker deserved at least that much.

Denny was still frowning but he looked wary now.

Smart guy.

"Okay," Zander said, taking a very deep breath and then blowing it out. "*Everybody* just needs to calm the fuck down."

"I'm calling your lawyer right now," Sawyer said, pulling his phone out.

"Whose lawyer?" Fiona asked.

He looked around. "Everyone's lawyer. She's going to be pissed she's not here."

Right. His wife, Juliet, was an attorney. That made Donovan feel better. At least the criminal he was in love with would be represented by someone who knew what they were doing.

"After you call Juliet, call Bennett and tell him I'm going to need bailed out," Kennedy told her older brother. "It might take a bit to convince him you're serious." Then she shrugged. "Or maybe not."

"Oh, hey, Dax, can I borrow ..." Maddie trailed off and looked at Zander. "How much is bail gonna be?"

"You're not going to need—" Zander tried to input.

"You know, stealing a dog can cost you three thousand bucks and ten years in jail," Denny told her. "You still want to take the fall for this?"

"Jesus, that's the *maximum* sentence," Zander said. "And no one—"

"That penalty only applies if the animal's worth is over five hundred dollars and sorry, yours isn't," Donovan told him. He'd spent time looking over *all* the laws around animal cruelty in Louisiana Wednesday night. He looked at Maddie. "That dog isn't worth over three hundred and that means less than five hundred dollars and six months in jail. At most."

"Six months..." Maddie looked at Owen.

"You look hot in orange. And I promise to make the conjugal visits worth it," Owen told her.

"Not funny," she muttered.

Owen leaned in and whispered in her ear, then gave her a hug.

Donovan remembered vaguely that Maddie's dad was in prison and realized that all of this, joking or not, was getting out of hand.

"Listen, let's just—" Donovan started.

"I need you all—" Zander said at the same time.

"Maddie didn't do it," Fiona said loudly. "It was definitely me. All my idea. I blackmailed the others into it. I've had fantasies about you and your handcuffs since the first day I met you," she told Zander, extending her arms, her wrists together. "Let's finally do this thing."

"Knock it off," Knox muttered.

She glanced at him but didn't say anything. She just wiggled her hands at Zander.

"Sorry, can't," Zander said. "I've only got one pair of handcuffs. And besides—"

"Fine. We don't need handcuffs. We're not resisting. Come on, ladies." Fiona pivoted on her heel and started for the front door "We'll meet you down at the station."

The other women, including Naomi, followed her across the room and out the front door.

The men all stood around, watching them go.

The door bumped shut behind them and there were a few seconds of silence.

Then Zeke asked, "So, they're walking themselves to jail?"

Zander sighed heavily. "I left New Orleans because this job was supposed to be *quieter*."

"Isn't having the criminals take themselves to jail pretty easy?" Knox asked dryly.

"I didn't say easy. I said quiet," Zander told him. "You really think my station is going to be *quiet* with all of them down there?"

Knox, Zeke, and the rest all nodded. Almost with sympathy.

"So can we get copies of their mug shots from you for the

scrapbooks of our trip down here or do we have to pull those off some public website or what?" Dax asked after a moment.

Zander just sighed.

What the hell had just happened? Donovan shook his head and started for the back door. He rounded the building as the women turned west and began walking toward downtown Autre.

Naomi was at the back of the pack with Jordan. Donovan reached her, wrapped a hand around her upper arm, and tugged her to the side of Ellie's.

"Hey."

"Just need a second."

Jordan hesitated but Naomi gave her a nod. "It's fine. I'll catch up."

When she met his eyes, he just studied her for a long moment. They hadn't talked in over a day. She hadn't confided in him what she'd done with the dog. But there was no question in his mind that this was the woman he wanted forever.

"What did you do?" he asked.

She rolled her eyes. "You know what I did."

He blew out a breath. "Yeah. I do. Generally. You want to give me specifics?"

"Do they matter?"

"Not really. I just thought... you were the steady one. And now here we are with you the one practically in handcuffs."

She simply nodded. "Yep."

"And I tried to talk you out of this bad decision and you didn't listen."

"Nope."

"So...what are we doing? You're taking risks and pushing boundaries and playing with danger. You're still upset with me about Brinkley?"

"No, actually. I just needed to stay with her yesterday because she needed lots of reassurance that she's safe and I didn't want to leave her alone again after she'd just been through that trauma."

He loved her so damned much.

"You didn't think you could tell me that?"

She shrugged. "I realized that I didn't need your help, or your approval, to take care of it."

Well, that was fair he supposed. "You didn't think I'd have your back?"

"I knew you would. And you did when I needed it."

That was...also good. He was pretty sure. "I don't know what's going on. I'm in love with you. You're in love with me. Are we really ending this over a dispute about what to do about Brinkley?"

"No."

"Oh."

He had never been in love before. Or had a long-term relationship. Or a break-up that he hadn't wanted to stick. So he was in uncharted territory here, he could admit.

"So help me out here. We're not over, but you're not sharing something pretty big with me. That doesn't seem right."

She thought about that. Then said, "Okay, I'll tell you exactly what this is."

He narrowed his eyes. "Maybe I don't want to know, on second thought."

"Well, now's a good time, since I might be in jail for the next few months."

"You're not...probably not...going to be in jail," Donovan said.

"Well, just in case, let me say this."

"Does it end with I love you?"

She gave him a smile and put both hands on his chest. "It does."

He blew out a breath. "Okay."

"You've been content to rescue animals and rehabilitate

them, and educate people about statistics and facts, and raise money for foundations, and get people active in organizations."

He frowned. "Because those are important things."

"Of course they are. But in spite of all those things you've done, you've felt restless. Like you wanted to do more," she pointed out.

"I wanted to keep growing and using my platform to make a difference."

"Right. Your platform." She rolled her eyes.

"Excuse me?"

"Rachel and Brent came to town to give you exactly what you wanted and you've been fighting them the whole time."

"They wanted to fake rescues!"

"They wanted to *recreate* rescues you've already done." She held up a hand when he started to reply. "It wasn't perfect and I haven't been happy either, but if you *really* just wanted a bigger platform and to do more of what you've already done, you would have gone for it."

Her voice softened. "But the truth is, while you've been in Autre, your platform hasn't grown but *you* have. You. Donovan Foster. As a person. You want to do more but not in a bigger, flashier way. In a more *meaningful* way. You said it yourself—you don't care if the animals are endangered and exotic or if they're raccoons and goats that show up everywhere all the time. You don't care if they're affected by a natural disaster, or they got their head stuck in a chicken feeder. You want to help them all. And you want to influence other people to help them.

"Knowing you inspired me to do this same work—to get my boots muddy and my hands bloody and my clothes covered in hair and fur—matters to you. A lot. Maybe more than anything else you've done. Even when it comes to me sneaking into some guy's backyard and taking his dog. Whether you admit that or not."

She moved in again, now practically standing on his toes.

She lifted a hand to his face. "And that freaks you out. You don't want me doing it wrong or risking the animal's safety or getting hurt or getting arrested because *you* helped me find this passion. So you suddenly pulled back and started dotting I's and crossing T's."

She ran her hand over his whisker-roughened jaw. "A few months ago, you would have taken that dog out of that yard and to hell with the consequences. But now you're in a new position...you're in love for the first time, you're part of a real, long-term team full of people who care about you and who you care about in return, and you're worrying about other *people* for a change. You're feeling responsible for humans for the first time. You're way more comfortable when other people are taking care of you rather than this way around."

Donovan felt emotions rolling over one another in his chest. He reached up and covered her hand with his, dragging it over to his mouth. He kissed the center of her palm as he stared into her eyes.

"How do you see all of this?"

"Because..." She paused and gave him a smile. "I love you."

His breath rushed out. "I love you too."

"I know you do. But that doesn't mean we're not going to disagree sometimes. That doesn't mean we're not going to worry about each other sometimes. And that doesn't mean that sometimes I'm going to *not* listen to you. And vice versa."

"Okay. Yeah. I can deal with that. Maybe. I'll learn."

"I know you will."

"And now I *really* need to kiss you."

She melted into him as he cupped her face and covered her mouth. The kiss was deep and hot and sweet and exactly what he needed. If Naomi LeClaire would still kiss him like this at the end of every day, he'd always know that everything was going to be okay.

He'd just started to walk her back to press her against the side of the building when they heard, "There you two are!"

Dammit.

They pulled apart and turned as Rachel and Brent stopped beside them.

"So this is a mess," Rachel said bluntly.

"What is?" Naomi asked, running her thumb over her bottom lip.

Donovan grinned at her smudged lip color and ran his own hand over his mouth, coming away with some berry color too.

Rachel thrust her phone toward them. "This."

It was the photo of Naomi, Charlie, and Jordan carrying Brinkley out of Denny's back yard.

"It's fine. They were actually taking possession of a dog that law enforcement put into their custody," Donovan said. He was ninety-nine percent sure that's what Zander was going to explain when he went back in and asked the cop what the hell was going on.

"What?" Rachel asked.

"Zander served a warrant at Denny Jenkin's house Wednesday night after investigating the reports of animal cruelty. That warrant allowed him to take possession of the dog. Law enforcement then turns the animal over to a custodian for fifteen days while the situation is more thoroughly investigated. After fifteen days, anyone interested in the animal can post bond that covers the expenses incurred during that fifteen day period. I, of course, intend to post that bond."

They were all staring at him. Donovan shrugged. "What? The law is easily found online."

"So you were made custodian of the dog?" Rachel asked Naomi.

"Uh..."

"Yes, she was," Donovan interjected.

"Doesn't matter," Brent said. "Jonathan is pulling his offer of funding."

"Because of all of this with the dog?" Donovan asked, scowling. "She hasn't been arrested or anything."

"Just... that. Everything. He thinks the goats are silly and the other rescues, except for the bobcat, are boring."

"The heron?" Naomi asked. "Come on."

"It wasn't hurt, it didn't even struggle." Brent shrugged. "He even said it would have been nice if there'd been a scratch or something from the bobcat but generally that one was good."

"Maybe a wildlife rescue reality show isn't something Jonathan should be producing," Naomi said, her eyes narrowing.

Brent nodded. "That's what he said."

"So...we're heading out. But it was nice meeting you both," Rachel said.

Then they turned and walked away.

16

Donovan and Naomi didn't say anything for several seconds. Then they looked at one another.

"You never signed any contracts or paperwork, did you?" she asked.

Donovan paused, realized she was right, and sighed. "Nope."

"And I didn't remind you or follow-up on it."

"You were too caught up in everything." He couldn't help but grin. She was right when she said that her having found a passion for this work mattered to him. It meant a lot. So much it had been overwhelming at times. It still was. But it was mostly amazing.

"So they can just...walk," she said.

"Yep."

They were quiet for another few seconds.

Then the front door of Ellie's banged open and Zander escorted Denny Jenkins out. In his one pair of handcuffs.

"Uh, I should maybe get downtown," Naomi said.

"Yeah, I'll...see you later?"

"Probably?" Then she laughed.

She rose on tiptoe and pressed a kiss to his lips and he knew, no matter what happened, everything was going to be okay.

He watched her take off at a jog toward Main Street, then he headed to Zander's car. "So what's really going on?"

Zander slammed the back door on Denny Jenkins' very angry face. "Well, if everyone would just shut the fuck up for a minute, I would have told them that the women aren't under arrest at all and that I'm charging Denny with several counts of animal cruelty. But, now I have a jail full of Landry women and their friends and my day couldn't get any weirder or more annoying."

Donovan winced. He wasn't sure Zander should tempt fate by saying that out loud.

"You gave Naomi custody of Brinkley?" he asked.

"Well, I was going to do it officially, but when I showed up at the house, she and Jordan and Charlie were already sneaking out with her dog."

Right. "So you knew it was them and where the dog's been all along."

"I probably could have gotten them for trespassing, but I was going to get the dog and take it to her anyway so she saved me some time. Plus I didn't actually see her enter the property." He shrugged. "The dog *could have* been out on the sidewalk when Naomi picked her up."

"So should I call Naomi and let her know that none of them are under arrest?" Donovan asked.

"Nah." Zander pulled the driver's side door open on his police car. "I'm gonna put Denny in the cell next to all the women for a bit. Figure he deserves that torture." He got into the car. "Tell the guys they can come get their girls in about an hour."

Donovan laughed, then headed back inside as Zander drove off.

The men were sitting around the big table in back, eating breakfast and drinking coffee as if nothing had happened. They definitely did not seem overly concerned about the morning's events.

"So now what?" Donovan asked the group at large.

Leo came up beside him and clapped him on the shoulder. "Now is usually the time that whichever guy is having girl trouble gets advice from the grandmother."

Donovan laughed. "I don't have a grandmother."

Realizations like that used to give him a twinge in the left side of his chest, but since coming to Autre those tiny flickers of loss had gotten less intense.

Leo chuckled. "Don't be ridiculous. You've got at least three. And a couple of grandfathers."

Donovan looked over at him quickly and saw Armand, Naomi's grandfather, standing next to him, nodding.

Donovan's throat tightened and he cleared his throat before saying, "Well, one of those grandmothers is down in jail next to the girl I'm trying to figure things out with."

"Yeah and another's going to have to be handling this bar by herself until that other grandmother gets released," Leo said, glancing over to where Cora was working behind the bar.

"No problem, I've got one for him. She's at home right now. Cooking." Armand gave him a wink.

Donovan's mouth immediately started to water, even though he'd just had breakfast. "Wonderful. Let's go." He felt contentment seep into him and, as he looked around the room and felt Armand's hand on his shoulder, he realized that he was home with his family. Whatever craziness happened, whatever worry and responsibility came with that, he was ready for it. In fact, he welcomed it.

A few minutes later, he and Armand climbed the front steps to Rosalie and Armand's house. As they stepped through the front door, Rosalie called from the kitchen, "About time you got here."

"I came for some grandmotherly advice," Donovan told her.

"I have plenty of that, along with coffee and dous makos."

He didn't even know what that was, but he couldn't wait. Just then he heard a *woof* and Rosalie saying softly, "Go see him. He's here for you too."

Brinkley came around the corner and Donovan grinned. "Hey, girl."

Brinkley trotted toward him, her tail wagging. He held out a hand and she immediately licked his fingers.

Yeah, he was here to see his dog too.

"This is inhumane!" Denny yelled from his cell.

"Little louder, ladies," Zander said. He had his feet propped up on his desk and was tipped back in his chair with a novel balanced on his lap.

The women in the jail cell next to Denny's—theirs with the door open, of course—launched into another round of "Jailhouse Rock".

Naomi shook her head, but still crossed to the bench on the far end of the cell and took a seat. She was all for torturing Brinkley's past owner—*past* being the key word there—but her mind wouldn't stop spinning over the fact that she and Donovan had just been fired from the TV show they'd been working on for weeks now.

Ellie Landry took a seat next to her. "Not an Elvis fan?"

"Elvis is fine. Though I am more a Johnny Cash girl."

The girls had also sung Johnny's 'Folsom Prison Blues' to Denny. Twice. They'd even done a poor rendition of Merle Haggard's 'Mama Tried', another song about going to prison, though Ellie was the only one who knew all the words.

"So, what's going on?" Ellie asked. "I saw Donovan go after you."

"He did. And I straightened him out."

"Good." Ellie paused. "How?"

Naomi laughed and stretched her legs out. "Basically told him that loving someone didn't mean you never fought and he didn't get to be right all the time anymore. But that he got me and all of you in exchange for putting up with having to be the one worrying sometimes now."

Ellie nodded. "Good." She was quiet for a moment, then said, "You know, for those of us who've been loved well and in spite of ourselves all our lives, we don't always understand or remember that doesn't happen for everyone."

Naomi looked over. She swallowed hard. "Yeah. You're right. He was loved though. They just left him too soon."

"And he didn't have people to step in like we do here."

"Griffin stepped in," Naomi said. "But Donovan doesn't think he deserved what Griffin did."

"Griffin might not have done a great job at it," Ellie said with a shrug.

Naomi's eyes widened. "But...he was there. He gave up all his plans. He adjusted everything to be beside Donovan. Griffin's great."

"Griffin is great. I love that boy like one of my own," Ellie said. She was watching the group of women in the cell with them. Some of them were her granddaughters by blood. Some were the women her grandsons loved. But they were all her family. "But we're not all naturally good at loving the people we love. And we have to love different ones different ways. We learn that over time."

"We can't just...love them?" Naomi asked.

"Feeling our feelings is one thing. *Showing* them those feelings and making sure they know we feel them are something else."

Naomi frowned and looked across the cell at Charlie. "Do you not think Griffin shows Charlie he loves her?"

"I think he does just great with that," Ellie said with a soft smile. "Because Charlie is obvious."

Naomi snorted. "She's obvious?"

"Charlie wears her heart on her sleeve. You always know how that girl feels about everything and I have no trouble believing that she tells Griffin exactly what she wants and needs." Ellie looked at Naomi. "A guy like Griffin needs that. He's straightforward and he needs a woman who will be straightforward with him. He'll give her the moon, but she has to tell him she wants it."

Naomi thought about that. Then about Donovan. "You don't think Donovan has told Griffin what he wants and needs."

"I don't think Donovan tells anyone what he wants and needs. And I don't think you do either. You two need to start talking more."

"I...I told him I love him. And that I want to work with animals with him. And that I'm not going to just go along with him and praise everything he does and that I'm going to keep calling him out on the risks he takes, but I'm also going to sometimes take risks when I need to. And I told him I think he's amazing and I want him to be happy."

Ellie gave her a big smile. "Good. Now keep telling him that. That boy needs to hear that all over and over. He hasn't had nearly enough of that."

Naomi wet her lips. "Okay."

Ellie laughed. "I know, that sounds like a lot for a woman who's kept her private feelings to herself for a very long time."

Naomi nodded. "I can do it though. I do feel all those things. I just need to get more comfortable being public and out there about them."

"Well, you know the perfect way to do it, don't you?"

"Record it all in a little speech and just let him play it whenever he needs to hear it?" she asked hopefully.

Ellie rolled her eyes. "No."

"Practice, right?" Naomi said. She could do it. She *would* do it. She showed her love in many ways. She carried her purse full of whatever anyone would need. She fed the people she loved. She was there for whatever plans her friends came up with. If one of them had called her to come help kidnap a dog, she would have showed up with no questions asked too.

She just didn't speak the words as often.

And Donovan needed the words. He hadn't had them enough. And she could do that for him.

"No."

Naomi focused on Ellie again. "No? No, I don't have to just say it over and over?"

"Well, that's good too," Ellie said. "But what you need to do to show him all of this—that you believe in him but that you're going to correct him when you think he's wrong, and you're going to encourage him to push himself, and you're going to pull him back when you think he's going too far, and that you share his passion for these animals—is to direct the TV show he's starring in yourself."

Naomi blinked at her.

Ellie just looked back.

"What?" Naomi finally asked. "I'm not directing anything. And there is no TV show. The producer pulled out."

"Well, good. Now you can *really* do it your way. You had all the ideas anyway."

"I...did?"

"I overheard you talking to Rachel and Bruce."

"Brent."

"Whatever. I heard your conversations with them. You had the ideas. You were already directing everyone anyway."

"But..." Her mind was spinning. Direct? She'd never

directed. Though when she'd been behind the camera for Boys of the Bayou, she'd found herself directing several times in small ways.

"The premise is that he and I are falling in love. So I need to be in front of the camera, not behind directing."

"You can't direct from in front? There's only one other star," Ellie pointed out.

Naomi shook her head, but she couldn't shake all of the ideas that were suddenly tripping through her mind.

"But we would still need producers."

"What do producers do?"

"They pay for everything" Naomi said bluntly. "Basically we would need people with a lot of money who were open to new ideas. We would still have the star power of Donovan and me, and the excitement of the animal rescues. But we'd still need money behind it. If we had that though..." She trailed off as she thought about how it could all come together.

"What?" Ellie asked.

"I guess we could still shop it around. I mean, I still have contacts in the business and so does Donovan. If we had the money..."

"You should totally pitch this to Dax and Ollie."

Naomi looked from Ellie up into the face of Piper Caprinelli.

"What?"

Piper nodded. "Ollie and Dax love this kind of stuff. They're always investing in new things. How do you think we ended up owning a snack cake factory in Iowa?" She laughed. "You should tell them about your idea. They love everything down here on the bayou. They've loved learning about the animals and they think Donovan is amazing. I can totally see them getting behind the idea of a reality TV show."

"Oh my God, Dax was already talking about how he

couldn't wait to watch it. He's been stalking the website videos and the Facebook page," Jane said, overhearing.

"She was just saying that she needs somebody to back them as producers for them to shop the idea around," Piper said.

"Oh my God, you should totally pitch this to Dax and Ollie," Jane said. "I mean, you already kind of have been the whole time we've been here. We've all heard the stories of the rescues you've done. And we were at the petting zoo with Henry and Didi when you fell out of the ceiling. It's all been so fun."

Naomi knew she was gaping at them.

Ellie reached over and used one finger to shut Naomi's mouth. "Looks like having some friends who are multimillionaires could be handy."

"Multimillionaires who are slightly crazy," Piper said with a nod.

"I'm... I'm not ready for a pitch and you guys are leaving in a day or so."

"What are we pitching?" Charlie asked, coming to stand with them.

"A possible TV show idea," Ellie said.

Charlie's eyes widened and started to actually freaking twinkle. There was nothing that Charlie Landry liked more than a big presentation.

"The TV show like the one that you and Donovan have been doing?"

"Yeah. Our producer pulled out. We basically got fired this morning."

"Oh my God, are you going to do it yourselves?"

"Dax and Ollie are going to back it financially," Piper said.

"You don't know that," Naomi said. "We haven't even talked to them about it."

Jane and Piper exchanged a glance. "Well, let's just say you have an in with the producers," Piper said. "And Ollie will love it. But even if he didn't, I have a few ways of getting Ollie to be very agreeable to things I want him to do."

Naomi couldn't help but laugh. She shook her head. "This is...amazing."

"But we totally need a kick-ass presentation so they know you're serious. We can take some of the video footage from our website and pull together stuff off of social media," Charlie said, speaking rapidly as she always did when she got an idea brewing. "We'll basically use everything that Rachel and Brent were going to use. They had a ton of the videos from us anyway." She whirled around and called, "Zander, we need your laptop and a whiteboard and markers."

"You can have the laptop and I've got sticky notes and ball-point pens."

Charlie rolled her eyes. "Pathetic. But okay."

She turned back to Naomi. "Can you get a hold of that Sara girl and her friends and see if they have any additional photos or videos we could use?"

Naomi realized that Charlie Landry was about twenty steps ahead of where she was, but she couldn't deny that her heart was suddenly pounding and she felt an excitement that she hadn't felt in all the time that Rachel and Brent had been in town filming.

"Okay," she finally said, looking around all of her women friends. "Let's do this thing."

Two hours later, the women walked back into Ellie's. The guys were still there, still sitting at the back table, seemingly completely unconcerned about the fact that their wives, fiancées, and girlfriends had been sitting in jail.

Donovan was up and out of his chair the minute he saw Naomi though.

"Hey, is everything okay?"

She gave him a bright smile. "Everything is wonderful. And I have something to show you."

"Okay. Do you want to get out of here?"

"Actually, I would love it if you would go back and sit down. We want to show everyone."

He lifted an eyebrow. "Not the kind of show and tell that I was hoping for."

She gave him a little smirk. "That's for later."

He obviously sensed her playful mood and he gave her a grin. "I'm on board. With whatever this is."

She nodded. "Keep that attitude."

He started to turn away to return to his seat, but she reached out and grabbed his wrist. He looked back.

"And I love you."

He looked surprised for just a moment, but then he said, "I love you, too. "

"I just want to say that. A lot. And I want you to know that what I'm about to show you is another way that I plan to show you how I feel."

"Again, not exactly the actions I would expect to follow those words. But I can't wait to see what you've got."

Damn. She really was madly in love with him and it was not going to be a hardship to tell him that, and *show* him every single day, the rest of her life.

Everyone settled into their seats, and Ellie and Charlie cleared the wall of a couple of posters, and a few photographs so that they had a blank space to function as a screen. They set Zander's laptop up and within minutes were projecting their new video onto the wall.

It started with a shot of Naomi. She was standing outside behind her house.

"Hi, everyone, I'm Naomi LeClaire and this is my hometown. In fact, this is my backyard. And this is my everyday view."

The film cut to a shot of Donovan stripping his shirt off as he got ready to jump onto an airboat from one of the Boys of the Bayou docks.

The guys around the table whistled and clapped. Donovan grinned and sat back in his chair, linking his fingers on his stomach. He looked cocky and she loved it.

The camera came back to Naomi's grinning face.

"I know, right? Well, stick around and I'll tell you how I went from a child TV star working with trained animals to just a regular girl to a wildlife rehabilitation expert raising a tiger—"

The camera cut to the tiger pacing around in his outside pen.

"A baby seal," Naomi's voice said as video of the seal pup swimming in his pool played.

"A colony of endangered penguins—"

The next shot showed the entire penguin enclosure and all of the Galapagos penguins they were raising in Autre.

"And so much more."

Then it cut to a clip of Donovan again. This time he was looking at the camera and saying, "Hey, Naomi, are you coming?"

Then Naomi's grinning face was on camera once more. "And yeah, you get to see a *whole* lot more of that guy too. Tune in and we'll take you along as we get a little...wild...on Main Street, USA.

The final shot was of the goats trotting down Main Street, Autre, Louisiana.

The video faded out and Naomi turned to face the group at the table.

There was only one beat of silence before the entire bunch erupted into cheers and applause.

"You looking for investors?" Dax asked. "Because I want in on this."

"I am. We'd like to shoot three episodes and start shopping it around." She looked over at Donovan. "Donovan will be the main star. I will be his costar and the director."

He lifted a brow at the word 'director', but then gave her a smile that said he was all in.

"I'm in," Ollie said simply.

"And I assume this means we can come down and visit you at any time," Dax said.

Naomi actually felt tears well up in her eyes and her throat tighten. She nodded. "Of course. You're part of the family now."

Suddenly Donovan shoved his chair back and stalked toward her. He stepped up to her at the head of the table in front of everyone, cupped her face, leaned in, and kissed her deeply. Then he let her go, bent at the waist, and lifted her over his shoulder and started for the door.

"Hey, where you going?" Owen called.

"Staff meeting," Donovan said. "Naked staff meeting," he said for Naomi's ears only.

"Wait!" Jill yelled. "That's not fair!"

Donovan turned back. "What's not fair?"

Jill looked around the table. "Well...what happens now with..."

"Everything!" Zeke filled in. "The zebra, for one!"

"And Brinkley," Charlie added.

"And the Galapagos Islands," Jill said.

"And Naomi's wildlife rehab certification," Jordan said.

"Oh, well geez, okay," Donovan said, settling his hand on Naomi's ass as she started to wiggle. "Naomi will take her test next week and pass with a perfect score, I'm sure. I'm not going to the Galapagos. They already have someone else lined up. The zebra, tiger, and seal all stay—we're going to need names for the zebra and tiger, by the way. And Naomi and I are adopting Brinkley. She's sleeping on her new dog bed at Rosalie's right now, in fact." He waited a beat. "Anything else?"

They all looked at one another, then a few shook their heads, while others shrugged.

"I guess not," Jill finally said.

"Okay then. We'll see you all later. *Much* later."

Donovan pivoted toward the door again, but he only made it halfway across the room before the door opened and someone swept into the building.

Someone who stopped Donovan in his tracks.

"Hey," Naomi said from where she was hanging over his shoulder, her view blocked by his back. "What's going on now?"

This time he shifted her, letting her slide down his body, then turned her to face the newcomer.

The woman was drawing everyone's attention. She was gorgeous. Like the type of gorgeous that drew attention wherever she went. She also had an air about her that said she was so used to it, she didn't even notice.

But Naomi had to think that her appearance today was unusual.

For one, she was carrying a large pet carrier in one hand and was dragging a suitcase in the other. She was also wearing a huge very sparkly tiara on her head that, for some reason, Naomi was certain was made up of real diamonds.

And she was wearing a wedding dress.

"Hi. Can we help you?" Ellie asked, coming forward.

"I assume so," the woman said. "I'm looking for Donovan Foster."

Naomi's eyes widened and she turned slowly to look up at her boyfriend.

"Swear I've never seen her before in my life," Donovan said. Then he stepped forward. "I'm Donovan. "

The woman looked slightly relieved. She thrust the pet carrier at him. "Here, I brought this to you. I'm surrendering it."

Donovan took it with a frown. "What is it?"

The woman gave him bored look. "It will be very obvious when you look inside."

"Right." Donovan set the carrier on the closest table and bent to look into it. He straightened and turned to stare at the woman. "No way."

She shrugged. "He's all yours. I brought him here specifically to you. I know you are an expert and that you have a sanctuary here."

Then she turned and started back for the front door.

"What is it?" Naomi asked.

"It's..." Donovan shook his head and just opened the latch and reached inside. He pulled the animal out and held it up for everyone to see.

"I kind of feel like that opening song from *The Lion King* should be playing right now," Owen said.

Because sure enough, Donovan was holding up a lion cub.

"Come on," Knox groaned.

Naomi glanced at the table.

Zander had slumped down in his seat and pulled his hat down over his eyes.

"I guess...we have a lion now," Donovan said.

"Just like that?" Knox said. "People besides you are going to be bringing stuff here?" he asked Fiona.

Fiona shrugged. "She's surrendering him to Donovan. He is a wildlife expert and we are an animal sanctuary. She can do that."

"Without knowing where she got it? What if she stole it?"

"Why would she be bringing it to Donovan if she stole?" Fiona asked.

"Why would she just have it in the first place?" Knox shot back.

"Well, those are really good questions to ask her."

They both turned to look at Zander.

The cop didn't say anything.

"Did anyone else notice she was in a *wedding dress*?" Maddie asked.

"And pulling a suitcase?" Jill added.

"Might be a good idea to just *ask* if she's okay too. You know, if there's any particular reason she's here in that dress without, you know, a groom," Charlie agreed.

"Maybe he's outside waiting," Zeke offered.

"Why's she pulling her suitcase around then?" Kennedy asked. "He could at least hold her bag."

"And he's sending her into a strange bar alone? With that tiara on her head?" Jordan added. "No way. Either he's a huge asshole, or he's not out there."

"Someone really should probably go find out," Fiona said.

Now they all looked at Zander.

He sighed. "What?"

"This kind of seems like something maybe you should follow up on, doesn't it?"

"Wearing a tiara and a wedding dress isn't illegal."

"*Zander!*" about twelve people said at once.

He sighed again. Even more heavily this time. "I just wanted to go fishing today."

"Alexander Raymond Landry," Ellie said, taking a step toward the table.

"Okay, okay, geez." Zander shoved to his feet and straightened his hat. "Let's not all go gettin' all worked up. We wouldn't want *that* to happen."

He started for the front door after the woman, muttering something under his breath that Naomi was sure none of them actually wanted to hear.

Donovan, cradling the lion cub against his chest, turned to Naomi.

"Our staff meeting is maybe going to have to wait."

She laughed. "I kind of expect to hear that a lot over the... rest of our lives."

At the words *rest of our lives,* heat and emotion flickered in his eyes.

He leaned in close and said with a little growl, "There's always the couch in my office at the rehab center."

"We really should probably get this lion up there and check him out."

"We really should."

"And, Donovan, something else that you should get very used to hearing a lot over the rest of your life?"

"Yeah?"

"I love you very much."

"And I love you very much." Then he leaned in and kissed her.

Until the lion cub between them made a weird part growl, part meow, part squeaking noise.

She looked down, then back up at Donovan. She was in love with a man who was now holding a *lion cub* between them. And it was just another Friday in Autre, Louisiana.

Yeah, she had definitely fallen for the right guy.

EPILOGUE

Caroline Holland stepped out of the bar/restaurant/whatever-it-was, whipping the train of her wedding gown out from behind her before the door could close on it.

She was in a tiny, nowhere town in Louisiana, wearing a tiara that cost fifty thousand dollars, trying to roll her stupid suitcase, deal with the train on her wedding dress, *and* handle a pet carrier with a four-week-old lion cub inside it, all at the same time.

Today was going pretty much exactly as she'd expected.

At least now the lion cub was taken care of.

Now she just had to decide what to do with...the rest of the mess she was in.

Thank you so much for reading Sealed With A Kiss! I hope you loved Naomi and Donovan's story!
And yes, Zander and Caroline are coming up in **Say It Like You Mane It!**

But up very **next** is **Head Over Hooves,** a Christmas story from Autre featuring Rory Robins and Drew Ryan—from the Hot Cake series!

You can also get **more from Dax and Ollie** and the rest in the Hot Cakes series! You can check it all out on my website, www.ErinNicholas.com... including the FREE series prequel, Sugar Rush!

HEAD OVER HOOVES

You know in movies where the big city girl lands in a small town for the holidays and falls for the hunky guy who saves Christmas?

This isn't that story.

But this guy does look fantastic in flannel. And out of flannel...

Grab it now!

Find out more at
ErinNicholas.com

♡
And join in on all the FAN FUN!

Join my **email list!**
http://bit.ly/ErinNicholasEmails

And be the first to hear about my news, sales, freebies, behind-the-scenes, and more!

Or for even more fun, join my **Super Fan page** on Facebook and chat with me and other super fans every day! Just search Facebook for Erin Nicholas Super Fans!

IF YOU LOVE AUTRE AND THE LANDRYS...

If you love the Boys of the Bayou Gone Wild, you can't miss the Boys of the Bayou series! *All available now!*

My Best Friend's Mardi Gras Wedding (Josh & Tori)

Sweet Home Louisiana (Owen & Maddie)

Beauty and the Bayou (Sawyer & Juliet)

Crazy Rich Cajuns (Bennett & Kennedy)

Must Love Alligators (Chase & Bailey)

Four Weddings and a Swamp Boat Tour (Mitch & Paige)

And be sure to check out the connected series, Boys of the Big Easy!

Easy Going (prequel novella)-Gabe & Addison

Going Down Easy- Gabe & Addison

Taking It Easy - Logan & Dana

Eggnog Makes Her Easy - Matt & Lindsey

Nice and Easy - Caleb & Lexi

Getting Off Easy - James & Harper

If you're looking for more sexy, small town rom com fun, check out the

The Hot Cakes Series

One small Iowa town.

Two rival baking companies.

A three-generation old family feud.

And six guys who are going to be heating up a lot more than the kitchen.

Sugar Rush (prequel)

Sugarcoated

Forking Around

Making Whoopie

Semi-Sweet On You

Oh, Fudge

Gimme S'more

————————

And much more—

including my printable booklist— at

ErinNicholas.com

ABOUT THE AUTHOR

Erin Nicholas is the New York Times and USA Today bestselling author of over forty sexy contemporary romances. Her stories have been described as toe-curling, enchanting, steamy and fun. She loves to write about reluctant heroes, imperfect heroines and happily ever afters. She lives in the Midwest with her husband who only wants to read the sex scenes in her books, her kids who will never read the sex scenes in her books, and family and friends who say they're shocked by the sex scenes in her books (yeah, right!).

Find her and all her books at
www.ErinNicholas.com

And find her on Facebook, Goodreads, BookBub, and Instagram!

CPSIA information can be obtained
at www.ICGtesting.com
Printed in the USA
BVHW080931191021
619298BV00008B/261